DIVINE HERETIC

Also by Jaime Lee Moyer

Brightfall

JAIME LEE MOYER

DIVINE HERETIC

Jo Fletcher
BOOKS

First published in Great Britain in 2020 by

Jo Fletcher Books
an imprint of
Quercus Editions Ltd
Carmelite House
50 Victoria Embankment
London EC4Y 0DZ

An Hachette UK company

A CIP catalogue record for this book is available
from the British Library

TPB ISBN 978 1 78747 924 1
EBOOK ISBN 978 1 78747 926 5

10 9 8 7 6 5 4 3

Typeset by CC Book Production
Printed and bound in Great Britain by Clays Ltd, Elcograf S.p.A.

MIX
Paper from
responsible sources
FSC® C104740

Papers used by Quercus are from well-managed forests and other responsible sources.

For Susan Jett, who loves this book. Thank you for reading my story.

The first time that I heard this Voice, I was very much frightened.

Jeanne d'Arc

Before the creatures who claimed to be angels spoke to me, I'd thought their visit was a sign of God's favour, but I was only a little more than five. I was still innocent and believed all my grand-mère's stories were true.

Mama had sent me out to collect twigs and small branches for the fire, a task even a child my age could do easily. Two of Papa's older black-and-white herd dogs guarded me, their ears up listening to every sound and bright blue eyes watching the trees. Anytime I took more than a few steps towards the dryads' grove, they herded me onto the path again. The box mounted on my small sledge was nearly full when I started back to the house.

A thin crust of snow crunched underfoot as I trudged towards home, but the weather had warmed enough that parts of the path were more bog than solid ground. Getting the sledge over those patches without spilling all the wood I'd collected was hard. Once, the box did tip too far, and I was near tears before I got the sledge righted and the wood back inside. The dogs stayed close, nervous and watchful as the sun dipped low, and twilight made the tree shadows creep over the path. I hurried as quick as I could, knowing Mama would worry if I was gone much longer and send my oldest brother, Henri, to find me.

The curve in the path ahead meant I didn't have far to go. I

1

whispered a prayer of thanks to Holy Mary, just as Grand-mère Marie had taught me, and pulled my shawl tighter. As the sun set, the wind picked up and the air got colder. I kept going, too stubborn to abandon the sledge and send my older brothers out to bring it the rest of the way, or leave the task half-done. Mama would fuss and rub warmth back into my fingers once I got inside the house, but Papa would be proud I'd finished what I started.

Both dogs growled as we neared the curve, the sound fierce and menacing, and the biggest dog, Luc, herded me back a few steps. Remi, the smaller dog, stood in front of us, seeming to bark at air. A great light bloomed in the middle of the path, bright as the midday summer sun, blinding me and filling my eyes with tears. The dogs whimpered once and were silent. When I could see again, Papa's dogs were sprawled on the ground, still and unmoving. I wasn't sure Luc or Remi were breathing, and that frightened me.

Three blazing lights stood in front of me, each one vaguely man-shaped and all of them taller than my father. All I could think of were Grand-mère's stories of angels. Picturing graceful white wings rising up and behind the creatures confronting me was easy. The light was brightest where their faces should be, but some of the stories I'd heard said angels' faces were too beautiful and terrible to look upon. I couldn't imagine another reason why angels would hide their faces – but I'd never thought one of God's messengers would come to me.

I dropped to my knees near Luc, trembling with more than cold, and waited for them to speak.

'Jeanne d'Arc, God has chosen you to free France and win a king his crown!' His voice rang with thunder and raging winds, scaring me more. 'You have a great destiny to fulfil as the Maid of Lorraine. You will lead a mighty army and drive the English out of France forever!'

Little girls didn't lead armies. I'd listened to enough of the old men's stories they told on market days to know that armies were led by kings and dukes, not peasant girls. Confused, and wondering why an angel would lie, I stared at his light and didn't say anything.

The light at his right hand spoke next, her voice full of ice and the return of winter. 'You've been chosen for a great task, but take heart, the prophecy says you won't battle France's foes alone! Pledge to obey us, Jeanne, and Saint Michael will teach you to fight and be a fearsome warrior. You need to be ready when the Maid's sword comes to you.'

'Fate has chosen you to be the Maid, Jeanne d'Arc!' The third voice was full of pealing bells, but I thought she sounded a little sad. 'You've no choice but to embrace your destiny. The sword will remain hidden until the glorious day you travel with the Dauphin. Do your duty for France and give Blessed Catherine your pledge to obey.'

Papa's voice came from further down the path, shattering the need to answer without asking questions or taking the time to think. Lantern-light marked how far my father had come searching for me. I scrambled away from the angels on hands and knees, closer to the sledge and the dogs. An icy wind ruffled their fur, but Luc and Remi still hadn't moved.

Tears slipped down my face as I thought of telling Papa how his dogs had died. He wouldn't believe an angel had struck them dead.

'No,' I whispered. 'My grand-mère says I always have a choice between right and wrong, and I don't know which this is. I won't promise until I talk to her.'

Saint Michael grew taller and the thunder in his voice grew

3

deeper, louder. 'Remind Marie of the promise she made to us and think hard about making the same pledge. You can't escape your destiny, Jeanne d'Arc. You are the Maid.'

Their light flared, blinding me again, and the three angels were gone. I buried my face in Luc's fur, horrified at how cold and still he was, and cried.

Papa scooped me up an instant later, holding me tight and safe even if his hands shook. 'Shhhhh, little one, don't cry. I've got you now, Jeanne. I've got you.'

My second-oldest brother, Pierre, bent over the smaller dog, running his hands over Remi's side and face. He wiped a hand over his eyes before looking at our father and shaking his head.

I buried my face in Papa's shoulder, trembling with fear and cold. Dogs were loving and innocent creatures, free of sin. I couldn't understand why God's angels would strike them dead for trying to protect me.

'Let's get you home, little bird.' Papa pulled his heavy cloak around me and kissed my forehead. 'Mama and Grand-mère will be anxious to see you. Pierre, carry the lantern for me. Henri and I will come back for the sledge later.'

Pierre walked a few steps ahead, lighting the way. Our father carried me home in silence, the crunch of his boots on the ice-crusted snow the loudest sound to break the quiet.

My mother and Grand-mère made up for Papa's silence when he brought me inside. Mama cried, ran her hands over my arms and legs and asked if I was all right over and over again. Grand-mère prayed and loudly thanked God for bringing me home safe. Pierre sat at the long family table, watching me silently.

Papa said a quiet word to Mama, touched her face and went out the door with Henri. He'd said they'd bring the sledge back, but I knew he'd bring his dogs back too. My father wouldn't leave them for the scavengers or let them go unburied.

My mother stopped crying not long after they left and set me on a bench near the fire to get warm. Pierre sat with me, rubbing warmth back into my fingers the way Mama always did. By the time Papa and Henri came inside again, my mother and grand-mère were nearly finished putting supper on the table. No one said much while we ate. After the dishes were washed, we went to bed early.

No one asked me what had happened or how the dogs died. That confused me until I heard Papa whisper to Mama in the dark loft, repeating stories about the Fae being pushed south by the war and what ill luck it was that I was in the wrong place when they'd passed our village. His next words were full of gratitude that the Fae had only taken the dogs. Grand-mère snored softly in the bed we shared near the hearth, at peace, her faith that God had brought me home safe unshaken.

I couldn't find the courage to tell my parents the truth, or the will to wake Grand-mère Marie to ask if she'd promised to obey three sainted angels.

Not while three lights glimmered in the corner near the door, watching.

The angels appeared next when Grand-mère sent me out to feed the chickens late the next morning. Blessed Catherine gave me all their names again and demanded I pledge to obey them. Merciful Margaret tried to coax me into changing my mind about needing to talk with Grand-mère before making promises, while the Arch-angel Michael watched silently, his light brightest of all. They all frightened me, but Michael scared me most.

Fear and the churning in my stomach convinced me that some-thing was wrong; angels shouldn't terrify me or push me to make pledges I didn't understand. I shook my head no, the only answer I could give, and ran back for the house.

I got used to Michael, Catherine and Margaret dogging my steps, being there when I fell asleep, still present when I woke. Most days they didn't speak at all, just watched me, but winter lingered overlong in Domrémy that year and I spent most of my time inside with Mama. My family wasn't as large as some, but I'd learned quickly that my voices stayed silent when my parents or my brothers were with me. Someone was almost always with me, a blessing.

A handful of weeks later, spring arrived in a rush. Snow melted away almost overnight, giving way to fuzzy patches of new grass and bright flowers. The apple tree near the sheep pens blossomed and all the trees in the dryads' grove unfurled deep-green leaves, giving shelter to songbirds and their nestlings.

Staying inside grew harder as the sun shone brighter and the days warmed. Catherine and Margaret confronted me each time I stepped into the yard to feed the chickens or fetch wood for my mother, while the Archangel Michael stood back, silent and watchful. I prayed each night that these creatures would grow as weary of my refusing to obey as I was of saying no.

The last of the snow had melted when Papa and my brothers began opening the gates on the winter pen each morning, and with the help of our dogs took the flock to graze fresh pastures. I watched them leave the yard each day, the need to follow them an ache that wouldn't stop. No matter how I begged to go along, my father said no.

'Grow a little taller and you can come,' Papa said. 'The rams are all much bigger than you are, Jeanne, and even a few of the ewes top you by almost a head. Your mother would have a hard time forgiving me if you got hurt. I'd have a harder time forgiving myself.'

Mama rested a hand on my shoulder as we watched Papa and Pierre whistle up the dogs, and Henri helped get the herd moving. She leaned down and kissed my cheek before going inside. 'Don't be in such a rush, little one. You'll spend all your days working soon enough. Enjoy the sunshine while you can, but don't wander too far.'

After being inside all winter, Mama knew how much I longed to feel the sun on my face and run barefoot in the grass. I searched carefully for any glimmer of the voices' light, prepared to stay with my mother if I saw them, but I didn't find any sign they were near. A few instants later, I'd fetched the thick stick I pretended was a shepherd's staff and hurried across the yard.

My mother hadn't forbidden me from going to the dryads' grove, so that's where I went. The tree spirits slept all winter, but on a warm day like today, they would be awake and filling the clearing at the heart of the grove, as eager to run and play as I was. Best of all, I wouldn't be alone and the voices wouldn't speak to me.

I'd seen smiling faces in tree bark or looking down from the tops of trees since I was very small, when I left the house only in Mama or Papa's arms. As I got older, the little tree guardians let me play chase with them or join in when they danced. They weren't any bigger than I was now and I always left the grove breathless with laughter and running and wanting to go back.

Grand-mère was convinced playing games with the tiny guardians was sinful and they would lead me into wickedness. Papa had to tell her to stop scolding me each time I came home with flowers in my hair.

'There's nothing wicked in the grove, certainly nothing that will hurt her,' he'd said, his tone stern. 'Let her be, Mama. Jeanne won't be a child for ever.'

The tree spirits rushed to meet me as I slipped between trees and ran into the grove. Two of them joined hands with me and we skipped around in a circle. All the rest formed a ring around us, singing. I couldn't understand the words, but I laughed at the faces they made.

A clap of thunder stopped the singing and a painfully bright light flared. When I'd blinked away the dazzle in my eyes, all the tree spirits had fled to the safety of their trees. Michael, Catherine and Margaret were haloed with flame, fallen suns that drove back the shadows. Fire rippled up and down the sword the archangel held in front of him, wilting the leaves over his head. I wanted to run home too, just as the tree spirits had, and hide in my mother's arms, but I couldn't move. Couldn't speak.

I was already afraid, but the thunder in Michael's voice burned fear deep into my skin. 'My sisters begged me to give you time, Jeanne. They said you were too young to understand duty or sacrifice but that you'd learn. My patience is at an end. The prophecy requires that you pledge to obey us and that you follow the path we show you. You've much to learn, but only you choose if the lessons are easy or hard.'

I blinked and Catherine's light stood behind me. She gripped my shoulders, driving cold into my bones and filling me with dread, but I still struggled to get away.

'You can't escape destiny, Jeanne,' she whispered in my ear. 'Promise to obey all our commands and we will teach you to be a great warrior. Stop fighting and promise.'

I started to cry. Tears froze on my face and my teeth chattered, but I found the breath to answer, 'No, this is wrong. I won't promise! Let me go, you're hurting me. Stop hurting me!'

Michael's sword vanished. He cupped my face in his hands, cold burning my skin and fear spiking into my chest. I think he meant to hurt me, and didn't care if Catherine hurt me too. Between them, my heart slowed as it turned to ice. I waited to shatter and be lost.

'There is always a price to pay for defiance, Jeanne,' Michael said, his words wrapped in thunder. 'You are the Maid, *La Pucelle*, and others must pay the price in your place. Remember, you chose this lesson.'

Catherine held me fast when he let go and moved to stand in front of the nearest tree. He pushed his hand through the bark and deep into the tree, singing words that reminded me of Father Jakob's prayers on Sunday. Michael yanked his hand out, clutching a weeping tree spirit.

His song grew louder, full of keening winds and the sound of lashing rain and hail, until the tempest in his voice filled the grove. The dryad's tree froze and cracked, splitting down the middle and falling to the ground in pieces. I screamed as the tree spirit he held crumbled to dust and was carried away by the gale.

Twice more Michael pulled a tiny guardian from its tree while I screamed and cried, struggling against Catherine's hold and begging him to stop.

He ignored me.

Margaret's voice whispered in my head, her bells hushed and frozen lips moving against my ear. 'He wants your pledge, Jeanne! Tell him you'll do as he wants before he destroys the whole grove. Promise him!'

He was reaching towards another tree when I found my voice.

'I promise, I promise,' I screamed. 'I'll be good! I promise I'll be good! Please don't hurt them. Please!'

The creature named Michael turned to face me, silent and judging.

Catherine's frozen fingers caressed my face. 'You promise to obey, Jeanne? To bind yourself to the Dauphin's cause and free France?'

I didn't understand what she meant – but even sick to my stomach, shivering with fear and grief, I knew what Blessed Catherine wanted me to say.

'I promise.' She let go of me. I curled up on the grass at her feet and shut my eyes tight. 'I promise.'

Emptiness filled me; the archangel and Blessed Catherine were gone. I could still see Margaret's light even though my eyes were closed, but it appeared faded and dim, her voice sounding far away.

Fingers brushed my cheek, the icy touch so light I wasn't sure I'd felt it. 'Remember your promise, Jeanne. Remember how afraid of Michael you are this day, this moment, and be wary. He won't hesitate to punish you again and you're too young and weak to defy him. Being the Maid won't be easy. Learn all you can as you grow older and grow strong. Survive.'

When I finally opened my eyes, I was curled up under the apple tree at home. A pile of young pups slept against my back, paws twitching as they dreamed of chasing butterflies and grasshoppers. Their mother kept watch over all of us, her head up and blue eyes missing nothing.

The yard was quiet without the sounds of sheep bleating in the pen or dogs barking. Papa and my brothers hadn't come back yet. I hadn't been gone long, no matter that it felt as if days had passed.

I rolled onto my back, searching for a sign the voices were

nearby, but not a faint shimmer of their light showed. The place they'd filled inside was still empty as well.

One of the puppies woke, making scared little noises, and I helped it climb onto my chest. I put an arm around the pup and began to cry.

I was home and safe, if only for the moment. That didn't erase the fear and grief welling inside, or make me forget the dryads' screams as they turned to dust.

But I was only five, too young to cling to the horror of what I'd seen for long, and the spirits let my memory of the dyads fade. They never let me forget my promise.

Part One

I fear nothing for God is with me!

Jeanne d'Arc

The lamb bleated non-stop, a sound that made my heart race and thud against my ribs. I followed the cries and the growing stench overwhelming the normal stink of pigs and cow shit on a hot day. The smell kept getting stronger, threatening to gag me.

At the edge of the wash I stumbled over the ewe's body. A gaping, bloody hole was all that was left of her belly and chest. An older carcase a few strides away was the source of the smell, but the ewe would stink as much by morning. Tracks circled the two dead sheep – more of the English army's dogs. The dogs had eaten their fill, and moved on.

Gone for now didn't mean gone for ever. The dogs and the soldiers might come back, or another group might come this way. Far too many hunting hounds followed the English soldiers, and rumour said their commanders didn't hesitate to set the dogs on stray sheep. English soldiers slaughtered cattle for themselves, and their dogs ran down their own dinner of mutton. If the peasants starved, so be it.

That morning, my brother Pierre had chosen a grazing pasture we hadn't visited in weeks. The field was called Shepherd's Haven, a large pasture ringed with tumbled rocks and full of new spring grass. Hidden among the boulders were shrines dedicated to the shepherds' guardian spirits and saints, one for each herding family in the village. Many had crumbled with disuse, abandoned by men afraid of Father Jakob's disapproval, but my father and older brothers didn't fear the village priest's disapproval. Pierre and I left new offerings each time we brought the flock to graze.

I'd barely set the fresh offering in place before one of my voices, Margaret, sent a vision, showing me a pregnant ewe was missing and which way she'd wandered. After telling my brother, I set off to look for her. I'd been too late to save the ewe, but the constant bleating said the lamb was very much alive. We needed every newborn this season to replace what the English stole.

Picturing the mother placing herself between the pack and her lamb wasn't hard – Papa's sheep weren't easy prey: he'd spent years working to make sure that was true. Ewes used their big, curling horns to defend themselves as often as the rams, so sheep who didn't grow up to have horns were the first ones sold at market.

Old bone crunched underfoot as I moved away from the ewe's body. Lynx, red fox and badger hunted in the valley and all kinds of prey found themselves driven to the edge of the wash and trapped. Rumours of a wolf pack had surfaced when sheep first started disappearing, but the stories quickly died.

Scuff marks showed me where the lamb had gone over the rim and slid down into the wash. Finding a way down I could manage without falling and that wouldn't trap me was hard. I considered sliding down a clear section of the wash wall, the way the lamb had, but that left the problem of finding handholds to climb out again. Whatever I did, it needed to happen soon. The baby's distress cries were more frantic and at the same time weaker.

The day was warm for early spring and growing warmer, making the smell of the dead sheep stronger. I fought back the need to retch and muttered a plea for help, hoping this time one of the spirits would answer. They didn't always. Other times they said no and left me to wonder why.

They'd said no when I'd begged them to save my mother and refused to answer when I begged again, pleading to be told why they'd let Mama die. I'd feared and hated them since I was five. I hated them even more for letting my mother die.

'Margaret, you told me where to look. Please help me find a way to save the lamb.'

A great light always heralded a visit from my voices and now it came near to blinding me, even at midday. When the brightness dimmed, Margaret spoke. 'Keep searching, Jeanne. Look for a place where the wash narrows.'

Flowering bushes crowded the edge at the narrowest point and I almost went past the spot. Fat black bumblebees buzzed in my ears, all of them upset at being disturbed as I pushed between the branches to the edge. A small yet sturdy tree jutted from the side of the wash only a foot or so down, giving me a starting point for climbing. Rocks and thick gnarly roots jutted from the soil all the way to the bottom of the wash.

The gradual slope I saw was different from the straight drop. I was tall for thirteen, my hands strong from working with the sheep, as well as weaving and spinning. Picking out a way down, one where I didn't have to stretch too far for handholds, or places to put my feet, got easier the longer I stared at the rocky wall. Even so, I'd need to be careful.

'Thank you for your generosity, Margaret,' I muttered.

I scrambled over the edge before I had time to lose my nerve. Getting to the bottom wasn't easy. Twice I slipped and slid before I caught myself. A wasp's nest clung to the wall a little over halfway down, its muddy shape and dull grey walls nearly invisible. The nest was out of the path I'd taken, but wasps buzzed and droned ominously. I scurried down the rest of the wall faster.

My arms shook and I was drenched with sweat by the time my feet touched the bottom of the shallow wash, but rest could come later. I wiped sweaty hands on my tunic and hurried to collect the lamb.

The lamb was only hours old, and it was desperate to be fed. All I had was the warm water left in my water bag, but I managed to drip some into the newborn's mouth. That would have to do until I found a ewe willing to nurse an orphan. I tucked the baby deep into the sling I always carried and made sure it couldn't wiggle out as I climbed. The bleating stopped right away, a blessing. I hurried back to the place where I'd climbed down.

Going up the side of the wash was easier than going down. I breathed a prayer of thanks as I reached the top. The voices' light flared bright, making my eyes tear, and Margaret spoke again.

'Tell your father what you found today and warn him the English grow bolder. Watch what your father does, Jeanne, and learn what you can when he arms himself. You're an obedient daughter, but never forget you aren't destined to be a shepherd's wife. Do you remember everything the archangel told you?'

I wasn't likely to forget, not when he'd told me again and again ever since he'd first appeared to me. Michael wasn't a real arch-angel, but his face was too terrible and beautiful to look upon, just as the priest said an archangel should be. He always held a flaming sword up before me to make sure I paid attention. Where Margaret's voice was wind-stirred church bells, Catherine's ice and winter-bare branches, Michael's was thunder and lashing winds. His voice always made me tremble head to foot. I never saw any of their faces – only the light – but confusing them with God's angels and saints, no matter what they claimed or wanted me to believe, was equally impossible. There was nothing holy about these creatures.

'I . . . I remember,' I said. 'Michael said Grand-mère was born to be the Maid before me, but Charles VI went mad and couldn't be crowned. Now it's my destiny to drive the English out of France . . . and I need to accept my fate and obey the way she did. I'll lead a brave army, and put a king upon his throne. Others will doubt me and mock my cause, but I'm the . . . the Maid in the prophecy.'

The light pulsed brighter and in a frost-touched voice, Catherine said, 'Not everyone will doubt. All of France knows the prophecy of the Maid of Lorraine and men will flock to your banner. But your path won't be easy, Jeanne. Hold tight to the people who believe in you. We'll tell you when the time is right to find the Dauphin.'

'And will you teach me how to fight, and tell me what to do, Catherine?' My voice trembled as hard as my hands and my heart pounded even faster with fear, but I needed to know. 'I'm only a girl. My grand-mère taught me to spin and sew, how to help a ewe give birth and how to make bread. I'm expected to marry and have children of my own. That's my life – my future. I know nothing of war.'

'You'll learn to fight,' Margaret said. 'The three of us will guide your every step. Now go home before Marie starts to worry. Tell your father to be ready to protect the village.'

The light flashed, making the midday sun look dim, and the emptiness inside said the voices were gone for now. They'd first come to me when I was innocent enough to believe when they claimed to be God's angels and too young to think it strange when Catherine made me promise to obey them. She'd said obedience was God's will, and that the Lord would bless me above all others.

I hadn't felt blessed then, and I felt less so as I got older. The visions they forced on me of the war I was supposed to fight terrified me, while the idea of taking a life – any life – horrified me to the point I couldn't speak.

My doubts about destiny, and the rebellious streak Grand-mère worked so hard to control, rushed in to replace fear. I slipped a hand into the sling to pet the sleeping lamb.

'The Dauphin will be the first to mock me,' I whispered. 'I'm not a prophecy fulfilled, I'm a peasant girl. That's all I'll ever be.'

Thunder sounded in the distance and clouds crowded the horizon, a promise of rain before dark. I turned back the way I'd come and ran for home.

All but a few families in Domrémy herded sheep. The land far beyond Scholar's Field and all the way to the village was kept free of fencing or stone walls by decree of the Lady of Lorraine. People had their garden plots, animal pens and small pieces of land near their cottages, but the land outside the village was open pasture for all of us to share. We had enough troubles with the English freely roaming our land and the lady didn't want the peasants under her rule squabbling over good grazing land or locked gates.

Other than the streams winding towards the river, nothing blocked my path as I ran home. As our house came into view, I breathed a prayer of thanks I hadn't run into trouble on the way.

My older brother, Pierre, had driven the flock back to the enclosed pasture near the house and now the beasts milled around inside as he filled troughs with water and hay. Normally we'd have stopped penning them overnight by early April, but the English dogs and nearby raids made Papa cautious. We'd already lost too many – if we lost the entire flock, that would set us back years.

We'd been fortunate the English had only taken a handful of cattle so far, but that was pure luck. The herd grazed the large pasture beyond the sheep, but we couldn't keep them confined more than another day or two. Half the grass inside was eaten down to the roots, which meant every time it rained, the ground turned to mud, which was made worse by the cattle moving around in a fenced-off space. Each time, new growth took longer to sprout, and the number of bare spots increased. The land needed time to recover – and the cattle needed more food.

Shaggy black-and-white herd dogs sprawled outside the sheep pen, blue eyes bright and pink tongues lolling out the side of their mouths. Two of my favourite dogs trotted over and nosed the sling cradling the lamb, tails wagging. The tiny sheep woke, remembered her stomach and began to bleat non-stop.

Pierre heard and his head came up. Relief that I was home safe, disappointment at not seeing the ewe and resignation moved across his face rapidly. He went back to feeding the sheep we still had.

The dogs nosing the lamb slipped into the pen with me, keeping the flock from rushing out of the gate. I touched the protection charm hanging from the gatepost, a crude sheep-shaped figure woven from honey-soaked straw, and muttered thanks the ewes had delivered safely and we hadn't lost any lambs. Tomorrow I'd burn the old charm, sending away the bad luck it had trapped, and hang a new one. For now, I went straight to the cluster of sheep under the lean-to at the back of the pen. One of the older, more experienced ewes who had given birth that morning let the orphan lamb nurse side by side with her own newborn.

'Thank you, little mother.' I scratched between her ears. 'God's blessings on you.'

I hurried to help Pierre fill the last of the water troughs. My arms were already sore from the climb in and out of the wash and hauling heavy buckets of water from the pond didn't ease my aches. We finished the last of the chores fairly quickly and my brother waved me out the gate.

He put an arm over my shoulders and led me to the apple tree growing between the two pastures. New leaves filled the branches and the ground was carpeted with freshly fallen blossoms. Tiny green apples, no bigger than the end of my finger, already showed on the branches.

Pierre said, 'Sit and tell me where you found the lamb, and what happened to the ewe as well. Papa will want a full accounting.'

I put my back against the tree and slid down the trunk to the ground. 'I found both the lamb and her mother in the middle of Scholar's Field. The lamb was at the bottom of the wash that slices through on the north end, near the spring and the slate quarry. A pack of English dogs had torn out the ewe's throat, and made a meal of the rest. You and Papa can go and look at the tracks, but I'm convinced that's what happened.'

My brother scowled. 'Papa will want to go look, but not because he thinks you're wrong. He'll want to know how close to the village they've made camp.'

Fear tingled under my skin, cold and hot at the same time. I'd forgotten all about Margaret's message and telling Papa to prepare. If Pierre was right, I wouldn't have to say anything.

'Do you think the English are planning a raid?'

'I don't know.' Pierre stretched out in the sparse shade and closed his eyes. 'They could be moving through on their way to one of the cities or bigger towns and not camped near us at all. The English can find richer targets without much effort, but that won't keep them from stealing what's under their noses. Put it out of your mind until we know.'

Grand-mère rang the big bell mounted next to the back door, and my stomach responded by growling loudly. Pierre laughed and helped me up, and the two of us strolled up the hill from the pasture to the house.

Our house reflected all Papa and Mama's hard work and my father's status as a village official. Papa, not the local lord, owned the land our house sat on and thirty acres besides. As my two brothers married, our father planned to build each a home of his own and gift them each with a piece of land. Five acres wasn't a huge amount, but enough to give his sons a start in life.

Pierre had a parcel all picked out on the far north edge of the land, covered in trees and good grass for grazing. Henri, the eldest, had declared he'd let his future wife choose where she wanted to settle. I secretly hoped Anaïs, the girl he'd been courting, might be wiser than Henri and have the common sense to build as far from Pierre's house as possible. My brothers loved each other, as most brothers did, but they quarrelled constantly.

The house Papa had built for Mama boasted stone walls, not wattle and daub like most of the village. A real glass window was mounted in the middle of the long wall of the main room: Papa's wedding present to my mother, carefully wrapped in Paris and transported hundreds of leagues so he could surprise her.

Papa still told stories about that day and the look on her face, but now there were tears in his eyes as he remembered. Mama had bled to death a little over a year ago; the baby born too soon had died with her. I glanced at the cradle near the fireplace each time I came into the cottage, battling fresh anger that the spirits wouldn't save her and wondering if Mama would greet me in heaven.

Crusty bread from the morning's baking, a wedge of yellow cheese and a crock of mutton stew crowded the centre of the table. Papa said a prayer of thanks, filled the bowls and passed them around. My mouth was full of the sweet, creamy cheese long before my stew, big chunks of mutton, diced shallots, dried parsley and thick slices of turnip, was passed to me at the far end of the table. I finished by mopping up the broth with a piece of Grand-mère's bread.

Papa and Pierre had their heads together at the other end of the table. Knowing what they were talking about didn't keep me from worrying about the serious expressions and frowns on Papa's face. They worried Grand-mère Marie even more.

'Jacques, don't keep secrets from your mother.' Grand-mère could always get away with wagging a finger at him, but no one else could. 'Tell me what's wrong. Maybe together we can fix it.'

'Dead sheep and roving packs of English dogs aren't easily fixed, Mama.' He leaned back in his chair and crossed his arms. 'Jeanne saved the lamb, but not the ewe – we can't afford to lose any of the flock, so this is especially bitter. I only hope she bred true.'

Grand-mère snorted. 'A sheep is a sheep and all your tinkering with putting ewes and rams together won't change God's plans. I worry more about losing the wool and the meat than big horns. You should do the same.'

Pierre and I exchanged looks, but kept quiet. Grand-mère and Papa had this argument at least once a week. She wanted to leave everything in God's hands and accept whatever came as a part of His plan – good or bad – with grace.

Papa didn't see anything wrong with nudging the Lord's plan along in the right direction. I'd heard him argue with Grand-mère over horns on sheep and choosing which rams covered which ewes

24

more times than I could count. Those arguments almost always led to bitter fights about the offerings my father and my brothers insisted on leaving at the small altars and shrines on our land. Neither would give an inch.

Our oldest brother, Henri, sighed and changed the subject. 'Scholar's Field is a good distance from where the flock grazed this morning. How did you know where to look, Jeanne?'

My hands were tucked into my lap, out of sight. I dug my fingernails into my palms, a small penitence for a partial lie. 'I . . . I prayed and asked for guidance to show me where the ewe had wandered to. The lamb was crying and I could hear she was a long way away from Scholar's Field. I found her in the wash and I prayed until I found a place I could climb down and get her out. Then I ran home as fast as I could.'

Much like Grand-mère, Henri never let things go easily. He drummed his fingers on the table and stared. 'You hate high places – and yet you managed to find a way to climb to the bottom of this wash and climbed out again with a lamb in your arms. Another sainted miracle, Jeanne?'

I opened my mouth to explain, but Pierre put a hand on my shoulder and shook his head. Staying quiet in the face of Henri's scorn was hard, but I'd do as Pierre asked. He was a little more than two years older than me, but he was already treated like a man by everyone in the village.

Everyone, that is, but our brother Henri. Pierre had stopped attempting to keep the peace in the family, refusing to back down when Henri played the bully with him. Then, when not long after Mama died our older brother decided I was an easier target, Pierre had taken it upon himself to defend me too.

'I've seen Jeanne drive a badger away from a ewe who'd just

given birth,' Pierre said. 'If you were in the pastures more often, you wouldn't question our sister's courage, Henri. I'm thanking God the English and their dogs weren't waiting for her in that field.'

Papa cleared his throat. 'We should all give thanks for that, Pierre. There are worse things than losing a beast and I'm grateful we don't have to face any of them. What we need to know now is if they set up camp close by, or if they kept going on their way north. If they're planning to raid the village cattle, we need to be ready.'

A stern look from Grand-mère pushed me to get up and help clear the table and start washing the bowls. She made sure the task was well begun before she went out to feed the chickens. For once, I didn't mind doing the washing-up. I was free to listen and no one could claim I was eavesdropping.

Papa and Pierre discussed how best to search for the English. Henri listened carefully, but only spoke up to ask questions, or when he disagreed with something Pierre suggested. Their biggest worry was what to do if they found the soldiers camping nearby, or signs that more troops were moving towards our village.

Driving the village cattle to our lord's castle until the danger passed was high on Papa's list. He argued that the duke wouldn't want the people under his protection to starve. Dead peasants didn't pay taxes, or tithe a share of the harvest. Getting the entire village to agree was the problem. Papa's influence only went so far.

I'd finished cleaning up by the time they were ready to leave.

'Papa? Can I come along?' I asked. 'I could show you where I found the lamb.'

'Not this time, little bird.' Papa touched my cheek and smiled. 'We might be gone until long after dark and I can't swear we won't be braving the lion in his den. Look after the sheep and your grand-mère. If anything happens while we're gone, the two of you run for the caves near the river. Promise me you'll stay with Grand-mère and make her go with you.'

'You think the English will attack today?' I tried to sound calm, and not let on how my heart raced.

'Only God and the English know the answer to that, Jeanne. They may never look our way.' Papa sighed. 'But I want a promise from you anyway. Stay with your grand-mère, no matter what happens. I need to know the two of you are safe if fighting starts.'

My stomach dropped as light filled my eyes. I braced myself for a vision that might show who in my family would die if the English came, but the light faded and took the vision with it. The angels had often shown me my future as the Maid, and other things too, some meant only to frighten me. I was strangely reluctant to promise my father anything, but I knew he'd keep asking until I agreed.

'I promise, Papa. I'll stay with Grand-mère.'

Both my brothers had armed themselves, threading sheaths with long daggers onto their belts, then buckling on swords; Henri fiddled with getting his to hang just right and not tangle his steps. He was never comfortable with weapons.

Pierre held our father's blade, watching me and waiting. He knew me best, and I didn't doubt he understood why I'd hesitated to give promises to our father. At times I thought my brother saw all the hopes and fears I hid in my heart.

'Tell your grand-mère where we've gone. May God watch over both of you.' Papa kissed my cheek. He took his sword from Pierre and the three of them went out the door.

'May all the angels keep you safe, Papa, and the guardians bring you home again,' I whispered. 'Margaret and Catherine, please protect my father and my brothers. Bring them back to me safe and sound.'

Silence was the only answer they gave, but I hadn't really expected one. The voices only spoke when it suited them.

Light, bright as midday, filled the loft where I slept. Michael's rumbling voice yanked me awake. 'Your first trial is beginning, Jeanne. The English troops are outside the village and you don't have much time. Wake Marie and keep your promise to take her to the river caves. Go quickly now!'

I'd gone to sleep still fully clothed, too nervous to risk changing and having to hurriedly dress again in the dark. Michael's light lasted long enough for me to tug on my boots and hurry over to the ladder. A sling packed with the few extra clothes I owned was looped over the top of the ladder's side rail. I slipped the strap over my head and climbed down to the main room.

Grand-mère's small bed was in the corner near the hearth, the warmest place in the cottage. Soft snores filled the semi-darkness, but I could hear distant shouts and faint screams as people in the main village woke.

Breathing fast and straining to hear any sound from outside, I shook Grand-mère's shoulder. 'Grand-mère, wake up! Wake up!'

'I'm awake, child. No need to rattle my teeth.' She yawned. 'What's wrong?'

'The English are raiding the village,' I said. 'Listen: you can hear them! We have to get to the river.'

Screams from within the main village mixed with men's shouts now, all of them sounding closer and louder. Grand-mère threw off the blanket and rolled out of bed.

'Light a candle, Jeanne. Find the market bags while I get dressed. Hurry now.'

I grabbed them from the peg where they always hung and piled them in the middle of the table. Grand-mère, who had already tugged on a tunic and skirt over her chemise, began stuffing them with food. When I tried to help, she waved me away.

'Let me do this, child,' she said. 'I know better what will keep and what to leave behind. Sit near the fire until I'm finished.'

I perched on the edge of a wobbly bench and hunched over my knees, eyes shut tight. Forcing myself to sit there, still and quiet and doing nothing, was almost more than I could bear. Sounds of the English attack continued to fill the cottage, growing louder as the fighting moved closer. Women were screaming and babies crying while men on both sides shouted orders. I smelled burning: the smoke blowing in around the shutters was thick and dark and full of ash, smelling of thatch and wool and charred meat. The stench made me sick.

Doing nothing made me furious, nervous and afraid. I guessed Papa and my brothers would be in the thick of the fighting. Letting the English take what they wanted without being challenged wasn't like Papa or either of my brothers. They'd fight back.

Grand-mère Marie muttered prayers under her breath. Yesterday had been a baking day and she packed all the fresh loaves, the cheese and what was left of the dried apples. Silence signalled she'd finally come to the end of our meagre stores, or at least what wouldn't spoil quickly.

'Get up, Jeanne, and help me,' she said, shoving a handful of the bags at me. 'We can't wait for your papa. We have to go right now.'

I slipped my arms into the straps and balanced the load on my back. I was strong as a grown woman, but Grand-mère still took the larger share. The sling sat snug against my chest. I couldn't help looking around the room, not wanting to forget any of what I saw, wondering if everything we owned would crumble to ash by daybreak.

'Stay with me, child.' Grand-mère touched my cheek. 'God and his angels will protect us.'

A faint halo of light warned that my personal guardians – Margaret and Catherine – stood near the door. When I was much younger, I'd imagined the two creatures looked like the angels in the small stained-glass window behind the church altar, or the saints offering blessings on the painted wood panels hung inside the sanctuary. All angels were tall and beautiful, with long dark hair and black eyes, dressed in bright white robes, and they radiated peace and comfort.

My spirits brought little comfort and no peace. The one thing I was certain of was that their words had nothing to do with God or His angels, but I wasn't convinced they were the demons Father Jakob warned about.

These creatures were something else. The thought they might be the Fae I'd heard stories about, the *Dames Blanches*, creatures said to be cold and uncaring about the people who lived on the land they guarded, made my insides quiver.

Smoke dimmed the waning moon and made the night even darker as Grand-mère led me outside. Flames jumped hungrily from rooftop to rooftop in the main village, igniting summer-dry thatch. Herd-dogs barked non-stop, loud even over the sound of panicked sheep bleating at the top of their lungs.

'Grand-mère, wait.' I pointed up the hill. 'If you can manage the gate for the cattle, I can let the sheep out and start them moving towards the pastures we've been grazing. The dogs will take care of the rest.'

'Smart girl. If we left the herd penned, the English could take what they please. Traipsing through the hills to gather them up again is better than losing the lot.' Grand-mère patted my shoulder. 'I can manage the cattle gate. Whistle up the dogs and put them to work.'

A few of the youngest dogs were as panicked as the sheep, but Pierre and I had spent hours training them and when the older, steadier ones responded to the three quick whistles, the signal to drive the sheep towards the high pastures, the youngsters calmed down quickly and fell in line, belly down, in the grass on either side of the gate. As soon as the sheep poured out of the pasture, they were bunched together and pushed in the right direction, the oldest dogs collecting the straggling ewes and their lambs and the young rams trying to head off alone and driving them back to the others. I made sure the flock was well in hand, then ran to check on my grand-mère.

I needn't have worried. The last few cattle were running into the darkness, encouraged to move faster by the long switch in Grand-mère's hand. I breathed a prayer of thanks.

The fighting was much closer, the clank of swords on shields and men swearing easy to hear. Grand-mère took a firm grip on my hand and we ran towards the river. Most nights I could smell the wet earth in our yard or hear the ducks calling from the reeds along the banks. Tonight, all that was lost in the smoke and screams.

Twice full-grown men running in blind panic came close to knocking me down, but Grand-mère helped me stay on my feet. The crowd pushed us towards the woods and away from the river, a tide difficult to swim against. French soldiers with blood on their faces or gaping wounds in their calves, sides and arms swelled the stream of villagers trying to escape. A few carried torches. Older children carried the babes while their mothers took those too young to run or keep up. One woman hurried past with a toddler in her arms and the younger son on her back.

Fear transformed the faces of people I'd known my entire life, neighbours and friends now a parade of strangers – I couldn't remember their names, or which house they'd lived in.

My own anger and terror played a role in forgetting. I didn't want to die, but Michael's voice rumbled in my head, ordering me to find a sword and fight and promising I'd be victorious. Running away made me feel a coward, but Papa had made me promise to stay with Grand-mère. I wouldn't break my word.

Bundles of flaming brands streaked overhead and landed on roofs, spreading the fire until every house in the village was burning. Domrémy was prosperous, larger than most villages in Lorraine and according to Papa, a prize the English were eager to seize – but now the enemy were destroying their prize, leaving the villagers with next to nothing. I needed to ask Papa or Pierre why, but they hadn't found us yet.

Then I saw them just ahead, standing at the edge of the woods. Blood on the blade of Papa's sword glistened in the uncertain torchlight, and more blood showed on Pierre's. They were trying to turn people aside from their headlong rush into the woods. Some heeded the warning. Most didn't.

Papa saw me, waved, and sent Pierre over to us. At sixteen, my brother was broad-shouldered and taller than our father, already one of the strongest men in the village. He ploughed through the crowd, careful of the women and children, but none too gentle with any man who wouldn't get out of the way. He was breathing hard when he reached us.

'Thank all the heavenly saints you're both safe. I was afraid we'd missed you in the dark.' Pierre's fingers flexed around the sword's pommel. He put his free arm around my shoulders and pulled me in close. 'We need to fight our way towards the river, not into the trees. The English are moving this way through the woods. Papa feels obligated to try and warn the entire village, but most of these idiots won't listen.'

'Then they'll die,' Grand-mère Marie said. 'God have mercy on the children. Lead the way, Grandson. Maybe a few of the smarter idiots will follow.'

'What about Papa?' I asked. 'And where's Henri?'

'Don't worry about Henri. He knows where we're going and how to find us. Papa will follow soon.' Pierre's eyes searched the darkness. 'Stay clear of my sword-arm, Jeanne. If it comes to a fight, you and Grand-mère run for the river. Do you remember where the cave I showed you is?'

'Up the small hill, hidden between the oak and the cracked boulder.'

Pierre smiled. 'If we get separated, wait for us there. Let's go.'

Pushing through the mob of villagers trying to reach the woods wasn't easy, but Pierre's shoulder made an effective battering ram and his sword made people wary. A man with two torches reluctantly surrendered one to my brother, who passed it to me. We broke through the crowd and into the clear and Pierre set a faster pace until the three of us were running. He kept an eye on Grand-mère to make sure she didn't fall behind and a tight hold on my hand to keep me from stumbling.

A brisk wind gusted off the river, blowing most of the smoke back towards the village. The moon grew brighter as the smoke thinned. Being able to see, even just a little, was a blessing. Pierre's shoulders relaxed and he slowed enough to allow Grand-mère to keep up easily. I realised he'd been worried that more English troops might appear out of the dark.

Shouts and the sound of running horses came from the way we'd come. Pierre slowed down to look back and I ducked under his arm so I could see too. Two English nobles were chasing Papa down, getting closer with each stride their horses took. A roar filled my ears and my head swam as Papa found a place to stand his ground and faced the two mounted men, sword raised, chest heaving and a snarl on his face.

Grand-mère clung to Pierre's arm as he moved away, holding him back from going to help Papa. The two of them began to argue and shout as the faint shimmering light I associated with the voices appeared. They silently watched Papa confronting the mounted knights.

'Please, Catherine and Margaret, I beg you, Michael, help him.' I couldn't look away from my father, but they listened. 'Don't let Papa die. I beg you, please, save his life.'

Catherine's winter-gale voice spoke first. 'Jacques d'Arc is at the end of his days. His fate is sealed as much as yours.'

'Your father shackles you to your old life,' Margaret said, a hard note dulling her bells. 'You cannot fulfil your destiny while he lives.'

The English nobles walked their horses in circles around Papa, laughing and forcing him to constantly turn in a circle to keep them in sight. The spirits' light shimmered through my tears.

'But if the three of you are truly angels, you can save him! Nothing is beyond God's power or an angel's miracles. Please, *please* don't let my father die.'

'Don't beg us for heavenly miracles; we won't give you one,' Michael said. The anger and command in his voice left me shaking.

'You are the Maid. If you want him to live, you must save him yourself!'

I'd never touched a sword or used any weapon to defend myself, yet Michael's command sent me staggering towards my father before terror froze me in place again.

The English knights were taunting Papa, trying to anger him and force him to make a mistake. Papa stayed calm and backed away from them slowly, careful to keep his distance and just as careful not to lead them closer to Grand-mère and me.

A cold hand gripped my shoulder and Catherine's voice hissed in my ear, 'Find your courage and fight for him, Jeanne. Fight – or watch him die.'

Courage had nothing to do with the way I trembled. The thought of watching Papa die was unthinkable, and laying the blame on my shoulders was monstrous, evil. I couldn't save him without weapons, or knowing how to use them.

And God's will had nothing to do with the compulsion to obey my voices, even if obedience meant my own death, or how Catherine's hand tightened on my shoulder until I couldn't breathe around the pain.

One of the knights spurred his horse and charged my father. My stubborn refusal to obey them crumbled under the creatures' compulsion and I ran towards Papa. I wouldn't let him die while all I did was watch.

I couldn't.

My brother yanked me back. The torch flew out of my hand, already sputtering, hit the ground and went out.

'Stay with Grand-mère!' Pierre shouted. 'Go to the caves and wait.'

I twisted out of his grip and dodged to the side, but Pierre caught me after only a few steps. He picked me up, ignoring the way I kicked and squirmed, and deposited me at Grand-mère's feet. 'For once in your life, listen to me, Jeanne – stay with Grand-mère, as you promised. Get her to the cave and keep her safe.'

Pierre touched my face, then turned to run towards the fight. I waited, counting steps until he was too far away to come back, before breaking free of Grand-mère's hold and running after him. All three spirits let me pass without a word, but my grand-mère's scream of frustration filled my ears, declaring she couldn't follow. I was running too hard to hear all she said, but I thought she was yelling at Michael and Catherine to let her go.

The English lord circling Papa was mounted. He had a longer sword and wore chainmail, putting my father at a huge disadvantage. Papa kept a two-handed grip on his short sword, battering away the Englishman's blade each time the lord attempted to impale him. The sword lashed out again and again as the knight toyed with him. Papa was already tired and winded after his run, and dancing out of the way was getting harder. My heart stuttered each time he had to try.

Pierre was younger, quick and nimble, and the knight he'd goaded into chasing him more reckless. Taunts and insults drew the English soldier further and further away from Papa – and his companion. The knight wore a helm and no chainmail and his mount wasn't armoured at all. A quick sword slash along the flank turned the horse into a demon, rearing up and bucking, turning and twisting in circles. The beast went all the way up on his hind legs and Pierre darted in to draw his sword across the animal's throat. Both horse and rider crashed to the ground.

The English knight struggled against the horse's weight pinning his legs, desperate to get up, or to roll far enough to the side to reach his fallen sword. Pierre watched for an instant, his expression grim, then smashed his boot heel down on the Englishman's face, breaking his nose, before drawing his knife and cutting his throat.

Pierre wiped his knife on a clump of grass and ran towards Papa.

My stomach flipped and I gagged, choking on bile. I'd never seen that much blood or heard the horrible sounds a man made as he bled and drowned and died. Real war was nothing like the stories old men told in the marketplace. I couldn't understand how men found glory in killing each other over a piece of land.

I forgot all about the dying man when Papa screamed. Blood was streaming from his shoulder and his left arm hung limp. He swayed on his feet as the English noble watched, waiting for him to fall – waiting for an easy kill.

'No . . . NO!' I yelled. 'Leave my father alone!'

The Englishman glanced my way, but all he saw was another unarmed peasant girl in a dirty tunic, her braid coming undone and dark hair hanging in her face. Papa was more of a threat, even wounded, and Pierre was running towards them as fast as he could. The nobleman ignored me and split his attention between my father and my brother. Without a sword or a long knife, I was easy to dismiss.

That didn't mean I was helpless. I dropped to my hands and knees and searched the ground for something, anything, to throw and distract the enemy until Pierre reached our father.

'Please, I beg you, give me a weapon I can use,' I whispered. 'Please.'

My fingers closed around a heavy stone, the perfect size to fit my hand. More rocks were stacked less than a handspan away. Younger boys used them to hunt rabbits and partridge so it wasn't strange to find the missiles they'd thrown scattered around, but I'd never seen them stacked and waiting this way.

I shivered. Questions about whether my plea for help had been answered by one of the river spirits or my hated voices filled my head. I was even more afraid of not knowing. The top layer of stones rattled and danced, making me jump, calling for me to take what I'd been given. My hands shook badly, but I filled the big pocket on my tunic and scrambled to my feet.

The horse's head cover was cloth, not chainmail, and festooned with fluttering silk ribbons. I begged God's forgiveness and threw. The first hit was a glancing blow; the horse tossed his head and danced in place, but his rider kept him from bolting. My second and third throws hit squarely and the English noble swore loudly as he fought to keep the horse from rearing up and throwing him off.

One last stone found its target before Pierre closed the distance. He came at them from the back while the rider was still fighting for control, drew his blade across the horse's back legs and darted away.

I'd never heard a horse scream before. The sound went straight to my heart.

The animal sat back abruptly, bellowing his pain at the sky. Pierre cut the horse's throat, putting the poor animal out of its misery. He ripped open the Englishman's helm as soon as he fell. The noble knight opened his mouth to curse my brother and Pierre filled it with a sword. I looked away.

Papa went to his knees and the sword fell from his fingers. Pierre and I reached him at the same instant and eased him onto his back. He hissed through tight-clenched teeth, but didn't cry out. I stared at the blood soaking Papa's tunic and couldn't stop crying.

'We have to bind the wound before we can move him.' Pierre

offered his knife, hilt first. 'Cut strips off the knights' tunics and search their purses for any coin you can find. Quickly now.'

I took a step back. 'You want me to rob the dead. That's . . . That's—'

'They brought the war to us, Jeanne, and right now we don't have any choice. More soldiers will come and all of us will die then.' He looked me in the eye and offered the knife again. 'They don't have any use for tunics and silver coins now. We do. Hurry.'

Taking the knife and approaching the first dead soldier left me sick to my stomach. Tugging his tunic free from underneath the chainmail was easier than I'd feared, but most of the fabric was soaked in blood, leaving very little safe for binding wounds. I took what I could, before looking for his purse. At first I couldn't find it, but the leather bag was hanging from his saddle. I breathed a prayer of thanks it wasn't trapped under the dead horse and cut the ties without a thought. The weight of the English nobleman's purse surprised me and I almost dropped it. Coins shifted inside as I tucked the bag into my sling.

Robbing the second man was easier. His tunic was cleaner and I gathered a good supply of binding strips. He had little coin, but a folded square of linen tied with silk ribbons was worth taking. I slipped Pierre's knife through my belt, freeing my hands to carry all the cloth I'd gathered, and ran back to my brother.

A faint light showed the voices still stood with Grand-mère where I'd left her. I'd expected to turn around and find she'd come to help Pierre and me with Papa, but she hadn't moved. Being afraid wasn't like her; all I could think was the creatures were still holding her back.

Getting Papa on his feet again after binding his wound was hard, but my brother and I managed. Wringing her hands and loudly imploring God to hear her prayers, Grand-mère watched us limp towards her. The spirits waited silently, but didn't offer me any hope or words of encouragement.

I'd done what Michael and Catherine asked and fought for my father's life, using the only weapon I knew how to wield. Their silence shouted that I hadn't been brave or ruthless enough, or done anything they deemed worthy of earning Papa's life. The idea that I could save him was another lie, one I'd wanted and needed to hear. Now I couldn't convince myself Papa might live out the day, he'd lost too much blood.

Even with the bindings pulled tight as Pierre could get them, Papa was still bleeding. More darkened his tunic with every step and I remembered how my mother's blood had soaked into the mattress before she'd died. I prayed to Holy Mary to save him, or for God to grant our family a miracle, but the empty ache filling my chest was the only answer.

No one could save him. My father was dying.

The sun was beginning to rise by the time we reached the narrow trail leading to the caves. Getting Papa up the hill and into the cave was the hardest part. He grew weaker with each step and leaned heavily on Pierre. The trail wasn't wide enough for me to be of much help until we'd almost reached the top. We all gasped for breath by the time we got Papa inside and settled on the soft brown sand covering the cave floor.

Sunbeams found their way through the entrance to light the inside, picking out crude drawings of stags and horses and men hunting shaggy beasts with tusks. I'd never seen most of the creatures drawn on the walls, but someone had. The drawings snaked up the walls to the top and black lakes of soot on the ceiling told a story of torches burning at night. Other people had lived inside this cave in the distant past: knowing that made me feel a little safer.

'Rest, Jeanne.' Pierre touched my face. 'Sleep if you can. I'm going to sit outside and keep watch.'

Grand-mère sat next to Papa and rested a hand on his arm. 'Do you think we were followed, Grandson?'

He shook his head. 'Not by the English. I want to watch for Henri and a few of Papa's friends. He told them where to find us. Some . . . some of them may need help getting up the hill.'

I crawled into the back of the cave to try and sleep. The drone of Grand-mère's prayers followed me: *Áve María, grátia pléna, Dóminus técum; benedícta tu in muliéribus . . .*

When I was very small, I'd found the prayers comforting. Mama and Grand-mère Marie would pray together at bedtime, making me feel safe and protected by God and family. Now Mama was dead and buried and Papa was barely hanging on and the words grated, making me jumpy and on edge. I wanted to scream at Grand-mère to stop, to just be quiet, or if she had to say something, to explain why she'd never told me about these creatures or being the Maid – but I couldn't say the words.

Instead, I stared at the pulsing outline of the creatures standing over me, knowing there was no help or consolation from any of them, and likely no answers.

I asked anyway.

'I don't understand why you forced me into a fight I couldn't win, or why you lied about my being able to save my father. Is making me watch him die punishment?' I whispered. 'Taking away the people I love won't make me your willing servant. If anything, I'll have more reasons to hate you and fight harder.'

Margaret spoke in my ear. 'Hating us won't change your destiny, Jeanne.'

A light flared brighter and Michael's voice filled my head. 'And fighting us is another battle you can't win. Will knowing what's ahead make obedience easier?'

Frost-touched Catherine spoke up, her voice woven around the rattle of winter-bare branches. 'It's not time.'

Margaret appeared to shake her head. 'Too soon, too soon.'

The brightest light moved closer and a touch of icy fingers numbed my cheek. 'Let Jeanne speak.'

Michael's touch filled me with dread and loathing, not the peace and blessings Father Jakob preached an angel brought. Twice before he'd touched me: at five when the voices first appeared, and again at nine when I'd refused to obey a command. Both times had left me trembling, frozen to the bone and terrified.

Margaret came to me later and warned me not to challenge Michael. I'd heeded that warning until today. They'd already taken my mother from me. Now my father. Drowning in grief, I'd little left to fear.

I shut my eyes tight, unwilling to discover what might lie beyond the light hiding Michael. 'No, I won't obey. I . . . I'm not your servant.'

'If that's your choice, Jacques d'Arc will breathe his last tonight,' Catherine said, her voice a howling storm.

'You could have saved him,' Margaret's bell-filled voice tolled.

'Liars, all of you,' I said. 'You wanted Papa to die!'

A sob, quickly bitten off and silenced, interrupted Grand-mère's prayers and convinced me she'd heard. Her prayers started again an instant later, leaving me to wonder who she believed – me or the voices. I was afraid of the answer, but more than that, I was scared she'd deny these creatures existed.

Her faith brought comfort, but for the first time I wondered if faith shielded Grand-mère from admitting she'd once been tied to these uncaring spirits as tightly as I was now. I desperately wanted to talk to her, to ask questions and find out what she knew about them, but I wasn't sure she'd answer.

Worse, she might force me to tell Father Jakob everything, or tell him herself. He'd see little to no difference between guardian spirits, devils and demons.

The creatures' light pressed hard against my skin, a weight I could feel. The pressure lifted again as the three spirits vanished. When I dared open my eyes, the cave was dimly lit and full of comforting shadows.

I rolled over and faced the cave wall, fighting panic and deeper grief. The voices hadn't said my life still rested in their hands, but they didn't need to say the words; I knew. Whatever they'd planned for my future wasn't anything I wanted or imagined, or came close to being what was best for me. Mistrust of anything they thought was preordained in my life swelled to fill me and burrowed deeper inside.

Once before I'd begged them to save someone I loved – my mother, when the midwife couldn't staunch the blood soaking the mattress. My mother's screams had filled the house and echoed in the yard and the protective charm the midwife hung in the window had crumbled to dust as I watched. I'd tried to escape the knowledge my mother was dying by huddling with the herd dogs and weeping, but there was no escape.

I'd despised these creatures before that day. Listening to my mother's screams grow weaker, I'd hated them more than ever. They'd ignored my pleas and let my mother die, just as they were allowing Papa to die now. No matter how frequently they'd lied about being angels and saints, the truth was, they were far from holy.

A few village women, older and less devout than Grand-mère, told stories among themselves that my grand-mère never wanted me to hear. I'd heard them anyway, sitting at the old women's feet and pretending to watch the jugglers on feast days. Stories of the *Matres* and the *Dames Blanches*, Fae guardians neither completely good nor evil, were frowned upon by the village priest: at one time, our ancestors had worshipped the *Dames Blanches* as goddesses, which gave Father Jakob even more reasons to wipe their memory away. The *Dames* and the *Matres* were said to protect the land and water of France and turn away invaders, but they were largely indifferent to the people living on their land.

Five years old was too young to have heard and remembered all the women's stories, or the warnings woven into the tales. My promise to obey meant I'd bound myself to them without knowing what I'd done.

Rebellion churned inside. These spirits didn't have the right to take away people I loved, break my heart or terrify me into taking up the sword. The thought of ordering men into battle, likely to their deaths, and fighting myself made me ill. My brother Pierre had a warrior's heart – I didn't.

I'd argued with the voices repeatedly about what Grand-mère and my mother had taught was the proper role for a girl – finding a good man to share my life with, having children and a home. Each time they'd scolded me harshly about resisting my fate, reminding me of my childhood promise to obey and warning I'd regret being selfish. The only thing I regretted was the day these spirits came into my life.

Mourning all they'd taken from me was something else entirely.

Father Jakob and Grand-mère had always urged me to trust in God, but I hadn't seen any evidence He meant to protect me from the voices, or save me from the English. Even so, I started to pray now, hoping to fill the emptiness in my heart with God's grace.

I fell asleep muttering Grand-mère's prayer. *Áve María, grátia pléna, Dóminus técum; benedícta tu in muliéribus . . .*

Hoping, this time, God would answer or give me a sign.

Grand-mère stopped praying when Papa died. Even as grief overwhelmed me, the silence was a relief.

We'd used the square of linen from the nobleman's purse to cover Papa's face. That was easier to bear for me, and I suspect it was easier for my brother as well. Grand-mère objected when Pierre insisted on placing copper coins over Papa's eyes.

'Sending good money into the grave with a man is pagan foolishness,' she said. 'The Lord will judge Jacques for his sins, not be bribed into letting him into heaven.'

The muscle in Pierre's jaw twitched and he clenched his fists, but he didn't yell. 'Let it go. Papa would have wanted me to send him off properly. Greux is half a day's walk from here. A few of us are leaving now to buy what food we can, and cloth for shrouds. We can argue over coppers after people have buried their dead.'

Grand-mère didn't know about the coin I'd taken from the dead Englishmen. The two purses held more money than either Pierre or I had ever seen, enough to feed the village for a year, and buy seed and supplies to help rebuild many of the survivors' houses. Pierre made me promise not to tell Grand-mère, a promise easy to make and easy to keep.

Both of us knew she would insist on giving the money to Father Jakob and we'd all starve if that happened. The priest was the least charitable or practical man in the province of Lorraine.

'When will you be back?' I asked.

'As soon as we can. Bartering for what we need will take a little time.' Pierre brushed a tear off my cheek and pulled me into a fierce hug. 'I won't leave you on your own for long, promise.'

He left, and Grand-mère moved towards Papa's body.

'Leave the coins alone!' I said, my voice sharper than I'd intended. 'This is Pierre's way of saying goodbye. If two coppers mean the difference between starving or not, you can take the cost out of my share of food.'

Grand-mère's lip quivered and she wiped at her eyes before stalking out of the cave. She hid how deeply she grieved for her only son, masking her sorrow behind gruff words and anger over small things. Pierre said we needed to be patient with her, but the more Grand-mère snapped and argued, the less patience I had.

With Pierre gone, the duty of sitting vigil over our father's body fell to me. I sat cross-legged in the soft sand, as near Papa as I could bear. I still couldn't bring myself to touch him, but being close was easier with his face covered; a scorched wool blanket hid his blood-soaked tunic. Pierre had brought the blanket back this morning; it was one of the few things the fire in our house hadn't turned to ash. I settled in to wait for what was left of my family to come back.

Our oldest brother, Henri, had disappeared the night of the raid. Rumours were passed from person to person, and everyone told different stories about what happened to him. One claimed he'd been captured by the English and marched away with other captives to be hanged. Another said Henri had wounded an English nobleman and the lord's men had bound my brother hand and foot and tossed him into a flaming house to burn alive. Both stories horrified me and made me weep, but no one could swear they knew his fate for certain.

No matter which was true, the result was the same, Henri hadn't come home, and he would have if he was still alive. Grand-mère held out hope that God would bring him back to us, but Pierre and I mourned our brother along with Papa.

Grand-mère stomped back inside soon enough. She sat on the other side of Papa's body, a hand on the blanket covering him, and the drone of her prayers filled the small cave again. I stopped thinking.

Pierre and two other men walked all night to reach Greux and were back by midday with enough cloth for a dozen shrouds. I found the strength and courage to help Grand-mère wrap Papa in layers of the rough-spun cloth, pretending to myself the fabric was made of silk and we were spinning a cocoon he'd emerge from come summer. It was a harmless, childish fancy to blunt my grief.

Pierre waited outside until we'd finished. Grand-mère called him in and he carried Papa's body down the hill to a waiting handcart, and gently laid him inside. My brother had convinced the older men to buy the cart on their trip to Greux, arguing all the ways the cart would be useful in rebuilding and that they could bring back more food with the cart than on their backs.

Using the handcart to carry bodies to the graveyard was an afterthought. Papa wasn't the only one to die in the attack, or in those first few days after. The cart saw a lot of use.

I helped Grand-mère down the hill and kept hold of her arm as we followed Pierre to the churchyard. Grand-mère Marie had always been stronger than any of us, but she'd aged and grown frail in just a few days. The shadow of all the deaths around her – especially Papa's – had brought her own end closer, and that scared me. I hadn't thought about losing her before now.

A few of Papa's friends went to the churchyard with us, carrying spades to help dig his grave. The English had ridden away days ago now, but Father Jakob was still barricaded in the rectory. There hadn't been anyone to give my father – or any of the dead – last rites. People took it upon themselves to bury their loved ones in hallowed ground anyway. The priest could bluster all he wanted once he crawled out of hiding, but the graveyard was full of fresh graves, and his congregation was united.

Pierre and the other men dug Papa's grave next to Mama's. When the grave was chest-deep, he carried our father's body over from the cart. The scorched wool blanket was spread out on the grass and he set Papa's shroud-wrapped body in the centre. Each man took a corner and they gently lowered Jacques d'Arc into the earth.

I didn't cry until they started to fill the grave, each spade of earth a barricade between me and Papa, shutting my father away forever. One of the men started to sing a harvest feast song, another laughed and joined in and soon all Papa's friends were singing as they shovelled the grave full. I shut my eyes and cried harder, remembering Mama's laugh as Papa sang this song to her at her last harvest feast. Her belly was swollen large with the baby that would kill her, but he'd pulled her into his lap for a kiss anyway.

The song ended when the grave was full. Grand-mère turned aside right away and followed the well-worn path out of the graveyard. Papa's friends caught up with her and one of them took her arm for the walk back to the caves.

Pierre stood with me, holding my shaking hand. 'I'll start working on a stone soon as I can. His grave won't stay unmarked for long.'

'He's with Mama,' I said, and dried my face on a sleeve. 'That's the important thing. He'll forgive us if we put rebuilding the house and flocks before carving gravestones.'

'Let's go back, Jeanne.' Pierre crossed himself and took a breath.

'We'll have some supper and rest. Tomorrow is soon enough to start rebuilding.'

We turned to leave. A faint glimmer of light showed me where the guardian spirits stood near the churchyard gate. I kept my eyes on the path and refused to look at them, but that didn't keep Catherine's frost-touched voice from filling my head.

'Remember what the English took from you,' Catherine said. 'Be angry about what they've done here, and all they've done to France. Anger will make you strong.'

I took Pierre's arm and ignored the creature who called herself Catherine. Her disapproval crawled up my neck as we went past and my temper stirred. I was already angry about so many things, but anger wouldn't fix any of them or right any of a hundred wrongs.

These creatures were as much to blame as the war for taking the people I loved from me, even if an English hand had wielded the sword. Hating all King Henry's subjects wouldn't bring back my father, our oldest brother or the baker's wife and child. Not God and all his angels could work that miracle.

I wanted to concentrate on what could be mended, live my life the best I could manage, and count my blessings. Blessings were few enough. That was all the more reason to cling to them.

Part Two

For even if I had had a hundred fathers and mothers and were a king's daughter, still would I go!

Jeanne d'Arc

Each spring morning, I laid a fresh bunch of tansy and mallow on Mama and Papa's grave. Summer and harvest time I found other wildflowers and in winter I cut holly branches, part decorations for their resting place and part offerings to the hilltop spirits. My father taught that honouring the dead kept the restless spirits happy and less likely to cause mischief. He'd warned my brothers and me to stay away from the graveyard at night. Darkness freed the spirits to wander, a caution I'd no problem heeding.

My brother Henri had been braver – or more foolish. When he couldn't convince Pierre to go with him, he'd gone to the cemetery alone. He'd been no more than ten, if that old. The moon was full, illuminating the path up the hill and the graveyard, but moonlight offered no protection. Henri had run home, crying and babbling stories of ghosts dancing atop gravestones and spirits chasing him to the edge of the yard. Papa figured being scared almost to death was punishment enough. Grand-mère disagreed, but for the only time I could remember, she didn't argue with my father.

Remembering the story Henri had told made a chill run up my spine. I crossed myself out of habit and stood, noticing how many graves were neglected and forgotten. The stones on many were cracked or knocked over and it wasn't hard to imagine the hilltop spirits rousing the dead to dance.

Two years had come and gone since Papa died, yet time passing didn't make me miss him less. The same was true for my mother. If anything, the ache grew deeper. I'd honour their memories for the rest of my life.

Grand-mère Marie had died a month before, taken by a winter fever that wouldn't break. Pierre had fetched a herbwife from a hamlet downriver, but none of the woman's potions helped. Our grand-mère was out of her head by sunset of the fifth day, talking to people who weren't there. Father Jakob had come to the house to pray over her and give her last rites. She was gone before the sun rose again.

Grass was starting to grow on the rounded mound of earth over her grave and the soil was starting to settle after a month of rainy nights. Pierre had left a bunch of daisies this morning before starting work on a neighbour's new house. He mourned her as deeply as I grieved for our parents.

I missed her too, but not in the same way. Before she'd married but after the voices had released her, Grand-mère had lived in a convent near Vaucouleurs for a year. She'd been allowed to sit in the back of the schoolroom and listen to the nuns teach catechism to noblemen's daughters and the younger sons meant to take the cloth.

The nuns saw how bright young Marie was and thought to convince her to become a novice. She'd told me that she was seeking God's forgiveness for speaking to those she now saw as demons. Grand-mère had almost decided to confess to the Mother Superior and afterwards, join the convent – if they'd still let her – until meeting Grand-père in the market square put an end to all that. Life with the tall, dark-eyed shepherd was more appealing than a barren cloister cell.

Being a shepherd's wife didn't mean Grand-mère forgot everything she'd learned. I'd confided in her about the voices' visitations more than a year ago and pleaded for help. Grand-mère's idea of help was dragging me to kneel on the cold stone floor of the church sanctuary and telling me to pray for guidance.

She'd taken everything she knew about these creatures and the visions they sent into the grave with her. Just or not, I placed the blame for her silence at Catherine, Margaret and Michael's feet. In my darkest, secret thoughts, I blamed them for Grand-mère's death as well.

Three faint halos of light showed just behind Mama and Papa's headstone, watching and silently judging me. I wouldn't be sixteen for another month and I'd already failed them by refusing to leave our village and find the Dauphin. Michael and Catherine scolded me again and again, telling me I had to go now or risk losing France to the English forever. They insisted my destiny was to cleanse France of the blight every English soldier left behind, as if the beef-eaters were insects burrowing into an apple tree's roots.

Margaret tried to shame me into accepting I was meant to be a hero. I refused to listen or believe.

I'd discovered paying less attention to them meant they couldn't compel me to obey as easily – a blessing, and I took full advantage of it. Rumours of English companies patrolling the area, or packs of dogs raiding the flocks of neighbouring villages, prompted them to order me to steal my brother's sword and put an end to the raiding. Resisting commands that would either get me killed or goad the English into raiding Domrémy got easier as time went on.

But nothing stopped these Fae creatures from watching me day and night, listening in on conversations, or following wherever I went. None of it was fair, and their presence frayed my nerves at times, but they didn't care what was fair and what wasn't.

They wanted me to obey and they were losing patience with all my small rebellions and refusals to listen or follow their orders. I'd be well rid of them if these so-called guardians of France grew tired of tormenting me and left, but that hope was unlikely to come true. They were as determined to bring me to hand as I was to go my own way.

The church was on a hill, perched a fair distance above the main street and the market square. I could see the entire village and down to the river from here. Faded patches of fire-scorched earth still showed in a few places, marking where homes and shops once stood. Some of the people who'd lived and worked there had moved away; others had died in the attack that took my father.

Spring flowers, saplings and grass had reclaimed most of the empty ground and all the fields were fuzzy green with fresh plantings. New cottages were still going up inside the village proper, all of them built with stone walls this time; they would help hide the rest of the scars and soon all signs of the battle would vanish, as if it had never happened.

The English army had destroyed our village and our livelihoods and the coin I'd taken from the dead nobles was all that kept us from starving that first year. Gold had been mixed with the silver, an unexpected blessing. Pierre managed that money carefully, the way Papa taught him, and made sure none of those who stayed to rebuild went hungry.

Not a soul asked where the money came from. Papa was known for his thrift in putting coin aside for lean times, so everyone assumed he'd passed everything he'd saved on to Pierre. My brother didn't feel the need to tell them differently. Neither did I.

Gratitude led the older men to mutter that it was too bad Pierre was only eighteen and too young to head the village council or be declared mayor. He'd hold those titles one day, after marriage and age and children proved his worth to all our neighbours. I thought keeping them alive was enough proof, and said so more than once, but other than tolerant smiles, no one paid attention. Unmarried girls weren't allowed opinions.

The door that led from the graveyard into the main church creaked open. Father Jakob, and the village blacksmith, Claude, strolled out into the churchyard. The two men had their heads together, deep in conversation, and didn't see me.

Not being forced to exchange greetings suited me fine. The last few times I'd run into Claude on the street, he'd found excuses to keep me talking and his expression made me uncomfortable in ways I couldn't explain. I hurried over to slip through the cemetery gate, intent on not being noticed, but the iron hinges gave an ear-shattering squeal and froze in place. Startled, both men looked up sharply.

Father Jakob frowned. 'Is the gate broken, Jeanne?'

'No, Father, stuck.' I gave a tug to show the gate was frozen in place. 'It worked just fine when I came in.'

Seeing me struggling to get the gate open, Claude pushed up his sleeves and grinned. 'Allow me, fair Jeanne.'

Wanting to flee from the look in his eye, or the way being near him made my skin itch, didn't mean I could be rude or refuse his help. I hid behind an unmarried maid's modesty, murmured a thank you and stepped away. The voices' light stepped aside to let him work and moved closer to me, a courtesy Claude never saw and I wondered about.

The way Claude stroked his chin and winked before getting to work baffled me – until he reached inside his tunic and pulled out the love charm hanging from a cord around his neck. A sunbeam glinted off narrow strips of soft, thin metal, each piece woven in and out and around each other in a complicated knot. Scraps of red ribbon were twisted in with the metal, bright as a river of blood, to add to the charm's power.

Henri had paid a hedgewitch to have a love charm nearly identical to this one made the year before Mama died, determined to win the heart of a girl he lusted after. I'd never forgotten his bitter quarrels with Grand-mère Marie over whether love charms were evil or not. Papa had restored peace in the family by throwing the charm in the river.

My heart lurched when Claude looked me in the eye, smiled and immediately redoubled his efforts to free the gate. All the discomfort I'd felt around the blacksmith – his fumbling attempts at conversation and the queasy feeling left in my stomach afterwards – took on a new meaning.

Everything became clear: that love charm was meant for me.

This was my father's old friend, a man I'd known since infancy, not one of the young men who flirted with me at market or after church. The thought that I'd somehow misread how friendly he'd been since winter solstice horrified me.

I second-guessed every smile I'd given him, every time I'd laughed at his small jokes, looking for anything he might have taken as encouragement, but try as I might, I couldn't point at anything. I'd treated Claude as I treated all my father's friends, as fond uncles who shared my memories of Papa.

Lost in thought, I barely noticed when Claude gripped the gate in callused hands and began rocking the black iron back and forth. The muscles in his thick arms bulged, but the gate wouldn't move. He wiped his sweaty palms on his tunic and started again, his face growing bright red and the effort making him grunt. Father Jakob glanced at me and looked impatient, but didn't offer to help.

A small flare of light came from one of the watching spirits. Thunder rumbled in my ears – Michael – before the glow marking where he stood vanished. The gate popped free suddenly and Claude stumbled backwards. I'd no doubt the spirit had freed the gate deliberately, but I didn't understand why.

The blacksmith laughed good-naturedly and waved me through. 'Problem solved, Jeanne. Or I should say, solved until someone closes the gate again. With the good Father's permission, I'll come back before sunset to fix it properly.'

'Thank you, Claude,' Father Jakob said. 'I'd be most grateful to have this done right.'

'Don't give it another thought. I'd do it now, but I promised Jules his tools would be mended by midday.' Claude turned to me with an odd smile. 'I'm a man who keeps his promises.'

His intention to flirt, or, God forbid, court me was clear. My hands shook and I didn't trust what I might say. Studying the toes of my shoes or the tiny daisies dotting the grass was a safe thing to do, so that's what I did. The silence grew uncomfortable too, but I wasn't willing to be the one to break it.

Father Jakob cleared his throat. 'Knock on the rectory door when you come back, Claude. Just so I know you're here.'

'Yes, Father.' Claude jerked the gate open wider and squeezed his bulk through. 'I'll let you know.'

The blacksmith was well down the path before I made a move towards the gate.

Father Jakob called me back. 'I need a word with you, child.' He took my arm and pointed at a stone bench under the rectory window. 'Sit there while we talk.'

The priest loomed over me once I'd settled on the bench, arms folded over his chest and frowning. I couldn't decide whether the way Margaret and Catherine crowded in close or the sternness in Father Jakob's eyes was the most frightening.

'Is . . . is something wrong, Father?'

'I hope not, Jeanne. How well do you know Claude?' he asked.

'As well as I know any of Papa's old friends. We say hello passing on the street, or speak a little in the marketplace,' I said. 'Papa's friends have always watched out for me. Since Henri and my . . . my father died, his friends have checked on me more often and asked if there's anything I need. Most of them do the same for Pierre.'

Father Jakob's scowl deepened and he began to pace. 'And you've always acted the same with Claude? Search your heart, child, and be certain.'

One of the creatures – I was sure it was Margaret – put a hand on my shoulder, making me shiver. She'd never touched me before and I fought to keep my voice steady. 'Once I went to Claude's forge to pick up a pair of shears my grand-mère sent to be mended. Another time I took a knife Pierre chipped and wanted Claude to grind smooth. Is that what you mean?'

'You're still very young, and without a mother or grand-mère to guide you.' The priest sighed and ran his fingers through his thick dark hair. 'I don't approve of the charm Claude had made, but it shows he has serious intentions towards you. What I need to know is where he got the impression you'd be willing to be his wife. God will understand if you acted improperly without meaning to, or led Claude into lustful thoughts. Confess your sins and all will be forgiven.'

I stared open-mouthed. 'No . . . I've never . . . NO! He's three times my age!'

'Calm yourself, Jeanne, and at least try not to look so disgusted,' Father Jakob said. He fingered the crucifix hanging from his neck. 'Fifteen is young to marry a man Claude's age, but I've blessed such marriages before. I needed to be certain he'd chosen you for the right reasons.'

Both Margaret and Catherine huddled against my back now, terrifying me and chilling me to the bone. I couldn't stop shaking. 'No – he's chosen the wrong person, Father. I don't want to marry him. I can't.'

'You have a duty to marry, Jeanne. All women do, and the difference in your ages doesn't matter,' the priest said. 'Claude can be a kind, gentle husband if you honour him and do your duty as a wife, just as he was to Aline. I'll ask one of the older women to explain what a husband will expect of you. You'll have time to pray before the wedding and ask God to help you accept your husband with a glad heart.'

'Claude is older than Papa was. Why would he want to marry *me*?' I curled my fingers around the edge of the bench, trying to think and not let anger blind me or control my tongue. 'I can name five or six widows in the village, most of them close enough to his age they'd make a good match.'

Father Jakob cleared his throat and looked away, obviously uncomfortable. 'It's part of God's plan that women become barren past a certain age. You're young and can bear Claude's children – and if God blesses the two of you, you will give him sons.'

If the priest had spun a romantic tale of the blacksmith discovering he had a great passion, or even a deep fondness for me, I still wouldn't marry him, but I might feel a little sympathy. Instead, I was furious at being seen as breeding stock, with no say in who I married or who fathered my children.

61

I stood to leave and anger won the battle for my tongue. 'Tell Claude to find someone else. He doesn't want me as a wife, he wants a brood mare.'

'Enough! I won't tolerate that kind of talk or disrespect!' Father Jakob slapped me hard, splitting my lip and knocking me back onto the bench. Pain in my jaw spread up the side of my face, while blood from my split lip ran down my chin. I let the blood drip; I was too dizzy to do anything else.

Catherine and Margaret hissed and spat, a nest of vipers inside their halo of light. They formed a half-circle around Father Jakob, each sound they made and every pulse of brightness a threat the priest couldn't see. Whether they would hurt a man of God or not I couldn't say, but they were very angry. Marriage was one of the things they claimed was forbidden to me, although I'd always planned to defy them when I found someone to make a life with.

But the thought of spending my life with Claude, sharing his bed, turned my stomach. His age, knowing that my father had called him a friend, was part of it, so was his willingness to use magic to fool me into thinking I loved him. More than that, he didn't really want me. He wanted anyone young enough to give him sons and his eye had lit on me first. The way Father Jakob was now yelling about forcing me to marry the blacksmith made it even worse.

'Who you marry is not your choice!' Father Jakob said. 'You'll do as your brother and I tell you – and once you're wed, Claude will make the decisions. Your father spoiled you, Jeanne, but your husband won't make the same mistake. Now get up and go home. Tell Pierre I'll speak to him later about posting the marriage banns.'

The faceless voices continued to hiss and spit as I used the bench to steady myself and stand, and they followed me as I staggered away. I tried to hide how badly my hands shook and how my head spun, but the triumph in Father Jakob's small smile proclaimed he thought me cowed. He went back inside the church.

I was far from cowed, but the priest was bigger and stronger and he'd already shown he wouldn't hesitate to strike me. Being a man of God didn't mean he was gentle or peaceful – far from it.

Father Jakob was determined to drag me to the altar and see me married to Claude solely because that was what the blacksmith wished. What I wanted didn't matter and a chill went through me at how much the priest reminded me of the voices trying to control my life.

No matter how righteous and pious he appeared leading mass or hearing confession, Father Jakob wouldn't lose any sleep about what happened to me after the marriage ceremony either. I didn't have any faith that Claude, my father's old friend, would think better of claiming his unwilling prize.

My father had spoiled me, not by indulging me, but by showing me how deeply he loved my mother, and how much he respected her. They were partners in everything. Mama didn't spend a moment of their years together doubting that, or being afraid of what Papa might do if she disagreed with him.

I leaned against the gate to catch my breath before starting down the hill. Papa had spoiled my brothers exactly the same way.

'Pierre will never betray me,' I muttered. 'My brother will help me until I can protect myself.'

My voices didn't answer.

My head throbbed viciously by the time I found my brother and the pain unsettled my stomach to the point I wanted to vomit. The man Pierre was working for, Edmond, was another of our father's friends. I was relieved when he took one look at me and told my brother he had business in the village.

Pierre sat me in the shade next to Edmond's half-finished house while he fetched a basin of cold water, cloths to bathe my face and a mug of watered wine to settle my stomach. An angry mutter followed his first good look at my split lip and the blood on my tunic, but he didn't ask any questions, which was as well. I didn't know what to say.

The wine helped to both dull the headache and staunch the tears. Relief that I'd stopped sobbing filled my brother's face. Pierre had thought me safe in the churchyard, as I'd been every morning, but I obviously hadn't been safe today, and that scared him. It scared me too.

'Tell me what happened,' he said, and touched my face. 'Who hurt you, Jeanne?'

Light sparkled behind my brother's shoulder, a sign the guardians were listening. I didn't want to risk summoning the pain and dizziness back if the light brightened suddenly, so I closed my eyes.

Telling him about the blacksmith and the priest's determination to force me into marriage was harder than I thought. My voice broke telling my brother how Father Jakob struck me, and why. Pierre's sharp intake of breath, and the string of profanity that followed, jerked my eyes open wide.

'Pigshit-wallowing bastard! I should cut off Claude's worthless balls and feed them to the dogs. No true friend of Papa's would want to force you into his marriage bed!' Pierre said, his voice rising. 'That bastard is old enough to be our grandfather! I'll cut off Father Jakob's thrice-cursed hands while I'm at it. Only a coward beats a girl half his—'

Pierre caught sight of my face and stopped mid-sentence. He sighed.

'They both deserve a good thrashing, and if Papa were alive he'd help me give them one. The only thing holding me back is knowing the trouble it would cause. Things are different since Grand-mère died.'

Things were very different. We were alone, with no one to stand between us and the little we had left and those who sought to use our age as an excuse to take control of our lives. No matter how much respect Pierre garnered from the older men, or how promising his future looked, he was still a boy in their eyes. I had even less standing.

My brother touched my face and the look in his eye made me glad I didn't have a mirror. 'You've my promise, Jeanne, I won't let either one of them force you into a marriage you don't want. I will talk to that idiot Claude and if he keeps insisting, or bothers you again, he'll regret it. The same goes for that black-hearted priest.'

I nodded, still unable to speak, and that small bit of movement set my head to throbbing anew. Keeping my eyes open made the pain worse.

Pierre patted my shoulder. 'Give me a minute to gather my tools and I'll take you home. I was about done for the day anyway. Edmond won't take it amiss if I leave a little early. Sleep and some hot soup will help you feel better.'

He walked away. An instant later the light flared bright and Catherine's raspy voice filled my head. 'There's an easy way to save yourself, Jeanne. Confess to the priest that God's angels sent you a vision and you'll soon be leaving the village on pilgrimage.'

Merciful Margaret spoke next, her voice close to my ear. 'A story will spread that you're the foretold Maid of Lorraine and the time has come to seek the Dauphin and win his throne. The blacksmith will believe you've taken a vow of chastity and will not marry until Charles is crowned king.'

'Not even a black-hearted priest will quarrel with God's commands,' Catherine said.

Any suggestion from my voices about what I should do or say, no matter how mild or apparently harmless, made me uncomfortable. Catherine's words were threaded through with the feel of command and compulsion, while Margaret sought to convince me they had my best interests at heart.

They wanted me to lie to a priest during confession, but that was far from harmless – and far from easy. I rejected everything they'd said, knowing that they'd trap me in a tangle of lies if I claimed angels brought me messages from God. If I gave in, I'd never be free. Getting caught in a lie was even worse. All the horrible stories I'd heard about women accused of witchcraft filled my head and made me ill.

Ignoring the voices might be the only way out. I trusted Pierre would keep his word and protect me, and if things went poorly for us I'd leave the village, but on my own terms. I wouldn't drag my brother down with me.

The creatures' light dimmed and the jangle of Pierre's tools warned he'd returned. He smiled as I opened my eyes. 'Let me help you up, Jeanne. We'll get you home quick as you can manage.'

He got a hand under my arm and hauled me to my feet. The world spun, my stomach heaved and I almost fell face-first into a puddle of vomit. I thanked God Pierre caught me.

'Easy now,' he said. 'Keep your eyes closed if that makes walking easier. I won't let you fall.'

'I'll try.' I leaned against him. 'Why am I so dizzy?'

'Father Jakob's hand was open, but he's a strong man and he hit you hard. The whole side of your face is bruising and I won't be surprised if your eye is swollen shut by morning. We're lucky it's not worse. Do you remember when Cedric got hit on the back of the head with a spade? Takes time to get over something like that.'

Pierre put an arm around my waist and half-carried me home. He laid me on the bed near the hearth and tugged off my boots before pulling the blanket up to my chin. 'I'll warm some broth. You should be able to manage that without your lip pulling open again.'

I was asleep when he came back. He woke me long enough to take a few sips of the broth, but sleep claimed me as soon as I lay down again.

My dreams were full of faceless spirits forcing a sword into my hand, while men died all around me. Mud and rust flaked off the blade the second my fingers closed around the hilt, but it was far too heavy for me to lift. I watched helplessly as my father died a second time, and a third, and heard my oldest brother Henri scream as English soldiers laughed and watched him burn.

Pierre and a stranger appeared and the stranger took the too-heavy sword from my hand. The two of them took a stand and battled to protect me from the English pikemen and the knights galloping towards us.

Michael spoke in my ear. 'Who will die, Jeanne? Pick up the sword and fight your enemy, or lose them both.'

The sword was in my hand now and I gripped the hilt two-handed and lifted it high over my head, marvelling at how well it fitted my grip, the way sunlight played along the edge and shot golden sparks into the afternoon, laughing at how simple this was, how much power the sword gave me.

I struck at Faceless Michael first, plunging the sword into the centre of his light and taking off his head when he fell. Catherine and Margaret cried out, and I swept the blade through the centre of their light too. Flame danced along the blade's edge for an instant, then died, plunging the battlefield into the deepest dark.

When I opened my eyes, dawn was still hours away. Embers glowed softly on the hearth and pale moonlight leaked around the edge of the shutters, but I couldn't find a flicker of the voices' light. I sat up to search the corners, certain they were watching, and found nothing.

I lay back down and shut my eyes again, unable to believe that after years of wishing and willing them away, a sword in a vision had the power to banish them. They had oftentimes sent dreams and visions in an attempt to break my will, or push me into doing what I refused to do while awake. They still sought to make me obey.

But if all they'd wanted was to test my willingness to take up arms against my enemies, now they had their answer.

Pierre sent word to Edmond he was needed at home and stayed with me the next day, and the day after that. I tried to convince him to finish the work Edmond had for him the third day, but he clucked his tongue at me the way Grand-mère used to.

'Edmond's repairs will keep. Rest while you can, Jeanne.' He put a bowl of dried apple and cheese on the table and sat across from me. 'I don't want you doing much until your head stops spinning. Things are quiet now, but another week or so and we'll be up to our chins in labouring ewes. I'll need your help with keeping track of all the newborn lambs.'

'And I won't be much help if I'm still dizzy and stumbling,' I said. 'One more day should see me right.'

One more day became two and Father Jakob still hadn't visited to talk to Pierre about posting marriage banns. I asked once if they'd talked, but Pierre's scowl and quick head-shake told the story. My brother never said, but I suspected he wanted me well enough to defend myself before leaving me on my own. I was deeply wary of the priest and confronting him, and equally determined Father Jakob wouldn't catch me off guard again.

My voices were silent on the subject, content to watch and listen to our conversations from afar. They'd vanished for four days and if not for the faint glimmers of light near the hearth now I'd have thought them still gone. I didn't dare believe silence meant they'd ceased plotting.

There was plenty of work for Pierre around our cottage, both inside and outside, and new herd dog pups needed training besides. Having my brother to myself for three days felt selfish; even so, I couldn't bring myself to feel guilty. Pierre was all the family left to me. I understood he'd find a girl to marry soon enough and I'd have very little call on his time after that, and even less right to keep him talking deep into the night.

Pierre went out to work with the dogs as soon as we'd finished eating. The house stayed chilly until long past midday and I'd wrapped a heavy shawl over my shoulders before sitting at the loom. I'd tried to weave a little for the last two days running, but gave up when my eyes refused to focus and my head spun.

Today I really was better. Watching the pattern form and the fabric grow longer, I muttered a prayer of thanks. The fire that took the house had destroyed Grand-mère Marie's loom and Pierre had insisted on having a new one made. Grand-mère only used the new loom a few times, pleading ageing eyes and aching hands as a reason to pass the task to me.

She'd long told me I was a better weaver, with a better sense of pattern and an instinct for what dyes to blend for the richest colours. My brother took the fabric I'd finished to the monthly market across the river and always sold every scrap. The new cloth would help make up for Pierre's lost wages and ease my mind.

The clack of the loom didn't drown out the raised voices in the yard and I paused to listen. Pierre and Father Jakob were moving closer to the house, shouting at each other with every step. They stopped beside the glass window and I thanked God the shutters were closed. The fury in the priest's voice brought back the memory of the stinging pain of his ring splitting my lip and the burning in my jaw; the bruising had yet to fade. My hands began to shake hard. I set down the shuttle before I dropped it.

A bright light flared in the centre of the room and Margaret, Catherine and Michael stood between me and the cottage door. I trusted Pierre's protection far more than any these evil spirits might offer. And much as I disliked the priest and wanted his meddling in my life to stop, I didn't wish him harm. I still didn't know if they had the power to hurt a man of God.

Pierre was just as angry as the priest – if anything, he was yelling louder. 'Mother of God, Jakob! Do you ever listen to anyone or do you always ride right over what they say? The very thought of forcing Jeanne to marry Claude turns my stomach. I won't let this happen.'

'Be reasonable,' Father Jakob said. His voice became soothing, as if coaxing a child to take bitter medicine. 'Claude is willing to postpone the wedding until after Jeanne's birthday. Giving her time to get used to the idea of Claude as a husband, not just her father's old friend, will make this easier on both of them. Sixteen isn't too young for a bride.'

'Sixteen isn't overly young if marriage is the girl's choice and the man is someone she wants to marry,' Pierre said. 'I'd have to be brain-addled to believe a few weeks will change Jeanne's mind.

My sister will marry when she finds a man worthy of her. Tell Claude to look for a wife his own age.'

'Are you defying me, Pierre d'Arc?'

'Call it what you want, Jakob. Taking the cloth doesn't give a man the right to decide who his parishioners marry,' Pierre said. 'And there's something not right or natural about a man old as Claude mooning after a girl my sister's age. If you weren't puffed up like a partridge courting a mud hen, you'd be able to see that.'

Neither one said anything after that. Silence stretched on so long, I got scared. I crept over to the window and peered out the crack in the shutters. Pierre stood closest to the house, putting himself between the door and Father Jakob. He still held the staff he used to train puppies. Three of the older herd dogs sat at my brother's feet, tongues lolling out of the sides of their mouths, bright eyes staring at the priest. Out of the entire pack, these three followed Pierre's every step all day long.

The priest didn't know that. He stood a few feet away, red-faced and uneasy. His eyes darted between my brother and the dogs, almost as if he didn't know who might attack him first. He clutched the crucifix dangling from his neck, gathered himself and broke the silence.

'Think before you speak, Pierre. Now that your grand-mère is with God, the village council is within its rights to appoint a guardian to run your affairs and make decisions about Jeanne's future.'

'And you're hoping they'll ask you. Or maybe you favour Claude to take over everything my father built and marry my sister into the bargain. That would be a tidy little package.' Pierre laughed, the sound brittle and sharp-edged. 'I'd give a lot to know what you're getting out of this.'

'How dare you.' The priest's face flushed crimson and he clenched his hands into fists as he moved towards my brother. 'You'll regret insulting me.'

One of Pierre's dogs growled, a warning rumbling deep in her chest that froze Father Jakob in mid-step. My brother put a hand on the dog's head and left it there. The other two dogs crowded in close.

'Easy, Belle, easy. You're upsetting your sisters.' He gave a short whistle; the dogs dropped to their bellies and lay still and quiet, awaiting the next signal. 'Truth isn't an insult, Jakob. And before you try making me regret anything, you might want to remember that I'm able to give as good as I get. I'm bigger than Jeanne.'

I couldn't let my brother face Father Jakob alone, or allow my fear to keep me cowering inside the house. My hand was on the latch when the light from my voices flared bright and vanished. I stepped outside and their shining figures appeared behind Father Jakob, each one tall and menacing. These guardian spirits had never protected me, not once, but their light pulsed with anger strong enough that their rage prickled my skin.

Michael swelled even more, grew taller, brighter, and held his flaming sword over Father Jakob's head. I understood them: they would send me into battle, risk my life and hasten my death if it fitted their vision or moved me further along their pre-ordained path. These creatures weren't protecting me from Father Jakob; the priest threatened their cherished prophecy.

Catherine's raspy voice rattled in my ears. 'Put your doubts about us and your anger aside for a moment, Jeanne. Do you trust your brother?'

'He's my family – I trust Pierre with my life.'

Margaret spoke next, the bells in her voice muted and dull. 'Then

72

stay back and let him end this. You have reason to fear priests, and this one has already hurt you.'

I shook my head and frustration crept into my voice. 'I won't hide.'

'Fear whispers to the foul priest's black heart and tells him to strike first. He'll use you to distract Pierre if he can,' Catherine said. 'Your fates are woven together, Jeanne, and if one of you falls, you both do. This is your brother's battle to win or lose. You've no part to play here.'

Knowing these creatures, cold and uncaring as they were, named Father Jakob foul and black-hearted gave me pause. I remembered all the arguments between my papa and my grand-mère over how much he tithed the church – several times I'd come home to find them yelling because Grand-mère had given money Papa had set aside to the priest. Papa didn't fear Father Jakob, but for some unknown reason my grand-mère had.

I stepped back into the shadowed doorway to watch and listen, trembling head to foot and feeling like a coward. Heeding Catherine's warning was a kind of surrender, but I couldn't risk Pierre for the sake of rebellion or my pride.

'Something else for you to think about,' my brother said. 'Most of the men on the council are my father's old friends and a fair number have daughters. How do you think the council will take to you knocking Jeanne down, just for saying she didn't want to marry Claude?'

The priest sneered. 'Your father had the right to bring things up before the council, but you don't yet – and they won't take your word over mine.'

'Edmond has the right,' Pierre said quietly. 'I was working with him when Jeanne found me. He stayed out of the way, knowing she'd talk freer about what happened, but he heard everything she told me. I'd like to see you convince the council Edmond is a liar.'

Father Jakob's face grew even redder, his breathing harsh and fast. I watched his anger change to rage, and watched again as his fury drained away again when he couldn't see a way to win. My brother saw too, but he didn't relax.

The priest clutched his crucifix tight. 'What do you want from me?'

'Talk to Claude. Convince him it's for the best if he stays away from Jeanne and courts someone else. He'll listen to you.' Pierre paused for an instant, and went on, 'But if he keeps after her, I'll deal with him myself. Make sure he understands that.'

Father Jakob flinched at the threat behind Pierre's words. 'I'll speak with him today.'

'The same goes for you, Jakob.' He gave two short whistles and the dogs crept closer to the priest. 'Maybe get on your knees after you see Claude and beg God for forgiveness. The dogs will see you on your way.'

My brother pointed at Father Jakob, gave one long whistle and one short and the dogs slunk forwards, bellies barely skimming the ground. Our dogs were always gentle and had never attacked anyone, but the panic filling the priest's eyes was worthy of a pack of wolves chasing him across the pasture. He lifted the hem of his robe and took off running. The dogs stayed at his heels until Pierre called them back.

'You can come out now, little one. He's gone.' He got down on his knees to praise the dogs and scratch their ears, then glanced at me. 'If God is kind, that's the last we'll hear of marriage to Claude.'

I wanted to ask him when God had last been kind to us, but I settled for nodding and going back to my weaving. Pierre had more of Grand-mère's faith then I'd ever had. I'd leave that to him.

Faint shimmers above the hearth told me the creatures had followed me inside. I'd thought I was beyond being puzzled by what they said or did, but today they'd proved me wrong. Siding with Pierre and me against the priest I almost understood, but they'd let me make my own choices and not tried to compel me.

But their power to force me to do anything had dwindled as I grew older and more determined, less afraid of them. As a result, they spoke to me less and less.

Even so, their treachery hadn't grown less: I'd little doubt they spent their long hours of silence plotting ways to force me away from home to seek the Dauphin. I needed to stay wary.

Not all summer mornings dawned clear and cool so I muttered a quick prayer of thanks for this one as I hurried to early mass. This year was hotter and drier than most and I welcomed any relief, no matter how small. Driving the flock to the high pastures would take me most of the day; we'd be well into the afternoon heat before the dogs and I got the last ewe into the meadow. Setting up camp wouldn't take long, but it would be near sunset before the air cooled again.

Three years of hard work had allowed us to make up for the sheep we lost to the English hounds and the attack on the village. We'd trained more puppies too, and I had my own loyal pack of young dogs now, following me everywhere, just as Pierre's pack followed him.

Having the dogs made me feel safer. Reports of English attacks on villages to the west and cattle raids to the south had died down as spring became summer and the war moved in another direction. Wolf and lynx weren't the only dangers to guard against when I was alone with the sheep, but we'd decided it was safe enough for me to drive the flock to the high summer pastures as I always did. The narrow opening into the wide, sheltered valley would allow my dogs to keep the flock penned safely inside.

My father had laid claim to the valley not long after Henri was born. He'd built an altar to the shepherd's guardians at the mouth and we still left offerings, asking for help in protecting the sheep.

I'd made the trip each year since I was ten. One of my brothers had taken me the first few years, but after that it was my responsibility to watch over the flock, especially after Papa and Henri died. Much as I loved Pierre, I looked forward to the solitude, falling asleep to the sound of the wind in the trees and watching the stars fill the sky one by one. The guardian spirits followed me as they always did, but once I'd climbed into the hills, they rarely broke the silence. I didn't know why, but I didn't question the gift.

Early mass on Sunday was usually crowded. A well-attended service gave me an excuse to stand near the door at the back of the chapel. Father Jakob wasn't likely to see me until the service ended and everyone began to leave, an arrangement that suited me just fine. Some of the men and boys near the door still smelled faintly of the pig pens and horse stalls they'd shovelled before dawn, but they were easy to forgive. I frequently smelled of sheep.

Thanking God that the war had moved away so I could make the trip into the hills felt selfish, but I said a prayer and lit a candle for Holy Mary regardless. The priest saw me then and scowled, but I'd grown used to his dark looks. God would forgive my sins, whatever they might be, but Father Jakob never would.

Claude stood in the back of the nave when I turned to leave, watching me. I pretended not to see him and hurried out of the church. More than a year had passed and the blacksmith's silent pursuit of me hadn't flagged. He'd kept his word to Father Jakob and not spoken to me again, but he didn't need to speak for me to understand he wouldn't give up.

I shivered, thinking of how often I saw him staring at me from the shadow of a market stall or during mass. Most times I caught him watching, a light from my voices stood behind him – even inside the church. Not knowing why they dogged his footsteps as they did mine unnerved me.

Twice in the last year, when Claude had seemed poised on the edge of doing more than watching from afar, I'd told my brother. Pierre was furious, but had the good sense to ask Edmond for advice, and each time, Edmond and my brother went to Father Jakob and reminded the priest what would happen if he didn't keep Claude away from me. I hadn't seen the blacksmith for a full month after they'd visited the priest the second time, but he'd gone back to following me around the market before a second month passed.

His persistence frightened me, but I held on to a tiny flicker of hope that weeks out of his sight would cool Claude's ardour.

Pierre was stuffing the last of my supplies into a heavy travelling pack as I came around the corner of the chicken yard. His dogs sprawled next to mine in the shade next to the house, watching his every move and waiting for the signal to start the sheep moving. Our flock was bigger than any Papa had owned and it would take all the dogs to keep them together on the narrow hillside trails.

Pierre would return home tomorrow, leaving Belle, his oldest, most experienced herder, with me. My dogs were well trained, but they were still very young.

'Are you feeling properly blessed, little one?' His sly smile reassured me he meant to mock the priest, not me.

'Or properly cursed,' I said. 'I'm never sure after one of Jakob's sermons.'

'Take heart from knowing I'll be going in your place for the next few weeks.' Pierre cinched the travel pack closed, and gave an extra tug to make sure the cord was tight. He glanced at me and smiled. 'The priest's curse should wear off by the time you get back.'

'I'd keep whatever curse Father Jakob mixes into his blessings if Claude would stop watching me.'

He looked up sharply. 'What happened?'

'Nothing happened.' I hadn't meant to say the words aloud, but now that I had there was no taking them back. 'Nothing ever happens. He doesn't speak or try to approach me – he keeps his distance – but he's always watching me. Always there.'

'Claude sidles up to the line of his pledge and as long as he doesn't put a toe down on the other side, he believes he's kept his word. I think it's time Edmond and I had another word with that conniving priest – and this time I want Claude in the room listening.'

He grabbed the water bags hanging on a nail near the door and, with a whistle, took off towards the stream to fill them all, the dogs fast at his heel, while I went inside to take off Grand-mère's crucifix. I placed it back in the drawer before donning the travel pack and fetching my shepherd's staff. Light flared bright in the corner of my eye and I braced myself for whatever my voices had to say, but their light faded again and none of them said a word. I sighed – they liked to startle me, even when they had nothing to say – and went outside to collect my share of the water bags from Pierre.

We were well on the way and climbing towards the pasture long before the air grew too warm.

The muscles in my shoulders relaxed as we climbed higher,

the tension I didn't know I'd been carrying baking away in the sunshine. Birds sang from every tree and flowers nodded in the shade or peeked out of the long grass. Pierre began to sing at the top of his lungs, making me laugh.

By the time we chased the last stubborn ram into the valley and poured our small offering of ewe's milk and honey on the altar, I'd almost forgotten about Claude. If God was kind, the blacksmith would forget about me as well.

Part Three

The counsel of our Lord is wiser and safer than yours.

Jeanne d'Arc

The weeks went past in a rush, each day marked with a knife on a dead branch. I was busy from dawn to dark of night, but it was a good busy, the kind that let me sleep deep and free of nightmares. The worst thing that happened was a young lynx tried to take a half-grown lamb late one night, but the dogs chased the spotted cat off. Fewer dogs or a more experienced hunter and I'd have lost the lamb, but God had smiled on me that night.

Long warm days sitting in the sun and watching the sheep graze made me want to stay in the valley forever. Mornings smelled of damp earth and grass, while in the afternoons the air was full of the scent of flowers. Birds I never saw in the village sang from the tops of trees. At times I daydreamed about building a cottage up here, but the idea felt ever more foolish as the weather began to change.

I made a slash in the branch I used to mark time passing, then set it aside and pulled my shawl tight across my shoulders. The days were growing shorter, the nights colder and I could feel the chill bite in the air. Fewer birds sang in the dawn now and the squirrels and mice were frantically gathering stores for the winter, showing me my time in the valley was coming to an end. Another week, two at the most, and Pierre would arrive to help me drive the sheep home.

Strong, swirling winds and an early snowfall weren't unheard of this high in the hills, so I pounded the tent stakes deeper into the ground, all the while praying I was being over-cautious. Shifting the lean-to I'd been using for shade to better break the wind came next – I didn't want howling gales to carry our small hide tent off as the five dogs and I huddled together for warmth.

The dogs were restless tonight, stalking around the edge of my camp and peering into the darkness, ears up and listening, before coming back to the fire. I fed more wood to the flames and listened for signs of distress among the sheep, but only normal night sounds filled the dark. Whatever the dogs sensed, the sheep didn't seem to be aware of any danger, or bothered by the dogs' uneasiness.

Belle stretched out with her side pressed against me, her head and ears up. The younger dogs stayed quiet and watchful, but soft warning growls began to rumble in Belle's chest. An instant later, she was on her feet and barking, and the other dogs joined her. I gripped my staff tight, knowing the dogs could see in the night better than I could and trusting them to help protect me. Charging into the darkness, looking for danger I couldn't see until it was on top of me, would be stupid and reckless.

Whatever set the dogs off finally moved away and one by one, they quietened and lay down. Belle stayed next to me, watching the darkness and still sniffing the air, ears twitching to catch every sound. My heart raced until she began licking my face and whimpering, her tail thumping hard against the ground.

'Good girl, Belle.' I hugged her, grateful there was no one to see my hands shaking. 'Brave, brave Belle. Thank you.'

She wiggled out of my arms, curled up and went to sleep. Still holding onto my staff, I crawled into my tent, but sleep ran from me. A thousand reasons for the dogs barking circled in my head, from English soldiers sneaking into the valley to another lynx, or even a brown bear come down from the mountains. Another year, long ago, Henri and I had spent the night in a tree, out of reach of the bear scattering our belongings across the meadow and eating our food. But that had been very early summer, when the bear was still hungry from sleeping the winter away. Papa had sent only one young dog with us that time, and he'd run to the far end of the valley to protect the sheep.

A bear was less dangerous than English soldiers and the dogs with me now were better trained – and they'd chosen to stay with me, not to rush off to guard the flock, which made me worry about scouts creeping about in the dark, watching me sit next to the fire and knowing I was alone.

I chased the thought in circles for a long time, listening to the pop and crackle of the dying flames and the soft yips of dogs lost in dreams. Deciding to trust Belle and the younger dogs to warn me of danger finally let me fall into a dreamless sleep, for once – my dreams were frequently full of vengeful angels, hiding their faces behind a blinding light.

I yelped as two strong hands closed around my ankles, startling me awake. A man yanked me out of my tent and dragged me into the deeper darkness of the valley. I screamed and groped for my staff, but I was already too far away to reach it.

The little light given off by the dying fire showed me the dogs were nowhere to be seen, but I yelled for them anyway. 'Belle! Rene! Come to me – *Belle!*'

'Yell all you want, fair Jeanne. You and me are alone and there's no one to hear. I took care the dogs wouldn't bother us before I came for you.'

His words were slurred, but I recognised Claude's voice. He stopped dragging me across the dew-damp grass and straddled me; the odour of strong wine souring on his breath was vile enough to make me gag. I turned my face away, trying to shake off the fear he'd killed the dogs. The blacksmith was reeling drunk and the thought of being alone with him terrified me.

He chose that moment to try and kiss me, and missed. His face landed in my hair, but instead of the anger I expected, Claude laughed. 'You need to hold still, my dove. We'll not get too far with you squirming and wiggling away.'

'I won't hold still! Don't touch me!' I swung at him, trying to take his head off, but he caught my hands in his, and laughing, kissed each of my fingers one by one. His laugh was different from normal, high-pitched and piercing, not like I'd known it, and hearing it made me shiver.

Claude jerked me up off the ground and tucked me under his arm, the way I carried young lambs. I kicked and pounded him with my fists as hard as I could manage, but he didn't seem to feel the blows. He began to whistle a festival song, as if he didn't have a care in life and carting around a struggling young woman was a normal thing to do. Too much wine could make a man stagger and addle his mind, I knew, but the way Claude acted was very strange and I found it more frightening than if he'd been merely drunk.

He paused in the centre of the meadow and peering into the darkness ahead, he muttered, 'The cave's hard to see in the dark, but I'll find it right enough and we'll get settled in and comfortable. I've made us a nice soft bed for our wedding night. Even fetched a wool blanket from home so you won't take a chill without your clothes on. Ah, I see the opening now. Off we go, fair one.'

'No, stop! We haven't said any vows!' I started swinging at his face, cringing each time I landed a blow, but somehow I had to break free. 'You can't do this!'

Claude finally noticed I'd hit him when I split his lip. He scowled and tossed me over his shoulder to hang head down.

'In the name of God, please, please, let me go!' My heart thundered in my ears, I could barely breathe, barely think, and my hands hurt from beating him. 'You know this isn't right!'

'Isn't it now? Was it right for your brother to keep going to the priest when all I wanted was to look at you?' he asked. 'Then Edmond had me dragged before the council: him and your brother, they shamed me so that I can't show my face in the market. You can't tell me that was right either.'

I shook from head to toe, angry and terrified and exhausted. Claude ignored my fists beating on his back and the top of his legs, as unfeeling as a slab of stone. Even without wine in his blood, the blacksmith was one of the strongest men in the village – unless God granted me a miracle, I couldn't win this fight.

'I'm begging you, Claude, please, let me go! Hurting me won't make anything right. I promise I won't tell anyone.'

He dropped me then, and I lay there stunned, wanting to get up and run, but he'd knocked the breath out of me. The moon, little more than a thin crescent hanging in a pitch sky, gave off little light. I could just make out Claude's smile as he crouched next to me.

'It's not just making things right, Jeanne. An angel told me to follow you here and wait for him to bring an answer to my prayers. I've watched you bathe every day since I arrived, watched you sit by the fire at night, all the while trying to decide if God will forgive my eagerness and bless our bed. I have my answer now,' he said, and stroked my cheek. 'Aline was a reluctant bride too, but she stopped struggling after a few days.'

His mention of angels came near to stopping my heart. Michael and Catherine had warned of punishment and suffering if I didn't obey their command to seek the Dauphin. I'd defied them, as I had so many other times, and stayed with my brother. Even so, I couldn't imagine their punishment was to have Claude force himself on me, not when they had been so very angry when Father Jakob insisted it was my duty to marry the blacksmith.

A light slowly brightened near the valley wall and Catherine's frost-touched whisper filled my head. 'The blacksmith is mad, Jeanne, and the voices whispering in his head aren't angels. Help is coming, fast as they can. Fight hard, so that they may come in time.'

Claude bunched the front of my tunic in his fist and hauled me to my feet. He kept a firm hold while running the fingers of his other hand along my chin and down my neck, making me whimper with fear. I looked into his eyes as he smiled and knew Catherine was right: he was mad.

His smile got bigger as his fingers moved over my lips. I grabbed his wrist, sank my teeth deep into his hand and held on, taking satisfaction in the way he howled and the blood running over his wrist and down his arm. He let go and shoved me away and I caught my balance and tried to run, but he seized hold of my braid and yanked me back.

'You're so young I thought I could be gentle with you, Jeanne, maybe even kind. But you're as spoiled and stubborn as the angel warned. I'll have to teach you to be a good wife the hard way.'

He wrapped my braid twice around his hand and knowing I couldn't get away, started tugging me towards the cave. I dug my heels in and pulled back, even though I couldn't see through the tears of pain blinding me – having my hair torn out by the roots was a small thing if it kept me out of that cave.

Dogs barked in the distance, the sound faint but moving closer, and Margaret and Michael shimmered into view next to Catherine. I dug my nails into Claude's hand and arm until I drew blood, but although he hissed and swore, he didn't let go of my braid; instead, he looped his arm around my throat. Breathing hard, his voice was a raspy whisper in my ear. 'Scratch or bite me again and I'll lose the last of my patience with you. Only a few more strides, girl. Come along now.'

The barking grew louder. Claude tightened his arm so that all I could do was stumble along in front of him, and as we neared the cave, I started to choke. He didn't appear to notice even as I sagged against him, darkness clouding my sight.

Claude gently lowered me to the ground, kneeling at my feet as he watched me cry and cough and struggle for breath. He started to quietly sing a song, his voice too faint for me to hear the words.

'I'm sorry, fair Jeanne.' He tugged loose the rope holding up his breeches and tossed it away. 'I didn't want to hurt you.'

I whimpered when he crawled on top of me and pushed my skirts aside. I didn't have the breath to scream.

A snarling black-and-white form flew out of the darkness and Belle sank her teeth in Claude's shoulder. He roared and came up off me to throw the dog aside. Rene, behind her, was limping on his back leg, but he didn't hesitate to bury his fangs in Claude's calf – and now two more of Pierre's dogs streaked past, snapping and biting. The four animals herded Claude away from me and towards the mouth of the cave, to my brother, standing with his shepherd's staff in his hand.

I tugged my skirts down and managed to crawl a few paces away before curling into a ball, covering my ears with my hands so the sounds of the dogs snarling, my brother swearing as he swung his staff and Claude's cries were muffled.

Nothing could mute the thunder of Michael's voice ringing in my head. 'Refusing to follow the path we've set for you invites punishment, Jeanne. So does weakness. Hoping the blacksmith would grow tired of being ignored was cowardly. Each time you pretended not to see him watching fed his madness, strengthened the whispers saying he deserved to have you. He believed the voice keeping him from sleep over any warning the black-hearted priest gave.'

Michael's icy fingers wrapped around my wrists and pulled my hands away. He pressed his frozen lips against my ear and began to sing softly in Claude's voice, each quiet word forcing the chill deeper inside. My heart stuttered in terror but went on beating.

'Your brother has a warrior's heart, Jeanne. He deals with your enemy as a warrior should.' Michael caressed my face the way Claude had, searing into my skin the memory of each time the blacksmith had touched me. 'Remember this lesson, Jeanne – and that you brought this on yourself. Remember: you are *La Pucelle*.'

As suddenly as he'd appeared, Michael vanished. I curled into a ball, weeping, tangled in a web of memories and questions that wouldn't let me go.

If Claude was mad for believing in voices, so was I. And I didn't think I was mad; I clung too tightly to who I wanted to be and fiercely pushed away all my voices' attempts to control me. I fought Michael most of all, despite all his threats and promises I'd regret rebelling.

Michael was the voice whispering in Claude's ear; I was sure of that. Nudging the blacksmith towards doing what he already wanted was an easy way to punish me and try to break my spirit; Michael was more than cruel enough.

Covering my ears didn't stop me hearing Claude begging my brother to stop, much the way I'd begged him to let me go. His voice, choked with panic, was rising higher with each blow of the staff. Pierre ignored him, as I'd been ignored, and much the same way I imagined Claude had disregarded Aline's terror.

I couldn't bring myself to feel sorry for him.

Pierre had piled all my store of wood on the fire, determined not to leave me in the dark for a moment. He rested a hand on my hair, a normal thing for my brother to do, but nothing about this night was normal and I had to fight not to flinch. Pierre didn't know how to help me, or what to say that wouldn't make me cry again, but he was trying hard.

'Belle will stay with you until I come back. This shouldn't take long.' He began to coil the rope he'd unknotted from the lean-to. 'Once I have that bastard bound tight and the cave entrance blocked, we'll start for home. Are you sure you don't want to wait until daybreak?'

I huddled deeper into the blanket he'd wrapped around my shoulders. 'No, I want to go home. I don't feel safe here.'

'Then we go home.'

He hung the hank of rope on one shoulder, slipped my hatchet through his belt and lit the torch he'd made. I shut my eyes, hoping that if I kept them closed long enough, I'd never have to see he'd gone. Belle whimpered and licked my chin. She nosed the blanket away from my face.

When I opened my eyes, I found Pierre staring at me.

'I'm so, so sorry, little one. I kept dreaming about coming to get you, but I didn't think there was any rush, not until the weather started to turn.' My brother wiped his eyes on a sleeve and cleared his throat. 'And this was partly my fault. I should have kept a close eye on Claude after the council meeting. He was angry, but Edmond and I both thought he'd come to his senses if we left him be. I never . . . I never thought he'd . . . he'd—'

'Pierre . . . he . . . tried, but he . . . he didn't. Belle stopped him.' I buried my face in Belle's fur, trying to forget the sour smell of wine on Claude's breath and how heavy he'd felt on top of me. 'I'm still a virgin. God in his mercy spared me that final insult.'

He stood there silently for far too long before he walked away, giving me time enough to wonder if he believed me. Some villagers, including the priest, would doubt my word, thinking I'd willingly lie to avoid even more shame. But my brother loved me. I decided he still didn't know what to say.

I didn't know what to say either.

The blacksmith was still unconscious when Pierre first began to truss him up tight as a goose on a spit, but that didn't last more than a moment or two. Claude spat and swore each time Pierre pulled the ropes taut and each time my brother growled for the blacksmith to stay quiet. Sound carried in the valley, leaving me no choice but to listen.

'I should leave you out here for the wolves,' my brother said, 'but instead, I'll let the council punish you. Which do you think it will be for what you've done, Claude? Hanging or cutting off your balls?'

Claude began to curse loudly, using foul words I'd rarely heard and promising vengeance on my brother. I could picture Pierre dragging the blacksmith into the cave as Claude's voice became fainter, and I knew when he'd kicked Claude on the way out.

Belle's tail began to wag, letting me know Pierre was back. Rene and the two young dogs followed him, all three of them sniffing the air and a bit uneasy. I said a quick prayer that God wouldn't send more trouble our way.

Pierre fed more wood to the fire, filling the campsite with light that danced and jumped and brightened the night. He stomped around, gathering what we'd take back tonight and piling what was left inside my tent. I felt useless, but the scowl on his face said to let him be.

He finished stuffing my clothes, cooking spices and warmest blanket into my pack before he called Rene over to him and gently ran his hands over the dog's injured leg. I knew my brother would carry the dog all the way home if Rene was hurt too badly, but Pierre looked relieved when he'd finished.

'That bastard blacksmith lured the dogs by hobbling some late spring lambs and their mothers. My guess is Belle and Rene heard the sheep bleating and went tearing off thinking a wolf or a lynx was attacking the herd. We've never had the need to train the dogs to avoid nets or snares. They didn't know to avoid the traps he'd set.' Pierre scratched behind Rene's ears. 'Belle was caught too tight to work her way loose, but Rene was nearly free when I found them. Looks like he pulled a muscle, but nothing worse.'

The young dogs pushed in under Pierre's arm, looking for their share of affection, but Belle stayed with me. I suddenly realised that the three dogs I'd brought from home were still missing.

'Are the rest of the dogs guarding the flock?'

My voice was little more than a raspy croak and my brother couldn't hide his flinch. 'I couldn't find them, little one. They'd have answered my whistle if they could and I didn't hear a sound from any of them. Once I freed Belle and Rene, they were frantic to reach you and so was I. Edmond will help me search for the other dogs when I come back to collect the blacksmith. Daylight will make things easier. Let's get you home now.'

Pierre offered his hand to help me stand. I took it and he pulled me into a hug, holding on as if he feared I'd disappear when he let go. I clung to him just as tight, needing a moment to pretend Pierre could always keep me safe and life would go on as it had before.

We both needed that to be true. I recognised the lie in that wish, even if Pierre didn't. Nothing was the same.

No matter how hard I fought these creatures, there wasn't any peace for me, not now, maybe not ever.

The monster named Michael had carved the truth of that into my skin.

My brother and I didn't exchange more than a few words on the long walk back to the village. Talking hurt my throat where Claude had choked me and new aches woke every few steps, making me stiff and slow, until Pierre carried me the last half-league.

The dogs he'd left at home rushed out to greet us, milling around his feet with joyful yips, sniffing Belle and Rene nose to tail. Another time the dogs' greeting would have made us both laugh, but not this morning.

A sharp whistle from my brother dropped the pack to their bellies a few paces from the threshold. He unlatched the door and nudged it open with his shoulder. 'Belle, Rene, Lily, inside!'

As soon as the dogs rushed into the house, Pierre carried me inside and kicked the door closed again. He laid me on my bed and eased my boots off. 'I'm going to find Edmond first thing,' he said. 'He knows that cursed blacksmith wouldn't stop following you or leave you alone so he won't be in any doubt about who's at fault. Likely the only council member who'll need convincing is the twice-damned priest.'

Father Jakob had always taken Claude's side. He'd find a way to do so again, if for no other reason than because my brother and I had defied him. The story of what the blacksmith tried to do to me would spread and change and the truth would be forgotten. People would gossip, watching to see if I carried the blacksmith's bastard, or wondering if I'd found a herbwife able to purge me of a child.

All the young men who flirted in the market square would turn away. They would look elsewhere for a wife, many believing the rumours that I'd encouraged Claude's attentions or lured him to my camp. Either way, I'd be disgraced. An outcast.

Margaret, Catherine and Michael had come to me the first time in the guise of angels, but I'd always been right to think them less than holy. They'd finally found a way to make me give up everything I loved or wanted – a way I didn't know how to fight. I was frightened by how much I hated them for that.

Pierre brushed a strand of hair off my face. 'I'm leaving the dogs inside with you: they are the best guards I could wish for, and the three of them will keep you company. Rest, little one, sleep if you can. I should be back long before dark tomorrow.'

I squeezed his hand to let him know I'd heard. He gathered his heavy cloak and staff and left.

Belle jumped onto the bed with me as the door closed. Rene and Lily curled up on the hearth, ears up and listening for anything that didn't belong. I said a prayer to Holy Mary, asking her to watch over my brother.

Falling asleep was easier than I'd feared. Avoiding nightmares proved impossible.

*

The afternoon light filling the room when I woke was made brighter by the light surrounding the spirit standing next to my bed. Belle's hackles were up and she growled deep in her chest, the rumbling meant to warn the creature away. I didn't know what one of them would do if Belle attacked, so I looped an arm around the dog and kept her close.

The stench of Claude's wine-soured breath filled my nose. I thought I'd be sick, both from the smell and the fear filling me to bursting. Margaret's light never moved closer, but her cold lips brushed my ear. 'The blacksmith almost killed you, Jeanne. You need to be stronger and more ruthless than any enemy and rid yourself of this man. Ask your brother to seek Claude's death from the council. Tell Pierre you won't rest until the blacksmith hangs.'

'No – I won't do it, not when Michael drove the blacksmith mad and sent him into the hills to find me. To . . . to punish me,' I said. My voice broke and I trembled, but I wouldn't back down. 'Michael told me so himself. I know who my real enemies are.'

Margaret hissed and grew taller, looming over my bed. 'You foolish, stubborn child. I've warned you before not to defy Michael or make him angry. How much more you suffer is up to you.'

Her light flared, blinding me, and Margaret vanished.

My brother came home soon after. Pierre petted the dogs and sent them out to join the rest of the pack. He glanced at me as he leaned his staff in the corner and hung up his cloak, his expression full of shifting emotions, some of which I couldn't read. His anger was easy to recognise.

'What happened?' I asked.

'I failed you, Jeanne. Thinking that group of cowards would punish Claude was a mistake.' Pierre sat on the edge of my bed and took my hand, but he wouldn't look me in the eye. 'I should have made sure he couldn't hurt you or anyone else before we left the valley.'

My breath came too fast and I had to cling to what little courage being home gave me, but I needed to know all my enemies. 'Don't try to spare my feelings, Pierre, just tell me what happened. I need to know who aside from Father Jakob took his side.'

'Edmond and I took ten angry men with us into the hills. The priest came along at the last moment. Most of the men who went to the cave were even angrier after seeing the bed Claude had fixed for the two of you. They have daughters of their own – if they'd any doubts when we left, the piles of empty wine skins in that cave settled them.' Pierre sighed. 'Louis had thought to bring chains from the forge and he bound the blacksmith tight, knowing how strong that bastard is. Jakob just watched, all sour-faced, until they tied a rope round Claude's neck. Then he argued with them about dragging him down from the valley like that – but the priest didn't win that round.'

He stopped speaking and stared into the dying fire, but I was used to waiting Pierre out as he hunted for words or made sure he had things straight before he spoke.

My brother glanced at me and went on, 'The men holding the lead jerked hard when Claude baulked at going on, or when they thought he was moving too slow. Twice the blacksmith fell on his face and men kicked him until he got to his feet again. Jakob preached endlessly at them, going on about compassion and mercy, but he couldn't answer when they asked how much mercy Claude had shown you.' Pierre shook his head. 'No one questioned the blacksmith's guilt; the only argument was over how harshly to punish a man who'd tried to rape a seventeen-year-old girl. I'd have thought sure they'd all have voted to hang him, or flog him in the square, all without me or Edmond needing to say a word. Damned if I know how that changed, but when the full council gathered . . . well, it did.'

'Father Jakob changed their minds,' I said, knowing in my bones he'd had help from my voices. Leaving Claude free was another way to punish me, one I couldn't fight. 'He found a way to blame me.'

'The black-hearted priest never said outright you were to blame or that you'd tempted an older man until he'd lost his reason, but his meaning was clear. After Jakob spoke, there was no more talk of hanging.' Pierre's anger and scorn coated each word. 'The council couldn't bring themselves to sentence Claude to anything harsher than a day and a night pilloried in the town square. He's to pay me a fine of two gold and seven silver coins for the dogs we lost. Father Jakob agreed losing the dogs was a grave injustice, but what you suffered at that bastard's hands wasn't worth troubling over.'

Specks of light glimmered in the corner near the door. I rolled towards the wall and closed my eyes, unwilling to acknowledge the treacherous beings inside that halo. The light brightened, a weight I could feel pressing against my skin, and just as quickly vanished again.

My brother patted my shoulder and his weight lifted off the bed. 'Don't despair, Jeanne. Not every council member voted to let the blacksmith escape unpunished. Edmond and Papa's other old friends won't let him off this easy, and neither will I.'

Pierre went out, whistling for the dogs. Listening to the commotion the pack and my brother made moving down the hill towards the sheep pens made me remember the three young dogs who'd fallen prey to the blacksmith's traps, how they'd race ahead, then double back to make sure I wasn't lost before running off again.

The rest of the pack wouldn't remember them more than a day or two, but I would.

Two more short whistles: Pierre was putting the pack through their paces. He'd rest tonight and go back to gather our flock in the morning. Knowing my brother, he'd ask Edmond's wife or oldest daughter to bring food at midday and sit with me while I ate. He wouldn't leave me alone more than could be helped.

He'd do his best by me. My brother had a good heart; he grieved for me and wanted to set things right. In the end, I wasn't sure a good heart was enough of a shield against three Fae creatures and a soulless priest.

Part Four

You have thought to deceive me but it is you who are deceived.

Jeanne d'Arc

A small war of Edmond's making broke out in the village and refused to stay confined to the council chambers. He warned Pierre to keep me well clear, advice I both appreciated and didn't need. I wanted nothing more from life than to stay clear of Father Jakob and Claude the blacksmith.

At Edmond's insistence, the council debated whether to forbid the blacksmith to leave his house after dark, or to speak to any woman in the village unless she spoke first. The older men on the council, all my father's friends and all with daughters near my age, argued furiously that the blacksmith had got off too lightly. A few of the younger men maintained that the village couldn't risk losing their blacksmith for the sake of one girl. Others kept what they thought to themselves.

Father Jakob took the blacksmith's side, as I'd known he would. He stood up to defend Claude, reminding everyone that he had lived a blameless life until the demons of lust and loneliness had driven him into the hills to find me. Then the faithless priest lectured the men crowding the council chamber on forgiveness.

The final vote was a tie, but that didn't end things. No one would admit to carrying the story outside of the council chamber, but news of the argument spread. Not a woman in the village would speak to the blacksmith. They shunned Claude publicly, shooing their children inside as he came down the street, even refusing to serve him in the marketplace. Men and women alike shunned him at mass, leaving him standing alone in a circle of empty space.

Older women made a point of telling their daughters stories about Aline loud enough that everyone close by could hear, and how Claude had treated her poorly. He'd told me she was a reluctant bride, but I'd been fighting too hard to pay much attention. Women who'd known Aline said she'd run away twice the first month they were married, but the blacksmith had chased his wife down and dragged her back. Each time she'd wept for days afterwards.

The stories had been forgotten when the village burned and Aline died, but people remembered now.

Claude became the outcast I'd feared becoming, but I didn't take any joy from that. My life had still changed. I was afraid every time I saw him in the village or standing at the front of his forge, my heart racing with panic and memories. He was still here for the voices to use against me.

A month passed this way and I left home as little as possible. My brother did have a good heart and he spared me as much as possible, taking it upon himself to collect flour from the miller or whatever we needed from the village.

The first snow had fallen, painting the trees in lace and closing the world into winter's silence. We kept the sheep penned this time of year and other than feeding the flock or collecting eggs, there was little to do in the way of chores.

I spent most of my winter days carding last year's raw wool, combing it free of seeds, burrs and all the tiny twigs sheep snagged in their fleece. The more dirt and grit I removed, the softer the wool would be when spun and woven into cloth. Once the wool was clean, I divided each fleece into good-sized hanks for dyeing when the weather warmed.

My voices shimmered inside the hearth, silent for once and letting me work in peace. Pierre was outside repairing the chicken coop when Edmond called out a greeting. My brother answered, but something in his voice caught my attention and I stopped working to listen. A third man spoke: Father Jakob.

Light filled the room and Catherine and Margaret stood near the door, watching to see what I'd do. Scrambling up to the loft and hiding was what I wanted, but acting a coward would give them more reasons to torment me. Setting my work aside and pulling on my heavy shawl took courage, especially as I knew the priest never arrived bearing good news.

Edmond and my brother were red-faced with anger as I approached and I almost regretted my decision to face Father Jakob. For a man who'd taken vows to remain humble before God, the priest looked overly satisfied and sure, a man who'd won some great victory and was certain to win another. His expression became serious and solemn as I joined my brother, but the smug look never left his eyes.

My brother put his arm around my shoulders, pulling me close.

'Pierre, what's wrong? Has something happened?'

'Yes, little one. Something happened.' My brother sighed and traded looks with Edmond. 'Claude's dead. Father Jakob went to see him at the forge this morning and found him hanging from a rafter.'

I shut my eyes and crossed myself, hearing my grand-mère's voice behind the words I spoke. 'May God forgive him and have mercy on his soul.'

Edmond cleared his throat. 'Jakob insisted on bringing you and

Pierre the news himself, Jeanne. I came along so there would be no misunderstandings.'

I stepped away from my brother, sensing I'd be better off to look strong, not to lean on him. 'Misunderstandings about what?'

'About the questions I need to ask you, child,' Father Jakob said. 'I need truthful answers, Jeanne. When was the last time you spoke to Claude?'

My throat closed up and I reached for Pierre's hand. The priest could think me a coward if he liked. 'In . . . in the valley . . . when I was begging him . . . begging him not to—'

The priest cleared his throat to interrupt and frowned. 'You didn't speak to him at the forge last night?'

Shock and anger replaced memory and fear. I could barely get the words out. 'No . . . *No!* How could you ask that question?'

The priest stepped closer and reached for me, but Edmond planted a hand on Father Jakob's chest and none too gently pushed him back. 'That's enough. Being a priest doesn't give you the right to torment this girl. You've even less right to put hands on her. You know full well what Claude did and how he hurt her, and that Jeanne's hardly left the yard since. I can't fathom why you'd think she'd suddenly go and visit him.'

'Someone saw her. Or they thought they did,' Father Jakob said. He pinched the bridge of his nose, suddenly looking less certain. 'The midwife Camelia was on her way home from a bad birthing when she saw a young woman slip out of the forge – she wasn't wearing a shawl or any shoes, so Camelia asked the girl if she was all right, if she needed any help. The girl smiled and the old woman couldn't remember anything after that, or even how she got home, but she's convinced Jeanne is the girl she saw.'

'And a confused old woman was enough to send you to our

door?' Pierre's voice was an angry growl. 'Do you think my sister put the rope around the blacksmith's neck and hauled him up? You're more of a fool than I thought.'

'Claude died outside a state of grace,' the priest said. He fingered the cross hanging around his neck, nervous and fidgety. 'I can't ask God to forgive him until I find out why.'

'Guilt, Jakob. He couldn't live with what he'd done,' my brother said. 'A priest should know all about guilt, but trying to blame Jeanne for Claude dying makes me wonder if you've ever felt a shred of regret about anything.'

The muscles in Pierre's back were stiff with rage. I held tight to his arm and leaned against his shoulder until some of his anger drained away. 'I'll make this simple for you, Jakob. My sister went to her bed before I did. I finished sharpening my knives, banked the fire and barred the door before I went to sleep. Three dogs stay inside with us near every night. They'd let me know if Jeanne got up or decided on taking a walk. She was not at the forge.'

Edmond stepped up, his jaw clenched and shoulders set. 'You got your answers, Jakob. I think it's best if you leave.'

Father Jakob opened his mouth to speak, but faced with both Edmond and Pierre's anger, he thought better of it and instead, turned and strode down the hill towards the main village. His black robes flapped around his ankles, the hem looking worn and tattered even from a distance.

Pierre pulled his hammer out of his belt and flung it after Father Jakob, but the priest was too far down the hill to notice. 'Keep him away from me, Edmond. Save me from the temptation of beating that smug look off his face.'

'I think God might forgive you.' Edmond winked at me and started after Father Jakob. 'I don't know if he'd forgive me.'

My brother kicked a small snowdrift, swearing under his breath, and began the trudge down to retrieve his hammer. Pierre dug where he thought the hammer landed, but when he couldn't find it, his swearing grew louder.

Faint glimmers of light caught my eye, growing brighter when I turned to look. A smiling young woman stood barefoot in the snow, the shawl she should have been wearing crumpled at her feet. I rarely saw myself in a mirror, but there wasn't any question she looked like me.

'You're out of time, Jeanne. You have to leave the village.' Her voice was full of bells: Margaret's voice. 'The priest's twisted heart is set against you and his mind wanders pathways that all lead to your death. His dreams are full of witches screaming as he breaks them on the wheel, or young women weeping as he lights the fire at their feet. He won't forget the old midwife's story. He'll find a way to blame you for the blacksmith's death. Your brother won't be able to protect you if the priest names you a witch.'

'This is your fault,' I whispered. 'Will you drive everyone around me mad until I obey?'

A faint light blossomed next to Margaret. Michael's thunderous voice was hushed, sounding far away. 'Evil finds fertile ground in those who proclaim themselves holy. The priest drove himself mad thinking his duty lay in making his congregation perfect in God's sight. If he names you a witch, the village will turn against you and those who defend you will be judged guilty of the same sin. Leave, Jeanne. Save them if you won't save yourself.'

The two monsters faded out of sight, leaving me a view of Pierre flailing in the snow, still searching for his hammer.

I didn't believe that my life's path was set before I was born: God gave us the will and the ability to make choices for ourselves, for good or ill. But I couldn't risk my brother's life out of stubbornness or the need to resist my voices. I told myself that leaving was my choice, made because I loved my brother, not forced on me.

We all lie to ourselves at times.

Convincing Pierre that I had to leave was as difficult as convincing myself.

I'd told my brothers about my voices when they first came to me. I was both excited and confused, and wanting to share everything with them. Henri scoffed and told me to stop lying or he'd tell our parents. At almost ten, he was too old to believe the sister half his age was in any way special.

Pierre didn't question that God's messengers spoke to little girls like me. Visitations of angels fitted in with everything Grand-mère had taught him and he was more devout at seven than I was now. The voices warned me away from telling anyone of their visits soon after. When he asked me a few weeks later if the angels had visited again, I lied and told him no.

Now I found myself lying again and hoping God would forgive me. I spun a tale of angels appearing late at night, warning me to flee the man hiding a demon's heart, and Pierre believed every word. My distress was real enough, sparked by knowing my brother would fight to keep me here if he knew the truth, and the danger facing both of us. Keeping him safe meant leaving him behind and that broke my heart, but I'd make the sacrifice to keep him free of Father Jakob's madness.

I never said the priest's name, but Pierre slammed his fist on the table as soon as I'd finished, rattling the clay bowls and tin spoons. The string of curses he spat out left no doubt who he was angry with. 'Jakob started all your troubles by telling Claude you'd come around if he just kept after you. Lord knows what other nonsense he planted in the blacksmith's head! Now God's own angels are telling you to leave home so a thrice-damned *so-called priest* won't cause you more harm. I should have let that evil bastard taste my sword years ago!'

Gripping his wrist tight kept him from jumping up and running out the door, sword in hand. Making him listen was harder. My only weapon was the truth – or at least part of it.

'Father Jakob will tell people I'm a witch if I stay,' I said. 'He may have already done so, or come close enough to make no difference.'

Anger still blazed in his eyes, but he sat still and let me hold his hand. 'No one but a brain-addled fool will believe that, Jeanne.'

'Won't they?' I asked. 'How many people has the old midwife told about a girl going barefoot in the snow and not feeling the cold? A girl who looks like me. The priest already believes I killed the blacksmith. He just hasn't figured out how. I need to be gone before he stumbles over a lie everyone will believe.'

'Then we both go,' Pierre said. 'Give me time to sell the flock and the cattle and I'll follow you.'

'Selling everything means never coming back, or starting over with nothing.' I took his hand in both of mine. 'I need to know home will still be here when it's safe to come back.'

Pierre grimaced and looked away. He'd found the truth in what I'd said. 'All right. What do you need me to do?'

'Help me find a place to go where I can make my own way,' I said. 'And help me keep leaving a secret.'

'Weaving and spinning will let you make your own way. Let me think a moment.' Pierre chewed his bottom lip, a boyhood habit I'd thought long gone. 'Edmond has a cousin in Vaucouleurs – the old man and his wife are cloth merchants. If they don't need help, they'll likely know someone in the guild who does.'

'Is pulling Edmond into this fair, or even wise?' I asked.

My brother smiled. 'Edmond has his own quarrels with Jakob, most of them stretching back years. He'd help you no matter what, but getting a little revenge on Jakob will make it all the sweeter. Leave it to us: we'll see you safely on your way.'

Spots of pale golden light glimmered over his shoulder, a signal the three spirits were listening. I'd always been puzzled about why they always let me know they were there and listening, but most things about them were baffling. One thing I did know, deep in my bones: they'd follow me to Vaucouleurs, and beyond. Leaving home didn't mean leaving the voices behind. God wasn't ready to grant me that blessing.

More snow fell, deep drifts trapping all but the hardiest into their houses and keeping the priest confined to his rectory. Father Jakob despised the cold and went out as little as possible. He'd happily spend all winter sitting near the fire if the needs of his flock didn't pull him away.

Pierre's plan called for me to be gone in less than a fortnight and the turn in the weather made that both easier and more difficult. Those few people who left their homes were bundled up to the point of being unrecognisable, so no one, including the priest, noticed that my brother and I had stopped going into the main village or attending mass.

Edmond travelled to Vaucouleurs with one of the traders who travelled daily between far-off towns, and returned two days later with the news that he'd made arrangements for me to live above his cousin Georges' shop. His serious face was spoiled by the twinkle in his eye.

Monique, his cousin's wife, wove all the cloth for their shop, but age and illness were taking their toll, just as they had with my grand-mère. Edmond's cousin had been looking for an apprentice to ease his wife's burden, but when he'd seen a sample of my work, Georges had offered me a small salary as well as room and board.

'He sent a month's salary in advance, Jeanne.' Edmond pressed a small leather purse into my hand, unable to keep from grinning ear to ear. 'He wanted to make certain you had enough to pay your fare and get whatever you might need for the trip. Monique is just as eager for you to arrive. She is already speaking of you as if you're a long-lost granddaughter come home again.'

Tears filled my eyes as I counted the silver and copper coins, seeing in my head the clothes too threadbare for a city like Vaucouleurs and debating whether to replace them before I left or when I arrived. The thought of the questions people here would ask decided me. Surely prices wouldn't be much higher in Vaucouleurs.

'I don't know how to thank you, Edmond.' I tucked the bag of coins into the purse at my belt, covering everything with the hem of my tunic and shawl. 'You can trust I'll do all I can to be a blessing to your cousins.'

He put his hands on my shoulders and looked me in the eye. 'Don't think you need to know everything at once, especially when it comes to getting around Vaucouleurs. Ask Georges, or his hired man, to take you where you need to go. You can't trust most folk in a town that size – there are too many strangers with no ties or stakes in the honest people who live there. You're best off if you let people you know guide you.'

A ripple of fear slithered down my spine and coiled in my belly. The people I knew and trusted best were in this room or in the yard, feeding the dogs.

'I'll be careful,' I said. 'You've my word on that.'

Pierre came inside as Lise, Edmond's wife, put the last stitch in the newest patch on my winter cloak. She folded the cloak and set it aside before packing the mending needle and thread into Grand-mère's sewing kit.

'All fixed, Jeanne. That patch should last a year or two at least.' She kissed my cheek on her way to the door. 'May God watch over you.'

As soon as Edmond shut the door, I put my arms around Pierre and held tight. I shook hard, not solely from fear of travelling or being so far away, but from knowing everyone and everything would change while I was away. I'd change too.

But Father Jakob and the threat he posed had left me no choice: to keep Pierre safe, I had to leave him.

'Are you ready, little bird?' The smile in my brother's voice and the echo of our father's pet name for me was a gift that boosted my courage. 'Two silver coins convinced Emile to leave tonight instead of at dawn. He's waiting with the wagon in the trees beyond the big pasture.'

I stepped away from my brother and picked up two of my packs. 'I'm not ready, but Grand-mère Marie always taught that acting brave is the next best thing to having courage. I pray she was right.'

He shouldered the rest of my bags and packs and pulled open the door. 'Grand-mère was usually right.'

I took a last look around and hurried out the door. If I lingered, I'd never leave.

Part Five

Nevertheless, before mid-Lent, I must be with the Dauphin, even if I have to wear my legs down to my knees!

Jeanne d'Arc

We stopped at the guardian tree growing at the edge of our land and I wedged a copper coin into a crack in the bark. So many coins had been left as offerings over the years that the wood had grown around them and made them part of the tree. Papa had always insisted to Grand-mère that leaving coins in the tree was just a different kind of prayer, safe travels and good trading being too small to ask of God. She'd scoffed and called it pagan foolishness.

I'd spent my life caught between honouring my father's traditions and Grand-mère's faith and I couldn't start this journey without offering one of the coppers in my purse and asking for continued good fortune. The new coin glittered in our torchlight. I took that as a good omen.

The wagon wasn't far from the guardian tree. Pierre greeted Emile before stacking my bags in the wagon bed. One small pack held my spare clothes, but he'd insisted I take all the cloth I'd woven since harvest to sell in Georges' shop. The coin Georges sent and things I held dear – my grand-mère's rosary and Mama's wedding ring – were safe in the sling against my chest. Grand-mère's silver crucifix was around my neck, as always.

Flickers of light danced next to the horses' heads: my voices, letting me know they wouldn't be left behind.

My brother hugged me tight and whispered in my ear, 'You

won't be gone for ever. Remember that, Jeanne. I'll come and get you when it's safe to come home.'

He gave me a hand up to the driving seat and stood back to watch us go. I waved as the horses started, then swiftly turned around to face the road ahead. My heart was already breaking. Watching my brother grow ever more distant would undo me completely.

Emile's old wagon's wide iron-rimmed wheels made it heavier than most, but the wheels dug in deeper and kept it from sliding so much on icy or muddy roads, Emile told me proudly. He was looking forward to a full wagon-load on the trip back from Vaucouleurs, but my bags and a stack of thick woollen blankets were the only cargo as we left Domrémy.

A brisk wind blowing in our faces carried the smell of smoke from the village hearths and the scent of tree sap from branches snapping under the weight of snow. It had thawed a little in the pale winter sunlight, then refrozen, leaving a smooth icy crust that let the horses pull the wagon with ease. But the chill was biting through my clothes and my toes and fingers were numb and frozen before we'd gone a league.

Emile pulled up and motioned me into the back of the wagon. 'You're shivering hard enough I can feel you trembling through the seat, Jeanne. Make a nest of the packs and blankets and stay low. You'll be warmer out of the wind. If I'd been thinking, I'd have put you back there from the beginning. Come on now, I'll help you get settled.'

Emile was thin as a breeze and the wisps of fine white hair that escaped his woollen cap made him look frail, but despite his age he was near as strong as Pierre, and probably tougher. He'd been a trader since before Papa was born and knew the tricks of travelling in all kinds of weather. If he said I'd be better off, I wouldn't argue.

He sat me against the wooden front boards with my bags piled in a windbreak around me. Being out of the gale made an immediate difference, but Emile wasn't content with half measures. The blankets stacked in the back were thick and heavy, tightly woven from good woollen yarn, so two folded underneath me kept much of the cold from creeping up between the wooden boards. With two more on top and one under my head for a pillow, my shivering stopped quick enough.

'Try to sleep if you can, Jeanne.' He patted my shoulder before climbing back onto the driving seat. 'We've a long way still to go.'

Winter nights were quiet, as if all sound had been buried under the snow or frozen into silence by the cold. The horses' hooves pounded a quiet rhythm felt in my bones more than heard and the constant hiss of the wheels soothed me, making it impossible to keep my eyes open.

My dreams were full of home and the people I loved, alive and healthy, the way my heart wished they were. Mama bounced a laughing baby girl on her knee, Papa sang, filling the house with songs, and my brother Henri pulled the girl he'd been courting up to dance, making her blush. Grand-mère Marie sat at her loom, smiling.

Pierre and I watched them through the glass window that had come all the way from Paris, but we weren't allowed inside to join them.

Not yet. It wasn't our time.

We moved at a steady pace, but the day seemed to drag on. No one had travelled this way since the last snowfall and breaking a path tired the horses, slowing them down. We stopped frequently to rest them.

Emile ran out of things to talk about not long after dawn, or at least things he felt proper to say to a girl my age, and hours passed in silence. I watched the unchanging landscape and tried to imagine life in a town like Vaucouleurs. Edmond's words about strangers had stuck with me, but walking down the street and not knowing a single soul was a difficult thing to imagine.

Late-afternoon shadows slithered over the snow when Emile stopped to rest the horses again. He helped me down before pulling a pail and bag of grain out from under the seat. The horses' ears twitched as the grain rattled into the bucket, recognising they were about to be fed.

The cold wind had stopped some time during the night, which I was deeply grateful for, but sitting still all day had left me with stiff, cramped muscles and I was eager to stretch them out. Trees crowded the road's edge, but were more widely spaced not far ahead. I paced the length of the wagon and back, careful to watch where I put my feet, knowing a smooth, solid-looking surface often hid hollows or deep holes. The shadows made it harder to see what was firm ground.

'Jeanne, come claim your supper.' Emile held out a wedge of cheese on a hunk of bread. 'It's a cold meal for man and beast both tonight, but we'll make up for it when we get to Vaucouleurs.'

I smiled my thanks. 'Will we camp tonight?'

'I admit to being tired. The idea of a fire and a night's sleep is tempting.' Emile cocked his head to the side, eyeing the sky. 'But the air feels too heavy for me to consider stopping that long. My guess is we'll have snow again before dawn, and that'll make the horses' job harder. We might get stuck here if we don't keep going.'

'You know best,' I said.

The bread was a little stale, the cheese on the edge of frozen, but I wouldn't complain. Tucking the cheese under my shawl while I tore pieces off the bread thawed it enough to eat. I wasn't close to full when I'd finished, but we'd be in Vaucouleurs before this time tomorrow.

'Emile, I've a question for you.'

He looked up from checking the mare's front hoof and smiled. 'Only one? On a grand adventure like this I'd thought you'd have more.'

I laughed. 'One for now. It's taking us two days and a little more to get to Vaucouleurs. How did Edmond get there and back in the same amount of time?'

'Risking his life on the ice.' He patted the mare's nose and moved to inspect the gelding's feet. 'When the river's frozen deep enough, a man can make the trip in a day. I've done it a time or two, but that was years ago. The trick is knowing where the ice is thick enough and avoiding places where it's too thin. Luc has a two-man sleigh that's not more than a driving seat and harness for the beasts to pull him along. He took Edmond to visit Georges.'

'Oh.' I hugged myself tight under my heavy cloak, a little embarrassed at not knowing. 'He never said and . . . and . . . I didn't know.'

He stood and wiped his hands on his breeches before pulling on his gloves again. 'No, Edmond wouldn't tell you. It may be taking us twice as long, but we'll get there all the same.'

While Emile checked the harness, as he did each time we stopped, I kept pacing, as much to keep my boots from freezing to the ground as anything, and muttered a prayer to Holy Mary, thanking her for keeping Edmond safe.

'Time to go, Jeanne.' He smiled and offered me his hand. 'Up you go.'

My voices shimmered into view and stood between Emile and

me. Catherine touched my face. 'Listen and remember,' she whispered, and all three vanished.

'Hold, old man – don't move!' An arrow slammed into the side of the wagon when Emile turned to see who'd yelled. 'I said *don't move!*'

Two English bowmen stepped out of the trees behind me and three more soldiers stepped out ahead of us on the road, longswords drawn. A pair of English knights rode out of the trees after the foot soldiers. One forced Emile up against the wagon, while the other herded me towards the men on foot.

I tried to dodge around the horse and run into the trees, but the Englishman just laughed and danced the beast sideways, forcing me into a soldier's arms. He pulled my wrists behind my back, holding tight so I couldn't break free.

The knight who'd trapped me rode closer to the wagon. 'What are you carrying, old man?'

His words sounded as if they didn't quite fit in his mouth, but unlike the night English raiders burned Domrémy, somehow, I understood him and all the talk flying back and forth between the other soldiers. Catherine's touch and command to listen was to blame, though I didn't thank her for it. Knowing what was being said was more frightening than not understanding a word.

Emile's voice quivered with fear, but his eyes darted towards me, as if making sure I was paying attention. He spoke some trader's English and he must have hoped to talk us out of this. 'Only my granddaughter and her belongings, Your Grace. She's to be an apprentice weaver in Vaucouleurs.'

Two of the soldiers clambered into the wagon and began going through my bags, dumping my clothes and the cloth I'd woven onto the snow, then tossing the bags after. The blankets were handed to one of the bowmen.

'Nothing back here worth taking, Lord Thomas. Nothing but the blankets,' one of the soldiers said.

'Look up front under the seat. They must have some food at least.' Lord Thomas scowled. 'And search both of them. I don't like the look of that man. He's lying about something.'

One soldier searched under the driving seat and quickly came up with Emile's pail and sack of grain. A bag with the leftover cheese and bread was given to the second English knight. What we had left wouldn't be more than a few mouthfuls for them, but hungry men eat what they can find. Maybe they'd been caught short, perhaps even cut off from the rest of the army.

The other soldier climbed out of the wagon and began pulling at Emile's clothing, stripping off his cloak and tunic and turning them inside out. He pointed at Emile's breeches. 'Take those off too.'

'Please, sir,' Emile said, a whimper in his voice. 'Not in front of my granddaughter.'

'Do what I tell you, old man!' The English soldier hit Emile across the face, knocking him back against the side of the wagon. 'Her turn's coming next.'

Lord Thomas' mount shifted restlessly, ears up and listening. The English lord patted the war horse's neck, his sharp gaze fixed on the trees back the way we'd come. 'Get on with it, Ben. Ned, search the girl and see what she's hiding. Quick now, both of you.'

Ned spun me around to face him, the smug smile on his face waking panic, making my breath come hard and fast. I pounded him with my fists, but he tore open my cloak and shawl with one hand, easily holding me with the other. Seeing Grand-mère's silver crucifix gleaming, Ned closed his fist around the cross and yanked on it to break the chain.

I grabbed his arm and sank my teeth into his wrist. Howling,

Ned tried to shake me off, but I held on and bit down harder until I tasted blood. He let go of the crucifix, red-faced and swearing, and I ran.

He caught me before I'd gone far, yanking on my cloak to pull me off-balance, and when the cloak came off in his hand, slammed into me from behind, his weight carrying me to the ground – but my left foot got twisted underneath me as I fell and something snapped inside. I screamed, blinded by the pain, and screamed again when the soldier flipped me onto my back.

He straddled me and snapped the silver chain around my neck before yanking the sling off over my head, and emptying it onto the ground. My grand-mère's rosary and Mama's ring went in the bag at his belt, but my purse vanished down the front of his tunic.

Ned watched me sobbing in pain, much like a cat toying with a cornered mouse, before he shook his head. 'You should've just let me have it all. I wasn't going to hurt you this bad, leastwise, not so you couldn't get home on your own. Now you'd best hope his Lordship has Benny cut your throat, like he did with the old man. That's a quicker way to go than freezing.'

I turned my head to look at Emile, who was lying in a spreading circle of crimson snow. He hadn't even cried out. I said a prayer, asking God to welcome a good man.

Two of the foot soldiers had unharnessed Emile's horses and were hurriedly tying blankets onto their backs as makeshift saddles. Lord Thomas and the other knight watched the woods and snapped orders at them to hurry. One soldier said something to Lord Thomas and started towards where Ned had me pinned to the ground.

My voices flared into view on either side of Emile's body, but for once they didn't speak or urge me to fight Ned, or scold me for being weak. Perhaps all their lectures about fate and destiny had been lies and they'd brought me here to die. I shut my eyes, unable to stomach the sight of them with Emile. Somehow I knew they were responsible for the kind old man's death.

Pain and terror whispered in my ear that I'd been right all along. I wasn't *La Pucelle*; I was only another French peasant girl about to die at English hands.

Men shouted and a horse squealed in pain. I opened my eyes to see one of the soldiers running towards Lord Thomas fall with an arrow in his leg. Two more appeared in his chest as a troop of soldiers in French colours charged out of the trees and fell upon the outnumbered English.

Lord Thomas and the other knight kicked their horses into a gallop and sped away, but there were close on a dozen French riders at their backs.

Ned was tugging at the knife in his belt, but never got it free. His eyes widened when an arrow sprouted in his neck. An instant later, a second arrow sank in deep just below the first. He tugged and twisted, and broke off the thin shaft, looking at me in surprise as his warm blood sprayed my face and coated my hair. His eyes fluttered closed before he pitched forwards, his dying breath hot and moist against my throat. I screamed and tried to push him off me, choking on terror as his blood soaked through my clothing and cooled on my skin.

A young French soldier rolled the body off me and dropped to his knees in the snow, wiping blood and tears off my face, paying no heed to the gore coating me. 'Shhhh ... shhhhh, they can't hurt you now. You're safe with us, little sister, you're safe. Come away now. I promise you'll be protected.'

He started to pull me up to my feet, but stopped when I screamed.

'God strike me dead for being a thoughtless fool.' He eased me back down and brushed strands of hair off my face. Worry filled his dark eyes. 'How badly are you hurt, little sister?'

'The ... the blood is his.' The pain was coming in searing waves, making it hard to breathe, even harder to think. 'When he ran me down ... and ... and fell on ... my ankle ... something broke.'

'Then I'm twice a damned idiot. I should have asked if you were injured before trying to get you up. Forgive me for hurting you.' The corners of his brown eyes crinkled when he smiled. 'I promise I'll do better from now on.'

An older man ran up, the chainmail stretched tight over his belly rattling with each stride. He stopped short as he caught sight of the blood. 'Ethan ... ? How badly is she hurt?'

'She thinks a broken ankle, which is bad enough. Her cloak is behind us, Robert – hand it to me, if you would.' Ethan pulled me into his lap as gently as he could and draped the cloak over me. 'I'm told the blood belongs to the English dog.'

'Thank Blessed Mary for that. I was afraid ... Well, never mind. She'll heal and that's what's important.' He crouched next to Ethan. 'Lady Maud has a physician at the castle. I'm sure His Grace can persuade the countess to have the man attend her.'

'I'm sure he can. She likes being in his debt almost as much as she likes being in his bed.'

I didn't completely understand why Ethan sounded amused or why Robert flushed scarlet, but I guessed something in the conversation must be vaguely scandalous.

My false guardians chose that moment to brighten into view behind Robert, forcing me to squint. Catherine's frost-rimmed voice echoed in my head, making me shiver harder. 'You have found the first of your champions, just as the prophecy foretells. Trust Sir Ethan above all others. He will protect you when others lose faith and flee your side, Jeanne.'

Her voice and the lights faded, leaving me to gaze up at Ethan's face. I stared, trying to understand why I thought I recognised him, why I wanted to trust him – and I remembered the warrior fighting next to Pierre in my dream, the Maid's sword in his hand. Pain had left me muddled and confused, but though the thought of tangling him in the monsters' cherished prophecy horrified me; I doubted either of us had a choice.

Ethan saw me watching and smiled. 'I need a favour, Robert. Coax one of the taller pages to give up a tunic and a linen shirt so we can get her out of these clothes, and please ask His Grace to order Giles to share a drop or two of the poppy mixture he has hidden in his luggage. Remind them both she's not a mercenary. I won't ask her to get drunk on brandy and bite a piece of leather if her ankle needs to be set and splinted.'

'Done. The beef-eaters tossed all her clothing on the ground, but if the pages don't have anything to spare I might be able to find something that isn't soaked through.' Robert glanced at the men near the wagon, his lips pulling tight. 'Giles won't like giving up even a drop of poppy, but I can pull rank if it comes to that.'

'If it comes to that, I can draw a sword,' Ethan said calmly. 'Go, quickly now, before she and I both freeze.'

Robert trotted back to the group of soldiers milling around Emile's wagon. More men on horseback had arrived, and with them, a line of wagons loaded with barrels and chests and what I guessed were rolled-up tents and pavilions. I'd seen a noble progression pass through Domrémy the year I turned ten: a bride and her ladies, travelling to Nancy for her wedding who'd hoped to avoid notice by English troops. Her luggage train was a fraction of what I saw now.

Two men spread one of Emile's blankets on the ground and placed the old trader's body in the centre. They wrapped him up tight in his woollen shroud and laid him in the wagon, which gave me hope he'd find a proper burial.

I started to sob again, overcome with grief and guilt over Emile's death, convinced he was dead because of me. My voices shimmered into view next to the wagon, silently judging me, which made me cry harder.

Ethan pulled my head against his shoulder, rested a hand on my blood-sticky hair and let me weep. I ran out of tears eventually, too tired and heartsick to cry any more.

'I'm sorry, little sister. Was the old man your grandfather?' he asked.

I shook my head and wiped my face on the inside of the cloak, smearing blood and snot both on the lining. 'An old friend of my father's, doing a favour for me and my brother. Papa was killed by a knight when the English raided our village.'

'Then I'm twice sorry. Too many good men have died for the sin of being born French.' He sat up straighter, watching the men coming towards us. One of them was Robert. 'Will you tell me your father's name? I'll light a candle for him.'

'Jacques d'Arc, son of Jules and Marie.' I had to swallow to finish. 'Father of Henri d'Arc, who died the same day.'

'I'll light two candles when we reach the castle.' He smiled again, and I decided the lines around his eyes meant smiling was a habit. 'I should know your name too. That will make introducing you easier.'

I took a breath, unsure why telling him my name felt as dangerous as stepping off a cliff. 'Jeanne d'Arc, daughter of Jacques and Isabelle, sister of Pierre d'Arc.'

Robert reached us first. He was carrying some long, straight branches and some of my own cloth, as well as one of my older shawls. A bottle of wine was tucked into his belt.

A handsome young man followed at Robert's heels, squinting against the sun, and a sour-faced man of middle years trailed slowly behind the two of them.

No one needed to tell me which one was Giles. He stayed well back, not bothering to hide his disgust as he eyed the blood on Ethan and me. 'Is a peasant girl worth all this trouble, Your Grace?'

The young noble exchanged glances with Ethan, clearly holding fast to his temper, and knelt near my feet. 'I say she is, Cousin. She wouldn't have needed rescuing if you'd finished off that pack of dogs when I gave the order. Give me the bottle of poppy and go back to the wagons. We'll speak again later. See if you can find a little mercy in your heart before then.'

Giles slipped a hand into his purse and pulled out a small glass vial. He stared at the bottle for an instant, then with a small bow reluctantly placed it in his young cousin's hand. 'As you wish, Your Grace.'

He turned to walk away, but not before I saw the hate-filled look he parcelled out between Ethan and me. I shut my eyes so I didn't have to watch him go and concentrated on steeling myself for the pain I was sure would come.

Robert set down the branches and cloth and unhooked a battered tin cup from his belt. He poured two fingers of wine into the cup and handed it to Ethan.

The nobleman pulled the stopper out of the glass vial and held the open bottle over the cup. 'One drop or two, Ethan? You've acted as battlefield surgeon more times than I have.'

'Two, I think: a little more is better than not enough.'

The drops sounded heavy as they landed in the cup. Ethan swirled the wine to mix in the poppy before holding the cold tin to my lips. 'Drink it all, Jeanne. One big gulp if you can manage.'

The sweet smell of poppy masked the scent of wine, but even so, I thought I'd be sick as it hit my stomach. At first I had to fight to keep it down, but warmth and numbness slowly crept thought my body, spreading until I forgot about pain and floated outside myself.

Ethan used the Englishman's knife to cut my boot and my wool sock away from my horribly swollen foot. He ran his fingers over my leg and ankle, careful to move them as little as possible. I felt everything he did, but it was as if I watched from the cloud-tops.

'I don't feel any broken bones in her ankle,' he said. 'Her foot is too swollen to tell if it's broken or not, but the swelling makes me think it is. Pray that God is kind and what she felt wasn't a tendon snapping. I'll wrap everything up tight to keep it from moving too much. Hold her foot straight once I get it aligned right, Charles, and don't let go. Robert, you'll need to keep her still. Even with the poppy this is going to hurt.'

I'd heard him, but the return of pain – sharp and deep and agonising – was still a surprise. How hard I struggled against their grip was even more of a surprise to them. The three of them had to hold me down until I finally passed out.

When voices – Ethan and the man he'd called Charles – woke me again, the pain had dulled to merely a bone-deep ache.

'You have to do something about him, Charles.' The frustration in Ethan's voice made me pay attention. 'Giles undermines your authority at every turn.'

'I will do something when the time is right, but until then I need his troops,' Charles said. 'He has five full companies under his command, more than five hundred men. I can't ignore him or send his soldiers away.'

'Those men have sworn their loyalty to him, not you or the Crown.'

'And they fight like fiends for him, Ethan. The English would have forced my army into the sea without Giles and his troops.' Charles sighed. 'But I'm not blind to the change in him.'

'Deal with him soon, my lord. Giles is too fond of strong drink and bragging to his followers. Given how closely he guards his store of poppy, I'd venture he's overly fond of that too. One day he'll find courage enough to declare himself the Dauphin in your place and if that happens, you'll end up fighting two wars.' Ethan lifted my foot enough to knot a last strip of cloth. 'This is done. Robert should have a tent up by now and some water warmed. It's past time for me to get her cleaned up and out of the wind.'

Ethan picked me up and carried me in his arms, but poppy sap mixed with wine kept the pain floating just out of reach. The snow crunching under his boots tried to lull me back to a deeper sleep, but my brain raced, struggling to understand what I'd overheard – and I needed to understand.

'Let me get one of the cooks to clean her up, Ethan. Or Father Géraud.' Charles sounded hesitant. 'She's young and might misunderstand. You shouldn't risk your good name.'

He snorted. 'I lost my good name when I became a mercenary.'

'You're also an earl's heir, Ethan. You really don't have to act as nursemaid to this child.'

'She's close to my age, Charles. That's long past being a child. I'm not sure I trust anyone else enough to bathe and dress her – aside from you, of course, and you're ill-suited to the task.' Ethan's arms tightened around me. 'And it's a point of honour. I told her I'd protect her, that she'd be safe with me. I plan to keep my word.'

I was trapped at the border of sleep, unable to cross from one side or the other, but I knew when we entered the camp: too many people talking at once, raising a din that made me long to cover my ears. Men shouted orders, pages recited messages they'd memorised and cooks scolded their helpers for not working fast enough, and all of it was louder than anything I'd heard at home. A baby began to cry, making me realise the idea of children travelling with an army was something I'd never considered before. I found myself confused at how anyone was able to pick out just one voice above the others.

'The poor waif needs a Paladin among this mob,' Charles said. 'I can make the appointment official if you like. Count Paladin is an old and respected title, going all the way back to Charlemagne.'

Ethan laughed. 'Paladin is surely a better title than nursemaid, but no one addressing me as such will be able to keep a straight face. I'm not Roland or one of Charlemagne's loyal knights; I'm the baseborn son of an earl. We both know people will still ask why Jeanne needs me to defend her. The rest will doubtless mutter about "young mistresses".'

'You're only baseborn because the Church wouldn't let your parents marry until after you were born.'

'Faithful sons of the Church don't fall in love with Moors, Your Grace. My father kept after the archbishop only because he was determined not to let the priests rob me of my inheritance. They were just as happy without saying vows.'

'God blessed them with that.' Charles lowered his voice. 'Don't underestimate your value to me, Ethan. The title is yours, whether you use it or not. A royal decree making her your ward should silence the worst of the gossip. I'll announce it when the commanders meet in my pavilion tonight. Look, isn't that Robert? Up ahead on the right.'

Their voices faded as Margaret whispered in my ear, 'Sleep, Jeanne. You refused to leave home, but the prophecy has brought you to Charles nonetheless. Gather your strength for the battles ahead. Your Paladin will guard your rest.'

Icy fingers brushed my cheek. I stopped chewing on words I only half understood and worrying whether Charles was the Dauphin the monsters wanted me to find and let sleep take me.

My lips were dry and cracked when I opened my eyes and a foul taste coated my tongue. The silence outside said it was far past midnight and that other than the sentries the camp was sleeping. Horses snorted and shook their heads; dogs barked and were quickly hushed. The sentries' fires flickered and danced outside the tent, casting shadows on the walls that mimicked the flames.

A small oil-lamp hung from the ceiling, filling the inside of the tent with a dim yellow light. Ethan sat on the edge of a cot across from mine, shirtless and barefoot despite the cold, with his head in his hands. At first I thought the dark lines marking his shoulders and upper arms were scars, but the patterns were too uniform and regular and they looked like they were meant to stand out on his brown skin.

Old men at home told tales of the fierce warriors their grand-fathers had faced in the Crusades. Those warriors believed the symbols inked into their skin would protect them in battle, and if the tales were true, those beliefs made them fearless. Father

Jakob had always scoffed at the stories, saying only godless fiends held to such nonsense. I couldn't picture Ethan as godless or a fiend – not after he'd saved my life – but I didn't have any trouble imagining him as a warrior.

I stretched my arm over the edge of my cot to touch the rich carpets covering the tent floor, but I was afraid moving more than that would wake the pain. The thick pile was warmer than bare ground, a luxury common soldiers in Charles' army wouldn't share. The cot creaked as I moved and Ethan's head came up quickly. I saw relief fill his brown eyes before he smiled.

'Are you warm enough, Jeanne?' He moved to sit on the carpet next to my bed, fussing with the blankets and making sure they were well tucked under the thick felt pad covering the cot. 'I can find another blanket if you need one.'

'I'm warm.' My tongue felt thick, but the mist was clearing from my brain. 'How long did I sleep?'

'Two days, a night and well into the second night,' he said. 'Long enough for me to worry that I'd given you too much poppy.'

My skin and my hair had been washed clean while I slept, but whoever had bathed me hadn't dressed me again. The wool against my bare skin felt odd, scratchy to the point of wanting to claw my skin off in some places, but almost as soft as a linen chemise in others. My clothes were nowhere to be seen. A page's tunic was tossed over a stool, but even from a distance I saw it was much too small.

I shut my eyes and turned away from Ethan, blessing the dim light and praying he wouldn't see me blush – I'd never expected to wake up naked in an army camp full of strangers. Feeling trapped and helpless frightened me, but it also made me furious. As long as I stayed angry, I could be brave.

'Is something wrong?' Ethan leaned close and brushed strands of hair off my face. 'Are you in pain again?'

'Is this how you keep your pledge to protect me, Sir Ethan? Where are my clothes? Did someone steal them?'

He sighed and rubbed his eyes. 'No one stole your clothes. The blame lies with the English tossing all you owned off the wagon. Half of Charles' army trampled your things into the mud, until there wasn't anything worth saving. Robert's sister and her ladies tried to scrub the blood out of what you were wearing, but they ended up burning everything. I'd thought to find a page's tunic to fit you, but Father Géraud forbade it. He declared dressing you in men's clothing would be heresy and put your immortal soul in danger.'

My voices had warned me to be wary of priests and I had good reason to be so, but avoiding them was proving impossible. Now another meddling cleric who thought he knew what was best for me had crossed my path.

I couldn't stop the panic and bitterness dancing under my skin, or keep my voice from shaking. 'What does this priest expect me to do?'

'I thought on that all through one long night and I cannot tell you. No doubt he wants you to rely on God's mercy, but I've never had much luck with that.' Ethan ran his fingers through his short dark hair. 'But the English didn't ruin all the cloth the old man was hauling and I've never known a noble lady to travel without needles and thread, or a pair of tailor's shears. I asked Lady Elise and her ladies if they'd be kind enough to make you something new to wear. They should be done by tomorrow.'

My throat closed up thinking of the English soldier dropping my purse of silver down his tunic. Even if Charles' men had searched him, I'd no proof the coins were mine.

'Ethan – I can't pay them.'

'Don't fret over payment, Jeanne. The cloth belonged to your friend and Elise said the work was a gift. Most of the ladies are bored silly. They welcome something useful to do,' he added. 'Elise didn't want to risk moving you and causing you pain, but she took what measurements she could. She asked me to warn you the clothes might be a little big, but better big than too small. There are plenty of seamstresses at Lady Maud's castle and we can get things altered.'

I said a prayer of thanks and asked God to forgive me for being foolish with the same breath. Blaming fear and pain or the way poppy muddled my head were a child's excuses for speaking without thinking. I wasn't a child and I couldn't act like one, not if I wanted to survive the monsters' plans for me. I needed to beseech Ethan's understanding.

'I've no reason for doubting you, not after all you've done. I hope you'll forgive me,' I said. 'I'll find a way to repay you – and Lady Elise.'

He smiled and brushed a hand over my hair. 'It's not all so serious as that, Jeanne. I've nothing to forgive and you've nothing to repay. If you'd like to give Elise a gift, tell her where she can find more of the cloth she's working with and the person weaving it.'

'The cloth came from my village.' My thoughts raced in circles, dogs chasing their own tails. I couldn't imagine why Lady Elise wanted to know. 'I . . . I wove it all. Why is that important?'

Ethan's smile became a grin which drove some of the tiredness away from his face. 'She wants to offer the weaver a position in her household. Elise pays her craftsmen fair wages and she treats them well too.'

'Emile was taking me to Vaucouleurs – I was going to weave

for a cloth merchant. He sent money so I could travel and . . . and a-a-a soldier took it.' I pressed the heels of my hands against my eyes, hoping to hold back the panic rushing to fill my chest. 'I can't work for Lady Elise until I have repaid him – b-b-but I don't know the name of his shop, or what part of the city it's in, or how to find him.'

A bright light flashed and Catherine spoke, her voice a winter gale that filled the tent. The blankets held me close, but I couldn't stop shivering. 'Fate brought you to the Dauphin's side and fate will keep you there,' Catherine said. 'Don't torture yourself by thinking you have a choice of where to travel, Jeanne. The English must be driven out and Charles must be crowned at Reims. You and your Paladin will be at his side, just as the prophecy says. Fighting your destiny will only cause you more pain. More punishment.'

My hands still covered my eyes, but I saw the light flare and heard thunder rumble as she left. Knowing the monster was gone didn't stop me from trembling, or ease the throbbing that woke in my ankle and travelled up my leg.

Catherine's threat terrified me. Emile had died to bring me to Charles' side, and so had my father and grand-mère, Henri, even Claude. One way or another, my monsters had killed them all to drive me to this place, this moment.

Continuing to resist what they wanted me to do – to *be* – meant someone else would die. Giving in meant losing myself.

I didn't know what to do. I didn't know who to sacrifice. Panicked and floundering, I began to sob.

Ethan leaned closer, stroking my hair. 'It's all right, little sister,' he whispered. 'You're safe, I promise. I'm here, Jeanne, I'm here. I won't leave you alone.'

He began to tell me stories about growing up near the sea with his four brothers. I found myself imagining fog creeping in off the ocean, bright-coloured shells lined up on the window ledge, the cry of gulls echoing off strong stone walls. Hearing Ethan tell how he quietened his small brothers' fears helped calm mine.

I fell asleep to the sound of his voice, less afraid and less alone.

Ethan had decided not to travel until I could ride with him without being dosed on poppy or in intense pain. He urged Charles to go on without us and the Dauphin agreed that, as my guardian and protector, that was Ethan's right. Then Charles declared that he had no intention of leaving us on our own: the army, and the court, would rest here until we could all leave together.

Giles sneered at his cousin's concern and proposed tossing me into the back of a crowded wagon and letting me bounce like a sack of grain. That started a loud, angry quarrel with both Ethan and the Dauphin. My voices made sure every bitter word between them filled my ears. The argument ended when Charles, annoyed and increasingly furious that Giles was questioning his judgement, ordered his cousin away.

'I'm sorry, Charles.' Ethan sighed. 'I didn't intend to cause you so much trouble. We really will be fine on our own until Jeanne can ride.'

'You're not the one trying my patience,' Charles said. 'I've waited too long to give my cousin a lesson in obedience. Not that I have much faith Giles will take it to heart, but watching him fume will amuse me. We'll leave when I'm ready to leave, and the more my dear cousin protests, the longer we'll stay. If that gives Jeanne time to recover, that's all to the good.'

Between the two of them, Ethan and Charles found ways to stall, buying me time to heal. Theirs was an open, cheerful conspiracy, but a conspiracy nonetheless.

No one but Lord Giles would openly question the Dauphin's word or his decisions, and as the days dragged on, he was wise enough to keep quiet. Charles found a host of reasons not to break camp, everything from a small snowfall or reports of bandits in the woods to organising a hunt for wild boar that brought him back to camp with flushed cheeks, and a joyful grin on his face.

He insisted on dressing the boar himself, a task that took most of a day. Roasting the enormous carcase took another two days. All in all, the future King of France wasted almost two weeks doing nothing but flirting with ladies-in-waiting, or listening to his soldiers tell stories, and seemed to have a great time of it.

Elise and her ladies hadn't thought to make me the plain tunics and skirts I'd worn my whole life. The two gowns they'd fashioned from my cloth were unadorned, but suitable for the ward of a future earl to wear at court. Lady Elise and one of her ladies came to help me dress, and Elise helped me braid my hair. Far from being too big, both gowns fitted perfectly.

By the time they finished and let Ethan back into the tent, my leg was throbbing with each heartbeat and I had to fight back nausea. He took one look at me sitting on the edge of the cot and eased me down to lie on my side before pulling out the bucket I'd needed before.

'Thank you, Lady Elise,' he said, covering me with a blanket. Ethan winked at me before he turned to Elise and smiled. 'You have my deepest gratitude, but Jeanne needs to rest now. Let me escort you back to your pavilion.'

Elise laughed and took the arm he offered. Their conversation drifted back to me as they walked away. 'You take your duties as guardian very seriously.'

'I swore an oath to protect her, Elise. I can't take that lightly.'

Light began to shimmer in the corner of the tent and I shut my eyes, too miserable to cope with monsters or their prophecies. They let me pretend to sleep until I wasn't pretending any longer.

For a few hours each day, Ethan let me sit in a camp chair just inside the tent entrance. Swaddled in blankets and mostly out of the wind, my foot propped up on a small chest, I could feel the sun on my face and watch the life of the camp. Ethan sat with me when we could, answering questions and explaining what I didn't understand. Charles and his cousin baffled me the most.

Giles might have stopped pushing Charles to leave but that didn't mean he stayed quiet. I began to recognise the stiff way the Dauphin held himself meant they were arguing again. Ethan insisted I was better off not knowing why they quarrelled so often and why Giles grew bolder.

'He does what he can to drive a wedge between me and Charles,' Ethan said at last. He held his knife up to the light and peered at the blade before going back to filing out a nick in the edge. 'The reasons why aren't important. All you need do is stay out of his lordship's way.'

'Staying out of his way is easy when I rarely leave the tent,' I said. 'But my father taught it's always best to know your enemy better than they know you.'

'Did he now?' Ethan glanced my way, his expression close enough to a smirk as to make no difference. 'Do all fathers in your village teach battle strategy to their daughters?'

'No, but Papa taught my brothers.' I blushed, ashamed of how close I'd come to a lie. 'He didn't mind that I sat with them and listened. I paid more attention than Henri.'

'And likely remembered more.' He finished with his knife, wiped the blade clean and slipped it back in the sheath before he stood and grabbed his cloak. He gave me a small bow before putting it on. 'I shouldn't tease you, Jeanne. How you learned the lesson isn't important. You're not wrong about Giles and in all honesty, it might serve you better to know more about him.'

'But you're not going to tell me now.'

He smiled. 'One of Elise's ladies has asked me to supper. If it's warm enough, we may go for a walk and find a quiet place to talk. I'm already late.'

'Oh – my apologies. I didn't know.' I wasn't child enough to think talking was all they meant to do. 'I shouldn't keep you.'

I managed to slide out of the chair and onto my cot somewhat gracefully and stretched out facing the wall. My heart beat too fast and I struggled with a sharp-edged sense of betrayal I didn't understand.

Ethan covered me with the blanket and sat on the edge of the cot, his hand on my shoulder. 'I need you to listen to me, Jeanne, and remember this. Charles' court is split into factions, all of them hungry for power, all of them fighting a war in the shadows. You can't look at anything that happens between factions without thinking of it as a skirmish. That's what spending an evening with Elise's lady is: a skirmish.'

I rolled over and stared at him. 'I don't understand.'

'I didn't expect you would.' He took a breath. 'Lady Talia doesn't want me in her bed. My mother was a Moorish princess, but my skin's too dark and my father's blood isn't noble enough to suit her. But Talia's bored and she's not above using me to get closer to Charles.'

A year after our village burned, a young widow was caught committing adultery with a trader who came to Domrémy every few weeks. Father Jakob had scolded the man and sent him away, but the widow was pilloried and shamed before the entire village. Memories of Grand-mère's scandalised voice lecturing me on carnal sin filled my head. Punishment of one sort or another always fell most heavily on the woman. I didn't feel scandalised that a noblewoman would plot to bring Ethan to her bed; I was confused.

But nobles followed different rules and the Dauphin's court was full of traps and currents I didn't understand. I thanked God I had Ethan to guide me.

'And you'd let her use you,' I said. 'Why?'

He shrugged. 'I'm bored too, but the only thing an hour with me will get her is a pleasant memory, or if her luck runs out, a dark-skinned bastard. Charles knows where I'm going and why. We both suspect Giles put Talia up to this. Until the Dauphin chooses a bride, every unmarried woman in court indulges the fantasy of becoming queen. Giles encourages those noblewomen he thinks he can control.'

I burrowed deeper under the blanket, taken by a sudden chill. 'Why are you telling me all of this?'

'Because given a chance, Giles will use you too, little sister.' Ethan stood and draped another blanket over me. 'Sleep if you can. We'll talk more tomorrow.'

'Ethan.'

He turned and waited.

'Was your mother really a princess?'

'She was the youngest child of the king of a small kingdom. A Castilian prince took my mother and two of her five brothers hostage when she was just a little girl. The Castilian held them for three years while he waged war on her father, eventually driving her father from his throne.' He turned away, apparently watching the wind rippling the tent flap, before giving me a smile. 'When her brothers were ransomed, her father promised he'd come back for her. She was nine. She believed him.'

'Blessed Mother Mary . . . Her father never came back?'

'No, little sister, he never came back. The Castilian ordered that my mother had to be useful if she wanted to eat and sent her to work in the kitchens. On his way home from a pilgrimage, Atu stopped at the Castilian's castle. My mother was seventeen, half-starved and defiant when my father first saw her. He paid her ransom, bought a second horse and told her she was free to go if she liked. She chose to stay with him. Atu treated her like a princess for the rest of her life.'

Ethan smiled again before he pushed through the tent flap, letting in a quick blast of frigid air and the sharp scent of smoke from the sentry fires. My voices' lights shimmered into view, blocking the entrance and standing watch.

I rolled towards the tent wall, shutting my eyes. Three monsters guarding the entrance didn't make me feel any safer. They were there only to remind me I couldn't escape.

Robert lifted me into Ethan's arms. The gelding was well trained, standing calm and still while Ethan helped me settle onto the front of his saddle and draped a blanket over both of us. This was my second day of riding with him. My leg was still wrapped tight, but the splints were gone. The deep purple bruises covering my ankle and my lower calf would take weeks to fade, but I could hobble a few steps if I clung to someone's arm.

For a man of his size, Duke Robert mounted with unexpected grace. I was surprised the first time I saw him get ready to ride out with the Dauphin, but the duke was full of surprises. The man who talked tactics and battle manoeuvres with Ethan deep into the night was sharp and witty and kind. I'd overheard Robert called a fool and a bungler, but he was far from either.

Lord Giles and some of his advisors were already mounted, waiting for Charles to give the signal to leave. He didn't attempt to hide that he was staring at us, or keep his obvious contempt off his face.

'Why does he hate me?' I asked.

'It's nothing you've done, little sister. His lordship hates everyone.' Ethan smiled, the lines around his eyes crinkling. 'The people he hates most threaten his power or his influence over Charles.'

'I still don't understand,' I said. 'How could I threaten his power? And the idea of me having influence over Charles is laughable.'

Robert and Ethan traded looks, but neither said anything. A shout came from the front of the line and the procession of horses and wagons packed full of people, tents and luggage began to slowly move. The air had warmed over the last week, taking some of the bite from the air. Sunshine melted the snow a little more each day, leaving patches of bare earth and dead grass. The ground was still rock-hard, but that was a blessing, keeping us from bogging down in mud.

Seeing Lord Giles and his men take their place around Charles at the head of the line, I whispered a prayer of thanks to Blessed Mary and relaxed against Ethan. Having Giles staring at me wasn't exactly frightening, but he made me uneasy and the impulse to guard against him was too strong to ignore.

Ethan cleared his throat. 'Something else for you to remember, Jeanne. You may think you've no power or influence in court, but that's not how his lordship sees things. Charles overrode Giles when the duke wanted to turn his back and leave you. The Dauphin appointed me your guardian and charged me with keeping you safe, giving you status you'd not had before. That alone is a near unforgiveable challenge to his standing as far as Giles is concerned.'

I didn't know whether to laugh or cry. 'And that's why he hates me? Because the Dauphin showed mercy for one of his subjects?'

Robert's barking laugh was quickly silenced. 'May God Almighty bless you for always speaking truth, Jeanne. If it's any comfort to you, his lordship hates me and Ethan even more because Charles trusts us over his cousin.'

'Charles wishes his cousin anywhere but at his side and he's not making the effort to hide how he feels.' Ethan walked the gelding around a mound of melting snow. 'Don't waste your energy fretting over this, little sister. Robert and I worry enough for all of us.'

'God's truth, Ethan.' Robert watched the countryside, keen-eyed as a hawk. 'You've travelled this way before. Will we reach Father Michel's church before dark?'

'Unless something delays us, likely by mid-afternoon. His Grace plans to sleep in Lady Maud's rooms tomorrow night, but he's eager to gather what news he can before we arrive. He doesn't want to ride into a trap, no matter how weary he's grown of sleeping alone.'

Robert laughed, but didn't say anything more. I burrowed deeper into the blanket, attempting to hide the heat burning in my face and neck, a flush that grew deeper when Ethan began to sing. The light-hearted song was about a lonely mercenary and his quest to lure the farm maid he loved into his bed. Robert joined in, adding verses of his own, and it didn't take long before half a company of young soldiers were singing along with them.

I shut my eyes and tried not to listen, but my mind kept circling around why the song bothered me. Verse after verse told the story of a mercenary determined to prove his love to the coy young maiden, but by the time she realised she loved the soldier, he'd found someone else. The story wasn't remotely the same – and I'd never have loved him – but I couldn't stop thinking about Claude and how he'd hunted me. Remembering made me tremble.

Light danced behind my eyelids and the monster Michael's voice rumbled in my ear, 'The only way the blacksmith can hurt you now is if you dwell on his memory and embrace the ghost of his deeds. Tell your Paladin why you're afraid. Tell him why you left home. The prophecy says he will protect you.'

Michael's light faded away, leaving me looking into Ethan's worried face. He leaned close to whisper, 'What's wrong, little sister?'

No matter what the prophecy said or how great a warrior Ethan was, he couldn't save me from my past. No one could, not even myself.

'It's nothing you can guard against or fix.' My voice shook and he frowned. 'You can't protect me from memories, Ethan.'

His arm tightened around me, but he stopped frowning and slowed the gelding's pace to little more than a slow walk. Robert looked up to see what was wrong, but Ethan shook his head and the duke rode on.

We dropped far behind, the soldiers' songs and the rattle of wagons bouncing over hard ground faded by distance before he spoke. 'How old are you, Jeanne? Fourteen? Nearly fifteen?'

If he meant to offend me, he succeeded. I fought to keep the edge out of my voice. 'Nearly three months past seventeen. I'm not a child, Ethan.'

I couldn't read his expression before he turned away to watch the forest, much the way all the soldiers did. The wagons and riders pulled further ahead, making me nervous as the silence around us deepened. When he finally spoke, I jumped.

'I'd never call you a child, Jeanne,' he said. 'A child wouldn't leave her village and all she knows behind. If I'd thought, I'd have realised that you were driven from home, much the way I was near your age. My apologies, little sister. I was too wrapped up in shielding Charles from his troubles to see what was in front of me.'

His apology confused me. 'How could you know? I never told you.'

'I was barely fifteen when I left my father's manor, running from things I'd witnessed and hadn't been able to stop.' Ethan looked me in the eye. 'Being the oldest son didn't mean I could lift a guardsman's sword, let alone use it. The captain of my father's guard forced me away from the keep or I'd have died in that English raid along with most of my family. I've lived with nightmares about my mother and brothers being cut down ever since. I should recognise the signs of suddenly remembering, but I put the blame on your pain, or being among strangers. Forgive me for being witless, Jeanne.'

I'd listened to my mother scream and sob until the screams stopped and the sobs stilled, watched my father bleed to death on a cave floor. I'd lost my brother Henri and Grand-mère Marie – and yet a mad blacksmith, a faithless priest and three faceless monsters drove me away from home. Away from Pierre.

Ethan wasn't witless, I was. Thinking no one would question why a girl my age was so far from home, alone and without protection, was foolish. Naïve. I couldn't answer without lying, a sin my grand-mère taught would weigh on my soul until forgiven.

I wasn't sure God would forgive me for lying to Ethan, or that I could forgive myself.

A soft whistle prodded the gelding into motion again and before long the back of the last wagon appeared ahead. The voices shimmered into view as well. Their light never seemed to move, but kept just ahead of us on the trail, listening to see how much I would tell Ethan. I felt their disapproval that I still hesitated about telling him, but they didn't threaten or try to force my hand. The prophecy said I needed Ethan. They wouldn't do anything to jeopardise that.

Father Jakob had come close to accusing me of using witchcraft to murder Claude. I trusted Ethan, valued his counsel and protection, but I hadn't known him a full month. Telling him the truth was a risk.

But in the end, I decided not telling him was a bigger risk. I didn't want to lose his trust.

I took a deep breath. 'Ethan, wait. I need to tell you why I left. You may not want to be my guardian when I've finished.'

He pulled the gelding back to a slow walk. 'I can't imagine you doing anything that terrible. Tell me the story, little sister.'

We had dropped far enough back again that birdsong and my halting, choked words were the only sounds. I told him how Papa died, about Father Jakob trying to force me into marriage with a man my father's age, how for more than a year Claude was always watching. Telling Ethan about the blacksmith attacking me was hardest, harder even than the tale of Father Jakob thinking I'd somehow bewitched Claude into hanging himself.

The only thing I left out were the three monsters watching us. If they'd truly tangled him in the prophecy, I'd be forced to tell him eventually – but not now. Not until I didn't have another choice.

I didn't understand the language Ethan spoke when I'd finished, but I recognised he was swearing. My father and brothers had all sworn occasionally and the angry tone, the way each word was bitten off and spat into the world, was familiar.

Ethan ran short of anger or ran out of words and shut his eyes, breathing hard. He surprised me by kissing the top of my head before he kneed the gelding into a distance-eating canter. We caught up with the wagons and riders quickly and Ethan slowed his pace as we came alongside Robert.

Charles and Lord Giles were just ahead and the Dauphin stopped long enough for Ethan to reach him. He looked at me and frowned. 'Is everything all right, Ethan? Robert said you were tending to Jeanne, but you were gone a long time. Between bandits and the English having the run of these woods, I was beginning to worry.'

'My apologies, Your Grace.' Ethan gave a small bow from the saddle. 'I never meant to worry anyone. Jeanne and I had things to discuss and I thought it best if we spoke in private.'

Giles forced his horse between Robert and Ethan's and looked down his nose at me. 'Discussing things with a peasant is a poor excuse to keep the Dauphin waiting. Nothing she has to say could be that important.'

'Enough, Cousin,' Charles said. 'This is none of your concern.'

'If Lord Giles is that curious, I'd be happy to tell him what we talked about.' Ethan's cold, menacing tone matched his smile. The arm that held me in the saddle tightened, but he never looked away from Giles. 'Jeanne told me about her father facing down two mounted English knights, his only weapon a shortsword. Her father died defending his family, but her brother killed both the English dogs. Discussing their bravery was important, even if they are peasants. And she told me the names of the men who've wronged her. One is already dead, but I've sworn to kill the others.'

'Ethan!'

The command in Charles' voice surprised me, but the tension coiled tight in Ethan seeped away. I realised then that men like Ethan and Robert were loyal to the Dauphin because of the man he was, not just because they hoped to gain something by being close to him.

He looked away from Giles and bowed to Charles. 'Your pardon, my lord. My temper got the better of me.'

'Elise has been asking after Jeanne,' Charles said. He pulled up the hood of his cloak, casting his face in shadow. 'Take Jeanne up the line to visit her for an hour or so. Flirting with her ladies will help cool your temper. We should reach the church by late afternoon. I'm sure Father Michel will grant permission for us to make camp on the edge of the grounds.'

A golden halo appeared around Charles' head, a heavenly crown that gave off sparks and nearly blinded me with its light. Michael appeared behind the Dauphin, his fiery sword forming a wall of fire behind the future king. Many of the visions they sent me were confusing, the message unclear, but this one was easy to understand: Michael meant to put Charles on the throne, no matter what the cost.

Ethan touched my shoulder and the vision vanished. Charles and Giles had disappeared as well and when I looked for them, they were three wagons behind us and obviously arguing. Robert sat his horse a few strides away, making a point of acting as Charles' bodyguard and scowling at Lord Giles.

'I'm sorry,' Ethan said. 'His lordship has always been an arrogant swine, but I shouldn't have lost my temper that way. You didn't need another enemy.'

I watched Giles, red-faced and sputtering, grab Charles' arm – then quickly back away again when Robert calmly drew his sword.

'Don't be sorry, Ethan,' I said, and crossed myself. 'He was always my enemy.'

Part Six

Courage! Do not fall back . . .

Jeanne d'Arc

Father Michel's church was surrounded by winter-bare trees and gardens sleeping under a deep layer of hay. Another month, two at the most, and the gardens would be thick with flowers and herbs and the air heavy with their scent. Fully leafed, the trees would cast shade on the stone benches placed underneath and along the path.

Robert lifted me out of the saddle and helped me balance on one foot until Ethan dismounted. I was stiff and sore after riding all day, but insisted that he let me try limping over to the nearest stone bench.

'The longer I wait, the harder it will be,' I said. 'And I won't know how much I've healed if I never put weight on my leg.'

'She's right, Ethan. Let her try and see how it goes.' Robert took the reins of both horses and led them towards a large pond at the far edge of the grounds. 'You'll know if she's ready or not quickly enough. Just make sure you catch her if she falls.'

Ethan watched him go and shook his head. 'He's worse about reminding me of simple things than my father ever was. Are you ready?'

'Yes.' I took his arm and held tight. 'The bench under the oak is closest.'

The first step convinced me I'd made a mistake. My ankle

throbbed with each beat of my heart, but the pain didn't make me want to scream, and the next steps were easier. I'd almost made it to the bench when my leg suddenly grew weak and wouldn't hold me.

'Easy, easy.'

Ethan picked me up and carried me the last few strides. I was shaking when he set me on the bench. He settled next to me and put an arm around my shoulders. 'You did well. Robert will be pleased to know I didn't let you fall.'

I laughed. 'I'm even more pleased.'

The crunch of gravel warned me someone was coming towards us. I looked up to see Charles striding up the path that led to the chapel, Lord Giles at his heels. Ethan stood and offered me his arm, but Charles waved me back down.

'You're not so recovered I'll make you stand or curtsey, Jeanne. We can save the ceremony for another time.' He smiled and turned to Ethan. 'Father Michel has given permission for us to camp on the other side of the pond. There's plenty of room in the meadow beyond, and if some of the troops spill into the woods, there's no harm done. Robert is organising getting everyone fed.'

'What would you have me do, Your Grace?' Ethan asked.

'Father Michel has granted the men access to the chapel to pray. He's offered to hear confession after supper if any of them feel the need.' Charles rubbed the back of his neck and glanced over his shoulder at the troops setting up tents and pavilions in the meadow. 'I need you to impress upon them that they are guests here and the contents of the chapel aren't to be touched. Any man who becomes unruly will regret it.'

'Yes, Your Grace. I'll make sure they know.' Ethan glanced at

Giles, who looked bored and impatient. 'Is there anything else you need from me?'

'Save some supper for me. I'll be hungry later.' Charles smiled and turned to leave. 'Father Michel's cook has the bad habit of burning even the bread.'

Ethan sat next to me, watching Giles and Charles greet the priest at the rectory door and follow him inside. He frowned and muttered under his breath, 'May God protect him.'

'From the priest or his cousin?' I asked.

He smiled and looked away. 'Likely from both. There were serpents in Eden's garden. I can imagine a nest hiding among Saint Catherine's flowers.'

My heart crawled into my throat. I'd dreamed of a church of Saint Catherine more times than I could count, dreams that always left me shaking and drenched in sweat, yet I could never remember what they were about. Being here now with the Dauphin wasn't an accident, and not knowing what would happen made me nervous.

'Is that this church? Saint Catherine?'

'Sainte-Catherine-de-Fierbois. Father Michel claims the chapel was built five hundred years ago, maybe more.' He watched three young soldiers strolling towards the door.

Ethan patted my hand and stood. 'Pardon me, little sister. I won't be gone long.'

He caught up with the three soldiers quickly. His back was to me, but the expressions on the soldiers' faces made it clear they weren't happy with what he was saying to them. Reluctant nods said they'd promised to obey his orders. By the time the three of them disappeared into the church, Ethan was back.

'Ask your questions, Jeanne.' He wrapped his fingers around the edge of the bench and stretched out his long legs. 'I can see the curiosity in your eyes.'

'What did Charles mean about warning the men to remember they were guests?'

'Did many soldiers visit Domrémy?' he asked.

I shook my head. 'Only the English troops who burned it down.'

He cringed. 'You didn't tell me that part of your story.'

'My father and brother died that night,' I said. 'I try not to think of the fire.'

Ethan sat up and took my hand. 'If you had more experience with soldiers, you'd understand the orders Charles gave. Dukes and princes seldom carry much wine or strong drink with them, and what they have isn't for their men. Drunken soldiers can cause more trouble than a drunken shopkeeper. Some soldiers are overly fond of wine and aren't above stealing any they find. Even from a priest.'

I stared, wide-eyed with shock. 'They'd steal the sacrament from the chapel?'

'Giles' men have, twice now. The last time, they beat a monk bloody when he tried to stop them. Neither of us is overly fond of priests, but the old man didn't deserve that.' He squeezed my fingers. 'Charles had the men responsible given five lashes in front of all the companies under Giles' command. He's not a cruel man, but he needed to make a point. The duke looks the other way, no matter what his men do off the battlefield. Charles won't.'

Shouts and what sounded like screams carried from inside the chapel. Ethan looked up sharply, stood in front of me and drew his sword. Relief filled his face when the rectory door opened and Charles ran out, followed by Father Michel. Giles strolled out an instant or two later, his knife in his hand.

Two of the young soldiers ran out of the chapel and fell to their knees in front of Charles and Father Michel, their eyes turned towards heaven and arms stretched high over their heads. Dirt caked their legs and their tunics.

'Miracles, my lord! Miracles! A bright light filled the chapel and an angel appeared to us! She spoke, my lord, she spoke!' The soldier wasn't much older than me. Tears streamed down his face as he reached for Charles' hand. 'Her voice was like bells, my lord, beautiful to hear – and she showed us where the Maid's sword was buried behind the altar, so we could dig it out. *Us!* Gérald's bringing it now!'

'Merciful God . . . no,' I whispered. 'Please, no.'

More people had heard the shouting and came hurrying to the churchyard. The two soldiers repeated the story, again and again, and other men passed it to friends crowding in at the back. Ethan watched the crowd around Charles nervously, but stayed with me.

The third soldier, Gérald, rushed out of the chapel, a mud-encrusted sword stretched across his palms. He lifted the sword above his head. 'Rejoice! The angel said the Maid is here among us – with this sword she will set France free!'

My monsters' lights flared near the chapel door and the glow spread until it touched all the men. The soldiers began to chant *The Maid! The Maid!* over and over again. I hunched over my knees, rocking, and wanting to retch. Ethan put a hand on my shoulder. He meant to offer comfort, to let me know he was there and I was safe, but it only scared me more.

Men reached for the sword in Gérald's hands, pushing each other aside as if they sought blessings from a holy relic. Their fingers brushed the filthy blade and the hilt – and the dirt crumbled to dust and fell away, leaving the naked metal as shiny as new in the afternoon sun, reflections dancing along the edge. Renewed cries of *A miracle! A miracle!* rose up, and ever more fervent calls for God to bless the Dauphin's cause.

The crowd of soldiers stretched all the way across the gardens now. Robert pushed through the throng to stand with Ethan, flanking me with drawn swords. Neither one knew swords couldn't protect me now.

Gérald turned in a slow circle, the blade still held over his head so everyone could see. A shaft of sunlight reflected off the gleaming sword, blinding me and lighting up my face. Joy transformed the young soldier's expression, filling his face with hope and belief.

'The angel's words are true!' Gérald pointed at me with the sword. 'There she is: the Maid is here! She's here!'

As he began pushing his way through the crowd, the men cheered and made way.

'Sweet Jesus, Ethan,' Robert muttered. 'They're all mad.'

'I know.' He sheathed his sword, picked me up and moved behind the bench. 'Stand with me, Robert. Don't let them get past us.'

An opening appeared at the front of the crowd of soldiers and cooks and drovers and Gérald stepped into the small space. It looked as if almost the entire camp had come to see what was happening. Gérald dropped to his knees a handspan from the bench, bowed his head and held out his hands, offering me the sword. The mob of soldiers behind him went to their knees too, still chanting *La Pucelle, La Pucelle . . .*

I saw Charles staring from the other side of the garden, confused, unable to understand what he was seeing. He'd drawn his sword too, but he held it loosely at his side. The Dauphin caught Ethan's eye, the question he was afraid to ask easy to see in his face.

Gérald stood and took a step forwards. He stopped with the

tip of Robert's sword pressed against his chest. 'Take your sword, sweet Maid,' he said. 'You will lead us to victory.'

Ethan swore under his breath. 'You all know her leg isn't healed and she can't hold a sword if she can't stand up. Give it to me. I'll keep it safe for her.'

The soldier hesitated, waiting for me to answer him.

Father Michel spoke for the first time, his voice carrying from the back of the crowd. 'The prophecy says the Maid will have a fierce defender, a champion. He will stand with her against all odds and long after others have forsaken her. The Dauphin tells me Lord Ethan has protected her since God decided their paths should cross. Give him the sword.'

Gérald stared at me, still waiting. The monstrous spirits would never let Ethan touch the sword before me.

'Put me down, Ethan. Help me stand so I can take the sword.'

He stared at me in shock. 'Jeanne . . .'

I touched his hand and spoke quietly. 'It's the only way to make this end without bloodshed. He thinks I'm the Maid. He'll only give the sword to me. Please, Ethan.'

'She's right,' Robert said. 'You can't reason with madmen. And there's a few too many for you and me to take on alone.'

'I don't like this,' Ethan growled in anger and frustration, the fierce sound a warning for the mob pressing forwards. He set me on my feet and slipped his arm around my waist to keep me steady. 'Lean on me if you have to, but make sure you have your balance. Swords are heavier than you think, even small swords like this one. Make sure you're ready for that, little sister.'

'I'm ready.' I took a breath, trying to steady my hand and failing. Once my fingers closed around the hilt, I couldn't let myself drop the sword. I couldn't let it slip.

Holding my hand out was frightening, but my monsters weren't leaving me a choice. 'Give me the blade, Gérald,' I whispered. 'I'm ready now.'

The young soldier bowed and put the hilt in my hand. Polished leather felt strange, hard and unforgiving against my fingers. I held on tight as Gérald backed away, but I was able to bring the sword up and show the crowd. My hand and arm shook, but no one seemed to care.

A deafening cheer went up, but it didn't last long. Charles and Father Michel began yelling for the soldiers to leave the gardens and finish setting up tents. Giles stood with Charles, scowling, but gave no orders of his own. The men began to stagger back to camp, most of them looking around wide-eyed, as if suddenly waking from a dream and not knowing where they were.

Giles muttered something to Charles and followed his men.

A few soldiers walked towards me, arms outstretched to touch me or the sword, but Robert's blade made them change their minds.

My arm began to shake harder and Ethan wrapped his hand around mine, helping me hold the sword and lower it without dropping it. 'Take it from her, if you would, Robert. If you don't mind carrying my sword, we'll keep that one sheathed and hidden.'

'I've never minded a blade in each hand. The idea of using them against our own men doesn't make me happy, but I'll do what I have to,' Robert said.

The duke took the Maid's sword out of my numb fingers and exchanged it in the scabbard for Ethan's sword.

'You did well, little sister.' Ethan picked me up again and made sure his cloak covered the sword. 'Not everyone can be brave enough to face so many men and head off worse trouble. You should be proud.'

I rested my head on his shoulder. 'I was terrified, Ethan, not brave.'

He laughed quietly. 'All warriors are terrified going into battle. Fighting anyway is what makes you brave.'

'Ethan!'

I kept my head turned when he faced Charles, hoping to go unnoticed, or at least be left alone for a time.

'Is Jeanne all right?' Charles asked.

'Frightened and a little confused.' Ethan stood up straighter. 'I don't think we can fault her for that, my lord. With your leave, I should take her back to camp now. Keeping her out of sight in the tent until morning would be wise.'

'Do what you think best.' Charles cleared his throat. 'One question before you go, Jeanne. What happened here?'

Light from my voices glittered under the tree behind Charles. These monsters were responsible for most of his army believing I was *La Pucelle*, but the Dauphin, Ethan and Robert would think me mad if I explained. I never got that far. A howling wind and clashing thunder filled my ears, warning me to take care. I asked God to forgive me another sin and unwilling lie. 'I don't know, Your Grace. Ethan was explaining the order you gave was about not stealing the church wine, then the men who'd gone into the chapel began yelling about angels and miracles. I was the only woman here . . . so a soldier decided I must be the Maid.'

Charles looked between Ethan and Robert. 'That was all?'

'Yes, Your Grace.' Robert looked the Dauphin in the eye. 'The boys in the chapel started yelling and the others came running to see what the fuss was about. It had nothing to do with Jeanne until one of them saw her.'

'All right.' Charles rubbed the back of his neck. 'Get her under cover. I'll do what I can to discount the story, but it may take a few days before this all quietens down. We'll speak later, Ethan.'

'Thank you, Your Grace.'

Tension knotted Ethan's muscles as we hurried back to camp. I buried my face against his shoulder to keep from seeing him and Robert attempting to watch all directions at once. My voices stayed silent, but I saw flickers of light from the corner of my eye. They hadn't slunk off to gloat over their victory. I guessed they were plotting how to close the trap around me completely.

Neither man spoke until we'd passed the pond.

'I can't help thinking Giles put his men up to this,' Robert said. 'What I can't understand is why.'

'To make Charles look a fool in front of his army and the court. A part of Charles has always hoped the Maid's prophecy was true, but hope isn't belief.' Anger leaked into Ethan's voice. 'His lordship wants the Dauphin to believe Jeanne is meant to hand him a kingdom and when that doesn't happen, to lose the heart to fight for his crown. Giles will find a way to use that to claim the throne for himself.'

'Anyone with eyes can see this girl's not the Maid!'

'No, she's not. But will that matter if eight battalions of soldiers declare it's true?'

The din and clatter of the camp grew louder, signalling that we'd reached the first row of tents. Calls for the Maid to bless them and pleas for me to drive the English from France followed us as we made our way through camp. Men dropped to their knees as we passed, hope shining in tear-filled eyes. Older, battle-hardened men simply stared, experience making them less willing to believe the rumour was true.

Robert drove away the dozen or so men gathered in front of our tent. Ethan carried me inside and set me in a camp chair, grabbed a blanket and draped it over my lap. I wasn't shivering with cold, but he couldn't know that.

He crouched in front of me and pushed dark strands that had escaped my braid off my face. 'You're safe in here. Robert will keep watch outside the door until I come back with food.'

I bunched the blanket in my fists, angry over feeling trapped and helpless. 'What am I going to do, Ethan? I'm not a warrior. I can't be the Maid.'

'Trust me to protect you, little sister.' He leaned forwards and kissed my forehead. 'I won't let them hurt you.'

He pushed through the tent flap, mumbled a few words to Robert about finding supper for all of us and was gone. The monsters slowly brightened into view, watching me, mocking Ethan's promise.

Charles ordered Giles' troops to ride at the very front of the procession the next morning, with his as the rear guard. Ethan kept me in the middle, near the wagons, where Elise and the other ladies of the court rode. Robert had arranged for me to hide among them if the need arose. I prayed that it never would.

Ethan had a solution for how to transport the Maid's sword, yet keep it out of sight. Spare scabbards and sword belts weren't difficult to find in an army and he knew how to string one so that the sword was angled across his back. The hilt showed just past his left shoulder, but his cloak hid the rest.

'Mercenaries carry an extra weapon like this all the time.' He reached over his shoulder with his right hand and smoothly drew the Maid's blade, then sheathed it again. 'If you lose your sword to an enemy's blow, having a second at hand can save your life.'

'Did an extra blade ever save your life?' I asked.

'More than once, little sister.' He held out a hand and helped me stand. 'Time to go.'

The day was warmer, the sun brighter and the sound of melted snow dripping from the trees surrounded us as we rode. Ethan did what he could to distract me, telling me stories of places he'd travelled as a mercenary and some of the wonders he'd seen. Robert added travel tales of his own, most of them designed to make me laugh.

Afternoon shadows, thin and skeletal, stretched away from the trees before Lady Maud's castle came into sight. I'd never seen a building so big, or with towers that reached into the sky, seeming to brush the clouds. Tall hills rose behind the towers and Ethan confirmed my guess that the castle and grounds butted up against them. If my endless questions about how the castle was built or what the towers were used for tried Ethan's patience, he didn't show it. His answers came with a smile, and a story if he had one that fitted.

'I'm told the stone for the castle was quarried in the mountains more than a hundred leagues away,' he said. Ethan pointed to a tower. 'Do you see the way the rock sparkles in the sun? The stone-masons look for just that kind of rock to bear the most weight. They believe the crystals make the stone stronger and keep the rock from crumbling. Crystals also make the towers more beautiful.'

'They are beautiful.' I watched the light flicker from stone to stone along the castle walls, as if cold candle flames were being stirred by the wind. 'How do the crystals get into the rock?'

Robert bit back a laugh and clapped Ethan on the shoulder. 'She may have finally hit upon a question you can't answer. I'll leave you and your student alone for a time. Pray that Charles has already decided where he wants the men to camp.'

A touch of his heel and Robert's gelding trotted towards the front of the line. Ethan watched him go, his expression one I couldn't read easily. He glanced at me, one eyebrow raised. 'Do you still want to know the answer, little sister?'

'You don't have to tell me.' My face burned hot. 'I know I'm talking too much.'

'My mother said I talked more than all four of my brothers together. I asked more questions too.' He tilted his head back to watch a hawk circling overhead, his voice growing softer. 'She never tired of answering. How else was I to learn?'

The ache of missing Papa filled my chest, a twin of the grief in Ethan's voice. 'How do the crystals get into the stone?'

'My father told me that even alchemists argue over how the crystals form. Most see it as a natural purification of elements.' He looked away from the hawk and back at me. 'My mother told me the true answer. God created the heavens and filled them with stars before He formed the earth. But He made too many stars and rather than let their beauty go to waste, God mixed them into the mud that formed the world. My mother believed the crystals were a gift, one meant to remind us not to be overcome by the ugliness around us. We need to remember beauty is hidden everywhere.'

I forced myself to stop staring into his eyes and went back to staring at the towers. The ache in my chest confused me, a mix of regret and sorrow both. I regretted so many things about my life – the path I was on, the things I couldn't change or escape – and mourned so many losses, yet now I was close to choking on emptiness and couldn't say exactly where it came from.

Or maybe it came from fear of losing more. I shied away from thinking about that.

'I wish I'd known your mother,' I said.

'My mother loved her sons, but she still wished for a daughter. I'd have liked watching the two of you together. You'd have stolen her heart, Jeanne.' Ethan put a hand on my shoulder and stood up high in the stirrups, looking ahead. 'We're near the gate. Depending on how much the farmers and merchants quarrel with Giles' commanders, we may sit here until dark. Most of them have been waiting to enter all day and won't like moving aside, but the Dauphin's wagons can't shift until the way is cleared.'

'They'd argue about making way for the Dauphin?' I asked.

'Some would.' He sat down again, frowning. 'Not everyone is loyal. Lady Maud and her people side with Charles, but some people living in the towns and farms around the castle are of two minds. Far too many would give the throne to King Henry and sue England for peace.'

I wanted to ask more questions, but Robert returned before I could. He pulled his horse up short, causing the animal to toss his head and dance sideways.

'Charles wants you with him, Ethan,' he said. Robert leaned forwards, murmuring in the gelding's ear and patting his neck. 'He's going to ride onto the castle grounds and let Giles sort how to get the wagons inside.'

'His lordship will take too much pleasure in bullying peasants, especially with an army at his back.' Ethan nudged his horse into motion. 'But Charles is better off inside the walls while Giles acts the villain. I'll breathe easier with Jeanne out of harm's way as well.'

Robert glanced back the way we'd come. 'I should send a company up from the rear guard to protect my sister and her ladies. Trouble won't travel that far, but Elise will never forgive me if she thinks I've forgotten her. I'll catch up soon enough.'

He wheeled around and nudged the horse into a gallop.

We neared the castle gate and Ethan guided his horse off the road and onto the rocky, weedy strip of dirt alongside. Trees – oak, beech and fir – pressed in close on the other side and twice Ethan had to ride deeper into the forest to avoid the peasants blocking the road.

Once we got close enough, he picked his way around carts and wagons as quickly as he could. Many looked at us curiously, some even staring rudely or making crude remarks about Ethan's dark skin, but I didn't see any danger. I'd known people like this my whole life. Most of the farmers and merchants were too busy scowling at Giles atop his tall horse, or the wall of troops blocking the road, to notice us.

'Where's Robert?' Charles asked.

'Surrounding Lady Elise and her ladies with one of his companies.' Ethan shrugged. 'He knows they won't need protection, but he'd rather not quarrel with his sister. He will join us soon, Your Grace.'

'I wouldn't want Lady Elise cross with me either. I'm not ashamed to say her temper scares me.' He nodded to the two guards flanking him and we all moved towards the entrance, one knight leading the way while the other followed behind as we entered the passageway. Ethan and Charles rode side by side, talking, while I gawked. I guessed the tunnel had been built long and narrow on purpose, so a whole army, with all its different companies, couldn't charge through from end to end. They'd need to send men in a few at a time – and those men would be easy targets.

The main gate burrowing through the thick outer wall formed a passage longer than our house in Domrémy. An iron portcullis hung at each end, ready to drop and seal enemies inside. I'd expected to see protection charms sketched above the gates or just inside the entrance, but the walls were bare. A ceiling of dressed stone rose to where I imagined the top of the wall to be. I spotted three trapdoors and thought of the stories I'd heard about castles under siege and how the defenders were forced to drop rocks on the invaders. Some of the old men had described how the enemy soldiers had taken hours to die, often screaming in agony up until the end. The grim duty of clearing the tunnel when the siege was over fell to the victors. I prayed I'd never live to see anything like that.

The sunny castle courtyard was more than twice the size of the market square in Domrémy and much more crowded. Armoured men stood sentry on either side of the main entrance into the castle, the tower entrances and the passageways leading to places I couldn't guess at. More soldiers walked the walls, carrying crossbows and pikes.

Men and women I assumed must be servants were hurrying away from the merchant wagons with full baskets and crates and everywhere I looked there were laughing, shrieking children chasing each other, darting between people's feet and ignoring shouts to stop. Every person I saw walked with the certainty of being home and knowing where they were going, though I didn't see how. I couldn't find an order or sense in any of it. The conviction I'd never learn to find my way from place to place fluttered in my chest.

Charles and Ethan worked their way over to one of the many passageways. It looked much like the others to me, but a pair of grooms appeared out of the shadows, only boys, little more than ten, but they knew how to handle the horses so the Dauphin and Ethan could dismount. The groom watched Ethan help me down, but didn't ask why or what was wrong before he led the horse away. Robert rode up a moment later, and a third groom appeared to take his gelding.

'Is Lady Elise safely under guard?' Charles brushed at the flecks of mud on his tunic. He glanced at Robert, not bothering to hide his amusement. 'I'd hate for her to take your head off for neglecting your brotherly duties.'

'My sister and her ladies are surrounded by some of my best soldiers. They're as safe from a band of unarmed peasants as I can make them. The company commander is under strict orders not to let any of the ladies wander away from the wagon, and to keep an extra watchful eye on Talia.' Robert frowned. 'Lady Talia seemed particularly afraid, for some reason. She begged me to bring her back to the castle, and as a reward for refusing, I was treated to a nasty tirade about Ethan and Jeanne.'

Charles frowned. 'A tirade about what?'

'Nothing I'd repeat in front of Jeanne, my lord.' He avoided looking at me, which told me enough about what she'd said. 'I will say it made little sense, especially since I know not a word to be true.'

'Interesting.' Charles crossed his arms and studied the scuffed toes of his boots, thinking. He looked up and caught Ethan's eye. 'Remind me. Talia's the woman Giles sent to seduce you?'

'She tried, Charles.' Ethan cleared his throat, glanced at me and quickly looked away. 'I'll do almost anything you ask, my lord, but even as bored and restless as I was, I couldn't bed her. I found another way to get her to talk freely. As it turns out, Lady Talia's as fond of wine as his lordship.'

Charles laughed, which made heads turn. 'No wonder she's been avoiding me. Talia likely doesn't remember what happened between you and she's worried I do.'

'And she's bitter enough to make up stories about Jeanne,' Robert grumbled. 'I'll get Elise to stop that. Sending her back to her father's house in disgrace will put an end to the gossip.'

Stories about me and Ethan could only have one purpose: to make Charles and the rest of the court question his loyalty and his honour. From the little I'd seen of Lady Talia I couldn't imagine her making up and repeating those stories on her own. I'd no trouble believing the stories came from Giles, or that he'd ordered her to spread them.

My monsters chose that moment to appear, their light brighter than the late afternoon sun. Looking at them blinded me, but hard as I tried, I couldn't look away.

Catherine's icy voice sounded in my head. 'Speak your mind, Jeanne. Whether you accept it with grace or not, you are the Maid, you will lead these men in the fight to drive the English from French soil. Do not let them treat you like a peasant girl who needs noblemen to direct her life.'

Her frozen fingers brushed my cheek and I shut my eyes tight, holding back anger. I loathed being touched by any of these monsters. They forced fear into my blood with a fingertip, and left compulsions behind I couldn't resist. I didn't have a name other than magic for the way these Fae creatures forced me to their will, and Grand-mère had taught me that all magic was evil, no matter the source. Catherine's light slowly dimmed and while all three vanished, the pressure to do her bidding grew stronger.

I spoke without thinking and without meaning to say anything. 'Lord Robert, it might be better to keep Lady Talia here for a time. Learn everything you can from her before you send her away.'

Robert stared, surprised I'd spoken, and likely more surprised by what I'd said. My face burned hot, but I stood as straight as I could, knowing I wasn't wrong.

Charles narrowed his eyes and watched me, his gaze sharp and piercing straight to the heart of me. He looked every inch a king in that moment. 'I'm not inclined to force Talia to admit she's been spying for Giles. We already know that.'

'Is trying to get close to you by using Ethan all that she's done, Your Grace? The instant she leaves court, her secrets go with her and Lord Giles can claim they have no ties. Lady Talia will be disgraced and branded the liar, not his lordship.'

Charles looked to Ethan. 'Well?'

'She's right, Charles,' Ethan said. 'Lady Talia's father will demand an explanation for why Robert and Elise sent her away and the truth will ruin the girl's life as surely as a lie. The count is too old to fight, but he is deeply loyal to the crown and he gives you the same loyalty. He won't take Talia siding with Giles against you at all well. He may even disown her.'

The Dauphin shook his head. 'Everything you say is true. The question becomes what to do with her.'

'Keep her close, Your Grace,' I said. My leg began to tremble, taxed by standing for so long, and I leaned harder against Ethan. 'Give her attention unasked for and unearned, to the point Lord Giles will question if he still has her loyalty. And enlist a woman you can trust to become her confidante.'

'Someone who can pretend to believe her lies,' Ethan muttered.

'And pretend to help spread them.' Robert stuck his thumbs in his belt. 'My sister is trustworthy, Charles, and I'm sure she will help. She complains often enough that I don't ask her opinion on important matters. Helping you would please her.'

'Speak to Lady Elise for me, Robert.' He waved to the tall, graceful woman standing outside the entrance into the castle and turned back to give me a smile. 'Thank you, Jeanne. I need more people around me willing to speak the truth. I'll ask Maud about the physician taking a look at your leg and having one of her stewards arrange a safe place for you to sleep.'

Charles hurried across the courtyard. He expected to be recognised and for people to give way and they didn't disappoint him. He bounded up the steps two at a time. He bowed over the hand of the woman waiting for him and took the goblet she offered, drinking deep while looking over the top into her eyes. She smiled and touched his face when he handed the cup back. The two of them joined arms and disappeared into the castle.

'God bless that boy,' Robert said quietly.

'Someone needs to,' Ethan said. 'He's already forgotten us and any promises he made. I can only pray Sarah has forgiven me.'

'That was almost two years ago. Sarah's a sensible girl: she'll have worked out by now that you were right.'

I looked between the two men, confused and determined not to stay that way. 'The court ladies gossip openly of the Dauphin needing to marry and don't care that I hear. Every person in my village knows marriage and the alliances he might gain will make his position stronger. What I don't understand is why both of you think Charles' fondness for Lady Maud is a problem.'

Robert sighed and patted Ethan's shoulder. 'Explain it to her. I'll hunt up Sarah.'

'You've done well, little sister, but I think we've taxed your leg enough. We'll sit down to wait. Sarah might be a long while in coming – if she arrives at all.' He smiled and pointed to a bench just outside the passageway. 'Walk that far and you can rest.'

Ethan helped me limp the few strides it took to reach a bench set flush against the wall. I shouldn't have been surprised when my bad leg tried to give out after only a few steps. The dull ache in my ankle never really left me, but it could become a raging beast, its fangs sunk deep and scraping bone. I held onto Ethan and kept going.

Sitting down was a relief. The air was a little warmer here, the sunshine a little brighter, and with my cloak tucked around me I began to stop shivering. We were far enough out of the crush of people in the courtyard that no one could overhear what we said. Ethan sat next to me and leaned back, eyes shut and long legs stretched out into the path. People stared, openly curious, but something about Ethan's posture, or perhaps memories of his last visit, kept them from venturing too close. He opened one eye and peered at me before he spoke.

'There is a long answer to your question, Jeanne, but we need time and privacy for you to hear it all. The shorter one will do for now. A king is not always allowed to follow his heart. No matter how much he loves her, the Church won't allow Charles to make Maud his queen.'

I spoke before I thought, another habit my grand-mère could never break. 'I can't see the sense in that. What reasons have the bishops for not letting them marry?'

'I should have known you wouldn't be content with half measures. More fool me.' He wiped a hand over his face and sat up straight. 'Nothing an intelligent man believes, but Lorraine's bishops never think beyond the gold dropped in their offering box. Gossip spread about Maud's mother being unfaithful with a common soldier and claiming the child she bore him belonged to her husband. Maud was just a babe in arms when the slander started and her mother freshly widowed. Her uncle, her father's half-brother, stood to inherit the title and lands if Lord Leon died without an heir, and he made sure the lies spread and were believed. Few outside the upper ranks of the Church dare Charles' rage by calling her baseborn, but that's the reason Bishop Monette gave for not letting them marry.'

'The castle and land didn't come from Maud's father?' I said.

Ethan shook his head. 'Her mother arranged a marriage for Maud. The count had been married twice before, his sons had died in infancy or in battle and he didn't care if he had another. Or so he said. Sarah was born within the year. All that Maud has, her money, her titles and property, came to her when her husband died in a battle with the English. That happened years before Charles and Maud met. She holds most of the land in trust for Sarah.'

I looked him in the eye, trying to come to grips with the unfairness of it all. Memories of my grand-mère telling me life was seldom fair didn't help. 'Is Lady Maud content to be his mistress?'

Ethan glared fiercely at a courtier who had ventured too close. He was as protective of Charles as he was of me. I didn't know if the man meant to spy or not, but I'd learned to read Ethan's moods. Hurrying away and not looking back was wise of the man.

'Neither one is content,' he said. 'They both know the cost of defying the Church, but if their son had lived past his second year Charles might have done so anyway.'

'Oh, Ethan . . . they lost a child? What happened?'

'A cough that wouldn't stop or let the baby sleep and a fever that wouldn't break.' He cleared his throat and looked away. 'They both took the baby's death poorly.'

'God have mercy on the little one's soul.' I crossed myself and took a breath, remembering all the small graves in the churchyard at home. The babes were safe in God's arms, but their parents were left with empty cradles and lasting grief.

'When do you think Robert will be back?' I asked. Sitting and waiting, not knowing if Lady Sarah would help me, fed all my fears. 'If I'm to end up sleeping in the stables, I'd like to claim a quiet corner.'

He smiled and squeezed my hand. 'I won't let it come to that. Last time I stopped here, I found Sarah hiding at the back of my practice yard. She was barely fourteen, Jeanne. She said she was in love with me and begged me to take her when we rode away the next morning. I told her no, and none too gently. Sarah didn't take my refusal well. She stole my belt knife and stabbed me.'

I stared, open-mouthed with shock. *'She stabbed you?'*

Ethan touched his left shoulder, but I couldn't read his expression. 'Here. The wound looked worse than it was, but I won't lie about how much it hurt. Lady Sarah doesn't do anything by half measures, including being angry with the mercenary spurning her affections, but all the blood frightened her. She ran out of the yard screaming for someone to help me. That was almost two years ago. I haven't seen her since.'

'I'm sorry, Ethan. That sounds terrible.'

'Don't be sorry for me.' He leaned against the wall again, watching the crowd in the courtyard. 'Sarah's reaction taught me how little I'd learned since my mother died. Never explaining, yet expecting her to understand why taking her with me was a bad idea, or how I knew she didn't really love me – that was cruel and selfish. At her age I'd been forced to become a man overnight. I never took into account how young she was, or how sheltered, and that was near unforgiveable. Yanking a knife out of my shoulder was an effective way to learn that lesson.'

I studied his face, trying to understand how the man I knew could be the same person who'd broken Sarah's heart. 'You were gentle with me.'

He looked away. 'What happened with you wasn't the same,

175

little sister. You were terrified and hurt when I found you, covered in an English soldier's blood and staring death in the face. All I could think to do was find a way to ease your pain and protect you. No one else riding with Charles saw you run from the soldier or heard you scream – I was convinced God meant for me to find you.'

Light shimmered in the corner of my eye, a sign my voices wanted me to pay attention. Robert was strolling towards us, arm in arm with a young woman who looked so much like Lady Maud she could only be her daughter. She was just as tall with the same green eyes, but her hair was a lighter brown with strands shimmering golden in the sun. Sarah said something in Robert's ear and he leaned close to answer, patting her hand at the same time.

Studying her face, my guess was she was nervous about seeing Ethan. I couldn't say if anger and nerves went hand in hand.

Ethan stood to greet her, bowing deeply when she stopped in front of us. His shoulders were tense and stiff, signs of his own nerves, but he smiled. 'Lady Sarah. I hope you're well. This is my ward, Jeanne d'Arc.'

She offered me her hand and I took it. Sarah squeezed my fingers and smiled. 'Robert told me how you were hurt. We'll have the physician look at your ankle this evening. I have an idea about a safe place for you to stay as well, but with your leave I need to speak to Ethan first.'

Ethan started to step back when Sarah turned to him, but a stern look from Robert froze him in place.

'I told Robert I wanted to settle this at the start. I need to know if you've found it in your heart to . . . to forgive me and if we can still be friends. I'm so sorry for what I did, for hurting you.' Sarah twisted a piece of ribbon around her fingers, nervously winding and unwinding the scrap of silk again and again. She looked

Ethan in the eye as tears started sliding down her cheeks. 'For the longest time I thought I'd killed you, or ... or hurt you enough you couldn't use your arm ... and ... and that's why you didn't come back. I'm so sorry, Ethan. It was a stupid, childish thing to do, and I ... I never meant to hurt you.'

The reserved, careful expression on Ethan's face surprised me. 'I've thought about what happened almost daily. I handled the situation poorly and was just as much at fault, and I hope you can forgive me too. But drawing a knife on me was more than childish, Sarah, it was reckless. If you'd had a little more skill with a blade you could have killed me, and if I'd had less control— Things could have ended badly. We were both lucky. I forgave you long ago, but we can't say a few words and pretend it never happened. Friends need to know they can trust each other, even in the heat of anger. That's not always quick or easy. Are you willing to try?'

Sarah wiped her face on her sleeve. 'I'm more than willing, Ethan. I've few enough people I can trust and call friends.'

He smiled. 'Then we start anew.'

She took his hand and laid her head on his shoulder, crying in earnest now. He patted Sarah's back and murmured in her ear, much the way he did with me when I needed comfort. Robert's bulk shielded them from onlookers and his fierce scowl discouraged the few men who did notice the lady's daughter sobbing on a mercenary's shoulder. Most of those men were soldiers, but their tunics were a different colour from those Charles' army wore, so I guessed they must be a visiting lord's troops.

Sarah finally stepped away from Ethan and sat next to me, drying her face on the inside of her cloak. She caught sight of me watching and laughed. 'That was a sorry welcome, Jeanne. Forgive me. My mother says my biggest failing is crying too much over trifles, so now you know the worst thing about me. At least I hope it's the worst.'

Her smile was warm and friendly and I trusted her instantly, just as I'd trusted Ethan. I relaxed for the first time since passing through the gates.

Robert snorted. 'Nonsense. Discovering you hadn't killed Ethan is more than a trifle. I'm sure he agrees.'

'He does.' Ethan went back to watching the courtyard, his face settling back into a frown. 'Giles has arrived, Robert, and it looks like he's brought half a battalion with him.'

'So he has. One would almost think Maud's people posed a threat to him. Pity that's not true.' Robert hooked his thumbs in his sword belt and stood shoulder to shoulder with Ethan. 'He also seems to have left my sister and her ladies outside the walls. I'd best go and get them before Elise realises she's been abandoned.'

'Maybe I can help with that, Lord Duke.' Sarah scanned the courtyard, her face lighting up when she spotted the person she wanted. 'Captain Lucien – a word please!'

The man she'd summoned towered over both Ethan and Robert. He bowed to Sarah and me and ran a wary eye over Duke Robert and Ethan. 'What can I do for you, my lady?'

She put a hand on Robert's shoulder. 'The duke needs a small escort to bring his sister and her ladies inside the castle walls. Half a squad should do.'

Captain Lucien glanced over his shoulder, frowning at Giles and his men. They'd dismounted in the middle of the courtyard and begun shouting for grooms to come take their horses, cursing the boys who came at a run and threatening them if anything happened to their mounts. Men in my village didn't get drunk often, but it was clear a drunk nobleman acted the same as a shepherd who'd had too much wine. The grooms managed to calm the horses and lead them away, but I deemed that a bit of a miracle.

The captain turned back to Robert, obviously thinking as he rubbed the back of his neck. 'How far away is your sister's wagon, my lord?'

'No more than half a league,' Robert said. 'I can go alone if you're worried about trouble starting here. I do have men waiting with the wagon.'

'No, we'll get you there, my lord. I've had word of trouble on the road – I'll leave you to guess who stirred things up.' The captain whistled and one of the young grooms appeared. 'Bring the duke's horse, Paul. Hurry now.'

The monsters' lights glittered in the courtyard, bright and insistent and impossible to ignore, moving back as Giles stormed past and climbed the steps to the castle entrance. He paused long enough to speak to a guard before pushing his way inside.

Ethan swore under his breath. 'Charles will have his head if Giles disturbs him.'

'Only if Mama doesn't cut out his lordship's heart first.' Sarah shuddered. 'He scares me, Ethan.'

Captain Lucien scowled. 'You have good sense to be scared of that blackheart. I can post an extra guard near your rooms if you like, Lady Sarah. Just until he's gone.'

'Thank you, Captain. I'm in your debt.'

The groom appeared with Robert's oversized horse and the two men stalked off across the courtyard.

Sarah put a hand on my shoulder. 'How far can you walk on your own?'

'A few steps,' I said. 'More if I have help.'

Ethan smiled. 'And if the distance is too great, I can carry you, little sister. I've had a lot of practice.'

Sarah looked between me and Ethan and a flush filled my face.

'My quarters aren't too far,' she said. 'Do you want to try and make it on your own?'

Laughter filled Ethan's voice, as well as a hint of surprise that matched my own. 'Is that your safe place for Jeanne to sleep, my lady?'

'Can you think of any place safer?' Sarah got a hand under my arm on one side and Ethan the other. We moved slowly towards a passageway off to the right. 'Both of my maids married this year. Strange as it seems, they like sleeping with their husbands more than listening to me talk in my sleep. Putting Jeanne in one of their empty rooms is the perfect solution. She'll have a quiet place to rest and be alone when she wants, and she won't have to deal with strangers all the time.'

'You have a good heart, Sarah,' Ethan said, quietly. 'Thank you.'

My throat was tight and speaking a struggle. 'I don't know how to repay you.'

'There's no need to repay me.' Sarah slipped her arm around my waist, both holding me up and making me feel welcome. 'Everyone needs a friend, Jeanne. I'll gladly welcome your company, but the truth is you'll be doing me a favour as well. Mother will stop worrying so much about me sneaking in lovers with you staying in my rooms. If God is kind, she'll stop making surprise visits.'

'Surely you haven't grown so bold, my lady,' Ethan said, and smiled. 'Or old enough.'

'I might be bold enough, but I haven't found anyone worthy of my affections, Sir Ethan.' She winked so that only I could see and leaned around me to better see his face. 'Unless you've changed your mind?'

I'd never seen Ethan flustered or at a loss for words before, but I'd never heard a maid speak to a man that way either. The expression on his face made him look less like a mercenary, hardened by war and experienced with women, and more like a young man unsure of his ground.

Sarah laughed. 'I'm sorry, Jeanne. I couldn't help teasing him a bit and I hope you're not too shocked.'

'A little shocked,' I said, embarrassed to admit it. 'But you've known each other a long time. I don't know what's been said between the two of you in the past.'

Ethan sighed, the sound full of frustration. 'Nothing was said, little sister. You've my word.'

Sarah looked from me to Ethan, the same unreadable expression I'd seen before crossing her face. 'Ethan has far too much honour to ever say anything he doesn't mean. The only thing between us was in my head, nowhere else, and I outgrew the fantasy we were fated to be together the day he rode away with Charles. I should stop teasing him about it.'

The walk was longer than I'd hoped. The pain was increasing with each hobbling step, until a stumble had me hissing in agony and cursing the English soldier anew for how badly he'd hurt me. Ethan picked me up without me having to ask for help.

'Enough exercise for now. Too much is as bad for your ankle as none at all,' he said. 'How much further is your suite, Sarah?'

'Not far.' She pointed ahead. 'Through the next entrance there.'

The passageway was lined with arched doorways that gave access to the main body of the castle, which we'd bypassed until now. Sarah led us to the last door before the passage disappeared around a curve. Nearly hidden in the shadows, I saw the faint glow of a good-fortune charm dangling from a peg pounded in between the stones. Fresh charms, and those made with good intent, often glowed if the local guardian spirit agreed to grant the request.

Seeing this one made me feel better. The only other difference between this entrance and those we'd passed was the number of guards standing watch outside, and more were stationed inside. We'd barely stepped inside the entrance when the man I assumed must be the guard commander stopped us.

'Is something wrong, Tristan?' Sarah asked.

'Good day, my lady.' He gave Sarah a crisp nod, dismissed me with a glance and stared at Ethan. 'With the Dauphin visiting we're taking extra care with strangers coming in. I know who he is, but could I trouble you for the girl's name and ask what this man is doing with you?'

Sarah's tone was frosty. 'Are you refusing to let us pass, Commander?'

He gave her a quick glance. 'I have orders from Lord Giles, my lady, delivered by his own commander. The duke was very firm. I'm to know the name of everyone who comes inside and what business they have in the castle.'

I didn't know what to make of Lord Giles issuing orders to Lady Maud's castle guard, but Sarah was obviously angry. She clenched her hands into fists and her tone grew even colder. 'Lord Giles is not in charge here. Be sure my mother and Captain Lucien will hear about this, Tristan. The *girl* as you call her is Jeanne d'Arc: she was injured in an English attack and still has trouble walking. Jeanne will be staying in my rooms while she finishes recovering. The Dauphin himself appointed Lord Ethan to be her guardian. Looking out for her is what he's doing with me and all the reason he needs to be allowed inside. Lord Ethan is allowed to visit Jeanne whenever he pleases. Is that clear?'

'Lord Ethan is it now?' Tristan looked Ethan up and down, his hand resting on the dagger hanging from his belt. 'Last time he was here you stabbed him, Lady Sarah. Never heard what that was about, but I'm not sure you trusting a heathen to look after young girls is wise.'

Ethan met the guard's gaze calmly, not letting the other man see the tension making his muscles twitch and his heart beat faster. I realised he must have faced the same kind of scrutiny and mistrust before, the same insults to his honour.

'A practice yard accident, commander. I was teaching Lady Sarah how to defend herself from any who sought to take advantage or to bully her. Her skill outpaced my caution.' Ethan's broad smile was far from friendly and echoed the glimmer of anger in his eyes. 'She was an apt pupil and took to the knife immediately. I'd be wary of testing her patience, or of stretching mine too thin. Jeanne is in pain and needs rest.'

Mutters started among the men, but they weren't lack-witted enough to let their betters hear what they said.

A wave of Tristan's hand silenced them. He bowed to Sarah. 'Your pardon, my lady. I'll pass word to the other watch commanders about the guest in your rooms.' He threw a baleful glance Ethan's way. 'I'll make sure they know her *guardian* is allowed to come and go as he pleases.'

The guards scrambled to move away as Sarah shoved past Tristan before waiting to make sure Ethan and I were allowed to follow. She acted as rearguard until Ethan was a fair distance down the corridor, staring down the watch commander before stomping after us. I couldn't say if the colour in her face was anger, or embarrassment over being challenged.

She faced the two guards outside the door, her arms folded over her chest and glaring at them. 'Move, both of you. Stand away from the door until Lord Ethan gets her inside.'

'Yes, my lady,' the tall older guard said. 'Right away.'

They exchanged puzzled glances as they hurried to follow her order.

Sarah held the door open until Ethan had carried me inside, then turned back to the guards. 'Who sent you to watch my door, Kylian?' she asked.

The shorter man answered in a deep voice, 'Captain Lucien, my lady. Same as always.'

Ethan put me down in a chair piled with cushions. He'd flipped his cloak away from his sword and with his hand resting on the hilt, turned to watch Sarah standing in the doorway. The Maid's sword showed over his shoulder, but Lady Maud's guards wouldn't know what it was, not yet, at least.

Ethan relaxed a bit at the mention of Captain Lucien's name, but not enough to make me feel easy. Issuing orders to guards sworn to Lady Maud's service was bold, even for Lord Giles, and no doubt meant to cause trouble, although I couldn't see what his lordship had to gain by angering both Lady Maud and Charles.

Sarah glanced over her shoulder at Ethan and I couldn't tell if she was seeking reassurance, or something else.

'I need both of you to listen and do as I ask. One of you needs to find Captain Lucien for me while the other escorts my mother's physician to my quarters. The captain should be back from escorting Duke Robert's sister by now, but if not, wait for him at the gate – please tell him I need him now and this can't wait. I don't care which of you summons the doctor or finds the duke, but I need you to hurry.'

The older guard shuffled his feet and fidgeted, obviously uncomfortable. 'I don't feel right with both of us leaving, my lady. The captain will have us flogged if anything happens to you.'

'Bastian's right, my lady,' the younger guard said, his face just as worried. 'The captain's very strict about not leaving your post. Too much upset to take chances.'

Ethan stepped forwards. 'I'll stand guard until you return. Your captain is more likely to have you flogged for not doing what Lady Sarah asks. The guards watching the outside passage to Sarah's rooms are loyal to Duke Giles – their commander claims he has firm instructions from the duke about who is allowed in and who to keep out. Captain Lucien needs to know that right away. Carry the message. Lady Sarah will be safe with me.'

They hesitated another moment before the older man bowed. 'With the Dauphin in the castle, better not to take chances. I'll be back with Scholar Josue fast as I can. Kylian will find the captain for you.'

Their muffled bickering carried until they'd moved a good way down the corridor, Bastian arguing that Ethan was a better swordsman and a better guard than either of them, while Kylian was muttering darkly that Captain Lucien would still punish them. Sarah looked relieved when their voices faded out of earshot.

My leg hurt badly now that I wasn't distracted and afraid. I leaned back into the cushions and closed my eyes, wishing that God would answer my prayer to stop being a burden. I knew Ethan would never say that to me, but I was: a child among strangers needing everything explained to her.

I'd never understood people saying they were sick with missing home until now, but then, I'd never gone further than the high pastures. The longing to be home again, to know my place and not worry that each word said to me was a trap, was my only thought.

These nobles and their plots against each other would confound me to the end of my days. The need to laugh with my brother over an evening meal, to hear birdsong filling the pasture or to whistle a pack of herd dogs back to my side filled me to bursting and filled my eyes with tears I was determined I wouldn't cry.

The light heralding my monsters' appearance flared bright enough that I saw it with my eyes closed. All three watched me, feeding my despair, but only Margaret's voice filled my head. Her words were wrapped in the sounds of pealing bells, beautiful and serene, but I knew so well that beauty masked the cruelty Margaret and Michael visited on me.

'Rejoice, for the second part of the Maid's prophecy is complete! Your first champion travels at your side, now and always, and the one true friend you can trust has found you. Your brother is your second champion and he will join you soon. Lean on them when you have need, Jeanne. Their fates are tied to yours and they won't leave or betray you, even when your battles are won and lost again.'

The hated monsters vanished, leaving me sick and hollow. Their twisted idea of destiny was wrapped as tightly around Sarah as it was Ethan and now they meant to force Pierre away from home too. They might claim the prophecy foretold who was fated to fight at my side, but that was another lie.

'Jeanne?' I opened my eyes to see Ethan crouched next to my chair, a blanket tucked under his arm.

He frowned and touched my face. 'What's wrong, little sister? Is the pain worse?'

I had tried to tell him about the voices and how they frightened me late at night when we were alone, but each time, the treacherous monsters compelled me to silence. They wouldn't allow me to talk about my fate until they were ready.

They were the only things I'd ever lied to him about, and that by omission, not intent. Looking into his brown eyes and seeing the worry there, the need to tell him grew stronger than ever. The monsters planned to use him as they used me, but without ever revealing themselves to him.

Ethan deserved to know, but I told him the truth I was allowed to tell. 'I . . . I pushed too hard and need to sleep.' I fought the urge to cling to him. Leaning on him wasn't fair, not when he didn't know the reasons. 'I'm tired . . . and I don't mean to worry you, Ethan. With rest I'll be fine.'

'Then you should rest.' He smiled and brushed a strand of hair off my face. 'I don't want to tire you more. Would you show us the room Jeanne will stay in, Sarah?'

She stood four or five paces behind him, that odd expression on her face again. The look vanished as soon as he looked back at her. 'I thought Karine's old room would be best,' she said. 'It's furthest from my sitting room and bedchamber, it should be quiet for her. This way.'

Sarah took the blanket from Ethan before he picked me up and led the way down the hallway opening off her sitting room. There were two closed doors on the right and one at the opposite end on the left standing ajar. Inside I could see a small table and a large chest and when she pushed the door wide, I got a glimpse of mullioned windows, trees and a darkening sky. Ethan laid me on the softest bed I'd ever rested on. The bed coverings smelled of lavender and roses and for a moment I imagined the mattress was stuffed with the down taken from a thousand, thousand swans.

He eased off my boots and covered me with the blanket Sarah offered while she busied herself lighting a piece of tinder from the embers in the fireplace and moving around the room, touching the flame to the wick of an oil-lamp hanging over the table and two others set in niches carved into the stone walls. When the lamps were lit, Sarah pulled the shutters closed.

'The room is sunny during the day,' she said, 'and you'll be able to sit near the window and watch people stroll in the gardens without being seen. Most of those who use this garden don't speak to each other, so don't think of it as spying on their conversations. Gazing into each other's eyes and the old stories that the roses here help women conceive are the main reasons people walk in the garden. All the strangers staying inside the walls might make garden watching a little more exciting.'

A knock on the outside door got Ethan up and moving towards the sitting room before the sound faded. 'Stay with Jeanne, my lady.'

We both listened to him open the door and speak to the man standing in the corridor. I'd only seen him once, but I recognised Captain Lucien's voice.

Sarah sat on the edge of the bed, the tension in her shoulders gone. 'I know that's the captain, but Ethan will be cross if I come out before he says it's safe – and so will Lucien for that matter. I'll just have to pry the entire conversation out of one of them later.'

'Ethan will tell you what was said if you ask,' I said. 'He's no reason to keep it secret.'

'I have to admit you're probably right.' She took my hand and studied my face. 'And you sound very sure of him. How long have you known Ethan?'

'Not long.' I counted the days since I'd left home in my head. 'A month and a few days, maybe a little longer.'

'A month isn't very long,' she said. She glanced towards the open door. 'When did he start calling you little sister?'

I frowned. 'As soon as he found me. I was hurt and terrified, and Ethan tried to comfort me. Is something wrong?'

'I'm just being curious.' Sarah cleared her throat, turning away from me and appearing to study the toes of her boots. 'And maybe a little foolish. Forget I asked.'

I struggled to sit up, feeling helpless lying flat on my back and sensing something really was wrong and she wouldn't say. Sarah helped me without being asked, piling pillows and cushions behind my back so I could lean against the wall. She kept fussing over me until I grabbed her hand.

'Sarah, please.' I tugged her down to sit next to me on the bed. 'I don't understand. Tell me why calling me "little sister" matters.'

She sighed. 'Now I've upset you, which makes me twice as foolish. You're supposed to be resting. Let me shut the door. Ethan never told me to keep this a secret, but I'd rather not have him walk in and be surprised. The way they're yelling at each other, I'm not sure you'll be able to hear me with the door open, let alone sleep. I'll never understand why men discuss everything so loudly.'

Captain Lucien and Ethan were arguing over how best to handle Giles, and how much to involve Charles. Both of them were worried about his lordship replacing Lady Maud's men with his own, and puzzled about what made him so bold; that he felt free to bring his soldiers into the castle made them both angry. Their voices kept rising, each man trying to make the other listen and believe. Anyone walking in would be hard-pressed to know they were on the same side.

Sarah eased the door closed and came back to stretch out on the bed next to me, hands folded on her stomach and legs crossed at the ankles. She glanced at me. 'Has he told you about his mother?' she asked quietly.

'He told me how she came to be with his father and that the Church wouldn't let them marry.' Sorrow filled my chest. 'And he told me how she died.'

'Ethan doesn't tell everyone about how his family was killed. Only people he trusts.' She rolled onto her side to face me and lowered her voice. 'My mother and Charles shut themselves away for nearly a month when my younger brother died. Ethan spent a lot of time with me then, but he was the only one who acknowledged that I was mourning too. I think that's when I conceived the ridiculous idea I was in love with him and we belonged together.'

'I'm sorry, Sarah.'

She reached for my hand. 'Feeling sorry for me isn't the point, Jeanne. Ethan told me lots of stories his mother told him, old, old tales she'd learned in her father's palace and others she'd learned from a servant bound to the Castilian prince. The old woman did all she could to shelter Jasmina. Where others saw a hostage who would never be ransomed, she saw a frightened little girl.'

'His mother's name was Jasmina?' I asked. 'That's beautiful.'

'Ethan says she was more beautiful than her name, but all sons think their mother is beautiful.'

And daughters believe their fathers are heroes, as I had. I wiped my eyes with the back of my hand and hoped Sarah hadn't noticed.

'One of the stories the old woman told Jasmina was about a wandering soldier who'd roamed the world so long, he couldn't remember why he'd started. Ethan said it was always his favourite. The soldier was travelling through a wood when he found a fox caught in a hunter's snare. He asked the fox if the hunter was hungry and if that was why she hadn't been set free. She told him the man had plenty to eat, but he planned to use her fur to decorate a hat. That made the soldier angry, so he freed the fox and carried her away.'

More shouting came from the sitting room, swiftly followed by loud pounding on the door. Captain Lucien began to swear, and his boot heels rang on the stone floors as he stomped across the room and yanked the door open. A third man greeted the captain cheerfully and asked Ethan how his shoulder had healed – I guessed that must be Scholar Josue.

Sarah leaned closer and spoke in my ear, rushing to finish before Ethan and the physician came into the room. 'It's a long tale,' she whispered. 'From the start, the soldier shows his affection for the fox by calling her little sister and doing all he can to take care of her. The old woman often called Ethan's mother little sister. She always told Jasmina the name in the story meant devotion, commitment and a pledge to keep the fox from coming to harm. Only the two of them ever knew what it meant.'

Tears filled my eyes and this time I didn't try to hide them. 'I'm not a fox in a child's tale, or a princess abandoned by her father.'

'Of course not, and that isn't what I meant, Jeanne. I understand why he called you little sister when he first found you. He wanted you to feel safe. But Ethan still uses that name for you. Only you.' Footsteps came closer to the door. Sarah sat up and swung her legs off the edge of the bed so she could stand. 'His mother's story means something to him. I suspect you do too.'

The sharp knock on the door startled me. Sarah waited to answer until I'd had the chance to turn my face towards the shuttered window and pull the blanket up past my chin. Facing Ethan – or anyone else – with a cheerful smile was more than I could do right now. I wanted to believe Sarah was foolishly making too much of a name, but what I wished and what was true were often far different. My biggest fear was that my monstrous voices had pushed Ethan into caring.

An older man entered ahead of Ethan. The physician, Scholar Josue, hurried over to stand between me and the window, a place where I could see him easily. He was almost a head shorter than Sarah, stout, as older men often were, with wild, bushy white hair sticking out from under a strange round hat. I'd only seen eyeglasses once and I guessed the metal frame around glass circles bouncing on his chest were the same thing.

He wore ankle-length black robes similar to a priest's, but his were embroidered in suns and moons, blazing stars falling from heaven and symbols I didn't have a name for. My curiosity itched to ask what they meant, but I didn't want to give offence. A large satchel hanging from his shoulder had some of the same designs scratched into the leather, although faint and worn by use.

Grand-mère would have turned up her nose, declared him a fraud and hurried me away. Alchemy was close kin to magic or witchcraft in her eyes, but Josue's face was kind and his dark green eyes echoed the smile he gave me. Sarah trusted him and as I returned his smile, I decided I could trust him too.

Ethan had hesitated in the doorway, but now he stepped into the bedchamber. The scholar flapped his hands, shooing him away, but Ethan stubbornly set his shoulders and didn't move.

Josue came around the bed and planted a hand on Ethan's chest. 'Leave, my lord. Sarah can stay, but you need to go.' The physician's head didn't reach Ethan's shoulder, but his tone made Ethan step back. 'I don't want you making young Jeanne nervous while I examine her. You can come in once I've finished.'

Ethan glanced towards me and back at Josue, looking torn and unsure. 'I'm pledged to protect her, Scholar. What if Lord Giles—?'

'His lordship was deep in his cups when I passed by the dining hall. Given his current state, I suspect he may have indulged in more than wine. I doubt he could make it to Sarah's chambers, let alone get past you and Captain Lucien.' Josue patted Ethan's shoulder before pushing him towards the door. 'Wait in the other room, my lord. She's in no danger from me.'

Ethan looked at me, then nodded and left me to the old man's care. I shut my eyes so I didn't have to see him go, feeling foolish as I did so, but I couldn't ignore the thought that people who left me didn't always come back.

Josue set his satchel on the windowsill and began to rummage inside. 'Lord Robert's message said your leg and ankle were injured weeks ago. His lordship said Ethan couldn't find any broken bones at the time, but you were in a great deal of pain – and that you still are. Is that true, Jeanne?'

'Yes,' I admitted. 'The pain is worse when I put too much weight on my ankle or walk for too long, but it starts to fade once I lie down. Short walks are getting easier, but from the courtyard to here was too far.'

'Believe it or not, that's a good sign.' Josue smiled and went back to searching his bag. 'A broken ankle would take months to heal enough for you to take a step. My guess is you strained a tendon when you wrenched your ankle.'

He finally found what he wanted and pulled out three small vials, a scrap of linen, a small bag of powder and a stone bowl. Lined up on the window ledge, the collection looked a little alarming.

'How have you been getting around?' he asked.

'I rode with Ethan.'

He turned to look at me, a raised eyebrow and a questioning look on his face saying he expected more.

Heat rose in my face. 'When we camped and weren't on horse-back Ethan ... Ethan carried me.'

He smiled. 'Very practical for both of you. I've no wish to make you feel worse so I'm going to give you something for the pain before I examine your leg. Sarah, is there water in that pitcher?'

She picked it up and peered in. 'A drop or two, Scholar, but it may have been sitting here since Karine left. I'll fetch some fresh.'

As Sarah hurried away, Josue busied himself measuring powder into the stone bowl. He produced a thick glass rod from the satchel. He hummed a cheerful song as he worked, one I thought I recognised. Scholar Josue wasn't anything like I'd imagined a physician would be, and further still from the image of an alchemist Grand-mère had planted in my head.

Ethan held the door open for Sarah and stood in the doorway, thumbs hooked in his belt. Sarah set the water jug on the win-dowsill and came back to stand near me, tight-lipped and looking askance at both Josue and Ethan.

'A moment of your time, Scholar, before you mix your potion Then I'll go,' Ethan said. 'Go lightly if you plan to add poppy to the mixture. Charles and I gave her some before I splinted her leg. Two drops of poppy mixed in two fingers of wine put Jeanne to sleep for just short of three days.'

Josue frowned. 'Two drops? You're sure?'

'I mixed the cup for her myself, Josue.' He looked at me for a long moment before turning back to the physician. 'The second night her breath came so slow and shallow, I thought she'd stopped breathing. I was afraid I'd killed her.'

The shock on Sarah's face matched my own.

'You said I'd scared you,' I said. 'You never said why.'

He smiled, but the smile didn't hold any joy. 'I didn't see the need to scare you too. I'd been frightened enough for ten men.'

'I wasn't planning on poppy in the mix, and now I'm glad.' He smiled at Ethan, but the smile quickly became a frown. 'One last question before you go, my lord. Where did the poppy come from?'

'At a guess, Lord Giles,' Sarah said, and sat on the bed. She took my hand as the physician turned to her in surprise. 'Everyone in the castle knows the duke always has a ready supply and makes free use of it when he's here. I've overheard Charles complain to Mother that it's the same when they travel.'

'She's right,' Ethan said. 'The Dauphin had to force Giles to give up the vial.'

'Ahhh . . . that makes more sense. If his lordship was involved, I'd guess there was more in that vial than mere poppy juice.' Josue went back to his stone bowl. 'A simple sleeping powder will do for now. We'll talk more when I'm finished, Ethan. Shut the door as you go.'

The sleeping powder tasted of fennel and honey. Sarah took the cup when I'd finished. I shut my eyes and let the heavy feeling creep through me.

Josue asked me a question. I don't remember answering.

Part Seven

My Voices have told me that the enemy will be ours.

Jeanne d'Arc

The shutters were open when I woke, a bright spring morning flooding the room with light. Birds darted past the window, squabbling over what little food they were able to find this early in the season. The lucky ones still had seeds and berries stashed away, leftovers from the caches they'd made from the bounty of autumn and late summer. Sparrows and dunnocks complained as they scratched in the dirt under the trees, while others worked at opening the rose hips still left in the garden, until their bigger, longer-beaked brethren chased them all away.

Keeping my eyes closed, even for a few moments, let me pretend the birds were in the yard at home, that the bed I slept in belonged to me, not one I'd borrowed for more than a month. My leg was healing rapidly under Josue's care, although some of the potions he had me drink tasted bitter and foul. The pain was gone and if I didn't push too hard, I could go where I wanted and not suffer for it.

I thanked God each day for the great gifts he'd given me, for Ethan and Sarah, and time to heal in safety – but with all this bounty, I still wanted to go home.

Ethan sat in a chair near the window, just as he had every morning for the last five weeks. With Charles' blessing, he seldom left Sarah's suite – not unless we left with him for a meal in the

199

great hall, or Duke Robert took his place. The story going around the castle was that the Dauphin had asked him to guard both of us as the English drew closer. People knew keeping the lady's daughter safe was important to Charles and the care he took now added to the servants' gossip that he'd found a priest willing to marry him and Lady Maud.

Since I was Ethan's ward, few openly questioned the arrangement, at least, not where he or the Dauphin could hear. I wasn't sure many cared.

As far as it went, the story was true. The English were closer, their army swollen with men from Brittany and soldiers who had sailed all the way from England. Charles was planning to take Maud and Sarah out of the castle and hide them away, but a safe place for them was proving difficult to find. He needed to be certain he wasn't leading the two of them into greater danger. Too many nobles, once sworn to Charles and to his father before him, had turned their coats and pledged to the English king. The territory still loyal to the Dauphin was shrinking by the day.

That should have been the worst of the danger, but Ethan and Robert were convinced that Giles was close to open rebellion and continuing to allow him to stay in the castle was madness. Relying on troops whose loyalty was in question was a sure way to lose what ground the Dauphin still held.

Persuading Charles was proving difficult, but every brawl his cousin's soldiers started and every outburst Giles made in open court brought him closer to believing.

Ethan stayed close for another reason too, one that filled me with guilt. The story of the discovery of the Maid's sword behind the altar continued to spread, sparking hope in what appeared to be a near-hopeless cause. When I ventured into the courtyard, leaning on Ethan's arm, soldiers who'd been in the churchyard at Saint Catherine's dropped to their knees, begging me to fight for Charles.

Servants had gathered to watch, and even some of Giles' troops, until the crowd surrounded us and the castle guard had to move them away – but the number of believers kept growing. My voices watched silently, waiting for me to yield to the pressure and take up the sword. I knew they were responsible for the story continuing to spread; they meant to box me in until I had no choice but to admit I was the Maid.

Now my eyes were caught by a flash of silver as Ethan held up the blade he was polishing, angling the edge so it caught the light. I recognised the Maid's sword: the hilt was impossible to mistake. A quillon curved up on one side to protect the wielder's fingers and down on the other side to trap an opponent's blade. The grip wasn't large. Ethan said it had been sized to fit a smaller hand. A woman's hand.

I refused to think of it as being made to fit mine.

The sword fascinated Ethan as much as it horrified me. He'd spent hours cleaning the blade, bringing the pictures etched on the metal into sharper relief. A woman in armour knelt before a cross. Two shields bore a coat of arms he'd not seen. A much fainter line of crosses, five in all, marched down the blade on one side. The sword was old, much older even than Grand-mère Marie had been. I couldn't understand how anyone could believe it had been made for a girl of seventeen years.

Ethan caught me watching him and smiled. 'Good morning. How did you sleep?'

'Better,' I said. 'No nightmares, and no pain to speak of. God granted me a miracle when he put me in Josue's care.'

'Maybe I should start drinking the scholar's potions.' Ethan opened the large chest at the foot of the bed, placed the sword at the very bottom and piled the spare blankets and clothes on top. 'Sparring with Robert isn't easy. He was always a good swordsman, but he's becoming stronger and more focused. His lordship has broken two practice swords over my shield just this week. I pity the Englishmen who face him.'

He broke off at the sound of shouting from the rose garden and moved towards the windows, standing near enough that he could see out, but not so close anyone outside could see him. His slight frown rapidly became a scowl, which worried me.

I wrapped a shawl around my shoulders, slipped out of bed and limped over to stand with him. The voices were clear enough – Giles, Captain Lucien and a woman's I didn't recognise – but they were standing to one side and all I could see was Lucien's back.

'What's happened?' I whispered.

'I'm not entirely sure, little sister. I can't see much.' He glanced at me. 'From what I've heard, Lucien is defending Lady Talia from Giles and refusing to let the duke drag her from the gardens. The duke insists that Lady Talia is his wife and Lucien knows that to be a lie. His lordship is being charming as always: he's threatening to have the captain flogged for interfering.'

'The duke has to know Lady Maud will never let that happen,' I said.

'He does, Jeanne.' The smile he gave me was fleeting. 'And he knows neither will Charles, but it's an easy way to cause trouble. But right now, Lucien needs the help of someone with more rank to stand with him. Will you tell Sarah what's happening while I tweak Giles' nose? Make sure she doesn't follow me.'

Lady Talia's cries were growing panicked and Lucien's responses angrier, making my heart beat faster. 'Should I send the guard to the gardens?'

Ethan buckled on his sword belt. 'Keep Bastian at the door and send Kylian to raise the alarm,' he said. 'Promise to stay inside with Sarah. This will go badly if Giles' men arrive first.'

Light flared near the bedchamber door and I saw my three monsters – their menacing shapes had grown more recognisable in the last few weeks. Now when they appeared, I saw something close to, but not quite, a person wearing robes made of light. One day they'd suddenly opened their eyes, as if startled awake from a long sleep. Margaret and Catherine's were dark pits filled with swirling stars, and if I looked into them too long I knew I'd fall forever. Michael's eyes glowed red, full of flame and promises that if I failed him I'd burn.

I looked away, quick as I could. They'd always frightened me, but not like this. This was a nightmare that wouldn't let me wake.

'Ethan?' I hugged myself tight to keep from reaching for him. 'Be careful.'

He ran for the door, yanked it open and kept running as he shouted instructions at the startled guards. Then he was gone.

The guards crowded in the door, waiting. My voices watched silently as I told them what I needed. I'd never issued orders before, but Kylian and Bastian took them from me as if I'd always done so.

'Time is short,' I said. 'You need to hurry.'

Anger burned in the young guard's eyes when I'd finished. 'I can't know what his lordship is thinking, but there's not a man in this castle who will let Captain Lucien be lashed by Lord Giles.' Kylian bowed, and it took me an instant before I realised he'd bowed to me. 'I'll have a company in the rose garden fast as I can.'

The younger guard was shorter than Ethan, but he took off just as quickly and vanished down the corridor. I watched him go, suddenly afraid and not knowing why.

Bastian pulled the door open wide and waved me back in. 'No matter what goes on, you're safer inside, Jeanne. Try to make Lady Sarah see the sense in that. I've known her temper to get the better of her and, well, she's fond of Captain Lucien.'

'I will, Bastian, but Sarah has more sense than most think.'

'That's likely true.' He scratched the side of his nose and frowned. 'Tell her one more thing for me. Tell her to get ready to leave. Giles is a clever bastard and not above causing a fuss to hide what he's doing. If real fighting breaks out, Lord Ethan won't leave the two of you here. He'll get you out.'

He shut the door, closing me into the silent chambers. I could hear the shouting from the rose garden again: Lady Talia was sobbing, and the fear in her voice went straight to my heart and woke guilt along the way. If I hadn't convinced Charles to keep her here, she'd be home and safe, even if it took time for her father to forgive her. She wouldn't have been a pawn in Giles' schemes. God might forgive me for that, as He would forgive Talia, but I didn't know if I could forgive myself.

The clamour from the garden grew louder. Men yelled just outside my bedchamber window and the dread squeezing my heart said if I looked they'd be wearing Giles' colours. More voices began to fill the garden, now shrieking battle cries. *For Lady Maud! For Charles!* echoed through the sitting room.

I heard Ethan ordering the castle guard to rally to him; the Dauphin had been betrayed. His voice was full of rage.

I whispered a prayer as I rushed to Sarah's chambers: 'Blessed Mary, please keep Ethan safe. Please, I beg you. Keep him safe.'

*

Sarah tossed me a plain dark tunic before pulling on one of her own. She slid a long dagger into the sheath on her belt and a knife into the top of her boot before she went back to stuffing a pack full of clothing.

The skirt she'd given me was a little longer than the one I wore in the pastures, but it was still short enough to move quickly and not trip. She told me that dressing like servants was meant to keep anyone from looking at us twice, but Sarah didn't believe that any more than I did. Anyone looking for us would know who we were.

She'd been awake and already preparing when I'd pounded on her door. The pack on her bed was already stuffed with the little bit of food kept in the suite, and spare clothes. Bastian and the castle weapons master, Nicholas, paced nervously in the sitting room, listening to the sounds of battle while they waited for us. I listened too, remembering the night Grand-mère and I fled our house in Domrémy. Soldiers, all of them loyal to Robert, lined the corridor, to protect us as we moved to a tower in another part of the castle, further from the fighting and more secure.

Sarah pulled three long wooden tubes out of the chest at the end of her bed and slung their leather straps over her head so they hung on her back and left her hands free.

'Do you have a knife, Jeanne?'

I shook my head. 'I lost mine when I got hurt.'

'I have another in my workroom,' she said. 'I'll get it for you.'

'Workroom?' Even in my panic I was curious.

Sarah put a finger to her lips before pushing aside a large tapestry to reveal a small door. 'My maid moved out more than a year before I told Mother. I'll show you everything when they let us back in here, but you can peek inside while I find the knife.'

Five niches in the walls, much like the ones in my own

bedchamber, held much bigger oil-lamps than mine. Only one was burning, but it gave off as much light as all three in my room. If all five were lit after dark, the room would be nearly bright as day.

The reason for all the lamps made me stare. One wall was covered in maps and drawings, the likes of which I'd never seen. Pierre and Edmond often drew the things they meant to build, but never as fine and detailed as these. I stared at the one nearest the door, guessing the small sketches scattered across the parchment were parts for the finished trebuchet in the middle. I stepped further into the room, longing to study the maps and the shelves full of models, some still half-built, lining the walls. A long worktable took the place of a bed and I could not stop myself from gently touching the tools and the project strewn the length of the tabletop.

'You made all this.' I pulled my hand back, afraid I'd break something or make Sarah angry. 'Why are you hiding what you've done? It's wonderful.'

'A priest told my mother using too much use of my brain would ruin me for marriage. He feared I'd think myself smarter than any man.' Sarah pulled a knife and sheath out of a small wooden casket she'd taken off a shelf. 'I was much younger and I never made any secret about preferring drawing plans for war engines over embroidery. The good father is years gone to another posting, but his lecture on what noblemen wanted in a wife made an impression. Mother made me promise to keep my work out of sight, so this room was perfect. She also made it clear I'd have to give up my "foolishness" once I married.'

The faint smell of smoke wafted into the room. Sarah and I looked at each other and I realised she was just as frightened. She handed me the sheathed knife and we hurried to join Nicholas and Bastian.

My three voices blazed into view at the far end of the corridor, filling the doorway into my bedchamber with light. Michael's red eyes froze me in place and his voice rang in my ears. 'Do not leave the Maid's sword behind! You are *La Pucelle*, not the simple village girl you pretend to be. Deny your destiny and France will fall, poisoned and lost for ever. Your life will go on as you wish, bearing a poor shepherd's children and baking his bread, but all the people you love and care about will perish. Can you condemn them to death and not regret your choice with each breath?'

A vision filled my head, one that had the taste of truth: Charles dragged in chains to a block outside the castle at Reims, Sarah running barefoot in a field, fleeing from an English knight on horseback, Pierre with a pike through his back, Ethan screaming as they broke him on the wheel.

Michael hissed in my ear, 'Choose, Jeanne. You've no more time.'

When the vision ended, Sarah was tugging my hand, trying to get me to follow. She touched my cheek. 'What's wrong, Jeanne? We have to go.'

Looking into her worried face decided me. Too many of the monsters' visions came true and I couldn't take the risk this one was a lie, another skirmish in the war between us. This time the price was too high. I wouldn't sacrifice the people I loved.

'The sword in my room . . . I can't leave it.'

A shadow passed over her face and was gone again, making me cringe. Of course Sarah had heard the soldiers' stories, just like everyone else.

'Ethan keeps it in the large chest, doesn't he?' she asked.

With the smell of smoke growing stronger, Sarah ran into my room and together we heaved up the heavy lid, tossing everything aside until the only thing left was the sword. Ethan had replaced the sword belt and found a decent plain scabbard of the proper size from the armoury, and with Sarah's help I fastened them so the sword hung angled across my back, from shoulder to hip, a mirror of the tubes Sarah carried. I'd never be able to draw the blade as Ethan did, but I could move quickly and not tangle my legs.

The weapons master was fuming and cursing under his breath long before we dashed into the living room, but he eyed the sword on my back and the wooden tubes Sarah carried and nodded. 'Glad to see you didn't risk your lives for trinkets. Do you know how to use that sword, Jeanne?'

'No, Master Nicholas,' I said. 'Not yet.'

He frowned. 'Then leave it right where it is. You're safer drawing your knife if you get cornered, but trust I won't let that happen easily. Are you all right with carrying the plans, Lady Sarah?'

'Fine.' She took my hand. 'Mother will be frantic by now. We need to hurry.'

Bastian drew his sword and went to the door. 'Let the guard form up around you, my lady. Same for you, Jeanne. All you need do is stay in the middle.'

He opened the door and twelve men in Robert's colours came to attention. When Sarah and I stepped out, they formed a square around us, leaving Nicholas and Bastian in the centre with us.

Smoke hazed the air, growing thicker as we left Sarah's rooms, moving swiftly down passages that led to the walkways servants used outside the castle proper. The air was clearer there, making it easier to breathe without choking. Twice the sound of fighting moved towards us, and both times, Nicholas backtracked and found a different route.

The third time the battle grew nearer, we rounded a corner and came face to face with six men pelting towards us. Four of them sported Giles' bright green and yellow – but two wore colours I remembered with fear: English army tunics. They were as surprised as we were – they all looked back over their shoulders before they charged into Robert's men, almost as if they expected to see a demon chasing them.

Nicholas shoved Sarah and me more than twenty strides away, getting us clear of the fight. Once our backs were against the wall, he drew his sword and stood in front of us, while Bastian took a stand a few steps to the left.

'Stay there, both of you,' Nicholas ordered curtly. 'If I tell you to run, go back the way we came. You'll need to find your way to a place you can hide.'

Catherine whispered in my ear, making me shiver, 'Fight, Jeanne. Use the sword!'

'I don't know how,' I muttered, my words lost in the din of weapons shrilling against one another and men grunting with effort. 'I can't even lift it. Do you want me to die here, now?'

For once she didn't answer or argue, which was a blessing, and the emptiness inside told me she was gone. The sword was just a sword, not magical or blessed to perform miracles, and no matter what Catherine wanted, I hadn't been born knowing how to wield a blade.

Four more of Giles' men appeared, pounding down the corridor to join the fight. One pointed at Sarah, shouting, 'It's the lady's daughter – the duke has promised gold to the man who takes her unharmed!'

'Mother of God,' Nicholas said, and glanced at Sarah. 'Why would Giles put a bounty on you?'

Sarah drew her dagger and held it steady, but the hand clutching mine trembled. 'He's asked Mother for my hand at least three times and each time she said no, I wasn't old enough. Charles supported her decision. Giles wants my lands, the herds, my money and titles and if I can give him heirs, so much the better. He doesn't realise I'd gut him to keep that from happening.'

Bastian snorted and moved to stand shoulder to shoulder with the weapons master. 'You'll have to wait your turn at gutting him, my lady. His lordship's not a well-liked man, and after this . . .'

I drew my knife too, watching and praying. Robert's troops were better trained, but I wasn't fool enough to put too much trust in their winning the day. I'd heard too many stories about how desperate men fought from the old soldiers at home and I could see Giles' men were afraid, which was making them reckless. Only men who thought they were about to die would fight that way. Robert's men were dying in the face of that fervour, which meant the odds shifting towards the enemy.

The weapons master saw that too.

'Bastian, take Sarah and Jeanne and run for it.' He wiped his sword hand on his tunic before gripping the hilt again. 'That's an order, man – go! We'll keep them from following as long as possible.'

The old guard barely hesitated before shooing us back the way we'd come. 'Fast as you can, my ladies, but think about where we can get out of sight. As long as we're in the open, the risk of running into things we can't handle grows. Lady Sarah, if you know somewhere we're not likely to be found, I'd like to hear about it.'

'If we can get to the old warriors' cemetery behind the practice yard. I know a place no one will find us,' she said.

'Show us the way, my lady.' Bastian looked over his shoulder. 'Quick as you can.'

The racket behind us grew louder and footsteps pelted after us.

Bastian had taken my arm to help me keep up, but I still couldn't move as fast as Sarah. My heart sank as the cries behind us drew closer. Robert's men wouldn't be chasing us.

The shouting changed and the sound of running footsteps vanished. I'd begun to breathe easier, praying that we might get to safety without running into more of Giles' men, when someone stepped out of a doorway and lunged for Sarah. She screamed as the English soldier grabbed her, and fought hard to get away.

I didn't think twice before slashing my knife down the length of his arm. The man howled in pain as blood quickly soaked his sleeve, dripped off his fingertips and splashed onto his boots. Sarah kicked him hard and twisted out of his grip.

Bastian pushed her completely out of the way and plunged his sword into the Englishman's chest. Sarah stared as the man crumpled to the ground, his eyes fixed on her face as his life drained away. Bastian put a boot on the dead man's shoulder and tugged his blade free.

'Don't look, my lady.' He gently turned Sarah back the way we'd been running. 'Keep going. Jeanne and I are right behind you.'

She hesitated an instant before beginning to run again. Before we'd gone much further, she darted towards a small gate, Bastian and I at her heels. Sarah knew the castle better than anyone and she'd led us to a pathway running between Master Nicholas' quarters, the armoury and the library, smaller buildings which were set apart, not actually attached to the castle itself. There were other small buildings here too – a smithy, a cordwainer's, a candlemaker's and quarters for some of the castle servants, all crowded onto the same small piece of land.

Trees and flowering shrubs lined the gravelled paths, hiding the twists and turns ahead. This part of the castle grounds was a real maze, easy to get lost in, but I trusted Sarah, sure she'd never have brought us here if she didn't know the way.

My monsters kept pace with us, fading in and out of view. Whenever I thought they'd given up, we'd round a corner and I'd see them, still waiting and watching. The flames in Michael's eyes had dimmed to a flicker, but the star-filled voids in Margaret's and Catherine's eyes were darker, deeper. Running wasn't the only reason my heart raced.

We stopped to catch our breath at the entrance to the practice yard. The path was higher here, rising up towards the hills behind the castle grounds and continuing on out of sight. I could see a line of men below, passing buckets of water to douse a fire in the stables, sending white smoke rising into the air. I couldn't see any other flames; I prayed that the fires we'd smelled earlier were already out.

Mêlées and clashes dotted the castle grounds, easy to pick out from this height. Bodies lay where they'd fallen, most of them wearing Duke Giles' bright green and yellow. The fallen banners bore his coat of arms. Their bodies would be left until the battle was over or one side surrendered; I'd learned that from the old men at home.

I couldn't imagine the arrogant duke surrendering to his younger cousin. He'd likely fled to join the English when the tide turned against him, knowing he'd lost this gamble. Charles wouldn't be inclined to show Giles any mercy now. Siding with the English was unforgiveable on its own, bringing English soldiers into Lady Maud's castle would surely seal Giles' fate.

Prisoners were lined up along one side of the courtyard. I saw Lord Robert on his huge gelding riding up and down the rows and imagined him glaring at the men who'd turned traitor. There'd be no mercy for them either.

Bastian twitched at the slightest sound and tried to watch

everywhere at once. 'Let's keep moving, ladies. We still need a place to go to ground.'

'Are you sure it's safe up here?' I asked. 'I don't trust the quiet.'

He flexed his fingers on his hilt. 'You're right to be wary, Jeanne. Looking empty doesn't mean the whole place is deserted. Staying here's a risk, but so is making our way down to Duke Robert. We're better hiding up here for now.'

'We'll be safe.' Sarah pointed. 'This way.'

She pulled open the gate. The hinges creaked, spooking a hare that bounded away and came close to stopping my heart. I hurried after her and took her hand again, compelled to stay close to her in a way that made me nervous. The faint glimmer of my monsters' light on the far side of the yard added to my unease.

The warriors' cemetery was old, older than any I'd seen. Some of the graves were marked with tall cairns, others with a rough-hewn cross or a flat rock. Crude stone shelters, overgrown with vines and many missing a roof, took their place as we moved deeper in. Leering skulls and bleached bone greeted me when I looked inside one, rusty armour and rotting wood in another. Flecks of bright colours showed in some of the graves, tucked in amongst the rotted leaves and leather. I thought they might be jewels.

A few of the stone shelters had ruined or broken shrines and altars outside the entrance. I'd seen few signs of honouring the old ways inside the castle or the gardens I'd visited, but I saw them all around me now, and somehow, knowing people here held the same beliefs as my father made me feel less a stranger. A few shrines looked if not newly built, more recent, with the spoiled remains of offerings suggesting they were still in use. Most looked older than any in Domrémy, buried in dead leaves and covered in moss, the altar stones broken.

The need to ask Ethan about this place bubbled inside, followed immediately by a sick quiver reminding me he was in the thick of the battle. I breathed another prayer to Holy Mary to bring him back safe.

Sarah led us to the very back of the cemetery. We were even higher up and the stone shelters were set against the base of the hill. One had collapsed, the stones scattered and cracked, and the vines covering it were sprouting new spring leaves. She went a few strides past the ruined shelter, stopped and pointed at the tree growing just in front of the rubble.

'I was very small when my mother brought me here the first time.' Sarah grimaced and brushed a mass of cobwebs away with her knife before pushing her way into a barely visible hollow between the hill and the tumbled stone. Her voice was hushed. 'She said if I was ever scared, or thought it was dangerous to come inside . . . Mother told me to come here, that she'd know where to look for me. Ethan knows about this place too. One of them will come and find us when it's safe.'

A bigger hollow had been cut into the hillside, ancient chisel marks showing around the entrance. I thanked Sarah's ancestors for making a place for their children to hide. We were safe and hidden and Ethan knew where to find us.

Bastian looked around and nodded. 'There's something to be said for growing up in a place and knowing all its secrets. The two of you get some rest. This will be a hard place to find by chance, but I'll feel better keeping watch. I won't go far.'

The floor was covered in thick, flat stones. Enough afternoon light filtered inside to allow us to see, but once the sun set our shelter would be dark as a moonless night. I prayed God would be kind and that for Sarah's sake, Ethan would come before night fell. We found a stone big enough to seat both of us and brushed it free of dirt and leaves, wrapped ourselves in the shawls Sarah had brought and huddled together. Safe didn't always mean warm.

'God will protect Mother,' she whispered. 'Charles won't let anything happen to her. He won't.'

I put my arms around her when she started to cry, pulled her head onto my shoulder and held tight.

I woke with a start, my heart thudding against my ribs, thinking I'd heard Ethan's voice. Listening brought only the quiet sound of Sarah's breathing, birds welcoming the day and the tiny mouse I'd shared crumbs with the night before rustling through dry leaves, hoping for more. No one was calling my name.

The monsters standing just outside the shelter entrance watched me silently. Their light had shone in that spot all night, never moving, but if they sought to comfort me, their comfort hadn't extended to Sarah. The near complete darkness made it all too easy for her to imagine the worst, so I told her stories about my brothers and village life to distract her, and thanked Mother Mary when she finally fell asleep.

I stretched out next to her again. The Maid's sword was between us, and I couldn't help thinking it was between me and everything I wanted from life. The instant my fingers had closed around the hilt, my dreams of children, a home of my own and the chance to make a life with a man who loved me had crumbled. Lifting the blade out of the chest had been my choice, I wouldn't deny that, but making the decision to save Sarah, my brother and Ethan had sealed me to a bargain I'd never wanted to make.

Even so, I'd make the same choice again. Not for Charles and France, or because I believed in the monsters' evil idea of destiny.

I'd take up the sword and pretend to be *La Pucelle* to save the people I loved. I was at peace with what I'd done.

A low rumble of men's voices came from outside and one of them called my name. This time I wasn't dreaming.

'Jeanne! Sarah! Where are you?'

'Ethan—'

I was on my feet and scrambling around the collapsed stone tomb in an instant. Bastian was trotting towards two other men standing a hundred strides away when I came into view.

'Lord Ethan!' Bastian got his attention and pointed at me. 'Turn around.'

I watched relief fill his face as he saw me, and the tight, angry way he held himself leached away. He sheathed his sword and ran to meet me halfway. My heart thudded against my ribs as I caught sight of the blood-soaked bandage tied around his left arm, all that was left of his linen shirt. The deep scratch across his chest had wept blood all the way down his belly, while the shallow cut on his shoulder was still oozing dark red drops.

I threw myself into his arms, thanking God he wasn't hurt worse, as he stroked my hair and murmured in my ear,

'You're all right now, little sister. You're all right.' He kissed the top of my head and hugged me tighter. 'I'm sorry not to come for you sooner, but it wasn't safe. Is Sarah well?'

Bastian cleared his throat, letting us know he was there. 'Lady Sarah's fine, thanks to Jeanne. She was a few steps ahead when a beef-eater popped out of a doorway. He got a grip on her ladyship, but Jeanne didn't hesitate about going after him with a knife. The cur let go and that gave me the room to make sure he didn't try again.'

I felt Ethan's heart beat faster and his breath came quicker for a moment, but he was smiling when he let go and stepped back.

He brushed the hair off my face. 'I knew you were brave, little sister. Now I know your brother's stories of how fierce you can be are true. Not that I doubted Pierre's word.'

I stared, wide-eyed as a child, and his smile got bigger. 'My brother is here?'

'I'm here, little bird.' The bearded man I'd seen speaking with Bastian stepped forwards and grinned. 'Have you forgotten me so quickly?'

The words all jammed up inside and I couldn't answer, but that didn't stop me from rushing to him. He picked me up and swung me around, laughing the whole time and sounding so much like Papa I could barely breathe. Pierre was much thinner and dressed like a warrior, not a shepherd, and the curly black beard changed the shape of his face and made him look years older. His eyes were exactly the same, but everything else about my brother had changed since I last saw him.

He'd see all the changes in me too.

'How did you know where to find me?' I asked.

He put me down and looped an arm around my shoulder. Pierre cleared his throat and glanced at Ethan. 'We have Sir Ethan to thank for that. The first message telling me what happened to Emile, where you'd gone and that you were safe . . . it went missing. Father Jakob told the whole village Emile was dead and let me believe you'd died too. After Ethan's second message reached me . . . Edmond spent a long night convincing me to find you first and settle with Jakob later.'

'Your friend sounds like a wise man.' Ethan wiped a hand over his face and sighed. 'I'm too tired to rage right now or ride for Domrémy, but I'd be honoured to help you teach this meddling priest a lesson.'

Pierre's arm tightened around my shoulders. 'I'm in your debt, Ethan.'

Bastian led Sarah out of the hollow that had sheltered us for the night. He had the tubes holding her drawings and plans over his shoulder and her pack on his back. With a word to Sarah, he started back to the castle.

Sarah carried the Maid's sword in one arm, the way a mother carries a babe, careful not to let the tip drag on the ground. She glanced at Ethan, but I couldn't read the look she gave Pierre. The itch on the back of my neck said something was wrong, but I'd no idea what.

Sarah offered me the sword and I stepped away from my brother to take it. She cleared her throat, pulled herself up and folded her hands at her waist, suddenly tight-lipped, cold and aloof. Looking at her like this, I could well believe she was a noble lady's daughter. Then she spoke, and became someone I'd never known.

'Who is this man, Jeanne?' Sarah asked. 'I need the truth of how you know each other before I find my mother.'

I struggled not to cry, confused and exhausted, and hurt by her tone. 'I don't understand why you're angry.'

Her hands trembled, but her voice held steady. 'All this time I thought you were alone in the world, yet you obviously know this soldier well – very well. I have to wonder how he came to find you here now, just as the attack is ended – and with all these strangers who have suddenly appeared inside the walls . . . I need your answer.'

'Sarah! Stop now, before you say something that can't be mended.' Ethan's voice was sharp and stern, even more than the look he gave her. He took her arm and pulled her aside, but Pierre and I could hear every word. 'I don't understand your anger either. I've never heard you use that tone with a servant, let alone a friend. Pierre is here because *I* sent for him. You owe Jeanne and her brother an apology.'

Fear and lack of sleep had already stolen the roses from her dirt-smudged cheeks, but now what little colour remained in her face drained away. 'Her *brother*?'

'Yes, her brother,' he said. 'Who else did you think Pierre could be?'

'A lover or a husband – a stranger I'd never seen before. Someone who didn't belong with Jeanne.' She crossed her arms over her chest and looked away. 'He had his arms around her and . . . and he wasn't you, Ethan. I didn't think beyond that. I'm sorry.'

Pierre hooked his thumbs in his belt and watched Sarah silently. She was a stranger to him and I could well imagine he didn't know what to think. I didn't either.

Ethan took a step back, his hands balled into fists. 'I've little patience left, my lady, and even less desire to deal with you acting like a child. Apologise to Jeanne and Pierre, not me. I'm not the one you hurt or in need of protection.'

Sarah stood silent and unmoving for far too long. She finally turned to face me, tears of regret brimming in her eyes. 'I treated you poorly, Jeanne. Forgive me.' Sarah swiped at the tear sliding down her face. 'I'm a fool.'

She hurried back the way we'd come, picking her way around the fallen branches, trying not to slip on the stones and rock shards littering the ground.

'Forgive her, Pierre. Sarah's a good person who's done her best for Jeanne. She'll apologise properly when she's less afraid and less tired and the sting of how wrong she was fades.' Ethan rubbed a hand over his face, but it would take more than that to wipe away the weariness and pain I saw. 'I should go after her and make sure she gets back to her quarters.'

'Let me go. My guess is she needs to know she's forgiven.' Pierre touched my hair and started down the hill, following Sarah. 'Force him to let someone tend to his wounds, Jeanne. He refused to seek the physician until we had found you and Lady Sarah.'

My brother quickly caught up with Sarah, more surefooted on the hillside and better able to keep his feet. She slipped, going down on her hands and knees this time, and when Pierre helped her up, Sarah nodded and let him take her arm. I thanked God for lifting one worry off my heart. Glancing towards Ethan sent a hundred more rushing to take its place.

I couldn't fix the Maid's sword so it hung across my back, not alone, but I buckled the sword belt around my waist, managing to tighten it enough that it wouldn't fall off. The tip of the scabbard was less than two fingers off the ground, but I decided that as long as it didn't drag, that would have to do.

When I looked for him again, Ethan was perched on a rock, his head in his hands. The wound on his shoulder had opened and a thin stream of blood trickled down his back. I sent a prayer of thanks to Holy Mary he wasn't bleeding heavily and muttered another prayer imploring God to keep his wounds from growing foul.

'Ethan.' I crouched in front of him and touched his arm. 'Please look at me.'

He lifted his head and my heart ached at the bleakness in his eyes. Now wasn't the time to ask what fresh loss he'd suffered, or what new horror he'd witnessed. He would tell me when he was ready.

Instead, I smiled and took his hand. 'We need to go back while you can still walk. I can't carry you, my lord.'

That made him laugh. 'And I won't make you try, my lady.'

Getting him to his feet took two tries and Ethan was shaking badly by the time we managed it. We set off slowly, my arm wrapped around his waist and him leaning heavily on me. I was afraid not to hold tight, frightened at how weak he appeared. He'd likely pushed himself too far and bled more than he'd admitted. If he fell, I wouldn't be strong enough to get him up again, not alone, but not far past the practice yard, I found help. One of Robert's soldiers spotted us, and in less than a moment, two strong men had taken Ethan's weight from me and four more guards had formed up around us.

The oldest man bowed. 'I'll send a runner to find Scholar Josue. Where should he meet us?'

'Ask him to come to Lady Sarah's quarters, please – and have your runner tell him to hurry.' Giving orders and being listened to was strange, but I needed to get help for Ethan as fast as I could. I didn't like being seen carrying the sword, but I understood that was one reason they obeyed me. 'Put Lord Ethan in the room I was using. I'll find another place to sleep.'

I discovered that walking with my hand on the hilt of the sword was easier as the end tilted up, keeping it well off the ground. I watched Ethan stumbling along just in front of me, or stared at the backs of the men keeping him from falling, pretending not to hear the whispers following us or see the men falling to their knees as we passed.

The Maid wears her sword! . . . Praise God, the stories were true! . . . Have faith, boy! The Maid will put the Dauphin on his throne and save us all!

My voices blinked into view as we entered the corridor leading to Sarah's rooms, pressed back against the wall, giving the men half-carrying Ethan room to pass – and they gave me space too. I suddenly remembered the dream where I'd cut the monsters down with the Maid's sword.

They might be afraid of the sword – or afraid of me wielding it against them.

The truth in that settled around my bones and I promised myself I'd remember and use it when I could.

Part Eight

I fear nothing, except treason.

Jeanne d'Arc

I'd taken to sleeping in the chair by the bedchamber window from the first night, too worried about Ethan to leave his side for very long. Pierre tried to coax me away at first, but gave up soon enough, instead dragging in a second chair and more cushions, which he pushed together so I could stretch out if I wanted.

Ethan grew sicker in the next few days, not better, and the frown that never left Scholar Josue's face said I had reason to worry. Other men who'd fought at Ethan's side, including Robert, had sickened not long after the battle ended. All of them had been wounded in some way, but even men who'd suffered little more than a scratch had died. Josue told Pierre he suspected poison of some kind, but he couldn't say what poison, or whether it had been the English troops or Giles' men using tainted blades.

I asked Pierre to find out which local spirits and saints the altars in the warriors' cemetery honoured. I didn't own anything, not even the clothes I wore, and food meant for me was the best I could do, so fasting for a day and a night gave me a small offering. My brother agreed to climb the hill, plead with the spirits and leave the food as payment for Ethan's life while I stayed behind and prayed.

The fever that started on the fourth day had broken on the eighth, but a full twelve days after the attack Ethan still slept his days and nights away. He would wake long enough to drink Josue's potions or a little water, then drop back into a deep sleep. I'd never seen him so still and quiet. So silent.

I'd begun to fear he'd slip away and never wake. Finally came a day when Scholar Josue gave me more hope.

'We've one less thing to worry over, Jeanne.' He pressed his fingers against the pulse in Ethan's throat and shut his eyes, counting. 'His heartbeat is stronger and the potions are doing their job. He'd lost more blood then I first thought, but bleeding likely washed some of the venom out of the wounds and saved his life. Now it's just a matter of the last of the poison working its way out of the body. He'd be nearly recovered otherwise.'

I clutched Ethan's hand tight. 'Was Robert able to discover what the blades were coated with?'

He sat on the window ledge and shook his head. 'The English swords were clean. The noble knights taken prisoner were horrified at the suggestion they'd do anything so dishonourable. Some felt compelled to cut themselves with their own blades to prove they'd told the truth.'

'But Giles isn't worried about what's honourable,' I said. 'He wants the crown, no matter the cost.'

'So it appears,' Josue said. 'Not all of Giles' troops carried tainted blades. The duke kept the secret of what venom he'd used confined to a small circle. I suspect he gave orders to go after Charles and anyone he couldn't afford to lose, or the people closest to him. A small force tried to break through to Lady Maud, but Robert's men drove them off.'

Charles and most of the court had been blessed: they had escaped being poisoned. Ethan and Robert were the only close advisors Giles' men managed to wound, but they'd been in the thick of the fighting from the start, fighting alongside those men who'd rallied to their side.

In total, some threescore of Lady Maud's guard and Robert's soldiers showed signs of having been poisoned. Captain Lucien was one of the first to die, a loss that broke Sarah's heart. Lady Talia died a day later. The only wound she'd taken was a small cut on her hand, but the poison killed her just as readily. Stories that Lord Giles had cut her deliberately before he fled spread rapidly, fuelling the soldiers' anger. Those stories were all too easy to believe.

Josue couldn't save everyone, but he'd saved Ethan and Robert. No matter how selfish it felt, I couldn't help being grateful.

The physician held out his hand. 'Come away, Jeanne, and have supper with your brother and Sarah – servants are bringing in food from the banquet. You've barely left Ethan's side or eaten in more than a week. Time outside this room will be good for you. I don't want you to fall ill too.'

Three faint lights shimmered in the corner. My voices had been here most of the time, never moving and never speaking. I worried about leaving Ethan with them more than that he'd take a turn for the worse, for all the monsters still claimed he was fated to be my champion.

'All right.' I stood and watched Ethan sleep, relaxed and serene, for all neither of us had much peace in our lives. I asked God to give him happy dreams and followed Josue into the sitting room.

Pierre and Sarah sat side by side on the floor, their heads bent over a set of plans spread across a low table. My brother grinned at me, but went back to listening to Sarah explain the system of gears and pulleys she'd designed to improve the trebuchet's aim. The two of them had become fast friends after their rocky start together, according to Pierre, and they spent hours going over the plans Sarah had drawn and discussing improvements. Weapons Master Nicholas joined them at times, making suggestions for things he'd like to have and taking away any drawings of weapons he could have built for the castle armoury immediately.

Neither Lady Maud nor Charles had any idea that Sarah deserved the credit for the improvements, both big and small, that were making their war engines superior to those the English brought to the battlefield. Sarah had sworn the weapons master to silence and let him take the credit. The rest of us kept her secrets for reasons of love and friendship.

I ate my fill of spiced beef, cheese, dried berries and fresh bread, half listening to Pierre and Sarah cheerfully quibble over ideas I didn't understand, all the while half listening for Ethan. Josue checked on him twice, patting my shoulder on the way back to his seat to let me know all was well, but I still couldn't shake my restlessness and the need to do something, even if it was just watching Ethan breathe.

A knock on the corridor door set my heart to pounding. Sarah grabbed a piece of needlework off the chair behind her and went to the door. She waited until Pierre had moved over so it would look as if he'd been the one studying the plans before she pulled the door open.

Charles stood in the corridor, five guards behind him. The Dauphin smiled. 'My apologies for disturbing your evening, Lady Sarah. I'd like to visit Ethan, if I may.'

With a smile, Sarah ushered him in. 'Please, Your Grace, come inside.'

He waved his guards back and closed the door himself. Pierre and Josue had scrambled to their feet and were bowing, but I stood more slowly, strangely uneasy that he'd waited so long to visit

Ethan's sickbed. Given all the things he doubtless had to attend to after the attack, the thought was uncharitable at best, but the flutter in my middle wouldn't be ignored.

'He's still sleeping off the after-effects of the poison, Your Grace. He may wake if you speak to him, but don't be surprised if he doesn't.' Scholar Josue hurried to the corridor. 'His room is this way, my lord.'

'Thank you, Scholar.' Charles turned to me, and I thought the smile he gave me was forced, a bit brittle. 'Would you take me in to see him, Jeanne? I understand how hard the last two weeks or so must have been for you, but there are matters we need to discuss. It's important, or I wouldn't trouble you.'

The food in my stomach turned to lead, a bit of alchemy Scholar Josue couldn't accomplish with a few polite words. I swallowed and forced a smile of my own.

'Of course,' I said. 'Follow me, Your Grace.'

Charles didn't so much follow as herd me towards Ethan's room. He paused on the threshold, taking in the vials and bottles of potions lined up on the window ledge, the basin of water and stack of clean linen next to the bed, the soiled linens and bandages in a bucket on the floor. The future King of France stared longest at his friend lying there unmoving, and I dared anyone to say the worry I saw on his face wasn't real.

When he finally moved all the way into the room, I shut the door, knowing he wanted privacy. Charles glanced at me. 'I trust you to tell me the truth. Will he truly be all right, Jeanne?'

'Yes, my lord, he will. He still needs time to shed the last of the poison, but Ethan will heal.'

'Then God has answered one of my prayers.' He crossed himself and sucked in a deep breath. 'Sit down, Jeanne, and so will I. Neither of us needs to stand to watch him sleep.'

Charles dragged over a smaller chair from the opposite side of the room and positioned it so that he could easily see Ethan, then gestured me to the chair I normally slept in. He gripped the arms of the chair, his knuckles bled white and his jaw clenched. Whatever he wanted to say wasn't coming easily. The light from my voices flared bright behind him and I braced myself, dread growing inside.

His next words made my heart race. 'I need answers from you, Jeanne. I took Ethan and Robert at their word when they told me the men forcing the sword on you had found the sword by accident and overreacted: that made more sense than angels telling them where to dig. But rumours continue to spread about angels sending visions naming you as the Maid of Lorraine. One story claims you were carrying the sword the day of the attack. So I need to ask you directly: are you *La Pucelle*?'

He stared at me, hope flickering in his eyes. Charles wanted to believe as desperately as I wanted to deny having anything to do with the Maid or the legends surrounding her.

'Do you think I'm the Maid, my lord?' Tears filled my eyes. I held my arms away from my sides. 'Do I look like a great hero, Charles? Or a warrior who can drive the English into the sea and save France? I can barely lift the Maid's sword.'

He ran his fingers through his hair. 'I'm not sure what I think matters much, if at all. The men speaking of visions and angels believe, and their belief spreads to every man who hears their story. And I have to ask myself: why now, Jeanne? Why only since you came into our lives? Before Ethan brought you into my camp, I hadn't heard a whisper about the Maid since I was a boy. Now *La Pucelle* is on every soldier's lips and your name follows with the next breath. That must mean something.'

My mind raced, still looking for a way out and not sure how much of the truth I could tell Charles. He was Ethan's friend, not mine, and I didn't know how far he'd go to win the throne. 'I can't say why they chose me or what I think it means, but what I think doesn't appear to matter either, my lord. Are you certain the creatures sending these visions are angels?'

Charles looked up sharply. 'Do you know they're not?'

My monsters flashed into full view and yanked me into a vision: Michael stood behind Charles, a guardian with his flaming sword held high. Catherine held the Maid's blade pressed against my throat, while Margaret lifted a golden crown set with emeralds and rubies and set it on the Dauphin's head. Their light expanded to wrap Charles in a soft halo.

Catherine forced me to kneel at his feet and while I handed the new king the Maid's sword, she whispered lies in Charles' ear, each misdeed and bit of treachery worse than the next. I shut my eyes when he lifted the sword, but the blade never touched my neck. Instead, Ethan's head rolled to a stop against my knee. I screamed and screamed, the sound echoing around the throne room, and I knew I'd never stop.

'You made the choice to accept your destiny when you took the sword from the chest, Jeanne, a choice freely made and binding.' Catherine's icy fingers caressed my cheek. 'You can't go back. Jeanne d'Arc is the Maid, now and for ever.'

When I could see what was in front of me again, I found Charles frowning and still waiting for me to answer.

'No, my lord,' I whispered and tucked shaking hands into my lap. 'I don't know for certain they aren't angels. Fear got the better of me.'

His expression softened. He reached out and took my hand,

and the monsters' trap snapped shut. There would be no escape this time.

'You've never been in battle before and I'd worry if you weren't afraid,' he said. 'We'll find a way to keep you out of the thick of the fighting, maybe holding a banner on a hilltop to give the men something to rally around. Knowing the Maid is on the field will give them strength and hope.'

I watched Ethan's steady breathing, the only thing stopping me from curling into a ball and weeping. There was no answer I could give him. Even if I didn't fall in my first battle, others would die trying to keep me alive.

Charles cleared his throat. 'Put it out of your mind for now, Jeanne. Robert and I need to talk. You'll have plenty of time to get used to the idea. I won't leave Maud to go back into the field until I know she'll be safe.'

I looked at Ethan, sprawled across the bed and utterly defence-less, and the same fear I imagined Charles felt loosened my tongue. 'Did you discover how the English got inside the grounds? I've been with Ethan since the attack and not much news reaches me.'

Charles wiped a hand over his face before he stood. 'We did. An almost forgotten gate hidden at the back of the rose garden. Sarah's great-great grandsire ordered the gate bricked up years ago, but time and weather weakened the mortar. People walk in the rose garden at all hours. None of us guessed some were Giles' men searching for weaknesses along the outside wall. We should all thank God his lordship didn't bring the English in after dark.'

I shivered, imagining the panic caused by unknown enemies ram-paging through the castle in the dark, leaving death in their wake. Thanking Holy Mary for that blessing didn't seem like enough.

Charles paused before opening the door. 'I want to know when he wakes, Jeanne. Send word, if you would.'

'I will, my lord.'

He left then, and the monsters left with him, shutting me in a near-silent room to wrestle with thoughts of killing and death. The Maid's sword hung on a clothes-peg pounded into the wall behind the door, hidden from sight when the door was open. I stared at the blade now, imagining the weight in my hand, what the edge cutting into flesh would sound like and how the shock running up my arm would feel.

Pierre had killed the English knights who'd murdered our father and I'd watched that battle. I'd heard Papa's screams, the attackers' taunts and the horrible sound of a man drowning in his own blood. No matter how much I had prayed, I couldn't avoid my fate. Bile burned the back of my throat.

I kicked off my shoes and shoved my chairs against the bed so I was next to Ethan, something I'd never done before. Feeling alone frightened me more than someone seeing this and starting more rumours about me. About *us*.

Ethan's chest rose and fell, soft and easy, each breath a reminder of how hard he was clinging to life. I pulled a pillow into my arms, a poor substitute for holding him close, and rested a hand on his arm. He sighed and sank deeper into sleep.

Weeping didn't ease the ache in my chest; if anything, the pain grew worse. Keeping Ethan safe from the monsters controlling my life might mean making him hate me enough to leave.

I didn't know if I had the strength to drive him away, or what I'd do if my strength failed me.

*

Dawn light filtered through the shutters when I woke, tinting the walls in stripes of rose and indigo. Someone – likely Pierre or Sarah – had covered me with a blanket during the night and left me to sleep. They had watched me struggle with not being able to help Ethan and the fear of losing him; they understood why I needed to be near him.

Ethan's eyes were open, watching me the way I'd been watching him sleep all these days. His hand shook but he brushed the hair back from my face and smiled. 'Good morning, little sister.' His voice was rough and he had to swallow a few times before going on, 'Could I trouble you for a little water? Once I have a sip or two, you can crawl under your blanket again.'

The water jug was freshly filled and I blessed the person who'd tiptoed in and out while we slept, filled the mug and helped Ethan drink until he lifted his head and murmured, 'Thank you, that's enough for now.'

I eased him back down, terrified of hurting him or, God forbid, reopening a wound. He didn't take his eyes off my face as I tucked the bedclothes around him, studying my features as if he needed to remember who I was. He took my hand when I started to fuss with the pillows.

'Sit down and talk to me, Jeanne. Watching you move around is making my head spin.' He squeezed my fingers and let go. 'Please, tell me what's happened while I've been battling death.'

Sitting on the edge of the bed made me nervous at first, reminding me of times when I was much younger and Grand-mère scolded me for things I'd done in all innocence, calling them sinful. But Ethan took my hand in both of his and smiled and I found that I didn't really care what others thought. Aside from Sarah and Pierre, he was the only person I could trust, probably the only person in Charles' circle who wouldn't be willing to sacrifice me for the sake of winning the crown. I asked Mother Mary for forgiveness that I'd ever thought of sending him away.

'Where should I start?' I asked.

'Start with how long I've been in bed.' He frowned. 'I've taken much worse injuries and not been out of my head for days. Did the wounds sour that quickly?'

'No, my lord.' He deserved the truth, horrible as the truth was. 'Giles poisoned his soldiers' blades and sent a force after Charles and his close advisors. They failed to strike anyone but you and Robert, and both of you survived the poison. I'm afraid the men fighting with you took heavy losses.'

Rage filled his eyes, but I was sure the weariness pulling at the corners of his mouth would stop him from seeking revenge any time soon. 'How many died?'

'Sixty of Robert and Maud's men showed signs of poisoning,' I said. 'Scholar Josue saved all but twenty-six.'

'Twenty-six . . . Mother of God.' He crossed himself with a shaking hand. 'May God have mercy on their souls and grant them rest.'

Ethan was quiet a long time, his eyes shut and his head turned to the side. The only signs he hadn't fallen asleep again were the sound of his breathing and the throbbing vein in his neck. I guessed he was thinking about what I'd said and looking for a way around his anger.

At last he sighed and turned back towards me. 'You don't have to tell me Giles brought the English inside the walls. A man lacking honour doesn't care who he hurts. Do Charles and Robert know how they got in?'

I told him the story about the old gate in the rose garden, followed by all I could remember of the days he'd been sleeping.

The chamber stayed quiet, but unless Sarah and Pierre were shut away in her workshop, the silence wouldn't last. I needed peace and privacy to tell him about Charles' visit, and the Dauphin's conviction that I was the Maid of Lorraine.

Ethan was the only one I could trust to remain calm. My brother would fly into a rage and Sarah would follow, only a step or two behind at most. Challenging Charles and making him angry was far worse than where things stood now.

'What's wrong?'

I looked up, startled, and found Ethan watching me.

'Something else happened. I can see it in your eyes, Jeanne.'

'Charles came to visit you last night. I'm to tell him the moment you wake, but he came to see me too.' I shut my eyes and struggled to keep my voice even, calm. 'The Dauphin believes all the stories saying that I'm the Maid. Men in Maud's guard and Robert's troops are claiming angels have sent them visions, naming me *La Pucelle*. Charles is convinced that so many men having visions means something, especially now, and he's trying to decide how to make good use of what's happening. He wasn't jesting, Ethan. He meant it.'

Ethan frowned 'Making use of these visions means involving you, little sister. Did he say how? Even Charles must see you're no warrior.'

'He knows I can't fight.' Not that it mattered. 'Charles is going to meet with Robert so the two of them can best decide how to use me. He said something about holding a banner atop a hill.'

'Mother of God . . . Why does having royal blood make so many men fools? Charles doesn't even want to be king. If there were anyone to give the crown to other than Giles, he would.' Ethan tried to shift towards me and grimaced. 'Help me get onto my side, if you would. I've been in this spot too long.'

I piled cushions behind Ethan to keep him from rolling back again. Enough signs of pain left his face to prove that moving him was a good thing. I sat on the edge of the bed and he took tight hold of my hand again.

'Charles is a good man. I don't want to believe he'd do anything that would get you hurt,' Ethan said. 'But he also embraces wild schemes, only to abandon them later. Robert won't agree to put you in danger. I won't either.'

A flash of vision came to me: I stood on a hilltop, desperately clinging to a pole and struggling to keep a huge banner from flying away in the wind. My monstrous voices stood to one side, silently watching.

Ethan and Pierre stood shoulder to shoulder a few strides downhill, swords drawn and ready to defend me, and I remembered the dream I'd had a year before. This time, Robert's bulk was at my back. Cries of *The Maid! The Maid!* filled the air. The grim expressions on my brother's and Ethan's faces confirmed my fears. Not all the cries came from the Dauphin's army.

No more than an instant had passed, but the weary lines in Ethan's face were already deeper. Fighting to keep my hands from shaking, I pulled my courage close. Now wasn't the time to shatter his faith in Charles, or to remind him that kings often rejected wise counsel and did what they pleased. He might argue, but he still needed to be cared for.

I smiled and pulled the blanket up higher. 'Do you think you could manage a little food? Maybe some soft cheese, or bread soaked in wine?'

'Don't try to distract me, Jeanne,' he said. 'I gave my word to protect you from anyone wanting to do you harm, and that includes Charles. My promise still stands.'

I squeezed his fingers and stood. 'I'm not doubting or losing faith in you, but winning a battle of wills with Charles will be easier if you have the strength to stand. Food will hurry that along.'

The door opened quietly to reveal Pierre holding a serving tray filled with bread, a wedge of cheese and several small bowls. His eyes went wide at seeing Ethan awake, but a delighted grin quickly followed.

'Good morrow, my lord! Seeing you awake means my sister's prayers have been answered, and likely a few of Sarah's as well.'

Ethan laughed. The sound was breathless and thin, but still lifted my spirits.

'What about your prayers, Pierre? Did opening my eyes answer any of those?'

'One or two.' My brother carried the tray over to the window ledge and set it down before picking up the cushions and pillows from the chairs I'd slept in, tossing them in the corner and taking a seat. 'I prayed hardest that God would give my sister a reason to stop weeping. I'd have gone into hell and dragged you back if you'd died, all to keep her from crying again.'

Pierre sounded amused, but Ethan's expression was serious and solemn as he watched me. 'Were you that certain I'd go to hell, Pierre?'

'Father Jakob told me before I left Domrémy that all mercenaries go to hell. Then he tried to convince me I'd regret coming here. Once Sarah told me how you saved my sister and kept her safe, I knew Jakob was the one going to hell.' My brother shrugged. 'The priest also told me that you'd lead me into the same sins that already damned Jeanne, and for the sake of my eternal soul I should abandon her. God will likely forgive me for only knocking him down twice when I really wanted to beat him bloody.'

The fierce, feral growl I'd heard before threaded through Ethan's voice, fainter and weaker, but still enough to make me shiver. 'I'm not concerned with forgiveness. I've already vowed to kill this man for the wrongs he did Jeanne.'

My face burned hot, flustered to the point I turned my back to keep from seeing Ethan's expression. I'd told him about Father Jakob's lies and about Claude, but I couldn't shed the fear he'd think less of me after my brother's story and even knowing how foolish such thoughts were didn't help.

Not admitting, even to myself, why what he thought of me mattered so much made it worse. Mama had been less than a year older than me when she'd fallen in love and married my father and she'd known she loved him long before that – but my parents' lives were simpler than mine.

Telling Jacques d'Arc that she cared wasn't tangled around three monsters claiming Isabelle was the saviour of France, nor did the shadow of war dog her heels.

Nothing about my life was simple. I couldn't risk pulling Ethan deeper into the trap with me.

I busied myself with filling one of the bowls on Pierre's tray with food I thought might tempt Ethan to eat. The jug was watered wine. I half-filled a mug, took a breath to steady myself and turned around to face him.

Ethan was sound asleep again, looking relaxed and peaceful. I watched him for a moment before I shoved the mug and bowl of food at Pierre.

'Stay with him, please,' I whispered. 'Don't let him wake up alone.'

'I won't.' Pierre touched my hair. 'Where will you be?'

I pointed at the window. 'In the rose garden. Call if you need me.'

The garden was deserted this early. Hurrying down the gravel path felt too much like running away, so I forced myself to a walk. Finding a bench screened by dark green leaves and sweet-smelling blooms wasn't hard in a garden built for lovers.

As long as I kept my eyes closed, I could ignore the monsters standing at my shoulder. Birds chattered and scratched in the dirt, looking for seeds or insects, while others sang from the treetops. Squirrels dashed up and down tree trunks, feeding the young still in their drey. Warm sunshine washed over me and I tipped my head up, a wildflower tracking the sun, hoping to bake the grief out of my bones.

Choices freely made didn't come with fewer regrets – nor did the things given up hurt any less.

I'd sent a message to the Dauphin that Ethan had awakened, but six days had passed since then and Charles still hadn't found the time to visit.

Ethan's strength was returning, if slowly, and he still spent most of his day on the bed napping, or sitting in a well-cushioned chair. Scholar Josue was allowing him short walks around the suite, but so far had refused to let him venture outside. Ethan grumbled, but obeyed, which I took as a sign of how weak he still was.

Hoping to distract him, I'd asked a question about the places he'd travelled before joining Charles and he sent me to beg a map from Sarah. We'd spent time looking at the map each day since. Ethan taught me to recognise the countries where he'd travelled by their shapes and told me stories of the places where he and his band of mercenaries had stayed. Strange cities were full of unfamiliar things, strange foods and animals I'd never heard of, and his stories let me imagine seeing them myself.

Each distant land he remembered sparked more stories, delighting me and holding his growing boredom at bay. Not all the tales were happy ones, nor were they all centred around the battles he'd fought, but I wanted to hear them nonetheless, and taking me at my word, he didn't skip over anything.

Scholar Josue had just left Ethan's side and we'd settled into side-by-side chairs to study the map. I didn't think anything of the door opening, or the pause before it closed again, so looking up to see Charles standing there was a surprise. I hurried to untangle my feet from my skirts to stand but the Dauphin waved me back to my seat.

'Don't get up, Jeanne.' He tugged a chair from the corner over to sit near Ethan. Sinking onto the thick cushions, he grinned. 'No one but Maud knows I snuck away, but I couldn't leave this any longer. How are you, my friend?'

'Cranky and impatient, and a trial to all who have to deal with me.' Ethan glanced at me and smiled. 'Even so, Scholar Josue says I'm healing more quickly than he'd feared. Another week and he'll allow me to walk in the gardens. He promises I can go back to the practice yard to regain my strength soon after. I'm holding him to that promise.'

'Excellent news all the way around. I need your good sense at council meetings again.' Charles sat back, more at ease than I'd seen him in weeks. 'I have news as well, but I need a promise that the secret won't leave this room. Maud and I will have a child this winter – she says the babe should be here by Yule, maybe a few weeks before.'

The Dauphin didn't appear to notice Ethan's relaxed smile becoming guarded.

He regained control, and reached for my hand, a reaction to

Charles' news that surprised me. 'God has smiled on you, Charles,' he said. 'I know how hard you've prayed for another baby. Have the Church fathers relented?'

Charles shook his head. 'Heirs are required for kings or they end up fighting distant cousins for the throne. Even the bishops will see the sense in that and stop blocking our marriage. But I want this child for Maud as much as I want an heir. She still cries for our son.'

Now I understood why Ethan couldn't share his friend's optimism. He knew better than anyone that the Church wouldn't let Maud's child inherit the crown. Rome would force the Dauphin to put Maud aside, declare their children bastards and marry a woman whose noble blood wasn't tainted by scandal. Even kings were forced to obey the pope and if Charles thought otherwise, he was lying to himself – and worse, he was lying to Maud.

Ethan looked down at his hands instead of answering immediately and I could feel Charles' building annoyance over the continued silence prickling my skin.

I said the first thing to come into my head. 'Is Lady Maud well, my lord?' I asked.

'She's had a little trouble keeping food down, but nothing else has troubled her and even that is starting to let up. Both the midwife and Josue say all is as it should be.' He leaned forwards and braced his hands on his knees. 'We won't take to the field until Maud is safely delivered of child. I don't want to leave her alone before then. And that will give Ethan time to finish healing, and allow you to learn to ride, Jeanne.'

Light sparkled in the corner where Charles had found his chair, signalling the arrival of my voices. They'd left Ethan and me to ourselves most days and their appearance at that moment sent cold fear spiking into my middle. 'Ride, Your Grace?'

'Your leg is healed, Jeanne,' he said, sounding amused. 'You can't expect Ethan to carry you into battle the way he carried you here.'

Anger brewed in Ethan's eyes – a storm I feared – but his voice remained level and calm. 'I beg pardon, my lord, but I don't see the need for Jeanne to ride into battle at all. She's not a warrior and shouldn't be anywhere near a battlefield. I've heard some of the stories of angels and visions the men pass among themselves, but that's all they are: stories. The men naming her the Maid are desperate for God to provide miracles that don't exist.'

'If it were only a few men making these claims, I'd agree, but my commanders tell me that nearly my entire army believes, and many have had visions. Those men are loyal, Ethan, and they know better than to lie to me.' A muscle jumped in Charles' jaw, but he was still smiling. 'Angels sent the soldiers' visions revealing Jeanne is the Maid. A lot of them saw her carrying the Maid's sword the day of the attack. I can't blame them for believing God has sent them miracles and signs.'

'And you're willing to sacrifice Jeanne for their belief?' Ethan let go of my hand and gripped the arms of his chair instead, clearly angry now and struggling for control. 'She took the sword that day to keep Giles or the English from seizing it, not to go charging into the fray. Stop and think about what you're asking, Charles. She can barely lift the blade!'

'Enough.' The Dauphin's tone demanded obedience. 'I've no intention of sacrificing Jeanne or anyone else, or of sending her into the thick of the fighting, but the men need to see her on the field. Maud's women are making a banner for her to carry now.'

Ethan stared at Charles, his face still. 'You have always said you valued my counsel because I was honest with you. I'm being honest now, Charles. You're making a mistake. Don't do this.'

243

'Try being honest with yourself.' Charles shoved the chair back hard and stood, looming over Ethan. 'You're acting like a lovestruck boy, not someone I can rely on to make command decisions. The only mistake I made was not seeing what was going on sooner.'

'Jeanne – leave us, please.' He never took his eyes off the Dauphin's face. 'Would you wait in the rose garden until we've finished.'

'Ethan . . .'

'Please, little sister.' He touched my face and gave me a fleeting smile. 'Wait in the garden. I'll be fine.'

I ran to the rose garden, trembling head to foot and feeling like a coward for not staying with Ethan. Choosing a bench within sight of Ethan's window was foolish. I couldn't help but hear Charles' angry voice or the shameful things he accused Ethan of doing. Ethan's quiet answers seemed to anger the Dauphin more. He was shouted down, his words lost. Unable to bear listening to their friendship shatter, I fled deeper into the garden.

Pierre found me hours later, sitting at the edge of a pool and watching the small bright fish. Rainbows shimmered on the wings of insects skimming the water, though many fell prey to the fish just under the surface. It was peaceful here, and I'd been able to curl over my knees and pray without anyone seeing. My brother offered his hand, pulled me to my feet and into a hug.

'Is Ethan all right?' I asked.

'Yes, little bird. I made him promise to stop pacing the chamber while I searched for you. I hope he's fallen asleep.' My brother brushed my hair back. 'He's worried about what you heard Charles say. Given how long you've been hiding, I'd say far too much. Let's go back before he decides to hunt for you himself.'

Pierre put his arm across my shoulders while we walked. My monsters slowly brightened into view, floating along the path just ahead of us. I sent a prayer to Holy Mary, asking for courage, and turned my back on them to look into my brother's eyes.

'I need to know if one thing Charles said is true.'

He smiled. 'Ask. I won't lie to you.'

I fought to keep the tremble from my voice. 'Charles was yelling such terrible things. He accused Ethan of making me his whore, but Ethan said something I couldn't hear and Charles apologised – but that didn't end the argument.' I took a breath. 'He accused Ethan of making decisions because he loved me, not because they were the right thing to do or the best strategy. Is that true? Charles . . . Charles made that sound like the worst thing in the world.'

'Is what true, Jeanne?' Pierre looked at me solemnly. 'Making decisions to keep those you love from harm is far from the worst thing in the world. If you're asking whether it's true Ethan loves you – I don't know. I could guess, but that's all it would be, a guess. You really need to ask him, little bird. And before you do, ask yourself if you're prepared for the answer – *whatever* it is.'

My monsters hissed and spat behind me, whispering threatening reminders that I wasn't allowed to marry or seek happiness until Charles had claimed his throne. They wouldn't let go of their web of riddles and lies, but once I'd agreed to take the sword, they'd trapped themselves in what they'd spun as much as me.

They couldn't change the prophecy, and as long as I kept my word and became the Maid, they couldn't harm Ethan, Sarah or Pierre, not without taking the risk that part of their precious prophecy would not come true. They'd insisted I needed all three of my friends by my side to crown the future king.

I took my brother's arm and we started walking again. 'What do I say when I see him, Pierre?'

He laughed softly. 'Say hello or ask if he's hungry. Reassure him you don't think less of him for anything you heard Charles say. The rest will come in time.'

'You're certain?'

'As certain as I can be, Jeanne. I've a little more experience than you, but not enough to predict what will happen.'

The older guard, Bastian, saw us coming down the corridor. When he knocked on the door, Sarah opened it and stepped out, relief filling her eyes. She threw her arms around both of us, holding tight for a moment before she took our hands and pulled us inside.

She glanced in the direction of the bedchamber and lowered her voice. 'Ethan was still awake a few moments ago; I doubt he'll rest until he sees you. I don't know what Charles said to him, but I've never seen him like this.'

'Be glad you didn't hear. Charles destroyed their friendship with lies about the two of us.' I squeezed her fingers. 'If a scrap of it was true, I'd be on the road to Domrémy by now – Ethan might be afraid I left anyway.'

'He doesn't always remember how brave you are, Jeanne,' my brother said and smiled. 'Be gentle when you remind him.'

I didn't feel brave standing in front of the bedchamber door, but whispering a prayer for strength allowed me to slip inside the room. Ethan was stretched out on top of the bed, still wearing his boots, with one arm over his eyes and the other flung up over his head. I'd have sworn he was deep asleep, but I turned around after shutting the door to find him watching me.

Relief I was back, and grief over why I'd hidden away so long, flickered across his face. He was sitting on the edge of the bed by the time I'd crossed the room, studying the scuffed toes of his boots. A small tremor ran through him when I took his hand.

'I thought you were gone, little sister.' Ethan cleared his throat.

'Charles vowed you'd be sent away if I fought his plans to name you the Maid. You were away so long . . . I was afraid he'd kept his promise.'

'I lost track of time, Ethan. If I'd known you had reason to worry, I'd have come back long ago. I'm more sorry than I can say.' I leaned my cheek against his shoulder, breathing in the scent of him. He'd been inside for weeks, but he still smelled of sun-warmed leather and the oil he used to clean his sword. 'Charles will have to drag me into battle if he forbids me to see you, or forces me away from Pierre and Sarah. His men won't find that very inspiring.'

'I hope and pray God will turn him away from this foolish idea,' Ethan said, 'or that Robert can make him see reason. But Pierre and I will protect you, no matter what Charles decides. You've my promise, little sister. I'll keep you safe.'

We sat in silence until Sarah knocked on the door, but after making certain we were all right, she left again.

Neither of us felt the need to speak. All was well between us, or as well as the spectre of war and the monsters watching from the corner would allow. And I found I didn't need to ask Ethan if he loved me, or ask myself if I loved him. I knew.

For now, that had to be enough.

Part Nine

In God's name! Let us go bravely!

Jeanne d'Arc

My seventeenth summer flew past quickly, there and gone in a blur.

With the poison finally out of his blood, Ethan's wounds healed just as fast as the season vanished. Scholar Josue warned him to take it slowly, but neither of us was surprised that Ethan didn't listen. He spent hours in the practice yard, sparring with my brother, determined to regain his strength and agility. Twice in those first few weeks he'd stretched newly formed scars too far and Pierre had to help him back to the chamber, but despite that, he quickly regained his speed and skill.

That was probably for the best. None of us knew how much time we had before war called us away from the safety of strong stone walls.

Four times over the summer months, small bands of English soldiers made a show of approaching the castle wall as if gathering for an attack. The first time, Charles led a force out to meet them, but the English turned and ran into the woods. His commanders had the good sense to talk the Dauphin out of giving chase. Even angry and frustrated as he was at the enemy's refusal to fight, Charles listened.

Duke Robert, with Lady Maud's support, convinced Charles to stay inside the walls and let his commanders deal with repelling any future attacks. They feared – with good reason – that the squads attacking were nothing more than decoys meant to lure Charles out into the open. The war would end quickly if he was captured or killed.

By late summer, it was clear to all of us that we probably wouldn't leave the castle until spring. Maud's face and belly were growing rounder almost by the hour and the Dauphin was in no hurry to leave her. His commanders complained to Ethan and Robert about lost ground and opportunities, but none of them dared say anything to Charles. His temper grew shorter as Maud's confinement drew closer.

Our future king's patience was shortest of all with Ethan.

They'd come to a compromise of sorts since that horrible first argument, aided by Duke Robert. Charles agreed he would not set me atop any hills, or whatever passed for higher ground, alone. Ethan, Robert and Pierre would act as my personal guard while I was on the battlefield – the Maid's Champions, as Charles named them. I loathed the name almost as much as I feared what it stood for.

The friendship between the Dauphin and the mercenary remained broken, taking any influence Ethan had with it. Even small concessions were hard-fought and hard-won. I blamed myself, even though Robert insisted I shouldn't.

'Charles is entirely responsible for the rift between them.' The rose garden was nearly empty this early in the day, but Robert still kept his voice low. 'Ethan has tried to get His Grace to see you are the least likely warrior in France, but Charles descends into a raging fervour if anyone suggests you aren't the Maid. I never thought I'd say this, but I'm worried about him. He and Ethan almost came to blows the last time they spoke – over the number of spare horses in the stables, of all things. One of the commanders suggested we needed more, Ethan agreed, and that sent Charles into a rage. Thank the Good Lord that Ethan kept his temper and stayed calm.'

I didn't answer until we'd gone past a young couple screened by a double row of wildly blooming yellow roses. The sound of a breathless sigh, followed by a long, drawn-out moan followed us down the path.

Robert didn't comment on the flaming blush burning in my face, but he quickened our pace until the couple were out of earshot.

'Surely Charles' temper will cool once Maud is delivered safely, and God willing, he'll remember who his friends are,' I said. 'I can't believe Ethan and His Grace won't mend this eventually.'

Robert still looked worried. 'The quarrel with Ethan isn't the only reason I'm concerned,' he admitted. 'Charles' father and grandfather were both near his age when they suddenly went mad. Physics and clerics alike attested they were sane, rational men one moment and raving murderers the next. His Grace was just a baby when his father died and I had thought he'd escaped his father's fate, but now with his insistence that angels are delivering visions and you're the Maid of legend . . . well, I can't help but question his sanity. These are not the actions of a sane man.'

I stopped in the middle of the path, forcing him to face me. Catherine flashed into view behind Robert, her dark, star-filled eyes warning me to take care. The Dauphin's mad behaviour wasn't a puzzle to me. 'Give him time, my lord Duke. Charles is still young and more unsure than he wants to admit, not a madman. Ethan tells me he is under enormous pressure from the older lords to gather all the men he can and take the war to the English. And he's worried about Lady Maud – all of that combined would make any man lash out, even at friends.'

'I pray you're right, Jeanne.' He took my arm again. 'And I must say, you're being very generous. I don't know if I could be as kind.'

'What do you mean?' The sorrow and uncertainty in his eyes suddenly made my heart pound.

'The legend of the Maid I know . . . well, it didn't end well,' he said. 'The Maid in the story my grandfather always told fought hard and inspired the men battling at her side. She led her army to victory, saving France and putting the Dauphin on his throne. But the newly crowned king didn't sit easy on his throne and he forgot all she'd done for him. He sacrificed the Maid for more power and security. She died at the end of Grandfather's story.'

'And you're afraid Charles is mad enough to sacrifice me?'

'I pray every night that I'm wrong.' He tugged a jewelled cross out of his embroidered tunic and clutched it tight. 'I *want* to be wrong. But the way he fought with Ethan over sending you up that hill? That frightens me.'

'Ethan won't let me be sacrificed,' I said. The truth of those words settled over me, armour of a kind, against the wash of fear that wouldn't let me think. Wouldn't let me act. 'And neither will Pierre.'

Robert smiled but didn't answer. He bowed over my hand outside Sarah's chambers and walked away.

Lord Robert and I hadn't spoken alone since, but the conversation came back to me at odd times. I placed the blame on the monsters standing near the gate into the practice yard.

Most afternoons Sarah and I sat at the far end to watch Ethan and Pierre sparring. The days grew shorter, the light failing earlier as autumn approached. Now torches lit the yard, the flames wavering and casting rippling shadows as the evening wind picked up. My brother and Ethan didn't appear to feel the chill sweeping in with the wind, but Sarah and I did, even huddled under heavy wool shawls.

Sweat on Pierre's shoulders and back glistened diamond-bright in the torchlight, and Ethan's dark skin gleamed a hazy silver. His new scars were still red and angry, impossible to miss. I'd no experience with scars like that, but Scholar Josue assured me they didn't cause Ethan any pain, and with time they'd begin to fade.

Most days the four of us had the practice yard to ourselves and even if I were blind and deaf I'd recognise how Sarah and Pierre felt about each other. They were very careful around Charles or her mother and did all they could to keep the secret from anyone but Ethan and me – she was the noble heir to a castle and all the lands, far above Pierre in rank and status. My brother was training to be a mercenary and if anything, that was looked down on more than being a shepherd.

Her mother would never allow them to marry, not that I was at all sure needing permission to wed would stop them from being together, or finding a village priest to say the vows, at least, not for long. Sarah cared as little for her titles as Ethan cared about his and I suspected she'd give them up for Pierre without regret.

'There.' Sarah laid aside the stick of black chalk she'd used and held up a new drawing. 'As soon as Master Nicholas approves this, I'll draw the fine details in ink. We should have a decent-sized trebuchet built for testing by Yule.'

I couldn't read the labels and notations she'd left all over the parchment, but Sarah had explained how it worked often enough that I could understand the plans. 'The weapons master will be excited to get his hands on this one.'

'The company commanders will be even more thrilled.' She

rolled the parchment and slipped it into a wooden cylinder before collecting her charcoal twigs and pieces of chalk. 'Trebuchets are powerful, destructive war engines, but what you hit depends mostly on guesswork and good fortune. If this works the way we want, artillery officers will be able to hit what they aim at.'

We both looked up sharply when Pierre shouted 'Yield!' Ethan pulled back quickly, his wooden blade held high over his head. My brother dropped to his knees, head down and panting, and before too long ended up on his back. Ethan took advantage of the break and stretched out on a bench.

Sarah glanced at me and shook her head. 'Pierre claims banging wooden swords together and sparring with Ethan is fun. He does allow that the bruises gained while having *fun* hurt. Your brother is a lovely shade of purple from knees to shoulders, but he doesn't plan to stop practising.'

I swallowed the temptation to tease her about how she knew where my brother was bruised and went back to the sketch. 'You've been working on this new trebuchet since before I arrived. Is it finished now?'

She laughed. 'Unless Master Nicholas finds a flaw or the aiming gears bind or the release doesn't work – yes, I think it's finished, but I won't know if the mechanism needs more work until we test the model.'

Ethan groaned and sat up. 'On your feet, Pierre. The English dogs won't allow any rest on the battlefield.'

'Then I'll have to take care of them before I get tired.' My brother winced and hauled himself up. 'None of the English will be the swordsman you are. Dealing with them shouldn't take long.'

'Only if God smiles on you. Never underestimate a man fighting for his life.' Ethan saluted Pierre with his chipped wooden blade and began to circle around my brother, his sword ready. 'Now, attack, or I'll be forced to spend a candle-mark introducing you to the flat of my blade.'

Pierre laughed and the clacking sound of their swords filled the yard again. Sarah leaned forward to watch, her hands clutched tight together and resting in her lap. She'd been distracted by her plans all afternoon, but no longer.

'I worry about them,' Sarah whispered. She glanced at me, her eyes brimming with tears, then went back to watching them spar. 'Pierre tells me not to worry, that God will protect them, but I can't help it. What if they don't come back? God forbid, but what if you don't either?'

'We all worry.' I put my arm around her shoulders. 'But you're the only one brave enough to say so.'

She wiped her eyes on the corner of her shawl. 'What do you worry about, Jeanne?'

'Being alone. Losing Ethan. Pierre. You.' I cleared my throat, trying to speak around the honest words lodged there. 'All of that frightens me more than dying at an English soldier's hands.'

Ethan called a halt, but not to rest, instead talking Pierre through a sword manoeuvre for tight spaces, showing him how to stand, how to grip the sword. Ethan was a patient teacher, Pierre a quick student and the two of them had swiftly become easy in each other's company, friends as well as comrades in arms. Watching them together made me happy.

'Does he know how you feel?' Sarah asked. I looked up, startled, and she laughed. 'Well, does he?'

I shook my head. 'I don't know what to say. He's older – experienced – what if he laughs at me?'

'He's only two years older than Pierre, so not so old. And not as experienced as the gossip Giles encouraged makes him sound.' Sarah took my hand. 'Ethan won't laugh. The first time you say the words is hard, but it gets easier. I tell Pierre I love him at least ten times a day.'

The thought of telling Ethan I loved him, even once, left me quaking in terror, but I took Sarah at her word.

'Have you decided how to deal with your mother?' I asked.

'Her ladyship is too distracted by the child growing inside her to pay attention to her older daughter. Charles' efforts to find a priest who will defy the bishop and marry them takes the rest of her attention. She cares about me, but she cares about Charles and his child more.' She crossed her arms over her stomach and hugged herself tight. 'Mother has no idea where I am or what I'm doing from day to day, or . . . or that Pierre sleeps in my bed. I've always known my role in her life was to marry well and secure my father's lands, but only virgin brides have any value to old men. I destroyed that value weeks ago.'

I put my arms around her, feeling foolish and younger by years, and tongue-tied in the face of Sarah's confession. Pierre laughed at something Ethan said and I suddenly saw him standing at the altar with Sarah, and later, dancing with her at the harvest festival, their young daughter perched on his shoulders. This waking dream had the taste of truth, a promise for their future. I sent a prayer of thanks heavenwards.

'Don't look so sad, Jeanne.' Sarah kissed my cheek and stood. She gathered up her drawing supplies and the tube holding her finished plans. 'I've never been happier. Pierre and I will be married within the month, two at the most. Mother can yell all she likes, but she can't do anything once we've said our vows.'

Pierre was coming towards us, his tunic slung over a shoulder, a couple of strides ahead of Ethan. Sweat soaked his hair and beard, ran down his chest and back, but Sarah pulled his arm around her and leaned against him for the walk back. I watched them until they moved out of sight on the path and vanished, swallowed by the dark of a moonless night. The feeling of loss that suddenly filled me to bursting confused me. I should have felt happy for my brother and Sarah. I didn't understand why all I felt was grief.

'Jeanne?' Ethan looked down the path where Pierre and Sarah had disappeared before he sat next to me. He wiped his face on the tunic bunched in his hand and draped it over his lap. 'Are you ready to go back, or would you rather sit here a little longer?'

'Will it be too cold for you if we sit here?' I asked.

'I'll be fine.' He held up the tunic. 'Talk to me, little sister. I know you well enough to see something's wrong. Let me help if I can.'

'Can you help me feel less a child?' He frowned and I held up a hand in apology. 'I'm sorry, that wasn't fair. You can't explain how I feel if I don't know myself. We should go back.'

He took both my hands in his and twisted around to face me. 'What did Sarah say that upset you?'

'Likely nothing you don't already know. She and Pierre are defying her mother and getting married within a month or two. She said that ... that Pierre has been sleeping in her bed for weeks – and she's never been happier.' I swallowed to ease the ache and tightness in my throat. 'I should be happy too, but all I can think is that I've lost them both, and that makes me feel a selfish fool and a coward.'

He brushed a strand of hair off my face. 'Jeanne – you're not a selfish fool or a coward.'

'Aren't I?' I pulled my hands away and stood, angrier at myself than I'd ever been, and paced over to the practice yard fence.

'Sarah's younger, with so much more to lose, and she's not afraid to take the gift given her. You've no idea how much I envy her that. I can't find the courage to tell you I love you or . . . or to ask if you love me.'

My hated monsters were hissing and spitting threats the instant I said the words, but they didn't brighten into view. I prayed that meant they knew they'd lost this battle. They might force me down pathways I'd never travel willingly, but they couldn't control how I felt.

Ethan's boots crunched on the gravel path as he came up behind me and put his arms around me. My heart raced as he pulled me close.

'Sarah and Pierre are very different people to you or me,' he said. 'Bold and loud and announcing their presence to the world at all times, both equally quick to anger or to laugh. Being quiet doesn't make you a fool or a coward, Jeanne. I have grave doubts what silence says about me. Forgive me if I've hurt you – I'm twice the fool for not telling you that I love you.'

I turned to face him, resting my head on his shoulder and holding on to him. He smelled of salt and sour sweat and I didn't care. We stood silently in the dark like that until well after moonrise. The cold wind rose with the moon, sharp and cutting, chilling both of us to the bone.

We let go of each other reluctantly.

Ethan was shivering when he pulled on his tunic, but we were still in no hurry to go back to the bustle of castle life or face what fate had in store for me. Given the choice, I'd have walked away from all of it and taken Ethan with me. We'd go back to Domrémy or settle in some other village, raise children and grow old, and make a good life together.

I wanted that life so much my chest ached.

My voices would never let me walk away, not until Charles had won his throne and been crowned king. But so many things could go wrong; so many disasters lurked in the shadows, waiting to strike.

No matter what happened, Ethan would be at my side. He wouldn't leave me on my own to face the dangers or the uncertainty ahead: that truth nestled next to my heart.

Pierre leaned against the wall, patiently watching Ethan pace the length of the chamber, turn and come back. Both of them wore their swords, an odd choice of costume for visiting a priest and a hasty wedding, but I was fairly sure Lord Robert would have his on when he finally arrived.

Sarah tried to hide her amusement over Ethan's case of nerves, but I was just as unsettled. Saying vows right away had been Ethan's idea and once dawn lit the sky, he set about making it happen. Father Géraud had reluctantly agreed to marry us in the small chapel, but it had taken two glowering swordsmen, an unhappy lord and several gold coins from Robert's purse before the priest stopped grumbling. He'd had hours to change his mind.

A firm knock announced Robert's arrival. I'd been right about his sword, but the black velvet tunic and gold chains he also wore told me just how seriously he took the occasion. The duke bowed to me and held out a small bouquet of mallow and damask roses. Someone had wrapped the stems in yellow ribbon and tied a bow in a lovers' knot.

Tears filled my eyes as I took the flowers. 'Thank you, Robert. These are beautiful.'

'My mother always said a bride should have flowers to see her on her way.' He held the door and waved us out. 'My sister will meet us at the chapel. Elise will keep Father Géraud busy until we arrive, just in case the good father is contemplating a change of heart. After you.'

Ethan held my right arm; Sarah and Pierre walked on my left. Robert led the way, setting a stately pace that was far too slow for both me and Ethan. We still reached the chapel before sunset.

Lady Elise was as good as her word and Father Géraud even managed a smile as he greeted us and we set about saying our vows. The monsters watched from behind the altar, but that didn't dim my happiness or make me less sure. Marrying Ethan was the right thing, the best thing for both of us. Once Father Géraud had given the final blessing, the guardian spirits vanished in a blinding flash of light.

Pierre and Robert raised their swords and cheered when Ethan kissed me, making me blush. At the wedding feast Elise had organised for us in her chambers, Robert and Pierre both toasted us, we all laughed and joked and I cried more than once at things that were said or remembering people who weren't there. It was well past midnight when we said our farewells. Sarah was staying with Elise and Pierre with Robert, leaving us alone.

The walk back was quiet and dark, giving me too much time to think – too much time to remember the blacksmith's hot breath on my face, his touch and to be terrified all over again. I didn't want to be afraid with Ethan.

Bastian, who guarded our door as he did most nights, gave us his congratulations and wishes for a happy life. I smiled and thanked the old man, touched by his kindness, and went in, leaving Ethan to exchange a few words.

Setting my bouquet of flowers on the bedchamber table was easy. Unpinning the crown of ivy in my hair with shaking hands proved harder, but I managed to work it free. The oil-lamp over the table, the only one lit, was turned down low, but in the soft light the crown I'd worn framed the bouquet perfectly.

I stood in the middle of the room, trembling, unable to force myself to move or to take a chair or sit on the window ledge. Scolding myself for acting so foolishly did no good. Noting all the ways the room I'd slept in for months was different from the high pasture helped a little, but not enough to keep me from shaking. The light falling on the bed was too much like moonlight, the oil-lamp flame too much like a campfire flickering on Claude's tunic.

The door opened, bringing me the sound of Ethan's laugh and Bastian saying goodnight. I hugged myself as the door closed again and listened to his boot heels on the stone floor, trying not to cry. Ethan loved me. He'd never hurt me.

He wrapped his arms around me and kissed the back of my neck and I did cry then, shaking harder than ever, trying not to choke on the sobs filling my chest. Ethan froze, going still and quiet, as if afraid moving would send me running out the door. He wasn't far wrong.

'What's wrong, Jeanne?' he whispered. 'Have you changed your mind about wanting to be with me?'

I shook my head, terrified I'd hurt him deeply. 'No – no, I love you. But I'm afraid.'

'Of me?' He held me even closer, his voice as wounded as I'd feared. 'Jeanne, Jeanne . . . I'd never hurt you. I thought you knew that.'

'Not of you.' I closed my eyes, but that didn't shut the memories out. 'But I can't stop thinking about the valley and . . . and how Claude hurt me . . . and I'm afraid, Ethan. I'm so, so sorry. Please don't be angry with me.'

He turned me to face him and stroked my hair. 'I'm not angry – not with you, Jeanne. I should have remembered – I should have talked to you, made certain you were ready, not made you feel rushed. If you're not ready tonight, you're not. We have a lifetime of nights ahead of us.'

'Are you sure?' I asked.

'Very sure.' He kissed my forehead and smiled. 'My mother taught all her sons that loving a woman is a gift when freely offered. I can wait for you to offer.'

'I wish I'd known her.'

'You're very much like her: stubborn, strong. Beautiful.' He touched my face. 'I have many stories to tell about her if you want to hear them.'

'I'd like that.' Ethan started for a chair and I pulled him back. 'Will you hold me while you tell me? Please?'

'Anything you want, my love.' He leaned in to kiss me, soft and tentative, trying not to startle me.

We stretched out on top of the bed, my head on his shoulder and his arm holding me close. I shut my eyes, losing myself in the sound of his voice. Memories of all the reasons I'd fallen in love with him, his kindness and honesty, began to shove my fear and worries aside.

My parents had loved each other fiercely and completely. I'd grown up hearing whispers and laughter in the dark, the soft sounds that told the story of how much joy they brought each other. I wanted that with Ethan. I wouldn't let a mad blacksmith or anyone else steal that from me.

He stopped speaking in mid-sentence as I slipped my hand under his tunic. My fingers traced his scars and the raised lines of his tattoos, making his belly quiver.

'Jeanne—' Ethan trapped my hand in his and swallowed hard. 'Are you bored with listening to my stories?'

'You never bore me, my lord.' I pushed up to lean on my elbow so I could see his face. 'I'll happily listen to your tales for the rest of my life. But I think . . . I think I want to try now. If you're still willing.'

'I'm willing if you're sure,' he whispered. 'Be very sure, Jeanne, I don't want to hurt you. If you need to stop, say so.'

He let go of my hand and pulled me down for a kiss. There was nothing timid about that kiss or the way he touched me, making my heart race and my breath catch in my throat. Getting undressed sent me reeling towards panic, until Ethan's whispered reassurances pulled me back again. I stopped thinking about anything but showing him how much I loved him.

I woke just before sunrise. Birds sang the sun into the sky, each one in a different voice and with a different song. Pale pink and purple light leaked through the shutters. Even ordinary, worn things glowed in that light. This was my first day as a married woman and I took that as a happy sign.

Ethan slept curled around me. He'd pulled me up tight against his chest and wrapped his arms around me, his breath warm on my shoulder. I'd watched him sleep a hundred, hundred times, but I'd never seen him look this relaxed and content. This happy.

'Holy Mary, let it always be this way. Let our love last and hold us up in times of trouble.' The prayer was no more than a breath sent heavenwards on a sigh. I flung my leg over his and went back to sleep, warm, happy. Blessed.

Let it always be this way.

*

Midday had come and gone by the time Robert arrived at Sarah's chambers. Three men-at-arms unloaded a handcart bearing the remains of our wedding feast, setting the platters on the long tables around the edge of the room, and hurriedly left again.

Ethan slipped his arm around my shoulders, tight-lipped and tense, waiting to speak until Robert shut the door. Pierre and Sarah had taken much the same position on the far side of the room. The Dauphin's reaction would have an impact on their lives as well.

'How did Charles take the news?' Ethan asked.

'Better than I expected,' Robert said.

He piled a double handful of apples on a plate, sat in the chair he favoured and began to peel them with his belt knife. 'Which is to say he didn't yell for long. He was angry over not being consulted, but Lady Maud stepped in and helped smooth things over. She reminded Charles of the bishops forbidding them to marry and how he'd declared repeatedly he'd never inflict the same misery on a member of his court. That cooled his temper.'

Ethan glanced at me and turned his attention back to Robert. 'Hearing that Maud stepped in on our side surprises me, but hearing Charles calmed down is a bigger surprise. His Grace doesn't like having his words turned back on him.'

'Charles adores my mother – and he listens to her,' Sarah said. 'He tolerates comments from Mother that would set him to raging if said by anyone else. I've seen it.'

I looked between Ethan and Robert. 'So we're forgiven?'

'You will be, Jeanne. Charles just needs a little time. I wouldn't be surprised if he sends a wedding gift within the month.' Robert quartered the apple he'd peeled and started on another. 'It will take longer for me to win back into his good graces. I reminded him that not even the King of France can undo vows said before

God. He took offence at the reminder, but I've survived his temper before.'

The duke went back to the table and pulled the covers off all the serving platters, filling the room with the aroma of roast beef and spiced turnips, cheese and fresh-baked bread. My stomach growled loudly, making everyone laugh, and Robert waved us all over to eat.

'I promised my sister I wouldn't let the food go to waste,' Robert said. 'Eat up and we'll celebrate Ethan and Jeanne's first day as husband and wife.'

Talk turned to other things and for once no one spoke of the war waiting outside the castle walls. Our first day of marriage was a happy one, full of laughter and singing and love. When I fell asleep in Ethan's arms, I was still amazed and grateful that happy days were followed by nights full of new joys.

Charles wasn't a forgiving soul and in the midst of my happiness I still worried he'd take his anger out on Ethan; I knew Ethan was worried about the Dauphin turning his wrath on me. I saw the shadow that crossed his face when he thought I wasn't watching.

I couldn't blame him for being afraid for me when I was afraid for him. What gave me a measure of peace was knowing we'd face the chaos and uncertainty of what lay ahead together.

With God's help, we'd keep each other safe.

The nightmare started like all the others.

An army of French dead covered the battlefield. Men lay face-down in churned mud; others turned sightless eyes towards God, all of them lay still and bloating in the sun. I couldn't bear to look at their faces, terrified I'd see a man I knew.

The carrion birds barely noticed as the four of us stumbled past; the crows and the huge vultures my father called bone-eaters were too intent on their feast. One bone-eater pulled its head out of a man's belly, its feathers and beak dyed crimson with fresh blood and a strip of flesh in its mouth. The bird gave me a baleful look, swallowed its meal and dived in for more.

I wanted to weep, to retch, to throw stones at the birds and drive them away. My voices whispered for me to pull the Maid's sword from the scabbard on my back, to lop off the vultures' heads and exact revenge for the dead, but I had neither the heart nor the strength. The sword weighed me down, making me stumble, and made running harder. I wanted to fling the blade away, but all I could do was hold on to Ethan and flee.

Pierre helped Robert limp away from the rout. Blood seeped through the dressing around his thigh and his face was grey with pain, but the duke kept going. We all kept going. If we stopped, we'd die.

Charles waited at the bottom of the hill, mounted on a roan-coloured stallion I'd never seen before and held the reins of our four horses. Gold glinted on the roan's harness and the gold ribbons braided into the mane sent glittering sparks into the air. Our new king wore his crown and a disdainful expression.

The monster named Michael loomed behind Charles, his flaming sword held high and fire flickering in his red eyes. Not for the first time I wanted nothing more than to send him back to the pit in hell he'd risen from. Catherine and Merciful Margaret were nowhere to be seen.

We were less than fifty strides away when Charles pointed at me. 'This is your fault, Jeanne! You never so much as drew your sword. These men died because of you!'

'Please, my lord!' I fell to my knees at the stallion's feet. 'I don't know how to use a sword!'

'Coward.' Charles glanced at the monster named Michael. 'Kill her. She's useless to me.'

He kicked the stallion into a trot and left, taking our horses with him.

Michael stood before me, sword in hand and smiling. I wasn't a coward and I wouldn't look away as I waited to die. The monster's smile grew broader. He swung the sword so it passed over my head, cutting Ethan in two.

Catherine's winter-frost voice whispered in my ear, 'Fight, or this is how it ends. Once the English poison is cleansed from French soil and the king sits on his throne, we've no need of champions and protectors. You earn their lives by wielding the sword.'

'Please, I beg you,' I cried, 'I'm not the Maid!'

'Not yet.' Her frozen fingers caressed my face. 'But you will be soon. Fate put you on this path and you cannot turn away until your task is done. Fight, Jeanne, and win your freedom. Fight, and win their lives.'

A vulture landed on Ethan's body. I screamed and once I'd started, I couldn't stop.

I sat straight up in bed, blind with panic, still trapped in the dream, still screaming. Ethan woke instantly, wrapping me in his arms to keep me from scrambling off our bed and pulling me back down to lie next to him. I stopped trying to run and buried my face against his chest, weeping and unable to speak.

He rubbed my back and murmured in my ear, 'You're all right, love, you're all right. It's only a dream. You're safe.'

We'd been married a little over a month and the ring still felt strange on my finger. Terror was the price I paid for the joy of being Ethan's wife. The nightmares had started within a week of our wedding, growing more vivid and horrible as the days passed.

Pierre's voice came from outside our door. 'Ethan?'

'Just another bad dream,' he called out, pulling the bedcover up over my shoulders as my brother came in. Ethan's arms tightened around me as I cried harder. 'I've got her, Pierre. Go back to sleep. No need for all of us to be awake.'

The room was dark as pitch, dawn hours away. I couldn't have seen my brother's expression if I'd tried, but he'd looked after me since I was born and not being able to protect me from these nightmares upset him deeply. Pierre trusted Ethan, he loved and respected him in a way he'd never respected our older brother, Henri. Even so, Pierre was having a hard time knowing I turned to Ethan first to calm my fears.

'May God grant you both some rest,' Pierre said and pulled the door closed again. 'Call if you need anything.'

God had nothing to do with disrupting my sleep. I wasn't at all convinced even He could take these dreams away.

Ethan waited until I'd stopped crying before he asked the same question he had every night for weeks. 'The same dream again?'

'The same dream.' I stroked his arm, unwilling to fall back into that memory, but knowing I must. 'A battlefield full of French dead. Charles on a strange stallion, a false angel with a sword. A voice . . . a voice claiming the price I'll pay for not using the Maid's sword is that you, Pierre and Sarah will die.'

He swore under his breath, but the fresh anger in his voice surprised me. 'You might be able to rest if Charles would stop encouraging the fools spreading stories of angels. I'm not surprised you're having nightmares. You can't step into the courtyard or walk the gardens during the day without men falling at your feet. His Grace needs to put a stop to this.'

'I'm not sure he can stop it. He certainly doesn't want to. No matter what Charles may have said in the past, he wants to be king. I can see the desire to wear the crown in his eyes each time he speaks to me – and he's convinced I can give him what he wants.'

He stroked my shoulder and didn't answer. I could feel his heart beating hard and fast under my hand and I waited for his anger to cool as he thought things through.

'My father has asked me to come home for Yule. The earl is strong as a bull, but Atu claims he's feeling his age and wants to see me.' Ethan trailed two fingers along my jaw, a smile I couldn't see in his voice. 'And he wants to meet the woman strong enough to steal my heart. Knowing I'm married has likely awakened his dreams of grandchildren. Would you like to go? You'd be safe in my father's keep.'

'Will Charles let us leave?'

'I'm not thinking of asking him.' He trailed the same two fingers down my neck, distracting me and making me shiver. 'We'll go out early one day for you to practise riding and simply not come back. By the time His Grace realises we're gone, he won't be able to catch us. Pierre and Sarah can come too, if they wish. My father will be delighted at the company.'

He didn't need to say that being away from Lady Maud's castle would give them a chance to find a willing priest and marry, but it was my first thought.

'I'd love to meet your father,' I said. 'But Charles will be furious – he'll never forgive us.'

'I've stopped caring about his temper or what might upset him.'

He cupped my face in his hands. 'Say the word and I'll take you away from here.'

I loved him all the more for letting me make the choice. The room was too dark to look into his eyes, though I dearly wanted to, so I contented myself with kissing him instead.

'Take me away from here,' I whispered. 'Hide me away in your father's keep, my lord. I'd like nothing better.'

I shut my eyes and ignored the faint flickers of light near the sword hanging on the wall. For tonight, I wanted to pretend escape would come easy and all we need do was ride away. I held the lie as close and fierce as Ethan held me.

The truth would find me when it chose.

We went out on the horses every morning. Most days Pierre and Sarah went with us and the guards grew accustomed to seeing the four of us leaving the castle grounds. If Charles had people watching, all they saw was Ethan doing as he'd asked, teaching me to ride.

In the afternoons, Pierre and Ethan went out alone, each time carrying small parcels of supplies. Any who asked were told they were scouting for signs the English had moved back into the area around the castle. Not all of that was a lie: Ethan was worried that the beef-eaters would return and besiege the castle, keeping us from leaving.

The cache they built was at the top of a beech, well out of sight deep in the surrounding woodlands and high enough off the ground animals couldn't reach. As well as elm, tall oak and pine grew all around, rotting leaves and fallen branches filling the spaces between trees. The path was only wide enough to ride single file, so no one would stumble over his hiding spot by accident.

He'd borrowed one of Sarah's maps to show me the route he planned to take.

'My father's keep is here.' He pointed to an unmarked spot on the map. Two large roads crossed not far away. 'That's well south of Maud's lands, and if his message still holds true, the fighting has moved west and north. There's a carters' road near the far side of the beech grove. In summer merchants and farmers use it as a shortcut to get to the castle when they've got wares or food to sell to Lady Maud's people. It joins the main road here.'

I watched his fingers trace lines on the map and tap the spots I should remember. 'The craftsmen will be using the winter months to make their goods and farmers won't have anything spare to sell to the castle, will they?'

'Shrivelled carrots and turnips, if that. They'll feed those to the pigs before they make the trek to the castle.' He rolled Sarah's map and slipped it back inside its tube. 'I've travelled that way to my father's keep before. For two days I never saw another person.'

My mind whirled in circles, chasing thoughts that wouldn't hold still. 'Charles won't think to search a farmers' path.'

'Charles rarely gives a thought to peasants unless forced to. He doesn't know the track exists. Lucien would have known; he'd have thought to look for us there.' Ethan crossed himself. 'But the captain is with God and his replacement is about as smart as a stone. I doubt we'll see another soul until we reach the main road.'

I stood and paced our bedchamber, unable to stay still another instant. 'When will we leave?'

'If the weather holds, three days.'

He tapped the tube against his knee and watched me, knowing I'd come to terms with trying to escape – or tire of taking short, measured steps – soon enough. Three days wasn't a long time, but if I could, I'd have left now.

Ethan took my hand when I finally reclaimed my chair, just as there was a knock and Pierre stepped into the room. He was dressed in the torn old tunic he wore in the practice yard. 'Are you ready, Ethan?'

'Give me a moment.' He kissed my cheek and smiled before he stood. Ethan pulled his own sweat-stained fighting gear off the peg behind the door and began to change.

'Take your time. I'm in no hurry to lose again,' Pierre said.

Ethan laughed. 'Fight better and you won't lose.'

My brother made a face and turned to me. 'Did Sarah say how long she'd be with Lady Maud?'

I glanced at the window, trying to gauge how far gone the afternoon was by the angle of the light. 'She wasn't sure, but I thought she'd be back by now. I'll stay behind and walk over with her.'

'Thank you, little bird.' Pierre touched my hair. 'Sarah wasn't eager to visit her mother today, but the lady summoned her and she couldn't refuse. They quarrelled last time they spoke and nothing was settled. She said it was a minor thing when I asked, not important enough to worry me with, but being summoned certainly bothered her. Lady Maud finds reasons to start an argument each time Sarah visits and it's starting to grate on her. She's afraid her temper is going to get the best of her and start real trouble.'

It wasn't like Sarah to quarrel with her mother, even if provoked, and less like her to keep anything from Pierre. I saw the same puzzled worry in Ethan's eyes as he tugged on his boots.

'She'll be fine, Pierre. Mothers and daughters disagree about things at the best of times. All the fuss about the new baby is putting extra strain on both of them.' I stood and kissed his cheek. 'Worry more about besting Ethan.'

'You're probably right,' he said and hugged me. 'Are you ready, Ethan?'

The two of them left with their heads together, joking and talking as they always did. I gathered up my basket of combed fleece and the small drop spindle Ethan had found for me and sat down to spin and wait for Sarah.

I didn't wait long. Sarah burst into the suite, teary-eyed and breathless from running. She didn't do more than glance my way before she went straight to her bedchamber. I followed and found her standing in the middle of the room, silent and still as a statue, staring at the wall covered with her drawings.

She knew I was there, but didn't look at me or speak. When I took hold of her arm, she tried to pull away.

'Sarah, please, you're frightening me. Tell me what's wrong.'

How long she took to answer scared me more.

'Mother plans to disinherit me.' Sarah sniffled and wiped her face on her sleeve. 'She's generously offered a small dowry if I'll marry someone worthy, but she made it clear the offer disappears if I insist on marrying Pierre. I told her I didn't care about a dowry, I'd ... I'd marry him anyway. She was already angry, but I've never seen her fly into such a blind rage before. Mother ... Mother said that was my last chance to do my duty – she's done with me.'

'Oh, Sarah. I'm sorry.' I touched her arm. 'If you just give her a chance to calm down—'

But she was already shaking her head. 'There are conditions in my father's will – he left her everything to hold in trust for her child. *Any* child. My father never imagined Mother would pass

me over in favour of another man's get. My land, my titles ...
my entire inheritance is going to a babe she hasn't even birthed
yet.'

Cold shock slithered up my spine. 'Surely your mother doesn't
mean it – she's just angry ...'

'She does mean it, Jeanne. I meant what I said too. I want Pierre,
not money and titles.' Sarah pulled a small stack of crumpled
parchment out of her pocket. 'Mother threw these in my face – all
the plans I'd given to Master Nicholas over the last seven or eight
months. Then she made me beg to be allowed to pick them up.
I don't know how she got them, but it wasn't from the weapons
master. She threatened to have Nicholas flogged for helping me
defy her, but Charles told her that was going too far. His Grace
wouldn't let her burn them, either.'

Of course not: he knew what those plans meant for his army.
The thought might be uncharitable, but God would forgive me
for recognising the truth.

Sarah sat on the edge of the bed, unfolding and smoothing each
of her drawings, stacking them next to her. Tears streamed down
her face and dripped off her chin, but she managed to keep the
parchment dry.

I sat next to her, not knowing what to say or do.

She set the last drawing aside and stared at the smudges of
charcoal on her fingers. 'Mother ... wasn't finished. Someone told
her I was carrying Pierre's baby and she started raging at me – she
kept saying I was having "that filthy peasant's bastard". But I'm
not with child and I told her so – but who would tell her such a
cruel lie? She called me a lying whore, Jeanne, and she *struck* me.
Charles had to pull her away so she'd stop hitting me.'

I put my arms around her, rocking her the way my mother

had comforted me when I was small. Sarah stared at the ink and charcoal drawings on the wall and didn't make a sound.

My monsters filled the room, blinding me, and loomed over us so suddenly I couldn't catch my breath. Catherine reached for Sarah, her fingertips sprouting talons as I watched. Panicked, I curled over Sarah protectively, as if my body could protect her from whatever harm Catherine intended. I'd never heard any of these creatures laugh before, but the sound of pealing bells filled my head, leaving no doubt Margaret was laughing at me now.

'Enough!' Michael's booming voice made me tremble. Catherine pulled back her hand and Margaret fell silent. His next words drove shards of ice through my heart. 'I won't toy with you or your companions the way my sisters do, Jeanne. Heed my words. Any of us could stop Sarah's heart with a touch, steal Ethan's breath as he sleeps or guide an arrow through Pierre's eye. Taking the sword from the chest means *nothing* if you won't use it. Be the Maid in truth or they will all suffer in your place. They will all die. *There will be no more warnings.*'

A hundred visions, a hundred ways the people I loved might suffer and die, ran through my head, each more horrible than the one before, and more terrible than the nightmares that made me scream and weep at night.

The monsters vanished in another blinding light. I desperately clung to Sarah, muttering comforting nonsense and shivering.

Betrayal was another path to suffering, another way to inflict pain on the people I loved, another way to punish me for not charging into battle. I didn't know who my monsters had used to betray Sarah, but in the end, it didn't matter.

This was my fault. My monsters had told me again and again I'd no choice but to wield the sword. Warned me. I'd only yielded

277

to them in small ways, small surrenders that let me pretend to do what they wanted – and pretend that they didn't know I had no intention of doing what they demanded.

Whenever their patience grew thin, Michael, Catherine and Margaret had found ways to break my heart, hoping to break my will. I'd been too young to understand they had taken Mama, but I knew why my father died, and I was not too naïve to realise they'd used Claude to drive me into Charles' path. An English soldier cut Emile's throat, but these monsters guided the knife.

Now they'd given me more people to love, only so they could use them as weapons against me. I'd no doubt they'd hurt Sarah more, destroy my brother, take Ethan. The truth in that thought made me want to retch.

I wouldn't let that happen. I'd been selfish enough.

'Shhhh, Sarah.' I shut my eyes and rocked her. 'I won't let them hurt you. I won't.'

I pulled a blanket over Sarah and left her room as quietly as I could. If God was kind, I'd be back with Pierre before she woke again.

Bastian came to attention as I left the suite. 'Off somewhere, Lady Jeanne?' He'd bestowed the title on me the day I married Ethan; I'd stopped trying to break him of the habit.

'I need to get Pierre – he's sparring with Ethan. Sarah's not feeling well.' Enough of the truth that it shouldn't spark too many questions. 'She's just fallen asleep. Would you make sure no one bothers her?'

He frowned and scratched his neck. 'Should I send a runner to Scholar Josue?'

'Not just yet.' I smiled and pulled my shawl up over my head, an imperfect shield against cries of *La Pucelle* that would doubtless follow me across the castle grounds.

He dragged over the bench the guards used at night and placed it squarely in front of the door. 'Your brother and Lord Ethan are the only ones getting inside until you tell me different, my lady. Excepting you, of course.'

'I'm grateful. My guess is Pierre will beat us back,' I said with a smile, and hurried to the end of the corridor. As soon as Bastian was out of sight, I ran.

Night was falling in earnest now, and the few people still out and about didn't give me a second look. Getting to Pierre was the most important thing right now. Telling Ethan I didn't dare go to his father's keep for Yule would wait a little longer.

My bad leg rarely bothered me, but the steep hill to the practice yard slowed me down and running made my ankle ache. Even so, I reached Ethan and Pierre sooner than I'd feared.

Pierre saw me first, my face flushed from running, limping and out of breath. 'Hold, Ethan!' He looked down the path, searching for Sarah, uncertainty and a little fear freezing him in place when she wasn't there, but only for a breath. My brother ran to meet me, Ethan on his heels.

'What's happened, Jeanne?' Pierre put his hands on my shoulders and peered into my face. 'Where's Sarah? Is she hurt?'

'She's . . . in her rooms.' I fought for breath to reassure him she wasn't injured, but all I could do was cough.

Ethan put an arm around my shoulders. 'Go on ahead, Pierre. Jeanne wouldn't have run all this way if Sarah didn't need you. Why doesn't matter.'

He was running before the last word faded away, the wooden practice sword still clenched in his hand.

My leg hurt more than it had in months. Ethan helped me limp over to sit on a bench, frowning at how I was hissing in pain with each step. As he helped me onto the stone seat, his arm was all that kept me from falling.

He knelt in front of me, brushing the hair off my face and wiping away frustrated tears with his sweaty tunic. I pushed the tunic away, coughing harder.

That made him smile. 'Sorry. A poor choice on my part. Catch your breath, love. I need to be sure letting you walk back won't make things worse.' He poked and prodded my ankle before he sat next to me and pulled my legs onto his lap. 'I want Josue to look, but my guess is your leg isn't happy about you running after so long. The pain will pass. Do you have the breath to tell me what happened with Sarah?'

'I have the breath, but not the heart.'

He glanced at me and frowned. 'How many fights will I need to pull Pierre away from?'

'Not many.' I touched his face and looked away. 'Lady Maud knows about Sarah and Pierre. She offered money if Sarah would leave my brother, but Sarah refused and the lady put her aside as heir. Lady Maud accused Sarah of carrying a peasant's bastard and called her a liar and a . . . a whore when she denied carrying Pierre's child. Then . . . then Lady Maud struck her.'

Ethan looked up sharply, anger tightening the skin around his eyes. 'Does Charles know?'

'He was there.'

I swung my legs around off his lap and put my feet on the ground. Putting a little weight on my leg let me know I could walk, if slowly. 'Charles had to restrain Maud. The noble lady wouldn't stop hitting her daughter.'

'Christ's blood,' Ethan said, sounding shocked. 'As if visions and raging kings weren't enough. Sarah must be shattered.'

'Sarah doesn't care about the titles or land, but she's frightened her mother will make up a reason to have Pierre punished or banished.' I couldn't forget the fear in her eyes as she spoke, or the way she'd clutched my hand before falling asleep. 'Someone betrayed her, Ethan. She doesn't know who, or what lies they told her mother.'

'She has reason to be afraid: she's not yet sixteen and those few months do make a difference. If Lady Maud accuses Pierre of rape, no one will take anything Sarah says seriously. I doubt the magistrate will even let her speak.'

My heart sank. Too many of the men on the village council had sided with Claude. 'Is there anything we can do?'

'I'll speak to Robert,' he said. 'He's the only one who still has any influence with Charles. But I may need your help convincing Pierre to leave for my father's keep tonight. We'll follow with Sarah in a few days.'

Now wasn't the time to tell him I couldn't go. Making sure Pierre and Sarah were safe came first, but guilt gnawed at me nonetheless.

Ethan helped me take a first step and we started back. 'Once we get to the keep, I'll talk to Atu. Pierre would do well in his guard – he'd likely rise to captain when old Marcon retires. And Atu will be more than happy to take Sarah in.'

'Don't get her hopes up until you talk to him, my lord.' I leaned my head on his shoulder. 'You haven't seen your father in a long time. He may not be eager to take in a pair of young lovers.'

He laughed. 'The earl has always had a large soft spot for young lovers. Pierre and Sarah will remind him of the trials he and my mother faced to be together. I'll be surprised if he isn't making noises about adopting Sarah or making her his ward within a day or two – a week at the most. Atu wanted daughters as much as my mother.'

Each story Ethan told about his father made me want to meet the earl more. There'd be time later, if I survived the plots and plans of my hateful monsters. I couldn't bear to think I wouldn't.

Ethan didn't bother changing before going to find Robert. He had a quick word with Bastian, left me with a kiss and a smile and hurried away. I crept inside, as quietly as I could, not knowing what I'd find. Silence greeted me and my stomach knotted momentarily before good sense chided me. Bastian would have told me if Pierre and Sarah had gone out or if there was trouble.

Their bedchamber door stood part-way open. When I peeked inside to check on them, I saw bruised circles darkening under Sarah's closed eyes. She looked small and broken, curled up in my brother's arms, her back against his chest, her knees up to her chin. Pierre was wrapped around her, close as he could manage, a shield between her and a hurtful world.

I prayed that God would forgive me for the sorrow I'd brought into their lives. I prayed that Sarah and Pierre would forgive me too.

The room I shared with Ethan felt empty without him there, the bed too large. I made myself comfortable in the chair by the window. Owls called in the dark, a fox barked outside the castle walls and the wind rattled dying leaves and rose canes. My mind chased truth in circles, weighing how much to tell Ethan: I wanted him to believe me, but not drive him away.

I tried to deny the glow coming from behind the bedchamber door and what it meant, but chasing truth meant I couldn't lie to myself any more. I'd run out of time.

The sword was lighter than I'd remembered, but the burden

on my heart wasn't any less. I held the blade up and studied the grip, and how perfectly it fitted my hand.

Whispering in the dark felt foolish, but I believed down to my bones that I needed to say the words aloud.

'You have my promise and my pledge, I will do as you ask. I will learn to fight. I will be the Maid, wield the sword and win the king his crown. I will heal the damage and drive the English away. Believe that I will keep my word.' I gripped the sword with both hands and faced the shapes brightening in front of me. 'And believe this as well: I will keep that promise as long as you leave Ethan, Sarah and Pierre untouched. Harm them in any way and I'll use the Maid's sword to send you all back to hell.'

The monster Michael's eyes flared bright, but he didn't answer or move closer. Slowly, all three lights faded. I sheathed the sword with shaking hands, hung the blade back on its peg and got undressed.

I curled up on Ethan's side of the bed. His smell clung to the bedclothes and I fell asleep with his scent in my nose and memories of his laugh in my head. When I dreamed, they were dreams of Ethan holding a babe who had his smile. He whispered in the baby's ear, telling her stories. Making her laugh. I watched them with tears in my eyes. His mother had always wanted daughters.

Before he walked back to me, he kissed his fingers and touched the gravestone in front of him. I took his arm for the walk back to the keep.

A dream can be a promise, truth or lies. I couldn't know which one this dream held. Not yet.

Part Ten

Be not afraid!

Jeanne d'Arc

Ethan was watching me when I woke. The weary lines in his face made me doubt he'd got much rest. He brushed back my hair. 'Did you sleep well?'

'As well as I could with you gone. No nightmares. I pray they've stopped,' I said. 'Did you convince Pierre to leave before you?'

'Once Robert spoke to Charles, there wasn't any need. The duke thought we should go to Charles together – Robert to talk and me to stand back and look aggrieved.' He rolled onto his back and laced his hands behind his head. 'Charles appeared to be surprised we were worried for Sarah; he insisted that she was making a fuss over nothing. He denied Lady Maud even hit her daughter, let alone having to restrain the lady. "A normal quarrel between mother and daughter" is what he called it.'

'That was far from normal,' I said. 'Normal arguments don't leave you bruised and terrified.'

'I suspect Charles was embarrassed and trying to smooth things over. I refuse to consider his reaction as an outright lie, even if that's closer to the truth.' He frowned. 'His Grace wanted to show us out right then, but Robert refused to leave. If this was such a slight disagreement, the duke wanted a promise that Pierre wouldn't find himself in a cell before dawn.'

I thanked God for Robert's skill in handling Charles; avoiding pitfalls that would hurt all of us had become a habit.

'Robert must have got his promise,' I said slowly. 'You wouldn't be so calm otherwise.'

'He got more than a promise, love.' Ethan rolled out of bed and fetched a ribbon-tied scroll from the table in our room. 'Robert is Sarah's new guardian, with full authority from the crown to manage her affairs. Charles signed and put his seal to this. He claimed not to care who Sarah married or whether she chose to sleep with an entire village full of shepherds. His Grace believes making Sarah the duke's responsibility will lessen the strain on Maud.'

I couldn't read the scroll he opened, but I could recognise the Dauphin's signature and seal readily enough. Charles would have a hard time backing out of an agreement bearing his own seal. 'I trust you and Robert didn't pass on Charles' remarks to either Pierre or Sarah.'

He shook his head. 'Neither needed to know. The good news was enough.'

'Now tell me what's wrong.' I traced the tired lines pulling down the corners of his mouth with my finger. 'At a guess, you didn't sleep at all last night.'

He took my hand and kissed my palm. 'Maud went into labour before we got to Charles' quarters last night. Scholar Josue rushed in while the wax on the Dauphin's seal was cooling or I don't think he'd have told us.'

I crossed myself, memories of my mother's screams mixing with the sudden fear squeezing my heart. 'Holy Mary, keep her safe.'

'Amen. Josue didn't look especially worried, but he doesn't attend births unless the midwife sends for him.'

Ethan rolled up the scroll and retied the scrap of ribbon around it before getting out of bed. He pulled open the big chest at the end of the bed, rummaged inside and came up with one of Sarah's map tubes. Slipping the scroll inside and hiding it only took a moment. As he pulled out a clean tunic, the set of his shoulders and the way his mouth pulled into a tight line, coupled with the furtive glances he sent my way, said there was more bad news he hadn't shared.

I sympathised. Biding my time and waiting for an opportunity to tell him I wouldn't make the Yule trip felt dishonest and cowardly. The last thing I wanted to do was hurt or disappoint him, or make him angry. Learning to fight – being the Maid – was sure to do all three, maybe even drive him away, but I couldn't put it off much longer.

Ethan pulled on a clean tunic and sat on the edge of the bed to tug on his boots. He continued to sit there long after he'd finished, silently staring at the floor. I finished dressing and sat next to him.

'What else, Ethan?' I rubbed the back of his neck, feeling knotted muscles start to loosen under my touch. 'Don't make me drag every nugget of bad news out of you.'

'Older mercenaries used to joke that having a wife who knew you well was both a blessing and a curse.' He smiled, a small smile edged with sadness, but still didn't look up. 'I sent a rider to my father last night to tell him we won't be travelling to the keep for Yule. Robert has asked me to stay. The Dauphin is trying to convince his commanders to carry the war to the English – in the depths of winter. Robert needs my help to keep Charles from doing anything disastrous. I'm sorry. I know I promised to hide you away, Jeanne.'

I'd been grateful for Charles' behaviour towards Sarah and Pierre, but stories of the things he'd said and done were being openly whispered abroad now, passing from soldier to soldier, servant to servant, and doubts about his fitness to rule were being voiced. I suspected that if the Dauphin hadn't openly named me as the Maid and supported the stories of his men's visions, his army would have trickled away by now, man by man.

The pale flicker of light in the corner made me suspect my monsters had stuck their hand in to keep Pierre and Ethan near me. These creatures likely had a very different idea of what harming my husband or my brother meant.

'There will be other chances to visit.' I leaned my head on his shoulder and took a breath. 'And if Charles has changed his mind about staying inside the walls until spring, the fighting will spread. Much as I'd love to hide in your father's keep with you, I can't. His Grace will expect me to ride with him, take the field and to . . . to act as the Maid would act and to use the sword.'

'Nonsense.' The snap in his voice surprised me into sitting up. 'Charles will do what he can to press you entirely into his service, but you can refuse.'

'Charles isn't the man we knew last winter, Ethan. No matter how much he dresses the words in pretty phrases, His Grace expects me to obey. He already sees himself as king, with the God-given right to put out his hand and take what he wants. Refusing to play the part Charles has decreed for me will only end badly – and not just for me.'

Ethan stared at me, clearly shocked. Anger swiftly followed. 'Mother of God, Jeanne! Trying to use a sword against the English will end with you dead!'

He'd never yelled at me before, never even raised his voice in the slightest, but I wouldn't back away from him, nor concede this. I needed to stay calm, not burst into tears. I wasn't the same person I'd been when I left Domrémy. Silently, I cursed the monsters who'd forced me to this place. Saving the people I loved might break me.

'Ethan, he won't leave me a choice,' I said. 'And if I'm to be forced into battle, I want to learn to use a sword, at least well enough to defend myself.'

'No, I won't allow it.' Anger burned in Ethan's brown eyes and flushed his dark skin, while his voice filled with the angry growl I'd always feared being turned on me. He clenched his jaw and stood, looming over me. 'No! No matter what Charles wants, you're not the Maid and you don't have to sacrifice yourself. I won't *let* you.'

For the first time, my temper flared, rising to match his. 'Forgive me, Lord Ethan. I didn't know being your wife gave you the *right* to forbid me my own decisions. I should have asked more questions before agreeing to marry you, thought beyond merely loving you.'

He couldn't have looked more stricken if I'd stabbed him. I turned away, unable to bear the hurt in his eyes. I'd done this to him; I prayed God would forgive me.

'Jeanne, I *begged* Charles not to send you onto the battlefield with a sword in your hand,' he said. 'His concession to my plea and Robert's arguments was to make you a prize for every English dog in France. You're not the Maid, Jeanne. I beg you, don't let Charles' desire to be king kill you. *Please.*'

He reached for me and I let him take my hands. Ethan's anger hid his fear for me, I knew that, but so did mine. I wouldn't answer his fear with more anger.

'I'm not the Maid, but an entire army believes I am. You know that's true, Ethan. You've seen men kneeling at my feet or begging for blessings and miracles often enough.'

He scowled, but he didn't pull away from me, quietening a hundred fears. Waking a hundred others.

'The soldiers' belief that I'll put Charles on the throne is what will make the difference – and help keep me alive. It's those men who will stand between me and the English when I've need. Please, Ethan, teach me to defend myself until help arrives.'

'And you'd trust your life to vision-drunk fools?' He yanked his hand away and went to stand at the window, his shoulders stiff with fresh anger. 'Don't imagine you'll be shown mercy or given quarter by the English because you're a woman. If anything, the beef-eaters' soldiers will be even more cruel. Don't ask me to help you die, Jeanne. I can't.'

'Then I'll find someone else,' I said. 'I won't ask any man to follow me into battle until I at least know how to defend myself.'

A light flared between the two of us. The swirling silver was gone from Catherine's eyes, replaced by black pits that wouldn't let me look away or breathe. A warning shiver said I'd stepped wrong.

'The prophecy doesn't allow for you or Ethan to veer from the path. His part in winning the king a throne is as unchangeable as the Maid's.' Winter storms swirled in Catherine's voice and the room grew colder. 'Your brother is tied to you by blood and devotion, Sarah by deep trust and friendship. Ethan's bond is deepest and rooted in his heart. He's fated to be your teacher, your protector. Find a way to convince him. Fail, and you'll force our hand. Time grows short.'

She vanished in a blaze of light that left me half-blind.

I'd once believed I was the only one their poison could touch. Now the idea of them forcing Ethan to do anything horrified me. They'd already proved how ruthless and driven they were.

I'd fight with all my strength to let Ethan make his own choices – even if the only weapon I had was truth.

'The soldiers willing to follow my banner into battle aren't the only vision-drunk fools,' I said. 'Those same voices speak to me.'

He turned around slowly, a hint of fear in his eyes. By the time he sat next to me and took my hand, fear had been replaced by disbelief. 'Jeanne, please tell me you're making a jest.'

'I wish I was. The last ... the last—' My voice quivered and I had to swallow hard before I could go on. 'The last vision showed me how Sarah would die at the hands of an English lord and his men. I've been shown how the English will behead Charles in the courtyard of Reims, Pierre will fall trying to take Orleans, and how you ... you will suffer before the English make an end to your torment. The only way to save you all was to tell Charles that I was the Maid and agree to lead the army.'

He sat next to me and put an arm around my shoulders as if protecting me from myself. Disbelief and love warred on his face. 'Are these voices telling the truth? Are you the Maid?'

'Not in the way the men think. One ... one of the monsters admitted they chose me because there had been other Maids in the past, all of them my ancestors. My grand-mère was meant to crown Charles' father, but the old king went mad and the voices released her. I was only five when they chose me, Ethan – and I believed them when they said they were angels. Holy Mary, forgive me, I promised to obey them – but these voices are far from divine.'

I told him the old women's stories, the tales Grand-mère had never wanted me to know. Explaining how the voices had entangled me in a net of lies and prophecy was hard, admitting all my efforts to break free brought nothing but sorrow and suffering and death was more difficult still. He pulled me closer when I told him about Mama, and how they'd used Claude to punish me.

When I'd finished, he frowned, but didn't say anything right away. I guessed he was thinking, trying to decide what to believe – and what to say.

'My mother knew stories from her homeland about creatures like these, but she seldom told them. When I was eight or nine, I asked her why. She told me to speak carelessly of evil was to invite evil to share your bed. I was years older before I understood that she believed these stories were true.' He kissed my forehead. 'You and my mother telling the same story forces me to believe. So now the question is how to free you.'

I whispered a prayer of thanksgiving and relief. 'I'm free once Charles takes the throne. The prophecy will be fulfilled and they'll have no need of the Maid.'

'Forgive me, love, but I don't find that comforting.' Ethan yawned, his lost night of sleep catching up with him. 'This war has lasted since my great-great-grandsire's time.'

'The monsters told me Charles had to be crowned by midsummer or France will fall to the English. That's only half a year away.'

'And you believe them?'

'They've sent me too many visions of his coronation, each one exactly alike, not to believe.' I sat up and stopped leaning on him. 'The flowers on the altar are summer flowers, all bright pinks and reds. The cathedral windows are open to lessen the heat. You and I are at his side, unchanged from how we are now. Much as I might wish to, I can't just ignore what they show me. Too much of what I see comes true for me to feel easy dismissing these visions as shared madness.'

'Shared madness.' He ran his fingers through his hair and his frown grew deeper. 'Like those young fools finding a sword buried behind an altar and claiming an angel said it belonged to you.'

'Yes, just like that.'

All of it was mad, but saying so wouldn't convince Ethan to teach me sword-craft. I lay back on the bed, shutting my eyes and desperately praying God would aid me. If I wanted a long life with Ethan, children and a home – all the things my parents had shared – I needed to stay alive until midsummer. Half a year of struggle was a small price for a lifetime together.

Ethan had been quiet much too long. When he finally stretched out next to me, I thought he was going to say no again. He pushed my hair back and kissed my ear.

'I'll teach you to defend yourself, but I need a promise in exchange,' he whispered. 'You have to swear you will do all you can to avoid fighting. Promise me that drawing the sword will be your last defence. Promise me you will always listen to me in battle and do what I say. Promise me you will not stray from my side. Promise me you won't die. *Promise.*'

'I promise, my lord.' I kissed a tear off his face. 'And I ask for the same pledge: promise me you won't leave me, not until we're old and grey. Promise me you won't die. Promise.'

'I promise.' He kissed me softly, draped his arm over my stomach, closed his eyes and promptly fell asleep. I watched him for a few moments, listening to each slow breath. I prayed he'd have happy dreams.

The biggest of the church bells began to toll, slow and deep and mournful. A second bell followed the first, taking turn by turn. My stomach knotted.

One bell for the mother, one bell for the child.

Ethan's eyes opened wide, listening, before he pulled me close and buried his face in my shoulder. His voice broke under the weight of grief. 'No, God ... no ... not Maud. Angels watch over Sarah and protect us all. Charles ... Charles will be lost.'

Squeezing my eyes shut, I whispered, 'Mother Mary, welcome them and let them rest in your arms. Let those who loved them find comfort in knowing you hold them safe, free of pain and fear. Comfort Sarah in her loss. Guide Charles safely to the other side of grief. In the name of the Father. Amen.'

I wished Ethan could sleep longer: he badly needed the rest before facing Charles.

I feared how violently the Dauphin might mourn.

Charles had ordered Maud and their stillborn daughter buried in a manner befitting a queen. Workmen had toiled all day and far into the night in the church, carefully pulling up the flagstones near the altar and setting them aside so they could dig the grave. Sometime after midnight, the lady of the castle and her child were lowered into the chin-high hole.

A statue of the Holy Mother looked down on Maud's grave, her hand raised in blessing. Charles stood a silent vigil until the last flagstone had been replaced and a small stone with her name carved into the surface capped the grave. After speaking with the priest, then angrily telling Robert he wasn't to be disturbed, he vanished into his quarters.

Pierre and I stood on either side of Sarah at the funeral mass the next afternoon. Ethan stood guard in front of her, his scowl warning other members of the court to stay away. Lady Maud had died without carrying out her threat to disinherit her daughter and that made Sarah the new lady of the castle. She'd already received messages asking for favours and several unmarried men had approached Robert for permission to court her. The duke disappointed all of them.

Ethan, Robert and I were the only ones who knew, but Sarah and Pierre had been married not long after dawn. The scroll bearing Charles' seal meant no one except Robert could forbid them to marry – and he'd been the one to force the priest out of bed so they could say their vows. Sarah held Pierre's arm and leaned on him openly during her mother's mass, both because she needed him, and to send a message: she wasn't alone and helpless.

Father Géraud had been forced to wait for Charles before starting the mass. The future King of France finally emerged from his quarters hollow-eyed with grief and very, very drunk. He stood at the front of the church, reeking of wine and swaying on his feet. Rumours were already swirling through court; many were claiming the babe had been malformed and no matter how hard she'd laboured, Lady Maud hadn't been able to deliver the child. Charles' drunkenness today would fuel new gossip about his fitness to be king.

I'd overheard people wondering aloud if Charles was capable of siring a living heir – or if he'd somehow displeased God. For months now the noble members of his court had been whispering of his unpredictable moods and temper, his rash decisions. Servants, tradesmen and soldiers were no doubt spreading the whispers beyond the castle. His cousin Giles would surely be making the most of them.

Light filtered through the stained glass behind the altar, making the sanctuary feel blessed. The church wasn't any bigger than the one at home, but with vaulted ceilings that echoed the priest's prayers, it felt far grander. Touches of gilt graced the statue of Holy Mary and the smaller statues of saints in their niches. The altar cloth was a fine woven linen. Even the robes Father Géraud wore for the mass looked more suited to a bishop than a mere castle priest.

As mass ended, the bells began to toll again. Master Nicholas and Scholar Josue were among those offering Sarah their sympathies before taking their leave, but we stayed with Sarah while she lit candles and prayed. Her mother's last words to her had been harsh and bitter. I sent a prayer to Mother Mary to take those memories away and let her remember the mother she'd loved.

When she had finished her prayers, she trembled head to foot and Pierre's arm around her was all that kept her knees from giving out.

'Let me be strong for you, Sarah. I'll keep all those fools from bothering you.' He tucked her against his side as they left the church.

The future King of France hadn't moved from his place at the front of the church. Ethan started to go to him, but Robert held him back.

'Let me get him into bed,' Robert said. 'He'll tolerate my help and sympathy more than yours.'

Anyone who didn't know him would have missed the flicker of pain in Ethan's eyes, there and gone in a breath. 'From me he'd think it pity, not friendship.'

'That's not your doing, Ethan.' Robert gripped his arm. 'We'll talk tomorrow.'

Ethan nodded and we followed after Pierre and Sarah.

The afternoon was still touched by summer, warm with fair blue skies and bright sun. I thought it too fine an afternoon to bury Sarah's mother, but then, all the days I'd buried people I loved were too bright and fine for sorrow. We went to sit in the rose garden instead of going inside. Pierre should be alone with Sarah; even if we kept to our own chamber, they'd know we were there. Letting Sarah grieve in private was the only gift we could offer.

Our favourite place was at the far end of the garden. Trees grew thick between the stone wall nearly as tall as Ethan which rose behind the bench, curving around one end, and the castle's outer fortification. Today, the autumn leaves that clung to the branches were singing in the warm wind. Birds twittered along with the song of the leaves, adding to the sense of peace.

We were almost always alone this deep into the garden, free to talk or stay quiet as we chose. He'd teased me once or twice about wanting to ape the other lovers in the garden and exchange more than a kiss, making me blush, but it was nothing more; no matter what others may have thought, his years as a mercenary hadn't made Ethan any less of a private person than I.

We hadn't spoken for a candle-mark or more when he sighed and said, 'Tomorrow we'll start working in the practice yard. I can't say if Maud's death will make Charles more eager to take the field or less. He makes most decisions on a whim and with less thought than he gives to naming his horse. I won't take the risk of waiting to start your training.'

My heart thudded in my chest, but I'd wanted this: I'd pushed Ethan to train me. I'd no one to blame for being afraid but myself.

'All right. Tomorrow.' I took a breath. 'How much time do you think I'll have to learn?'

He shook his head. 'A week, a month – most of the winter? I can't say. Whatever time he allows you won't be enough to put me at ease.'

The sun was already setting, the light fading and the air growing chilly. I stood and offered Ethan my hand. 'Let me break the news to my brother. He won't be angry with you if he knows this is my decision.'

'Pierre will still be angry,' Ethan said. He took my arm and we strolled back towards the garden entrance. 'But he knows how stubborn you are. He'll know there was no talking you away from the idea.'

'Am I really that stubborn, my lord?'

His expression was solemn, but he couldn't hide the laugh in his voice. 'Profoundly stubborn. You might be the most wilful person I've ever known.'

Ethan hadn't meant insult or to mock me, but I still thought about what he'd said, trying to decide how I felt. 'After Mama died, my grand-mère scolded me for being wilful so often I stopped listening,' I admitted. 'Stubbornness was as big a sin as pride in her eyes. She did her best to break me of it.'

'She likely thought you'd live in Domrémy your whole life and wanted to protect you. I've met far more men like the mad black-smith in small villages than those like your brother and father,' he said. 'A warrior needs a stubborn streak to stay alive, Jeanne. I'm grateful she never managed to break yours. I doubt your grand-mère ever imagined you with a sword in your hand or having an army at your back. From the stories you and Pierre tell about Grand-mère Marie, she wouldn't approve. She'd disapprove of the brown-skinned mercenary sharing your bed even more.'

Everything he said was true, yet the sudden flash of anger towards my grand-mère was a surprise. When I'd pleaded for help with the voices, she'd refused, leaving me to find my own way. Railing at a long-dead woman that she'd no right to question my decisions was a foolish impulse and likely a little mad. How much I wanted to was maddest of all.

300

'The only approval you need to share my bed is mine,' I said, and hugged his arm. 'No one else matters.'

I just caught the relief flickering in his warm brown eyes in the fading evening light, which made me wonder what he'd feared I'd say – or if I'd done anything to make him doubt? He was the only one I wanted, now and always. I'd prove that to him as many times as it took for him to believe.

We didn't speak again until Ethan greeted the guard at our door. Silence met us when we went inside. I listened for the sound of Sarah crying as we went to our room, but all was quiet. I sent a prayer heavenwards, thanking God for giving her the peace of sleep.

Full dark came early in these first days of autumn. Ethan crawled into bed right away, piling pillows behind him so he could comfortably watch me unbraid and brush out my hair. By the time I'd finished hanging up my clothes and snuffing out all but the smallest lamp, the chill in the room was raising goosebumps on my skin. He pulled me close and kissed my shoulder.

'Rest well, my love,' he murmured. 'You'll need all your strength tomorrow.'

'I'll rest soon. Not yet.' I trailed my fingers down his chest. 'Tell me a story, if you would, Lord Ethan.'

'A story, my lady?' Quiet laughter wound around his words. 'What story would you like to hear?'

'I don't know what it's called, but it's about a mercenary and his lady. They fall in love, marry, spend their nights in each other's arms.' I quivered as his kisses moved lower. 'You can make up a new story if you don't remember the last one.'

'New stories are often best,' he whispered. 'I don't want you to get tired of the old ones.'

'Never, my lord.' I brushed his curly dark hair back from his face. 'Tell me the same story a thousand times and I'll ask you to tell it again. All I ask is that the story end happily.'

We stopped talking after that. I shut my eyes so I could pretend not to know the three monsters were standing in the corner, jealously watching all we did. I was as stubborn and wilful as Ethan claimed. I refused to let them win and drive me from his arms, or feel shamed knowing they'd seen us loving each other.

They'd stolen so much from me already. I wouldn't let them steal this joy.

The next day dawned bright and sunny and grew warm quickly. Early autumn often felt still, hot and airless, as if summer was refusing to leave. Sweat trickled down my back long before we'd climbed the hill to the practice yard.

He'd shown me the small shrine at the top of the hill weeks before. It was close kin to the one in the cemetery, but much smaller. Care had been taken to keep the niche in the rock shadowed, difficult to see – I knew not everyone approved of the men leaving offerings to the warrior spirits watching over the castle. I added the small flask of wine I'd brought to the other offerings and breathed a plea for courage and strength before following Ethan the last few strides up the path.

He stripped off his tunic once we went through the gate, the sweat already beading on his skin before he'd done much more than stretch to touch his toes.

Moving to the centre of the practice yard, he drew his sword, gripping the hilt with both hands. I'd seen the blade in his hands a hundred times, watched him sparring with Robert and Pierre, but suddenly this weapon was the most fascinating thing in the world.

'Stay clear, Jeanne, and watch what I do.'

I edged back all the way to the fence, half-afraid to take my eyes off him. Now that he'd finally agreed to teach me, I didn't want to miss anything, or have to ask him to repeat a lesson.

He glanced at me, making sure I was well out of the way, and began to weave patterns in the air with the sword tip, slowly at first, but moving faster as the movements grew more elaborate, until he was whirling and dancing with the sword, swinging the blade in circles, twirling the blade over his head, thrusting and slashing at an enemy that didn't exist, all with a strength and grace that left me breathless. Every now and then he would stop dead and, extending one arm, hold the sword out straight, all the weight hanging on air. The sweat running down his chest made the lines inked into his skin even darker, made his scars stand out even more.

Now his movements were slowing again, until finally he came to a stop with the sword held high over his head. He held the blade up as long as he could, his chest heaving and arms shaking before slowly bringing the tip down. Panting and out of breath, he shoved the sword into the scabbard and waved me over.

'Did you . . . Did you . . . watch everything I did?' he asked.

'Yes,' I whispered. My heart sank. I couldn't imagine how to master what he'd done. Still, I had to try. 'I . . . I don't know where to start.'

'Come with me.'

He was breathing easier by the time he reached a rack of wooden practice swords. A row of battered straw dummies sat twenty paces away.

'This is where you start,' he said. 'Choose a sword. Learn how the hilt feels in your hand, how the weight pulls at the muscles in your arm and shoulder. Then you'll start hitting one of these

303

straw men and feeling the shock running up your arm – learning to hold on when your hand is numb takes time. You'll attack the dummy again and again, until you're certain you can't even hold the sword, let alone lift it one last time – and then you'll swing it again.'

I stared, feeling my heart plummet to the ground. 'But if this is where I start, what was the point in what you showed me?'

'To show you how it ends, Jeanne.' He ran a hand over his sweaty face. 'Years of living with a blade in your hand, knowing that your life depends on your strength not faltering, will give you that skill – but you don't have years to practise, or the rage needed to be a mercenary. You just need to learn how to stay alive long enough for me or Pierre to get to you. That starts with being strong enough to swing a sword.'

I pulled a sword from the rack, surprised at how heavy even a wooden blade was. The hilt was wrapped in strips of rough linen and the wide blade was chipped and gouged. Any of the carpenter's efforts to smooth the blade had long been undone by hard use.

'Watching your mother die – is that where your rage came from?' I asked.

'At first,' he said. 'I found other ways to stay angry. Then I met Charles and thought I'd found a better reason to fight.'

Ethan moved to stand behind me, showing me how to wrap my hands around the rough hilt so that it wouldn't fly away when I landed a blow. He helped me take a first swing at nothing but air, and a second. 'Good.' He backed up fifty paces or so, folded his arms and smiled. 'Do battle with the air a little longer on your own. Keep the blade level and find your balance and try not to let the sword slip out of your grip.'

The first few swings I took without help went well. I didn't drop the weapon or send it flying across the yard as I'd feared. Years of working with the flock had made me strong, certainly compared with the court ladies, but I realised quickly that I'd need every scrap of strength I possessed and more besides to use a real sword. I wasn't at all confident the voices or Charles would give me the time I needed to build myself up.

I'd often wondered if merely thinking of them was enough to summon the voices. Now, as the three lights brightened behind the row of straw men, I cursed having turned my thoughts to them. I hated the idea that might be true.

None of them said a word, but their silent judgement made me angry.

Turning my back didn't ease the feel of their hold on me, nor did it lessen the anger that always bubbled inside when they appeared, not just for what they'd done to me, but for entangling the people I loved in their evil web. I adored my brother, cherished Sarah as if she was my sister and loved Ethan in ways that frightened me. They were my reasons to fight, to keep myself alive. The only way to free the people I loved was to free myself.

Panting and sweating, longing for the skill to take my monsters' heads off, I stopped swinging at the air and held the wooden sword out to point at a straw man. Unlike in Ethan's display, it wobbled madly. With a silent sigh of relief, I let the point drop for a moment.

Ethan watched me for an instant, then nodded. 'Be ready for the shock. Don't be surprised by the pain.'

When I reached the straw man, only the monster named Michael still stood there. His thunderous voice filled my head. 'You were always destined to take up the sword, Jeanne. Tales will be told about the Maid's great victories and all will praise your name.'

'I don't want praise and glory,' I whispered. 'I want all of us to be free of you.'

Michael's fingers trailed down my face, freezing my blood. 'Then fight hard, Jeanne. Freedom is yours to win or lose.'

His light blazed brighter and he was gone. I shivered, gripped the sword tight in both hands and swung. All my strength – all my rage and fear – went into the blow I aimed at the straw man's head.

My hands tingled and burned as the dull edge of the blade hit. The shock travelled up my arm, lodging in my shoulder. Again and again I swung at the straw dummy's head until I couldn't go on. My hands had cramped into claws and wouldn't let go of the grip, but I hadn't dropped the blade.

Ethan gently pried my fingers off the hilt so he could take the sword. One by one he massaged them until the feeling started to come back and he began working his way up my arms. As the numbness fled, sharp sparks of pain started in my fingertips and danced all the way up, as if I'd slept wrong for days. I'd done this to myself, so I clenched my teeth, determined to endure and not complain.

'A good session, love. If your foe had been made of flesh and bone, he'd have lost his head.' He smiled and kept rubbing my hands. 'Not many can land a blow that hard on their first day, let alone keep hold of the sword. Tomorrow we'll start work on control and knowing how much force is needed.'

'Tomorrow? We're done?' I swallowed, remembering the monster's words. 'I feel better – I can work a little longer.'

Ethan seldom gave me stern looks; when he did, it always came as a surprise. He let go of my hands and stepped back a pace, arms crossed over his chest. 'Can you open your hand all the way, Jeanne?' he asked. 'That is a simple enough test of whether you can go on or not.'

My right hand was cramping up again before I'd even got it halfway opened, my left wouldn't move at all. Trying to force it sent pain shooting to my fingertips. I curled over my hands, trying to breathe through the pain, and waited for Ethan to scold me. Instead, he put an arm around my shoulders and led me to the bench. Crouching in front of me, he began rubbing again, massaging my arm, wrist and hand until I could straighten my fingers.

'On the battlefield you won't have a choice, Jeanne: you fight until the battle is over. But this is your first practice. However eager you are to learn, I don't want you to hurt yourself in ways that won't heal. We're done for today. Tomorrow we start again.'

Ethan helped me to my feet, one hand under my elbow to support me while I found my balance, then held my arm for the walk down the hill, grabbing his tunic on the way out the gate.

'Did you ever hurt yourself in practice?' I asked.

'Of course. How do you think I got so wise?' He grinned and took my arm again. 'I was younger than you are now and every bit as stubborn, so I wouldn't listen to anyone telling me to go slowly, or suggesting that I still had much to learn. I saw pain as just another foe to overcome, not a warning that I'd pushed too far. My sword master got tired of me arguing and sent me away. Twice.'

'But he took you back.'

'I didn't leave him much choice. He caught me sneaking in to practise late at night,' he said. 'Instead of chasing me off or giving me a beating, he drew a sword and challenged me. He won that first night, and the second, and again and again, until I finally managed to win a bout – narrowly, but I did it. We were sparring every night by then, and when he threw me out the third time, it was because he didn't have anything else to teach me.'

My throat threatened to close, but I made myself look at him. We hadn't been married so long I took anything for granted. I prayed I never would. 'How will I know when you don't have anything left to teach me?'

He smiled, the corners of his eyes crinkling in that way I loved to see, and touched my cheek. 'You'll know. If a day dawns when you've grown weary of hearing my voice and seeing my face, tell me to go and find another teacher.'

I took a breath and tried to slow my racing heart. Not knowing how much time we'd have before Charles decided I'd learned enough sword-craft frightened me. 'Then we'd best make good use of the weeks ahead. Teach me to stay alive and that day will never come.'

Ethan wrapped his arm around my shoulders as we entered the now familiar corridor leading to Sarah's rooms. 'Are you sure, Jeanne?'

I didn't have a single doubt about Ethan and how I felt about him. Everything else that lay ahead filled me with dread. 'As sure as I can be of anything. We've barely started our life together. I can't imagine sending you away.'

Michael and Catherine suddenly filled the corridor with light, swelling so that I couldn't pretend not to see them. They'd forced us together and told me to cling to Ethan, to lean on him, and that the prophecy said he would still be with me when all others had fled. I'd never imagined falling in love with him, or that he'd love me in return. Now these monsters were angry their scheme had taken a turn they hadn't foreseen, and couldn't change.

The old guard watching our door greeted us as he always did, and Ethan stopped to talk, as he always did. I rested my head on his shoulder as he told Bastian about my first training session, that I'd done well, but still had to build up my strength. My voices glowered, but stayed silent.

I let them glower and ignored them. Ethan was as much a part of their prophecy as I was. Foul looks wouldn't change that.

Our lives settled into a new pattern. Ethan and I still went out riding in the mornings, but now we had to bundle up against the chill that lingered into midday. When they could get away, Sarah and Pierre rode with us, but the new burdens on their shoulders meant that happened less often.

Charles hid in his rooms for more than a fortnight after Lady Maud's burial, drunk more often than not, before Robert finally forced him out. The duke wouldn't ever say how he'd managed or what he'd said, but the future king began to attend briefings from his commanders again. Most days he sat silently and appeared more than a little sullen as his staff went over scout reports on where the English had set up winter camps, or where their troops still raided.

We were coming back from supper with Robert when Ethan told me the only time Charles brightened was if Lord Giles' name appeared in a report.

'We've known Giles was with the English for months, but His Grace is suddenly paying attention.' He waited for a minor official to pass us before going on. 'A thirst for revenge may be the only thing that pushes Charles into acting like a king again. He blames his cousin for Maud's death.'

I stared, fumbling for words. 'That makes no sense.'

'Good sense has nothing to do with it.' Ethan sighed. 'Charles needs to blame someone, love. Otherwise he's left blaming himself.'

Days after that walk home, I came out of the bedchamber to find

Sarah perched on the edge of a chair and staring at the parchment in her hand. She looked up as I came in.

'A message from Charles,' she said angrily, and set the parchment aside. 'He cites the press of his responsibilities as the reason for not coming to see me or offering his condolences on my mother's death. His Grace concedes that while he should have been consulted, marrying Pierre immediately was a politically wise move, then offers to make Pierre an earl. He worries marrying a peasant puts the legitimacy of our children in question.'

I sat next to her, remembering what Ethan had said about Charles, and wondered if he blamed Sarah for being happy. 'You were married in the church, with your guardian's blessing. That can't be true.'

'It's not true.' She wadded the parchment into a ball and threw it into the hearth. 'Not a word of this is true. Charles was too drunk to offer condolences at the funeral and now he's afraid to see me. I look too much like my mother.'

'What will you tell Pierre?'

Sarah watched the parchment blacken and curl before she answered, 'All of it. I can't keep this from him, Jeanne, and better he learns of Charles' foolishness from me tonight. I stand the best chance of convincing him that this changes nothing between us. I'll beg help from you and Ethan if necessary, but I don't think I'll need it. Pierre listens to me.'

'The way our father listened to Mama,' I said softly. The way Ethan listened to me.

'I owe your father a debt of gratitude.' She smiled and held out her hand. 'I have some new ideas on increasing storage space I'd like to show you. You can tell me if they're practical or not.'

The new lady of the castle had taken on the responsibility of preparing her people for both winter and war, bending her own special talents to shoring up the castle's defences and protecting the water supply, while deputing others to organise the food supplies, ensuring they had enough stored away in case of a spring siege. Although mourning her mother deeply, Sarah wasn't constrained by Maud's disapproval and pushed ahead with openly building and testing the new war-engines and weapons she'd designed. Weapons Master Nicholas became a frequent visitor to her quarters to report on progress.

We heard of the weapons master's visits, but by then we were rarely there to see him. Ethan and I had our own chambers now, a surprise gift from the lady of the castle.

Sarah had taken me aside one evening, telling me she wanted my approval on something. She insisted I had to wait to ask questions until later, so I followed her down a long passage I'd never used before. Sarah threw open a door to reveal a small sitting room next to a large bedchamber, with deep windows overlooking a private courtyard. When I entered the second room opening off the bedchamber, the first thing I saw was a well-used loom, already warped and waiting. Shelves stacked with baskets lined two of the walls, with a row of drying racks lined up underneath and bunches of dried flowers hanging from a rod near the window. There was a door into the courtyard in the far wall.

Sarah wrapped her arm around my waist. 'This is my wedding gift to my new sister.'

Memories of Mama and Grand-mère Marie, singing while they wove, filled my heart. 'These rooms are perfect, Sarah. I don't know how to repay you—'

But she was shaking her head. 'There is nothing to repay. Honestly, you know people arrive at my door at all hours of the night, demanding attention – they're keeping all of us from sleep. Once the sun's up, it only gets worse. All these people are my responsibility now – but that doesn't mean you should have to suffer too. You and Ethan deserve some quiet and privacy.'

'What about you and Pierre?' I asked. 'You shouldn't have to put up with this from dawn until the last bell.'

She laughed. 'You missed Pierre taking control yesterday while you and Ethan were in the practice yard. Pierre drove everyone away – he stopped short of drawing his sword, but only just. He told the guards to keep everyone but you and Ethan away from our door until he rescinded the order, so we had a private afternoon shut up in our room, just the two of us, and the only demands I entertained all day were from Pierre wanting more kisses.'

That sounded like Pierre: he was as protective of Sarah as he'd always been of me. I knew he would do everything in his power to stop anyone taking advantage of her, whether it was a minor nobleman or a castle official. My brother and his new bride were well matched.

'Do you think Ethan will like it here?' I asked.

Sarah smiled. 'Actually, I'm convinced Ethan would live in a cave as long as you were there. But you should ask him – can you find your way back here without me?'

'Yes, I think so.' I tugged her towards the door. 'If I can't, one of the guards will show me the way.'

I did get lost briefly, but soon realised my mistake and retraced my steps. My heart fluttered with excitement as I opened the door and waved Ethan inside. He explored the rooms silently, running his hands over the bed, the chairs, the loom and shelves and racks. I unlatched the door so we could step into the courtyard.

Ethan paced to the centre of the courtyard, folded his arms and stared up at the moon. He glanced at me and smiled when I came to stand with him, but went back to gazing at the moon.

'What do you think, my lord?' I asked. 'Is this a good place for us?'

'Will you be happy here?' He slipped an arm around my waist. 'I don't know how long we'll get to stay, or if we'll be able to come back any time soon once we leave. Rumours are flying about Giles and the English, and Charles warned his commanders today that we could be marching before Yule. I want you to enjoy our time together before we're forced to bow to his whims.'

Those whims, whether a grieving king's reckless decisions or the cruelty of the three monsters watching me day and night, ruled our lives.

I kissed him and ran my fingers through his hair. 'This is a good place for us, Ethan,' I whispered. 'I'll be contented here with you.'

We moved our things that night and set about being happy while we could.

Through the autumn and into early winter, Ethan, Pierre and I spent most afternoons, often well into early evening, in the practice yard. Pierre and Ethan still fought together each day, and now I sparred with both of them. They challenged and pushed me to improve, and although I'd never match either of them in skill or strength, I slowly learned how to stay alive against a taller, stronger fighter. I thanked God daily for their patience.

In the mornings, I'd work the loom. Sarah visited often, sitting with me and catching me up on all the gossip, especially the progress Nicholas was making with her war engines. I taught her to use a drop spindle that winter, which delighted her. My rooms became a refuge, a place for her to escape the burden of being the castle's lady, if only for a candle-mark or two. I was glad to let her hide away for as long as she wanted, and as often as she needed.

Eventually, the winter drove us from the practice yard early. Yule and New Year passed peaceably enough, but the freezing weather didn't show any sign of growing warmer. If anything, the air grew more bitter.

The small hearth in our bedchamber laboured to warm the room, but wrapped in blankets and furs, we kept warm enough. The thin, pale winter light leaked around the edges of the heavy wooden shutters but did little to aid the oil-lamps in brightening the room and illuminating the maps covering the table. Ethan was teaching me more than just sword-craft.

Pointing out Reims, Orléans and other towns between us and Paris, he explained, 'The terrain makes all the difference in how a commander approaches a battle.' His finger tapped the map. 'Taking your stand on uneven, rocky ground risks both men and horses stepping wrong. Broken legs and wrenched ankles are fatal for a horse and men who can't fight can be left behind. Every horse and man lost makes your force weaker.'

I looked at him in shock. 'Wounded men are left behind?'

'I've seen it happen, Jeanne.' He took my hand. 'A lot depends on the commander, how many men he has and the force he faces. Surviving is the only rule in battle. Commanders will withdraw if they're outnumbered and the fight is going poorly for them.'

A heavy knock echoed off the sitting room ceiling. I started to go and answer, but Ethan held me back.

'Stay here, Jeanne.' He threw off the blanket around his shoulders, leaving his hands and arms free. 'You can tell me I'm foolish later, but I'll feel better if I answer.'

The lights from my monsters suddenly flickered and brightened near the door, a signal he wasn't being foolish. I untangled myself from the furs and pulled my heavy shawl closer around my shoulders. It hid the knife I'd pulled from the sheath on my belt.

I stood just inside the bedchamber as Ethan yanked open the outer door. His back and shoulders stiffened as Charles pushed inside. Robert, only a step or two behind, laid an apologetic hand on Ethan's shoulder.

Charles moved past me without a word and went to the table in front of the hearth. After shuffling through the maps, he started tossing the furs and blankets we'd left on the chairs aside before moving into the loom room. We could hear him opening the crocks of dye on the shelves and moving things; he wasn't trying to hide his actions. I took the opportunity to sheathe my knife before joining Ethan, my only thought to keep the anger on his face from spilling over into rage.

Robert looked equally unhappy, but the Dauphin hadn't suddenly appeared at his door after weeks of silence and begun searching his quarters. I understood and shared Ethan's fury, but not knowing what Charles was looking for meant the unease writhing under my skin was stronger.

The door leading to the courtyard opened and closed, opened and closed again as Charles came back inside. He slid the latch home with a sharp click and walked back into the bedchamber. The Dauphin paused, staring at the Maid's sword hanging from a peg on the wall.

He seemed startled to find the three of us standing together, watching him.

Charles took the closest chair, his shoulders stiff. 'Sit, Jeanne.'

I held tight to Ethan's arm. 'Thank you, Your Grace, but I'll stand with my husband if you don't mind.'

Charles waved a hand in my direction, a vague gesture that took in all of us. 'All of you sit down then. I don't fancy craning my neck to look up at the lot of you. My head is already pounding.'

We rearranged the chairs so that we all sat facing Charles. He drummed his fingers impatiently until the three of us were seated, but stayed silent even after we'd settled. It felt strange sitting in front of him that way, as if he were judging us and had already found us wanting. I clung to Ethan's hand and silently sighed, remembering the days when we had all felt easy in Charles' company.

'I've had word the English are still settled in their winter camps.' Charles continued to drum on the arm of the chair. 'The snow has kept them from moving far afield, just as it's sealed us into the castle, but spring will arrive soon and the snow will melt. I intend to ride out as soon as the roads are passable, even before they are completely clear. Will you be ready, Jeanne?'

I'd never be ready, but I couldn't say that to Charles. 'As ready as I can be, Your Grace. I'll never be a warrior and sparring with wooden blades isn't the same as facing men with steel in their hands.'

'If Ethan and Robert defend you properly, you won't have any need to fight.' He shut his eyes and rubbed the back of his neck. 'Your brother will be there too. You've little reason to fear English blades.'

Robert couldn't hide his flinch, or keep from crossing himself. The only person who believed I'd nothing to fear was Charles.

'May I ask why you feel the need to hurry into the field, my lord?' Ethan kept his voice calm, but he was coiled tight, every muscle stiff with apprehension. 'Your cause might be better served waiting for the ground to dry out a little.'

316

Charles sighed, the sound weary and full of pain. 'Normally I'd agree with you, but my traitorous cousin is with the English. Giles has a lot to answer for and I won't give him a chance to slip away again. Not if I can stop him.'

He got to his feet suddenly and we all stood as well, but Charles was already at the door. The Dauphin left it standing open when he went out, trusting Robert to be at his heels. As expected, the duke was hurrying after him, muttering complaints under his breath.

Ethan swore quietly and closed the door against the chill wind. 'And we can add reckless to the list of Charles' sins. He used to have the best head for tactics of any commander in Christendom. He would plan every move carefully – that's how he won so many battles against larger, more seasoned armies when he should have lost. Now our Dauphin's need to avenge himself on Giles will have him chasing all over France without a thought for what he's doing.'

'And his army will have no choice but to follow.' I crossed myself. 'Holy Mary protect us all.'

'Amen.' He kissed my forehead. 'Let's get back to the fire. We've more study to do. The men will see what's happening with the Dauphin soon enough. They'll be looking for someone to lead them. Learning all you can now is what's going to help keep you – and them – alive.'

I stared. 'Ethan, I can't – I can't lead an army. I can't.'

'You may not have a choice, love.' He scowled. 'Charles is counting on the effect of the Maid – not just on his soldiers fighting harder for the Maid, but on new men flocking to the banner he expects you to carry. I don't think he thought about who would hold the soldiers' loyalty. Those men will fight to win Charles a crown, but they'll fight because *you* ask them to, not out of love for him, not any more.'

My monsters' light brightened, blinding me, and Merciful Margaret's bell-toned voice filled my head. 'This should come as no surprise, Jeanne. We have shown you again and again what must happen, the victories you will win and the men fighting at your side. Armies will follow you and win freedom for France. Listen to your Paladin and learn all you can.'

She vanished, not in a brilliant flash, but slowly fading away, to be replaced by blinding visions: Ethan fighting at my side, tents filling a meadow as far as I could see, me riding at the head of a column that stretched a league or more behind – and Pierre, Ethan and I walking into the cathedral at Reims with a hundred knights, while an army cheered in the courtyard outside.

When I could see again, the worry in Ethan's eyes woke the usual mix of guilt and regret and love. Knowing I'd worry him more, and often, made the ache worse.

'A vision?' he asked and held out his hand.

'Yes, my lord.' I walked into his arms, grateful beyond words he'd never once turned away from me. 'Visons of glory and easy victory I don't believe. The monsters left out the pain and death it will take to win.'

'Victory always has a cost.' He hugged me tight. 'Anything else is a lie.'

'Everything I did in these visions was in service to winning Charles a throne,' I said slowly. 'But I never see him there. He's never fighting with you or Pierre; he's never battling at my side. What do you think that means, Ethan?'

'If there's any scrap of truth in what you're shown . . . I think it means that we need to win without him.' He gave me another hug and stepped back. 'I don't know what else visions like that could suggest.'

I'd begun to suspect that, but I needed to hear Ethan say the words out loud. Foolishly, I'd believed Charles would fight as hard as any man in his army to win the crown. Recognising that the responsibility of command rested entirely on my shoulders meant asking more from Ethan and my brother. They wouldn't refuse me. That only made the guilt heavier.

'Will you teach me how to win, Ethan?'

'I'll teach you what I know, Jeanne.' He smiled. 'Winning is up to you.'

We sat in front of the fire until long after dark, studying maps in the yellow glow of the oil-lamps. I decided that listening to him talk about tactics, terrain and troop strength, supply lines and manoeuvres was much the same as listening to one of his stories. It was easier to understand after that.

Remembering all he said had to lead to victory, to winning our freedom from monsters and impulsive kings.

I had to win.

Part Eleven

Watch! When the wind blows my banner against the bulwark, you shall take it.

Jeanne d'Arc

The battlefields in my dreams and visions were always silent, full of fallen banners and dead men who would be for ever voiceless. No one thought to warn me about the noise.

Men screamed, pleading with God and their opponents for mercy or begging a saint for a quick death. Horses screamed too, rearing up on their hind legs or whirling in panicked circles, an arrow lodged in a flank or neck. Riders fell and were trampled and they screamed as well. Commanders bellowed orders; their men bellowed battle cries. And above all was the deafening clash and bell of weapons as the two sides crashed into one another.

I sat on the white mare Charles had insisted I ride, trying not to let the banner flapping over my head fly away. The line between dreams and true visions had blurred for me long ago, but I remembered dreaming about this battle, the crackling of silk in the wind and the struggle to hold on. His Grace had forced a white tunic and a white skirt split 'to make riding easy' on me before we left the castle. The fact I'd been married for months didn't matter; he wanted the Maid to be a vision of purity.

Ethan had quarrelled with him again over making me a target and a prize. The Dauphin lost his temper and threatened to leave Ethan behind in a cell if he said another word – until I got between them and made a few threats of my own. Charles had the sense to believe me when I said I refused to leave without Ethan. Something he saw in my face must have made him think better of shattering the Maid's purity by dragging me onto the battlefield in chains. Nothing else was said about Ethan staying behind, but he refused to relent on dressing me in white or putting me on a white horse.

Threats might have ended the quarrel, but they didn't settle anything; all the argument had done was to stoke Ethan's anger and growing contempt.

The hilltop Charles had promised me was little more than a rise in the middle of a rocky field. Robert's soldiers encircled me in two ranks, managing to keep a clear space between me and the main battle, but the press of English troops was driving them closer to me, pace by pace. The sweat trickling down my back had nothing to do with the bright sun overhead. I was terrified.

Ethan and Pierre stood together and watched the advance nervously, just as they had in the vision I'd had so long ago – although at the time I hadn't known the name of the warrior standing shoulder to shoulder with my brother, or that they'd both be ready to defend me to the death. Robert and one of his commanders had my other flank. My voices stood a dozen or so paces in front of the mare's nose, calmly watching the battle and enabling me to understand every shout and curse uttered by the English. I didn't take any comfort in their calm.

Every word that Pierre or Ethan said carried over the din as well, a miracle I wanted to lay at God's feet, but couldn't. Pierre swore non-stop, cursing both the enemy and Charles.

Ethan leaned in. 'Remember what I told you, Jeanne. Watch for a hole in the line, a place where the English troops aren't as thick. That's where we go if they break through the first ring of

Robert's men. Stay between me and Pierre. Don't be afraid, love. We won't let them hurt you.'

He repeated the same words, over and over. I didn't know if he thought I couldn't hear or if he needed to reassure himself all would be well, but in the end, it didn't matter. I sat on my white horse, trembling, listening to his voice and trying to find a place to run towards.

The battle never stayed still. Knots of soldiers surged from one position to another, always pushing to gain a few more strides of ground. I finally understood why the dukes dressed their men in such bright colours and why they took over whatever high ground they could find; it was the only way to direct the battle. Even a little height let me see where the English troops were strongest, but each time I thought I spotted a hole in their line or a place where soldiers weren't so close together, more men rushed to fill the gap.

English knights sat along one side of the battlefield, far back from the fighting, listening to messages brought to them by the young boys acting as runners. A line of archers ten rows deep stood in front of the knights, and in front of them was a triple row of pikemen. I recognised men dressed in Duke Giles' colours among the pikemen, archers and swordsmen.

No doubt Giles was one of the helmed knights watching the battle. I suspected that not being able to get at his cousin would push Charles to take even greater risks.

A stir of air was all the warning I had as an arrow flew past my face and tore through the banner. The last of my courage deserted me. I tossed the banner aside, screaming in terror.

Ethan grabbed the back of my tunic and dragged me off the horse. Pierre caught me and kept me from crashing to the ground.

The fear on their faces as Ethan pulled me up to stand behind them came close to stopping my heart.

His voice quavered as he touched my face. 'Are you hurt, Jeanne?'

I couldn't get a breath to speak, so I shook my head instead.

'Thank God.' He brushed back my hair. 'I thought I'd lost you.'

His relief lasted just an instant or two before the warrior took over again. He turned back to search the battlefield, still looking for a place to run. His eyes narrowed as he stared at a spot to the left.

'Pierre – over there!' He pointed and I saw the same recognition dawn on my brother's face. 'Give the signal and start calling men to us . . . then pray they come.'

My brother scowled. 'They'll come.' He gave two long, sharp whistles; the piercing sound carried over the deafening noise of fighting and dying.

As soon as the notes faded, Pierre began bellowing, 'To the Maid! To the Maid!'

Robert and his commander took up the call and the soldiers encircling us moved back to tighten the line, all of them shouting at the top of their voices. Soon the cry rose from other parts of the battlefield and I suddenly saw the flow of battle change: even to my untutored eye it grew more intense anywhere the men cried out.

Ethan took my hand and leaned close. 'We move in another moment or two. When we get close, Robert will send the horse charging through the line. Pierre will watch our backs. No matter what, stay with me – and remember your promise.'

I grabbed his arm. 'And you remember yours. I still have much to learn from you, my lord.'

Ethan's smile was there and gone in an instant, but it still lifted my heart. His shoulders tensed again as he stared, no doubt studying things I couldn't recognise as important, Muttering prayers under his breath, he tightened his grip on my hand and ordered, 'Pierre, Robert – *go!*'

Robert looped the reins around his hand and urged the mare into a trot. I had breath only for running, but everyone around me started yelling as they picked up their pace. The cry changed as we neared the fighting.

Victory for the Maid and France! – For the Maid, for the Maid!

The words mingled until it sounded like every French soldier on the battlefield was screaming one or the other.

When we were only ten or fifteen strides from the battle line, Robert dropped the reins and slapped the mare's rump with the flat of his sword. The poor horse picked up speed and crashed into the battling soldiers, scattering them to either side. Robert's men didn't hesitate to follow, helping the French soldiers to push the English back.

Ethan and Pierre charged straight into the opening, pulling me along with them, while Robert closed in behind. English soldiers were snarling as they fought to reach me, but our men held the line. Knowing the English all wanted me dead – not for anything I'd done, just for who they thought I was – sent fresh terror through me.

An English swordsman hacked his way through the French soldier blocking his way, lunged for me and grabbed my wrist. He yanked my arm savagely, pulling me off my feet and jerking me away from Ethan. I hit the ground hard, knocking out what little breath I had left after running.

Ethan and Robert drew their swords and stalked the soldier dragging me back towards the fighting. The soldier kept looking over his shoulder, searching for a path to escape, but any move by Ethan or Robert to come closer brought the point of his sword back to my throat.

'Let her go,' Ethan said softly. 'We will let you leave unharmed if you release her.'

'Don't burden your soul with the death of an innocent girl,' Robert said. 'Let her go.'

The soldier glanced behind him again and laughed, but I could hear the fear and bravado in his voice. His French was basic, his accent thick, but he was clear enough that Ethan and Robert could understand without the aid of my monsters. 'Innocent? Only whores travel with an army! Does she warm your arse at night, old man, or does she save it for the younger ones?'

Ethan growled, the angry sound rising from deep in his chest. No matter what happened to me, I knew this man was dead. 'Let my wife go, *coward*. Face me.'

'Lord Giles will pay good English gold to the man who brings him the French harlot.' He looked behind himself again, but this time his eyes widened in fear. The English line had fallen back a good way. 'His lordship is offering extra coin for handing her over alive. You going to pay me for giving her back?'

'I will.' Robert pulled his sword back. He never took his eyes off the soldier's face. 'Ten gold and five silver if you let her go unharmed.'

'Robert—'

The duke held up a hand, silencing Ethan. 'I have that much in my purse right now. Let Jeanne go and it's yours.'

The soldier stopped moving towards the English troops and his grip on my arm loosened, but he didn't quite let go. He pointed his sword at Ethan. 'What about him?'

Ethan scowled and began digging in his purse. He came up with a small handful of coins, all of them glinting silver in the sunlight, and threw them at the soldier. 'This is all I have. Take them.'

The silver hit the Englishman in the chest, bounced off and landed in the dirt. Coins glittered at his feet, but avarice shone even brighter in his eyes. He let go of my wrist and bent down to gather the silver.

Pierre slammed into the soldier from the side, sending his sword flying and carrying him to the ground. His knife was out and pressed against the soldier's throat before I could take a breath. I crawled away from the Englishman as fast as I could.

Ethan pulled me up to my feet and into his arms. We were both shaking.

'Ethan.' Pierre was still straddling the soldier, shaking with anger. All the colour in his face had drained away. He pressed the knife blade at the soldier's throat down harder. 'Get Jeanne out of here.'

I flinched, knowing my brother was the warrior I'd never be, doing what was needed to stay alive, never leaving a foe at his back. He'd not give an enemy a second chance to kill him – or me.

Ethan took my arm, steadying me as we moved against the tide of French troops rushing to join the battle. A squad of soldiers in Charles' colours ran past us towards the crumbling English line, followed by those in the livery of those loyal barons and dukes who'd pledged money and men to the Dauphin. They'd sworn to fight the English – and to die for his cause, if it was their time. Some of the soldiers cheered when they saw me and the chant started up again: *For the Maid! For the Maid!*

I stayed close to Ethan, determined not to let the crush of bodies separate us and even more determined not to let the soldiers see me cry and think me weak. Being the Maid would steal what was left of my innocence: it would tear out my heart and soul. I needed to be even stronger if men were going to kill in my name and call it glory, if Pierre and Ethan were going to kill to keep me alive.

Gradually we left the fighting behind. Ahead of us, still a league or more away, I could see the brightly coloured flags flying from our drab pavilions. Runners raced back and forth, bearing messages from the battlefield commanders to the assembled dukes and noble knights waiting in front of the pavilions, who then passed those messages to Charles. I'd no doubt the Dauphin already knew Ethan and I had quit the field.

Light glittered in the corner of my eye, a signal my monsters were demanding my attention. The last thing I wanted was to face them so soon after barely escaping with my life. Before any of the three said a word I pulled away from Ethan, deeply angry. I gripped the hilt and drew the Maid's sword before I turned to face them.

My three monsters looked more solid – more *alive* – than they had a day ago. I shuddered, convinced that they'd pushed me to go to war because each English soldier's death made them stronger, freer.

I'd never hated these creatures more. 'You have what you want: an army of French soldiers will follow where I lead. They will fight – and die – on my word. Too many good men will lose their lives because of me, but Charles will have his crown and France will be free of the English.' All the rage and loathing roiling inside filled my voice. I raised the sword, holding the blade in front of me. 'Now leave me in peace and let me win your war.'

Catherine's frost-touched voice burrowed under my skin, bringing fear with it. 'Are you so sure you'll win, Jeanne?'

'*You* were sure! How many times did you tell me to take up the sword? You said if I became the Maid, the English would fall—' My knuckles bled white as I gripped the sword even tighter. 'You swore it was my destiny. Was that a lie too?'

Behind me, Ethan sucked in a hissing breath and drew his sword.

I'd no doubt the monsters had allowed him to see them. He stood at my side, silent and watchful: on guard.

'Not a lie, Jeanne.' The bells in Margaret's voice were dull and hushed, the brightness gone. 'Winning means making your own battle decisions, leading your men to victory and rejecting the Dauphin's mad schemes. Today you nearly lost. Do what you must to make Charles listen. Time grows short.'

Menace filled the air as the monsters drifted closer. Without a word, Ethan and I both took a fighting stance.

Flame flared in Michael's eyes. 'You dare to challenge us, Jeanne?'

Ethan stepped in front of me. 'We both dare. You showed her the path to freedom. Now you say that's not enough. I won't stand by and do nothing while you threaten her.'

Margaret and Catherine vanished, but not before their laughter rang in my ears.

The flames in Michael's eyes leapt higher and his mocking whisper filled my head. 'I argued against allowing you to go to his bed, but my sisters insisted. Catherine chose your lover well.'

I shut my eyes, searching his words for a whiff of truth and my heart for the smallest doubt. Within a breath I knew.

'Liar,' I said and opened my eyes. 'I chose him.'

I gripped the sword and rushed past Ethan, fully expecting Michael would disappear before he let the blade touch him. All my hard-won strength and rage went into the blow and the flames in Michael's eyes sputtered as the sword sliced through his chest.

Light blazed where the monster had stood, as bright as if the sun had fallen to earth. Ethan flung a hand up to shield his eyes and swore; I closed my eyes and prayed.

When I could see again, Michael was gone. My arms shook, but I couldn't bring myself to lower my weapon.

'Mother of God, Jeanne.' Ethan stood at my shoulder. He clutched his sword as firmly as I held mine. 'Is he dead?'

Trying to explain how I was sure the monster named Michael still lived was near impossible. I didn't understand what tied me to the three spirits, but I could *feel* them. 'No, not dead, but I pray he's wounded enough to stay away.'

He sheathed his sword and I looked around one more time, hunting for glimmers of light that didn't belong, before I did the same. As we started towards the pavilions again, Ethan took my hand.

'I've always known you were brave, my love,' he said. 'Whatever power allowed me to see those creatures showed me just how brave.'

'Or perhaps it was meant to show me that confronting Charles doesn't take half as much courage.' I pointed ahead. 'He's riding out to meet us.'

He frowned. 'What do you want me to tell him?'

'Warriors need to win their own battles, my lord.' I squeezed his fingers before letting go of his hand. 'Charles won't respect me if I don't stand up to him. He needs to believe I'll walk away without a glance and that won't happen unless I make him believe.'

'Are you certain, Jeanne?'

'I am, my lord.' I stopped walking, folded my arms and waited for Charles to come to me. 'He needs to learn just how stubborn I am – and that when I say no, I mean no. Glower and look menacing if you like, but let me talk to him.'

Ethan barely held back his smile as he bowed. 'As you wish, my lady.'

'One last thing, if you would.' A shiver ran up my back, but I pushed away the memory of the English soldier dragging me

332

through the dirt. 'Will you find a place where we can be alone for a candle-mark or two? I don't want anyone else to hear me cry.'

Charles pulled his horse up no more than five strides away and waited for us to come to him. Ethan squeezed my shoulder, letting me know he'd heard. He didn't need to answer. That was enough.

I took a breath, matched my scowl to the one on Charles' face and went to do battle with the future King of France.

I climbed down from my mare and bid Robert goodnight. The short walk across the army camp had become familiar, but the ritual of showing myself to the men each evening, allowing them to greet me, still made me nervous.

Part of the bargain I'd made with Charles after that first disastrous encounter with the English was that I would be allowed to make my own plans, including choosing when to attack the English forces directly and when to draw them out of the towns they held. With Ethan and Pierre glowering at my back, I gained a pledge that he wouldn't attempt to override my decisions and that I would set my own strategy for the battles I commanded.

In return, Charles wanted the soldiers to see me off the battlefield, so they would know I was sharing the same hardships, suffering alongside them. He'd asked little of me that afternoon, appearing greatly relieved to have someone else shoulder the burden, but this was the one point he wouldn't consider compromising on. I'd agreed, likely too easily, rather than not reach a bargain at all.

Ethan was skilled at devising the best attack formations while Pierre proved adept at finding the best place for us to stand our ground. My brother and I had little experience of war, but because we viewed the battlefield with fresh eyes, we often came up with strategies the English hadn't been expecting. We might be guessing half the time, arguing over the best plans for attacking, but somehow, we made it work – and most importantly, we won.

Liberating Orléans was our first victory, in late spring. By the end of June we'd secured Jargeau, Meung-sur-Loire and Beaugency, putting the banks of the Loire back in French hands. The battle at Patay was our biggest challenge; the English had gathered a great mass of longbowmen, but we managed to catch them unprepared.

I took no pleasure in the slaughter that followed, but the victory cleared our way to Reims and to Charles' coronation in July. The monsters had told me he needed to be crowned by midsummer. I had believed that an impossible feat.

The soldiers who'd flocked to my banner shouting *The Maid! The Maid!* before we took Orléans were beginning to grumble as we moved towards Reims. More victories followed the first and we'd regained a great deal of French territory, but Charles' coffers were nearly empty. Robert and Ethan had managed to keep the soldiers fed, but none of the men had been paid in months. Their loyalty and their patience had worn thin weeks ago. All that kept them here was knowing Charles would be crowned tomorrow.

Not being the centre of their attention or expected to lead them to victory was a relief. All I wanted was some quiet before I had to deal with entering Reims tomorrow. Charles was to be anointed in the cathedral at noon. The archbishop was eager to help arrange the coronation, even if he was considerably less eager to deal with me. He'd eyed the chainmail, white tunic and split skirt I wore in battle with a mix of disapproval and horror. I'd let Robert flatter the cleric and stayed out of his way as much as I could.

My monsters conspired to make certain I got neither rest nor quiet, a petty sort of revenge for forcing Michael away for a time.

Arguments between soldiers started up again as soon as Robert and I returned to camp. French soldiers were never quiet at the best of times, awake or sleeping – I'd wager not a single man under my command had ever spoken in whispers to spare a comrade's feelings. I knew that wasn't going to change, even if I was the one the archers and pikemen were arguing about. Thanks to Michael and Catherine, I was able to hear every word. My marriage to Ethan, an endless fount of rumour and innuendo, came up daily, especially among the older men. Being the Maid of Lorraine wasn't just a title, according to the grey beards. They didn't see how I could be married and still be a maid, and so they quarrelled over whether I was still a virgin, whether marrying meant I was still following God's plan, whether it attracted divine favour or if heaven would turn away from me. Some had even started wagering on how often Ethan and I made love.

And yet these same men followed me into battle without hesitation or complaint, something that still left me very confused.

I went back and forth between being embarrassed and angry; I thanked God every day that Ethan and Pierre were spared hearing as much of this nonsense as I did.

A page wearing the garish colours of the Duke of Nancy took my horse when I reached the picket line. The mare would be groomed and fed before being allowed to sleep until dawn. I watched him lead her away before heading towards the tent Ethan and I shared. The page was about my age, I guessed, if not a year or so older. I was jealous of his freedom.

Stares and raucous conversations followed me through camp. I'd have been a total fool if I'd failed to realise how many of the soldiers were afraid of me. A lot were even more afraid of what the angels might say about them. All soldiers had to learn to live with death, otherwise they stopped being soldiers. Knowing the day and time and the manner of your death was another matter. Every man in camp had stories of divine messengers telling me who would live and who would die – and what was worse, I couldn't deny those stories were true.

Men often crossed themselves as I went past and more than a few made signs against evil, thinking I'd never see. I sympathised with them, but banishing the evil dogging my steps was going to take a lot more than twisting my fingers and spitting in the dirt.

And I couldn't blame the men who questioned how I could name who would live and who would die, how the battle would end and the precise moment to attack. Most days, I questioned myself, and why I still let the soldiers believe I spoke with angels or messengers from God. I'd damned myself a hundred times over with that lie. Keeping quiet would be the wiser choice.

The loudest voices belonged to the men who supported me without question, who scoffed at the doubters and always gave the same answer when challenged: *God wants her to know, fool. She is the Maid and angels whisper secrets in her ears. Even the Dauphin has faith in her: God's hand guides her! Now be quiet and eat your supper.*

Nine nights out of ten their utter faith and conviction stopped the arguments, but I would have rested easier every night if the bickering had never started at all.

A twenty-pace-wide space around my tent was kept clear by Robert's orders. Ethan and I were never really alone in the crowded camp, but I welcomed the illusion of privacy. A slightly scorched rabbit waited on a spit over the fire, angled to keep warm but not burn more than it already had. The cloth bundle atop the chest outside the tent held bread, and if I was lucky, a little cheese. I ate quickly, tossing the bones into the fire, and began to clean my weapons.

He came to sit with me not long after, kissing me before he settled cross-legged on the ground. I finished my sword and inspected the blade for nicks or cracks. Satisfied all was well, I put it aside and drew the long knife that hung on my belt.

Ethan watched me in silence as I dribbled oil on the whetstone and began stroking the blade back and forth, but his frown deepened with each pass of the blade over the stone. A shout from another fire made him turn his head sharply, but he went right back to brooding when the noise stopped.

'What's wrong?' I asked.

'At this moment? Nothing. Pierre had to stop a fight earlier.' Ethan held a hand up to keep me from interrupting. 'Pierre wasn't hurt, but the man who started the brawl – he won't live through the night.'

'May God have mercy on his soul.' I crossed myself, swallowing the bitter taste his words left on my tongue. 'Don't they get enough of killing in battle?'

'Amen,' Ethan muttered. 'Too much wine made him stupid and eager for a fight. He won't live long enough to regret what he said about you.'

I laid the dagger across my knees. 'Which of the English insults did he use? Am I a heretic, a Godless whore or a blasphemer? Or did he content himself with merely calling me a madwoman? Go ahead and tell me. Pierre thinks he's protecting me, keeping me clear of the filth being flung, but I've heard all the insults.'

Ethan almost squirmed. 'I hope you haven't heard this one. Are you sure you really want to know?'

'No, I don't really want to know.' I batted a fly away from my face. 'But if what this man said makes a hardened mercenary like you flinch, I think I need to know.'

337

'Jeanne—'

'Hiding things from me doesn't help, Ethan,' I said. 'The talk still goes on.'

'All right.' He sat up straighter and looked me in the eye. 'He called you a demon-fornicating whore and accused you of being a witch. Four other men in his company heard and . . . and he won't be calling you names again.'

'Sweet Mother Mary. Is that what the stories and gossip being passed around say?' I couldn't stop the tears filling my eyes, which made me angry at myself. 'No wonder you didn't want to tell me.'

Ethan wiped a hand over his face. 'I shouldn't have repeated his slander, even if you did ask. Upsetting you was the last thing I wanted. This was one loud-mouthed mercenary too deep in his cups. Take heart from the fact that he was surrounded by loyal, decent men – and that he can't spread the lies any further. Not every soldier repeats the filth they hear, Jeanne.'

I stood too quickly and the chair tipped over. 'I can't take heart or comfort or anything hopeful from a man's death. Too many men die because of me as it is.'

I kept my head down and ran towards the outer edge of the encampment, but no one challenged me or asked if I needed help and that bothered me until I realised: I was the Maid. No one ever challenged me.

I came to the banks of a swiftly running stream and had to fight the temptation to wade to the other side and vanish into the woodland. The only thing that stopped me from running away was knowing Ethan and Pierre would come searching for me. They'd both think I'd gone mad.

Perhaps I had. Escaping the whispers, the disapproving looks and rumours wasn't that easy: I'd have disappeared into a convenient forest long ago if that was all it took.

The stream bed dropped away where I stood, forming a deep, still pool full of fat trout lazing in the slow current and silvery minnows darting everywhere. Water leapt from rock to rock a few feet away, racing for the ocean, much the way I'd spent months frantically racing from battle to battle. I sat on the grass to watch the fish for as long as the light lasted, longing to make the quiet last as well. Too much of my life was spent darting from place to place.

I wasn't surprised when Ethan sat next to me, only that it had taken him so long.

'Jeanne . . . please, look at me.'

'I'm not angry with you, Ethan. I thought I was at a point where I could handle anything being said about me, but it seems I was wrong.'

'You shouldn't have to deal with slander of any kind. You've done nothing to deserve it.' The frown on Ethan's face was thoughtful, not angry and dark. 'Soldiers' gossip changes in the telling until the rumour finally dies. The stories about you haven't gone away or changed since before we left Orléans, so Robert tasked a few of his commanders to find out why. When they began touring the camp at night, they discovered local tradesmen and farmers telling tales around the cook fires. These strangers – they were agents for Lord Giles.'

'Inside our camp?' My heart beat too fast and too loud, but it always did when I was afraid. 'How did they get past the sentries?'

'Too easily.' He took my hand. 'They arrived during the day carrying loaves of bread, milk and cheese to sell to the cooks, and no one thought much about it when some of them stayed to trade news well into the evening.'

I crossed myself. 'Mother Mary protect us. It's Giles, keeping the rumours alive.'

'Worse.' Anger filled his eyes. 'The commanders forced one of the men to talk. His lordship started the slander from the start.'

Charles had chased after Giles for weeks before realising his cousin wouldn't be so easily caught, but stories still reached us about which English lord he was travelling with, the battles the duke had bravely fought and always won. As soon as the tales began, Ethan had been convinced the stories were false and deliberately spread.

Lord Giles was an honourless coward. He'd hide from confronting Charles until he saw a chance to stab the Dauphin in the back.

'The coronation is tomorrow.' Ethan put his arms around me and pulled me close. 'Once the ceremony is over and you're free, I'll find him, Jeanne. He won't sully your good name again: you've my promise.'

A chill ran through me. I looked around for the monsters, expecting to see them watching, reminding me I was not yet free, but they weren't there. I'd seen very little of them since striking Michael with the sword, an odd thing, but one I'd got used to quickly.

'Please don't swear revenge in my name.' I lay back on the grass and pulled him down with me. 'Swear you'll take me home and we'll visit your father at Yule, or swear you'll always love me and that we'll grow old together. That's all I want.'

I'd never seen Ethan look so unsure about what to say, but I could guess what the warrior in him was thinking, *never leave an enemy at your back. Never give him a second chance to kill you.* Since before we'd marched to Orléans, my husband and my brother had made sure the enemies at my back couldn't follow.

'All right,' he whispered and cupped my face in his hand. 'I swear

I'll take you home and we'll visit my father. If God is kind, we'll live to see our children grown and with children of their own. I swear I'll love you all my days.'

He started to kiss me, but someone I couldn't see cleared his throat and called out, 'Ethan—'

Ethan sat up abruptly, his knife already in his hand. I wasn't surprised to see my brother step out of the deeper shadows, red-faced and looking anywhere but at us.

'Forgive me, both of you,' Pierre said. 'Charles sent me to find Jeanne. He wants to speak to her about the ceremony tomorrow.'

I took a breath, trying to calm my galloping heart. 'Tell him I'll be there in a moment or two.'

'Tell him you couldn't find her,' Ethan snapped.

'He'll only send more men to search, my lord.' I touched his face. 'You know Charles won't give up until I'm found.'

Resignation replaced the anger on his face. 'Carry my lady's message, Pierre, if you would. We'll be along soon.'

'I'll take my time going back,' Pierre said. 'I really am sorry.'

My brother left and Ethan pulled me to my feet. He picked grass out of my hair while I brushed at my tunic. 'Charles has call on you for one more day, Jeanne. As soon as the crown rests on his head, we ride away. No one will pull you from my arms again.'

He held me then, fiercely protective and loving all at the same time, and I held him just as close. Charles would lose his patience long before I was ready to let go.

The words *tomorrow I'll be free* ran through my head all the way to Charles' pavilion, a wish and a hope and a prayer.

God would answer this prayer. I couldn't bear to think He'd turn away from me now.

*

Pierre, Ethan and I stood at the front of the nave, just to the right of the altar as Charles had ordered. Robert was on the left with his sister and other members of the court. The sanctuary was huge, long and wide, with vaulted ceilings that soared so high they might have touched heaven, but even with all that space the church was overfull. All the commanders in Charles' army and half the city of Reims had crowded inside to see the Dauphin crowned.

Foot soldiers and members of the city guard filled the side chapels, all of them vying for the best view. I understood now why Ethan and Pierre, Robert and his commanders all wore chainmail under their velvet doublets. They were there to guard the new king, not just honour him. Anyone meaning Charles harm could hide in that crowd and be swallowed up again just as easily when the deed was done.

I'd never seen Ethan dressed as a lord before. Much to his chagrin, I'd been staring openly since he'd got dressed. Black hose hugged his legs tightly before disappearing under a black velvet doublet that hung to his knees. Leafy vines were embroidered down both sleeves and around the neck in silver thread, and more silver graced the small cap covering his curly dark hair. The light pouring in from the windows overhead and on each side made the silver spark and gleam. Embarrassment flushed his dark skin each time he caught me watching.

Other people stared too, but not because they were overly fond of him. Priests and bishops who weren't part of the ceremony frowned, making their disapproval of his presence clear. We'd been in the field so long, I'd almost forgotten they'd named him a bastard and a Godless heathen, all because his mother was a Moor. They didn't know him, his kindness and good heart.

God might forgive His servants for judging Ethan so harshly, but I wouldn't.

The tall double doors at the back of the nave opened, flooding the church with light. A choir began to sing, their sweet voices full of joy echoing off the ceiling. Altar boys and young priests came through the open doors, each boy and man carrying a banner sporting the royal crest. Older priests and bishops were next, each man swinging a censer and chanting the opening prayers. Sweet smoke drifting through the air slowly spiralled towards the ceiling. The priests and bishops took their places behind the altar and looked towards the open doors.

Silence descended upon the cathedral when the archbishop appeared in the doorway, banged his gilded staff on the stone floor three times and repeated the prayers for high mass. His voice carried to every corner of the nave and into the side chapels, making me tremble. Ethan took my hand and Pierre stepped forwards to stand at my other side. They were as anxious as I was for the ceremony to be over, each for his own reasons.

The archbishop reached the end of his prayers and started the slow, measured walk to the altar. Young altar boys walked three abreast behind him, row after row filling the long aisle. Every child in Reims and the surrounding villages had been pressed into service for the coronation.

Charles was the last to enter the sanctuary. He wore the same heavily embroidered and jewelled white robes his father and grandfather had worn for their anointments. Light found every strand of fine-spun gold thread worked into his clothing, every facet of the citrines, emeralds and lapis sewn to his doublet and fur-trimmed cloak.

His hands were folded in prayer and pressed to his heart while his eyes focused on the stone tiles at his feet. The monsters named Michael, Catherine and Margaret followed Charles down the aisle, their light dimmed in this holy place. I didn't know if he could see them, or if they'd spoken to him, but Charles had never looked more humble or more afraid. I pitied him.

He knelt at the altar and the ritual of anointing him as king began in earnest. I clung to Ethan's hand, willing each step to be the last, praying over and over that the three monsters hadn't lied to me.

One of the bishops handed the heavy crown to the archbishop. He held it up and called down blessings on the rule of Charles VII of France, imploring God to guide the king's hand in all things. I held my breath until the archbishop placed the crown on Charles' head.

The cathedral dropped away and I fell through thick grey mist, terrified and screaming, unable to see the ground or catch hold of anything to stop my fall. I landed hard, flat on my back, unable to speak or breathe, waiting for the pain to start ... waiting to die.

Thunder quarrelled with frost and angry bells. Cold hands – Michael's hands – cupped my face, driving ice into my heart. Fighting him wouldn't save me, but I fought anyway, clawing at where his hands held me until I couldn't feel my fingers and tears froze on my face.

Catherine rested her hand on my heart, Margaret pressed both hands over my middle and the three of them pinned me to the ground. Something inside me broke and tore and agony filled every part of me. I prayed the pain wouldn't shatter me.

'Your task is finished, your bond broken,' Catherine said. 'You're free, Jeanne d'Arc.'

Margaret's bells were hushed, the joy faint and dulled.

'Remember: being free doesn't mean you're forgotten. Guard yourself as you follow your heart.'

'Freedom has a price,' Michael whispered. 'Sometimes the price is pain, other times it's death. Be strong, Jeanne. You won't be abandoned.'

Ethan cradled me in his lap when I opened my eyes. His back rested against an oak tree as he rocked me. The wind stirred the leaves overhead, sending shadows dancing across his doublet and his face. Pierre stood in front of us, glaring at anyone who so much as looked our way.

Bells were pealing joyfully from the cathedral's bell tower, announcing that France had a new king. The English would know by morning, but Charles would be far away long before dawn.

So would we. The need to be gone filled me to bursting.

'Ethan.' My voice was little more than a muffled croak, but he heard me.

Relief and concern warred in his eyes. 'Thank all the holy angels, Jeanne. I was ready to make bad bargains with God if you didn't wake soon.'

Pierre crossed himself. 'You scared both of us, little bird.'

'What happened?' I asked.

'You fainted the instant the cheering for Charles started.' Ethan kissed my forehead. 'One of the young priests showed me a side entrance behind the altar. It opened into one of the gardens. We brought you outside, but neither of us could rouse you. I thought it best to sit and wait until you woke on your own.'

'That was wise, my lord.' My head spun when I sat up, but settled quickly. The space filled by the monsters who'd controlled my life was strangely hollow, but I was free and that meant more than I could say.

'Help me up, if you would,' I said. 'We need to be leagues away from Reims before sunrise. And Pierre needs to be well on his way back to Sarah before then.'

He helped me stand and wrapped an arm around my waist. 'The horses are ready. Are you sure you can ride?'

'I don't have a choice,' I said. 'We ride – or we greet the English at the gates. They won't wait to search for Charles.'

Pierre stripped off his velvet doublet and hung it over his shoulder. He gave me a hug, holding on tight. 'Stay safe, little bird. I gave a trader a message for Edmond two or three weeks ago. I told him to expect you and your husband soon. He'll be looking for you. Sarah and I will visit when we can.'

'May God watch over you, Pierre.' I stepped back, smiling despite the pain of saying goodbye. 'Give Sarah my love.'

I watched my brother lope away, not knowing if I'd ever see him again. God didn't always answer my prayers.

Ethan touched my face. 'Are you all right?'

'No, but the monsters are gone. Being free will have to satisfy me for now.' I took his hand. 'Take me home, my lord.'

Less than a candle-mark later we led the horses out through a postern-gate in the southern wall. I wore a plain brown tunic and skirt and had my hair tied back in a dun-coloured scarf. Ethan wore his chainmail over his linen shirt, but neither of us would attract much attention. He paid the gatekeeper well for his silence and we headed south.

A league or two later, we turned west. We changed direction a few more times before we made camp in a small clearing, far from any well-travelled roads, villages or towns. If the English were hunting for us, we saw no sign.

I fell asleep with Ethan curled around me, the sound of wind-stirred leaves in my ears, and dreamed of being home.

Two, three more days' hard ride and home would no longer be a dream.

Part Twelve

There was neither sorcery or any evil art in anything I have done.

Jeanne d'Arc

We arrived in Domrémy four days after we left Reims. The house looked strange sitting dark and empty, without so much as a single candle burning, and too quiet with no dogs to welcome us. We carried the few possessions we had inside and Ethan tended to the horses while I made the two of us a bed in the loft.

The moon was high in the sky before I fell asleep. Ethan's arm held me close and his breath was warm on my shoulder, but I couldn't stop thinking about how much in my life had changed since I'd left home. How much I'd changed.

We walked to Edmond's house not long after dawn the next morning, hand in hand, the way Mama and Papa always strolled through the village. Few people were out and about this early, but Edmond was feeding the chickens. He dropped the pail when he saw me and rushed to meet me halfway.

Edmond threw his arms around me and picked me up, laughing and swinging me around just as he had when I was small. He put me down again but kept hold of my hands, still grinning wide enough for five men. 'Thank God you're here and safe! When did you arrive?'

'Late last evening.' I pulled my hands free of his grip and tugged Ethan forwards. 'This is my husband, Ethan.'

'You can't be old enough to be married, can you?' Edmond asked.

'Stop teasing her, Edmond.' Lise hurried across the yard to hug me. She stepped back and smiled. 'She's a grown woman now, not a little girl. Now introduce me so I can get to know her husband.'

Edmond sized Ethan up as Lise spoke with us, much the way I imagined my father would have. I didn't fool myself into thinking Papa's friend wouldn't wonder where Ethan got his dark skin and curly dark hair, but Edmond was already smiling and gripping Ethan's hand, silencing my fears. Everything would be all right between them.

Edmond took it upon himself to show Ethan around, introducing him to the villagers and making sure he knew who he could trust and who to avoid. The two of them spent hours trading stories while rebuilding the sheep pens near the house. Watching them together gladdened my heart. I worried less about Ethan being happy here.

The high summer days that followed were bright and overly warm, the nights gentle and full of the sounds I'd heard as a child. Owls called one to another; the howling screams of foxes were often followed by the barking of village dogs. Music and singing wafted into the loft after dark. Nights were when I felt most at home, welcome and safe.

Days and weeks sped past that way, taking summer and the first few days of harvest with them. If I never left our yard or never spoke to anyone but Ethan, Edmond and Lise, I could almost pretend I still belonged in Domrémy, but the years away had made me a stranger. I still held a faint hope of picking up my life, of filling my parents' house with children again, but each time I greeted someone I used to know and they hurried away, that dream faded a little more.

Early mass each week was as crowded as I remembered, shepherds and swineherds tending to their souls before tending to their flocks. A few of the women nodded hello before moving away, but the empty space at the back of the nave that used to surround Claude belonged to me now. But stubbornness and the need to feel close to God sent me back every week.

Ethan had counselled patience, urging me not to take any of the snubs to heart. 'People will remember you belong, Jeanne. Give them time. They never knew the Maid. They need to get to know Jacques' daughter come home from the war and married to a mercenary.'

A mercenary who must be a Godless heathen because of his dark skin, a bastard who claimed to be an earl's son and heir. If I'd heard the stories, he had too. Slander about Ethan was as plentiful as the gossip about me; our neighbours took no care to hide what they were saying.

Discovering Father Jakob was the source of the worst rumours making the rounds shouldn't have surprised me, but it did. My monsters had used the priest to drive me to Charles, just as surely as they'd used the hapless blacksmith, but they were gone now. I'd hoped Jakob's heart would soften towards me without them whispering in his ear, his judgement become less harsh.

But hate found fertile ground in some men's minds. Father Jakob didn't need whispers in his ear to harden his heart against me. The priest continued to scowl anytime he saw me – in church, or walking through the market with Ethan – and woke memories of being a frightened girl of fifteen. I wasn't that girl now. Most days I smiled in response to his glowering face, said good day and went on with my business. I'd tried to make peace with Father Jakob when we first arrived, but my attempts to set things right just made him colder towards me than ever.

Staying out of his way and doing my best not to cause trouble was all I could think to do. Much as I wanted to confront Jakob and end this wordless duel, the priest would make this an excuse to drag Ethan into things. That wouldn't end well.

I'd gone to market alone this morning, hoping that if I went early enough I could avoid seeing the priest. Ethan had travelled downriver with Edmond two days before as helper and guard on what was to be a short trading trip. Crowning Charles hadn't stopped the English from raiding, and rumours of a French lord – that Ethan said could only be Giles – leading squads of beef-eaters grew more frequent. Villages and towns came under attack less and less often as the French retook territory, but if anything, the bands of soldiers roaming the countryside grew bolder about attacking traders and travellers.

My plan failed. Father Jakob already stood glowering near the cheesemaker's stall. I couldn't dismiss the feeling he'd been waiting for me. The priest silently followed me around the market, watching everything I did and everything I bought. Feeling uncomfortable, I left the market sooner than I'd planned.

He stood at the edge of the square and watched me go. It was all I could do to keep from running.

Whether he meant to or not, the way Father Jakob was acting reminded me of Claude, and that bothered me enough that my hands shook hard. Hate made men do strange things, even men of God. I'd got out of the habit of always carrying a knife since coming home. Now I regretted not having a weapon at hand.

I'd long practise at working the latch with full hands and soon had the door shouldered open. The stench of old sweat brought me up short.

A hand clamped over my mouth and pulled me back hard against a man's broad chest. He was strong, taller than Ethan and stank as if he'd gone unwashed all summer. His other arm wrapped around my throat, choking me – but if he sought to keep me from fighting, I disappointed him. I clawed at his arm, determined to draw blood, and jabbed an elbow into his gut. He grunted and choked me harder.

Lord Giles moved around to where I could see him, dragging Lise with him. A fresh bruise was darkening on her jaw and he held a knife to her throat. The fear in her eyes came close to stopping my heart. I ceased struggling and Giles smiled.

He shoved Lise into the arms of a third man. 'Tie and gag this one, Crispin, and leave her in the loft. Make sure to use something strong enough to hold her. I need her alive to tell the earl's bastard who has his wife, but I don't want her raising the alarm too soon.'

Crispin was older, his grey hair chopped off short above his ears and gaps showed in his toothy smile. His tunic was faded and the emblem hard to make out, but his name and accent said he was English. 'I'll make sure, my lord.'

Lise didn't climb to the loft willingly. Crispin dragged her up the ladder a rung at a time and at the top, shoved her into the loft. A loud thump over my head told me he'd pushed her onto the pallet Ethan and I slept on. She was sobbing now and the soldier began to swear.

'Hold still, woman.' Frustration filled his voice. 'The duke didn't say I had to be gentle.' He came down the ladder a moment later. 'She won't get free on her own, Lord Giles, that's a promise.'

Giles bound my hands himself, pulling the knots tight. He leaned in close and his breath came close to making me gag. 'Behave and don't cause trouble, Jeanne. You can ride with Alec, or I can drag you behind my horse. It's all the same to me.'

I spat in his face. 'If you wanted me dead, you'd have stuck a knife in me by now.'

He calmly pulled a scrap of linen from his sleeve, dried his face and tossed the soiled cloth into the hearth. 'Any other woman would weep and beg for mercy. I'd forgotten how much time you spent in battle. I can't expect you to believe idle threats.'

He backhanded me hard across the face, splitting my lip and knocking me to the floor. Giles stood over me, a strange smile on his face. 'The English refuse to pay for your rotting corpse. They want you alive and well when they put you on trial. That limits how far I can go in making you obey, but don't think for an instant I won't hurt you.'

Giles waved the other man over. 'Pick her up, Alec. She's riding with you.'

Alec pulled me up off the floor by the front of my gown. The sour smell that coated the back of my tongue said he was man who'd grabbed me as I came in. My knees sagged and he wrapped his arms around me, holding me against his chest. I wanted to retch down the front of his filthy tunic, but I fought being sick.

A hinge on the cottage door squeaked and Giles spun around, dagger in hand. Father Jakob stood there, silently taking in the blood dripping from my lip and the way I sagged in the soldier's arms. Above us, Lise sobbed around her gag, the sound loud in the otherwise silent cottage.

The priest's mouth pulled into a thin line of disapproval. 'Explain yourself, my lord. The first time you visited, you claimed to be seeking Jeanne in order to take her to the archbishop in Paris to be cleansed of her sins. I would never have sent a message saying she'd returned home if I'd known you meant to give her to the English. And why is Edmond's wife crying? Did these knaves hurt her too?'

My head spun, but I still watched the duke's face, trying to guess what he'd do. Giles saw me and smiled before he muttered in Alec's ear. His smile scared me more than Alec putting a hand over my mouth again. My anger at the priest's betrayal was muted, put aside until I'd lived beyond the next few moments.

Father Jakob was dead no matter what else happened. If Giles didn't kill him now, Ethan would.

'I never lied to you, Father.' Giles spread his arms wide, his dagger held loosely as he stepped closer. 'Cleansing a woman of her sins isn't easy; she has to want to repent. Jeanne refused to go with me and tried to run. I had no choice but to stop her.'

He rested his left hand on the priest's shoulder and looked Jakob in the eye, a relaxed, pleasant expression on his face. His smile grew wider as his right hand slipped the dagger between the priest's ribs. Jakob's mouth opened in surprise, but he didn't cry out. He reached for the duke and stumbled forwards, his eyes open wide and lips moving in prayer.

Giles pulled the dagger out, watching the priest bleed and sway, and buried the blade in Jakob's heart. The priest gasped and blood bubbled on his lips.

'Father . . . forgive me,' he whispered and crumpled to the floor.

The duke wiped the blade clean on the priest's ragged black robe before shoving it back into the sheath. 'Crispin, get the horses.'

Duke Giles, cousin to King Charles VII, tipped his head to listen to Lise's muffled crying and shook his head. Fear he'd changed his mind and meant to kill her after all slithered under my skin.

'She'll have quite a tale to tell Ethan when he comes home. Quite a tale. The boy will be quite desperate to find you.' He patted my cheek and I prayed I was wrong about why his hand trembled.

Poppy always made Giles more unpredictable, more dangerous. 'I don't give much for his chances.'

Crispin led three horses to the door and held one for Giles to mount.

The duke pulled a ball of something dark from a small silver box he took from his saddlebag, pinched off a small piece and placed the morsel in his mouth. I shivered, feeling as if icy water was trickling through my veins.

A blissful fog filled the duke's eyes as the poppy took hold and he waited for me to be handed up to Alec. The two soldiers bickered about whether I should ride astride, my skirts hiked up past my knees, or if I should sit sideways. With my hands tied, I'd be at Alec's mercy either way, a truth not lost on me or Giles.

'Stop it, both of you. I don't care how she rides,' Giles said. 'Hold on to her and don't let her fall. Is that clear?'

'Yes, my lord.' Alec wrapped his arm around my chest and pulled me up tight against him. 'I won't let her fall.'

The duke mounted and we sped away, leaving the village and home far behind. I shut my eyes and prayed for someone to find Lise soon and for Ethan to find me once he knew. I even prayed for Jakob's black soul.

Ethan had to find me. I couldn't bear to think he wouldn't.

We rode for days that became weeks, always heading north, deeper into unfamiliar country. Always heading further from Ethan and home.

Alec kept me from falling, but he wasn't gentle about it and as soon as he realised the duke didn't care, he took all the liberties with his hands that he could. I bit the brute at every opportunity and drew blood as often as I could. Listening to him howl and complain was the only satisfaction allowed me.

Lord Giles forbade Crispin and Alec to go near me when we camped at night or I'd have suffered much worse. My feet were bound each night to keep me from running off and I was left in a small tent until dawn lit the sky. Alone in the dark, I let go of anger and let myself weep, even as I sent prayers to God and Holy Mary, pleading for them to guide Ethan to me and speed him on his way. As the days went on, I had less and less faith my prayers would be answered.

My dreams each night were full of Ethan and Pierre riding strange roads, searching for me in towns and villages I'd never visited. Pierre chased every scrap of rumour in the smallest of villages; Ethan hunted up old mercenary friends in bigger towns and cities, searching for stories of Giles and where he might have gone. My dreams all had the taste of truth and visions. At times bells pealed, distant and faint, but there.

The dreams collapsed around me every time Crispin dragged me from the tent and dumped me at Giles' feet.

Snow fell before we left the woods to find a wide, well-travelled road. We followed that road for more than ten days, skirting an unnamed village before the road turned back into the woods. Two more days passed before the road widened out again. I saw the tower long before I saw the keep's walls or the dark tunnel leading from the gate: a beast waiting to swallow me. Fear whispered that I'd never come out of that gate again.

The keep sat alone, far from any town or village. If Crispin hadn't been complaining that the nearest tavern was two days' ride, I'd never have known even that much. Walls of dull brown stone surrounded equally dull-looking buildings inside. I was surprised to find about half of the buildings were built from wood, bleached grey by time and weather. The stone tower belonged to a church, also of stone, with window and doorframes of wood. It looked newly built compared to the rest of the keep.

Clergy mingled with soldiers in the courtyard, each of them apparently with urgent business of his own. No one I saw wore French colours. Giles had carried me into an English fortress to collect his bounty.

'Holy Mother, protect me,' I whispered. *'Please.'*

Alec laughed quietly and clamped his hand over my mouth.

A richly dressed bishop waited at the base of the church steps. Other clergymen of all ranks and even a few brothers stood behind him, all of them watching us approach. The duke dismounted once we reached the steps, knelt and kissed the bishop's ring.

'Rise, Lord Giles.' The bishop stared at me and frowned. 'This is the fabled Maid of Lorraine?'

'So Jeanne d'Arc claimed while she was fighting for Charles.' Giles brushed off his knees. 'She's been married for close on two years, Your Grace, and she's no longer a virgin. You should know that before the court examines her.'

The bishop pursed his lips. 'The nuns will examine her and let the court know what they find. They will look for witch-marks too.'

At a signal from the bishop, a sharp-nosed young brother came down the steps to confront Giles. 'You're sure this is the right girl, Lord Duke? Bishop Cauchon is paying a large bounty and even a man such as you might be tempted to make false claims.'

The cleric didn't know to be wary of the smile Giles gave him, although I doubted the duke would cut the man's throat in public.

'I was with Charles when Jeanne joined his court, Brother

Jean. I saw her often: I believed her a witch from the start. She claimed to hold divine favour, that God sent angels to her, but the truth is she spoke with demons. I have witnessed her commit heresy time and again, dressing in men's clothing with no hint of shame.' Giles glanced at me over his shoulder, gifting me with that same smile. 'I would not endanger my mortal soul by making false claims. You've my word that this is the heretic Jeanne d'Arc.'

Bishop Cauchon nodded and waved a group of guards forwards. 'Take her to the cells. Go with them, Jean. The nuns and I will follow once I have settled with Lord Giles.'

Alec saved the guards the trouble of getting me down by shoving me off the horse, knowing I couldn't catch myself with my hands tied. Two guards jerked me up off the ground, wrenching the shoulder I'd landed on and forcing a cry of pain out of me. I wanted to be brave, to hide from Giles if no one else how afraid I was, but I shook too hard to pretend.

Brother Jean looked me up and down and sneered, 'No one here will pity you, witch. Search your heart and repent your sins and the bishop will show mercy and send you to God easily.'

'I'm not a witch.' I could barely get the words out as the guards took me away. 'I'm not a witch!'

Brother Jean didn't answer, instead following silently as the guards hurried me across the raised courtyard in front of the church and through a small side door. They dragged me down a short set of steps that led to cells built under the church building. I'd thought we'd be going deep underground, but the narrow windows at the top of the walls said I was wrong.

The stench hit me long before we reached the first cell: piss and rot, sweat and blood. Rats watched from the shadows, then vanished. I wanted to beg and plead and promise the priest any-thing not to be forced into one of those cells. I wanted to scream that I'd done nothing wrong; I didn't belong here, but even if I did, no one would listen.

One of the guards unlocked an iron door and the two men holding me shoved me onto the stone floor. Fear and the smell of the bucket full of shit in the corner did make me retch this time and I heaved until my stomach was empty. As I crawled over to an iron bed against the wall, I realised Brother Jean and two guards stood outside the cell, watching me. I turned my face to the wall so I didn't have to see their eyes.

There was no mercy in them, no room to believe I was innocent.

I needed to make my peace with God. I was going to die here unless He granted me a miracle.

Flecks of light glowed on the stone wall. Shutting my eyes didn't keep me from seeing the light dance, but this wasn't the miracle I'd prayed for. I'd felt the voices leave at Charles' coronation, the tie between us snap. Trying to think of a reason they'd returned added to my terror.

Bells, quiet and far away, sounded in my ear. I buried my face in my arms and wept.

The small window in my cell showed night falling by the time Bishop Cauchon arrived with four nuns. Brother Jean took the keys from one of the guards before he sent them away. He unlocked the door and stood back so the nuns could come inside.

All four nuns were tall and broad-shouldered, strong enough to hold me easily, no matter how I struggled. I'd hoped for a little compassion from the sisters, but they stripped me bare and pinned me to the bed, holding me there so one could force her fingers inside me and tell the bishop if I was still a virgin or not. He only nodded when the sister told him I wasn't.

'Get her on her feet again,' Jean ordered. 'Look for witch-marks.'

The strongest of the four nuns pulled my arms up behind my back and held them there while the other nuns poked and prodded me everywhere. One even pried my mouth open and looked for signs of witchcraft on my tongue. I couldn't stop sobbing.

Brother Jean and Bishop Cauchon watched everything the nuns did to me. Three faint lights shimmered behind the two men, silent witnesses to my growing shame. Brother Jean leaned in closer at times, his face flushed and sweating.

The sisters failed to find any signs of witchcraft. I'd known they wouldn't. Bishop Cauchon and the nuns left together, leaving me curled into a ball on the filthy floor. Brother Jean still stood over me, my chemise wadded up in his hands.

He crouched down and pulled my chin up, forcing me to look at him. 'You can't hide your crimes for ever, Jeanne. Every lie adds to your guilt. God will help the bishops and the law masters see the truth.'

'I haven't done anything wrong,' I whispered.

'Haven't you?' He stood abruptly and threw the chemise in my face. 'Cover yourself, girl. I won't have you tempting weaker men.'

Brother Jean, his jaw clenched and shoulders set in angry lines, slammed the cell door shut and rushed away. The lights vanished as soon as he did. I pulled on the chemise, then found my gown where it had landed in the corner and pulled it on as well.

I climbed onto the iron bed and hugged my knees to my chest. I couldn't let go. I couldn't lie straight. When I was very young, before the monsters found me, I'd imagined that if I made myself small enough, no one could see me. I was grown now and knew better, but I still tried to become so tiny no one would see me, or think to look for me, or remember I was there.

Small enough no one would hurt me. I wanted that more than anything.

Part Thirteen

I would rather die than do something I know to be a sin, or to be against God's will.

Jeanne d'Arc

A man arrived just after dawn to replace the bucket of shit sitting in the corner with an empty one. He left a clay jug of water just inside the door. Two guards waited in the corridor as the stranger scurried into my cell and out again. I stayed as far from him as the small space allowed, mistrust and caution burning in my chest. Not a soul in this place was a friend.

The guards waited impatiently for the man to load the full bucket on his pushcart. Mine was the last cell at this end of the building and I guessed the church guards were eager to return to their own amusements. I picked up the water jug as soon as the three men moved away, praying the water was clean and wouldn't make me sick. Good sense said not to drink all the water at once, to make it last – they might bring another jug tomorrow, or it might be days. I'd no way to know.

I was right to be cautious. No one brought more water or fed me, or so much as walked that far down the corridor, leaving me jumping at every sound. By the third day, my stomach was cramping with hunger, sharp and painful, and I slept as much as I could manage. I didn't remember my dreams when I woke, but I knew they had changed – but I wasn't hungry while I was sleeping and rats didn't watch me from the shadows.

When I awoke two days later, Brother Jean stood outside my cell.

My monsters were back too, standing inside, a few strides from the door. Twice now they'd appeared to watch the priest and what went on between us. My head spun too much to try and puzzle out why they'd returned.

I sat up, my back to the wall, and waited for the priest to speak.

'I've given you time to pray and repent your sins, Jeanne,' he said. 'Are you ready to confess your crimes against God and man? Admit your bargain with Lucifer and all will be forgiven. You will go to God with your mortal soul unblemished.'

He meant to send me to God whether I was innocent or guilty: I could see that in the eager, hungry way he watched me. This man didn't know me, but Giles had accused me of witchcraft and Brother Jean didn't need proof. He wasn't interested in truth, only in ridding the world of sin.

'I've made no bargains with devils or demons.' My hands shook, but stubbornness kept my voice steady. 'I've done nothing wrong, Father.'

Anger replaced the eagerness and hunger on his face. He'd make me suffer before I died, I was sure of that. I promised myself I wouldn't beg or confess to things I hadn't done. Others might betray me, but I wouldn't betray myself.

'The bishops and the law masters will have the truth from you, witch,' he said, as he had days ago. 'God will show them what hides in your heart.'

The priest went away again, leaving me alone with the chittering rats and the monsters.

I lost track of time after he left, confused when I woke about whether I'd slept for a night or a week. Being able to remember my dreams again left me with a jumble of memories and longing that made me ache: Ethan dressed in armour, a fierce and deadly warrior, Ethan making me laugh over supper, Ethan holding me close in our bed, whispering he loved me. I died in my dreams too, and watched Ethan mourn; I fled this prison and avenged myself on Giles.

Midday light angled through the window at the top of the wall when Brother Jean and three guards came to collect me several days later. They hauled me up off the bed and shackled my hands before dragging me away, weak after days without food or water. My monsters trailed behind, their lights brighter, but still silent.

High ceilings vanished into shadows overhead when we entered the hall. The tallow candles burning in huge iron sconces along the walls gave off more smoke than light. Bright sunlight streamed through the windows behind the dais, illuminating the rows of bishops, priests and law masters seated there, allowing me to see their faces as I was led forwards.

The only face I recognised was Bishop Cauchon. He scowled when the guards let go of my arms and I stumbled and swayed.

'Is Jeanne ill, Brother?' the bishop asked. 'We can hardly question her if she's too unwell to answer.'

I shut my eyes to stop the room from spinning, but not before I saw the glint in the young priest's eyes.

'A fast that went on too long, Your Grace,' Brother Jean said smoothly. 'I'd thought it would clear her mind and let her reflect on the state of her soul. I didn't realise she'd grown so weak since I last questioned her. My apologies, Your Grace.'

A murmur rose from the men seated behind Bishop Cauchon, but any hope that these holy men were concerned for my welfare or might try to find the truth shattered with the bishop's next words.

'Has Jeanne d'Arc shown any sign of repentance or remorse,

Brother Jean?' the bishop asked. 'Has she shown any willingness to make her peace with God?'

I turned to face him, refusing to cower in fear, wanting to look the priest in the face while he sentenced me to death. The sadness in his voice and on his face didn't match the triumph in his eyes.

'No, Your Grace.' Brother Jean folded his hands over his heart and bowed his head. 'She refuses to admit her guilt and cleanse the sin from her soul. I fear we've been too gentle to drive the demons out.'

Bishop Cauchon sat back and gripped the arms of his chair tight, his knuckles white and bloodless. 'As Deputy Inquisitor, I commend her into your keeping, Brother Jean. The Sabbath is two days from now. Use whatever method you see fit before then. Leave her in peace on that holy day to ask God's forgiveness and repent. We will all pray for her soul and hope to hear a different tale on Monday.'

Brother Jean bowed to the bishop, who waved the guards forwards. They gripped my arms painfully tight as they followed the priest out of the great hall. I muttered prayers to Holy Mary as they took me away.

I thought they meant to take me back to my cell, but Brother Jean went the other way at the bottom of the steps. We hadn't gone far when he turned down a corridor that quickly widened into a large room. Shackles hung from the ceiling and walls, and more were mounted on tables. A blacksmith's forge glowed bright against the back wall. Dark stains that could only be blood spotted the floor.

The courage that had come so easily while sitting safely in a cell faltered. I already shook from head to foot, and now my knees gave way. One of the guards cursed, having to drag me the last few strides.

Brother Jean was talking with a bearded man near the back of the room who looked me up and down, then said to the guards, 'Take her gown, but leave the chemise for now. Pin her left arm to the table.'

I struggled, but I never had a chance of winning. They took the gown and one of the guards forced me face-down on the filthy stone table with my right arm trapped under my stomach. He lay on my back, breathing hard in my ear, and used his weight to keep me from moving while the second guard stretched out my left arm, pinning my wrist and elbow. I cursed and swore and fought to get free, but it did me little good.

The man Brother Jean was speaking to picked up a pair of black-smith's tongs from a rack and stood waiting on the priest's word. My voices' light blinked into view, standing shoulder to shoulder with the torturer.

Brother Jean leaned down and touched my face. 'Confess now, Jeanne, and I'll take you back to the bishop.'

'I'm not a witch!' I was panicking, panting for breath. 'In the name of Mother Mary and all that's holy, I've done nothing wrong!'

He stroked my face again before nodding to the man holding the tongs. I whimpered as the cold metal closed over my finger.

A yank and a twist and my fingers snapped, the sound of breaking bone lost in my screams. The torturer and the priest took their time, giving me a chance to confess before snapping another bone. When I fainted from the pain, they doused me in cold water to bring me around and did it again. The monsters watched until the end, fading from sight only when Brother Jean gave the order to take me back.

My hand was a curled, useless claw when the guards dumped me on the bed in my cell. Brother Jean sent them away and stood over me, watching me struggle to breathe around the agony. He settled on the edge of the bed and brushed the wet hair back off my face, the tender gesture turning my stomach. I'd seen his face as my fingers were broken.

'Tell the truth, Jeanne, and this is over.' He forced my face around so that I'd no choice but to look at him. 'Confess and the pain will stop.'

'You . . . you know the truth. *I've done nothing wrong.*' I sobbed harder, hating him, and angry with myself for feeling helpless, for knowing he enjoyed hurting me and I was going to die. 'I'm not . . . not the one needing to confess.'

He stood abruptly. 'Then we start again in the morning.'

Brother Jean slammed the cell door behind him, startling the rats roaming the corridor. I cradled my ruined hand to my chest, turned towards the wall and prayed.

'Mother Mary, hear my prayer,' I whispered. 'Watch over Ethan when I'm gone, keep him safe and let him find someone else to love. Shelter a faithful daughter in your arms and let death come quickly.'

Sometime later, I dreamed of angels watching as Ethan and I raced our horses down a wide sandy beach, both of us laughing so hard we couldn't breathe. I rested easier after that.

God would keep him safe.

Brother Jean pulled the filthy chemise off over my head himself and balled it up in his arms. The heat from the forge beat against my skin as the guards forced my arms above my head and fastened the shackles around my wrists. I dangled there, my toes barely brushing the ground, and prayed for strength.

The man who'd broken my fingers checked the iron bars he'd

thrust into the coals, pulling them out one by one, then putting them back again.

Brother Jean moved closer, his expression solemn and serious. 'This is your last chance, girl.' A frustrated growl entered his voice. 'Confess your evil deeds.'

My eyes filled with tears. I'd refused to confess, despite everything they'd done, certain telling such a lie would stain my soul. I'd die either way, knowing Mother Mary would welcome me and hold me safe in her arms. I just didn't have the heart to refuse again.

Brother Jean looked into my eyes and flinched.

The torturer pulled one of the glowing irons from the coals and carried it over. 'Where first, Brother?'

Brother Jean's eyes grew hard. He put his hand on a spot above my breast. 'Here the first time, to either side the second.'

The heat blistered my skin even before the torturer's iron touched me. All my courage fled and I screamed, 'Holy Mary, help me – *please*, help me!'

I wet myself as soon as the red-hot iron touched my skin. The stench of burning flesh stole what was left of my breath and I passed out. When I came around, the guards were dropping me onto the bed in my cell. Lights flickered in the corner of my eye as Brother Jean pulled the cell door open wide.

'Leave, both of you,' he growled at the guards. 'Be quick about it.'

He stood over me as he had before, anger and something I couldn't name in his eyes, before he sat on the edge of the bed, terrifying me anew. He shook out the chemise he'd tucked under his arm. 'Sit up, Jeanne. You need to cover yourself.'

The priest eased the chemise over my head, taking care to get my arms into the sleeves without hurting me more than necessary.

I cried harder when he'd pulled the skirts down below my knees, confused about why he'd bother to be kind.

'Tomorrow is the Sabbath and no one will come for you. Pray hard and search your heart. I beg you to tell the truth when the bishop asks. He'll show mercy if you confess.' He brushed my hair back and stood. 'There are easier ways to die than burning.'

The priest shut the cell door and left, leaving me to struggle with terror, pain and despair. I couldn't say how many months had passed since Giles took me from Domrémy, but Ethan and Pierre would surely think me dead by now. They wouldn't look for me for ever – and soon there wouldn't be anyone to find.

Grand-mère had taught me that wishing for death was a sin, one so terrible that God couldn't forgive it – your family couldn't even lay you to rest in hallowed ground. Even so, I prayed death would find me before the priests and bishops dragged me to the stake and put flame to the pyre at my feet.

If God still had a crumb of kindness left for me, He'd forgive me for seeking an easier death. When Brother Jean took me to the bishop after the Sabbath, I'd confess the sin of witchcraft. I'd beg for mercy and hope mercy was granted.

I woke from troubled dreams in the dark hours between midnight and dawn, convinced I'd heard Pierre's voice.

A priest with a shaven head and a beardless face stood in front of my cell, arguing with one of the guards. Another priest beside him had the hood of his heavy black robes pulled up, covering his face and his hands tucked into his wide sleeves. I wasn't imagining Ethan's brown eyes watching me from underneath that hood, or that he'd nodded when he saw I was awake.

My heart pounded as the first priest – Pierre – shook a scroll in the guard's face. 'I have orders from the bishop to wake her. He needs the girl's mark on this parchment before morning services start. Open the door.'

The guard hooked his thumbs in his belt and planted his feet. 'Not until I get a look at that scroll. I know the bishop's seal even if I can't read much else. Let me see the seal and I'll let you in.'

Pierre shoved the scroll into the guard's hands. 'Read it then, but be quick.'

Ethan moved until he was less than a handspan away as the man fumbled with the scroll's ribbon; the guard's mouth fell open, his eyes wide in surprise. Fat drops of blood hit the dirty stone floor before the man dropped to the ground and pitched onto his face.

Pierre stripped the guard of his weapons and his keys and unlocked the cell door.

Ethan's long legs brought him across the room in a few strides and he dropped to his knees next to me, brushing my tangled hair back with a trembling hand. 'I couldn't find you or ... or I'd have come sooner. I'm so sorry, love,' he whispered. He reached for my shattered hand and stopped when I whimpered. 'How else did they hurt you? I don't want to cause you more pain.'

I was sobbing now, all the fear and anguish rising up at once, all the shame and hopelessness. As often as I'd prayed for God to send them to me, I couldn't believe Ethan and Pierre had really come. I was afraid this was another dream and that I'd wake to find Brother Jean standing over me instead.

'They ... they burned me,' I stammered and held my good hand above the burn. 'My shoul ... shoulder. The bis ... bishop wanted me to confess and Brother ... Brother Jean said I was lying ... and they wouldn't believe I wasn't a ... a witch ... and they kept hur ... hurting me, Ethan.'

'Shhhh . . . shhhh, love, we've got you now. We've got you.'

His voice was as choked as mine, but his hands had steadied. I closed my eyes when he eased the top of the chemise down to look at the burn. He wouldn't be able to hide his horror and I couldn't bear seeing that. Ethan sucked in a quick, hissing breath and covered the burn again.

Echoing booms sounded outside, followed by the sound of men shouting.

Pierre had shed his disguise to reach his weapons and watched the corridor, sword in hand. 'Ethan, they've started.'

'I hear.' He stripped off the priest's robes and took off the cloak he wore underneath. 'I need to bind her arm to her chest before I move her.'

Ethan drew his dagger and quickly cut the wool robe into long strips. He helped me sit up and wrapped the strips around me, fixing my arm in place against my chest so it couldn't move. When he'd finished, he wrapped me in his cloak and picked me up. I buried my face against his chest, unwilling to acknowledge the faint lights that shimmered into view over his shoulder.

'Lead the way, Pierre. We're with you.'

We reached the top of the steps before we were challenged. Ethan kept well back while Pierre quickly took care of the surprised church guards. The bleary-eyed men were no match for my brother's skill, but we'd be in trouble if they came after us in greater numbers.

Screaming had stolen my voice; it broke over every word. 'Put me down, Ethan.'

He frowned. 'Jeanne . . .'

I laid my fingers over his mouth when he started to argue. 'You need your sword arm free, my lord. Let me at least try to walk.'

He kissed my forehead, set me on my feet and drew his sword. Walking hurt more than I'd thought, even with Pierre and Ethan helping where they could, but I gritted my teeth and kept going. I trusted them not to let me fall.

The shouts outside grew louder. We were challenged twice more, first by guards, then English soldiers, and I thanked God that we won free both times. Pierre and Ethan knew where we were going, but I'd seen little of the building other than the great hall and the cells. I prayed for God to guide and protect us.

Tall arched doors filled the centre of the wall ahead of us, flanked by windows on either side, allowing pale pre-dawn light to spill across the smooth stone floor. The building began to shake. Panicked nuns and servants appeared, most likely fleeing their quarters and looking for a way out. The dust drifting down from the ceilings and upper floors was a fine-grained fog that coated everything it touched – everything but the monsters following us. The dust raining down on them touched the light and vanished.

As we got closer to the doors, the booms grew louder. Men fought within sight of the windows, the church guards greatly outnumbered by soldiers in Robert's colours. Gaping holes showed in the wall enclosing the courtyard. Bodies, broken rocks and boulders littered the paving stones.

A group of priests and bishops hurried down a staircase from the upper floors, Bishop Cauchon at the centre of the knot of black robes. Thick dark smoke followed them down. Blood stained Bishop Cauchon's face and he was limping badly. One of the priests helping him was Brother Jean.

I thought about pointing them out to Ethan, but I knew my husband too well. Rage would take over and doom every cleric in the building – not that I deemed any of them innocent of the horrors visited on me inside these walls: they had all known and kept silent. God would judge them. He would decide their fate.

We pushed through the heavy doors and the creatures' light dimmed and vanished. I watched a large rock sail over the court-yard wall and hit a row of windows at the top of the church, breaking every one. An instant later, three smouldering bundles followed, struck the wall below the windows and exploded with a loud boom. Flame licked the wood framing the windows and crawled towards the roof.

Pierre followed the line of the building, taking us away from the church entrance, towards the back of the keep and a few out-buildings. Robert's men still had the upper hand and the sounds of fighting rapidly fell behind us and began to fade. We came around a corner to find racks of fresh tallow candles near an overturned vat of wax, no doubt abandoned by the candlemaker when the fighting started.

'Ethan, wait.' My brother glanced back the way we'd come. 'This is far enough. Wait here while I give the signal.'

He picked me up to wait, listening and watching for signs the church soldiers were chasing us. I listened too, frightened I'd hear men shouting that they'd found the witch, and tried to slow my racing heart.

Pierre ran ahead another hundred strides or more before he stopped to let out three long, sharp whistles and two shorter ones, the way he used to signal the dogs. Pierre raced back to us as whoever waited on the other side of the wall answered with a barrage of explosions that shook the outer wall. Thick smoke and the stink of black powder filled the air, growing steadily worse as the bombardment continued.

Cracks began to appear first along the mortar lines, the gaps growing larger until entire sections of stonework began falling to the ground.

The men on the other side began pulling at the openings, making them wider. I choked back a relieved sob as Duke Robert and Master Nicholas appeared in the gap, their arms outstretched to help me out.

Angry shouts sounded from the way we'd come and a large force of church guards and English soldiers came into view. One of the guards pointed at me and shouted, 'It's the witch! Witch-craft's what made the walls fall!' Others took up the cry as they pounded towards us.

Ethan shouted, 'Get her out, Pierre – go!' and headed towards the enemy, sword in hand.

My brother lifted me into his arms and ran. Each pounding step woke the pain in my shoulder and jarred my hand, but I clenched my teeth to keep from screaming.

Robert's men had already started pouring through the new opening, but the duke still waited to help me out. 'She's hurt badly, Robert,' Pierre said and lifted me into the duke's arms. 'Get her to Josue, quick as you can.'

The instant I was safe with Robert, my brother was turning back to help Ethan, followed by more of the duke's troops.

Robert tucked Ethan's cloak more closely around me, trying to keep me from shivering, and set off to find Scholar Josue. I couldn't get warm – couldn't stop crying – overcome by terror and pain threatening to shatter me, far beyond Robert's efforts to comfort me. I'd found hope and safety in Ethan's arms, only to have him yanked away again.

I looked back over Robert's shoulder, hoping to see Ethan and Pierre, but they'd been swallowed by the chaos of battle.

Six large farm wagons spaced along the outside wall each held a trebuchet the height of a tall man and a squad of men to load and fire them. I recognised the hinges fixed in place with iron locking pins midway down the frame, designed to let the machines fold in half to make moving them easier. These had to be the models Nicholas built from Sarah's plans.

The wagons were placed so they could cover the whole length of the wall at the back of the church and the keep. Sarah's new aiming device meant the trebuchets could also send rocks into the back of the building. I leaned my head against Robert's shoulder, trying to watch as Nicholas shouted an order, the trebuchets shifted and the rocks flew toward targets higher up the building wall.

The smells of dried pigshit and blacksmith's tar, kitchen fat turned rancid and more black powder filled the air as bundles of sacking replaced the rocks and were set alight before being flung into the air. Flaming bundles went through broken windows at the top of the church, others stuck to the tower wall. I heard explosions and not long after, billowing smoke rose in a thick black column, spiralling higher and higher into the sky.

I prayed that no innocents had been trapped inside and asked God to forgive me when I couldn't include the torturer, the bishop or Brother Jean in my prayers.

Scholar Josue was pacing beside a canopied wagon when Robert found him. He looked both relieved and worried when he saw me. A set of folding steps Sarah had designed for him had been mounted on the back of the wagon; he scrambled up and waved for Robert to follow.

'Put her on the pallet,' he said. 'Gently, gently, Robert. How badly is she hurt?'

'God's truth, I don't know, Josue. She hasn't said a word.' The

JAIME LEE MOYER

duke laid me down as carefully as he could. 'Pierre said she was hurt badly, but other than her hand I don't know what was done to her.'

'My guess is it will take time before she talks to any of us.' Josue touched my face and frowned. He hurriedly soaked a piece of linen in the jug by the pallet and laid it on my forehead. 'She has a fever. Pray it's from ill-use and lack of water and not something harder to mend. Where's Ethan?'

'Killing anyone in that hellhole he can.' Robert scowled. 'A band of English soldiers came after her, all of them shouting about Jeanne taking the walls down with witchcraft. Pierre got her out and went back to fight at Ethan's side. Neither one is going to let those bastards hurt her again.'

'God protect them both,' Josue said.

'And give them peace now that they've found her.' Robert wiped a hand over his face and sighed. 'Those weeks of chasing after Giles made them both a little mad. His lordship was always a step ahead until ... well, if you can believe it, until Merciful Saint Margaret sent Ethan a vision. Giles was in a brothel, out of his head on poppy and wine, when Pierre and Ethan caught up with him. Had the drunken lout not been bragging about branding her a witch and selling her to the English, Ethan might still not have found her.'

I turned my head to the side, watching light ripple on the canopy and wondering if Margaret was listening, if saving my life was penance for all the harm they'd done. The sound of bells filled my ears, sweet and joyful, and gradually faded away. She was gone again, and this time I was certain she wouldn't come back. Relief I was truly free of the monsters warred with gratitude I was still alive.

Josue had been studying the way Ethan had tied the strips binding my hand, but now he looked up sharply and crossed himself. 'Angels continue to watch over this child. Did they turn Giles over to Charles? I know there's a bounty on his head.'

Robert hesitated before answering. 'They filled his clothing with stones, bound his hands and feet and tossed him into a deep pond. It's a test for witchcraft. If a woman drowns, she's innocent.'

'Christ's blood, Robert.' He went back to the bindings on my hand. 'Mind, I can't say Giles didn't deserve it.'

'Neither can I,' Robert said.

Ethan's voice filled my head. *Never leave an enemy at your back.* I pleaded with God to let this be the last time, and the last of our enemies.

'Give me plenty of warning if we have to move the wagon.' Josue began cutting the strips that held my hand still, and even that slight movement made me whimper. 'Now go away so I can take care of her.'

Robert left and other than my whimpering the wagon fell silent. Josue left my hand resting on my chest while he rummaged through a trunk behind my head.

'Ah, here we go.' He held up a stiffened piece of leather. 'Ethan did an admirable job keeping your hand still, but this will work better. When we get back to Sarah and the castle, I can set your fingers properly.'

I surprised myself by answering. My voice was still rough, raw and barely there. 'How did you know Ethan bound my hand?'

'The knots.' He smiled. 'Ethan learned to tie knots like those from his mother. Before I start on your hand, can you tell me where else you're hurt, Jeanne? It's important for me to know if I'm going to help and not do more harm.'

I bit back a sob. 'My shoulder.'

Scholar Josue was a physician, but he flinched when he saw the burn. 'I can't stop this from scarring, not completely, but I can help it heal cleanly and make sure the wound doesn't go sour. The first thing I'm going to do is help with the pain. Do you trust me to give you poppy?'

I nodded and shut my eyes, more afraid of the pain than of going to sleep and never waking up. He put a single drop of poppy juice on his finger and rubbed it on my gums. The pain became distant, as if the agony in my shoulder belonged to someone else. I wasn't sure if I fell asleep or finally passed out.

The wagon was moving when I woke. Ethan sat next to me, leaning against the wagon side and sleeping. He looked deeply weary, but didn't look to be hurt. I watched him sleep, thanking God he was safe.

Pierre's laugh sounding outside the wagon let me know he was safe too. I added gratitude that I hadn't lost either of them to my prayers and shut my eyes.

I don't remember anything else.

Part Fourteen

One life is all we have and we live it as we believe in living it.

Jeanne d'Arc

The next time I woke, I was in our chambers back at the castle. I'd no memory of arriving, or travelling to get here, or of Josue setting my broken fingers – he had to have set them, each one lay straight now, all of them bound tight in thin strips of linen and tied to a smooth board cut to fit from my fingertips to my wrist.

God had blessed me when Josue crossed my path. Healing the breaks would take months, but I might have use of my hand again.

That first awakening was ten days ago now. Sarah visited when she could, sitting quietly if that's what I wanted, or giving me news Ethan hadn't shared. The tide of war had turned in Charles' favour, aided by the fury his army felt when they'd learned of my capture. League by league, he was reclaiming his kingdom.

Neither Ethan nor Pierre would speak of the king, or carry news of his victories the way Sarah did, but my husband and brother both spoke freely when they thought I was sleeping. Charles had refused to aid in the search for me or to send troops to help rescue me. The bitterness in their voices told me Ethan and Pierre would never forgive him. Neither could I.

I needed less sleep as the days passed, often lying awake in the dark beside Ethan as he slept, remembering far too much. Tonight wasn't any different.

Ethan was stretched out next to me, one arm folded under his head and his other hand resting on my stomach. Night was far along and the only light came from a small oil-lamp on a shelf in the corner. Black circles still bruised the skin under his eyes and even in sleep new lines carved by worry and grief showed in his face. I wanted to smooth them away, but moving even a tiny bit woke the deep pain in my shoulder.

No one needed to tell me that his worry and grief were all for what had been done to me. Ethan saw my wounds and thought them the worst of it, and in some ways he was right. But I hadn't yet told him everything, and those were the things that haunted me. Poppy took away my pain, but it didn't take the memories or the nightmares.

He might not love me once he knew, not with the same hunger or tenderness he had before Giles carried me away. I couldn't stand that.

Ethan startled and came awake, alert and ready to do battle. He started to pull me closer before he remembered.

'What's wrong, love?' He touched my face. 'Should I wake Josue?'

'A nightmare.' I sniffled. 'Nothing important enough to wake the scholar or keep you awake. Go back to sleep, my lord.'

He pushed up on his elbow. 'My mother taught me that talking about nightmares helps take away the fear. Tell me about this one.'

I shook my head. 'I just want to go back to sleep.'

'How many nightmares have you had in the last five days, Jeanne? Or the last seven nights?'

Even in the dim light, I saw the frustration on his face when I didn't answer. He sat up in bed and piled pillows behind his back. There'd be no sleep for either of us now.

'I understood when Robert told me you wouldn't talk to him after we took you from that cell. I can almost understand why you won't talk to Pierre or Sarah.' He put his hand on my arm. 'But I don't understand why you won't talk to me. I love you, Jeanne – and nothing that happened in that . . . that place is so terrible you can't tell me.'

'Are you sure of that, my lord?' I was angry and didn't understand why. 'You weren't there. You didn't see . . . see what they did.'

He slid back down in bed and found a way to curl around me that didn't hurt my shoulder. 'I'm sure, love. I'm very sure. Tell me.'

Fear whispered that I should stay silent, but my stubborn streak rose up, telling me not to let the life I'd found with him go without a fight. And Ethan had never lied to me. I needed to believe him now.

'All right. I'll tell you,' I whispered. 'But please don't hate me, Ethan.'

Telling him about how humiliated I'd been, how helpless, when the nuns stripped me bare in front of the priests, the eager way Brother Jean watched them shame me, or how he'd looked at me afterwards – the times he'd brushed back my hair, stroked my face – I'd known that would be hard, that it would hurt. A hundred times worse was saying how ashamed I was to have a man, a stranger, on top of me, his warm breath on my face as my fingers broke, or how Brother Jean took my clothes – how he touched me as I hung naked in a room full of guards.

We were both crying when I'd finished.

'You didn't do anything wrong, Jeanne.' He kissed me, reminding me of how long we'd been apart and how much I'd missed him. 'You weren't the one to sin.'

Ethan told me stories deep into the night, making me laugh and feel safe, making me ache for him and love him more. I fell asleep knowing that with time, everything would be all right. He still loved me.

He'd always love me.

Our daughter Maryam was born in her grandfather's keep, the sound of the sea mingling with her first cries. Ethan's father proclaimed her the most beautiful child ever born.

The earl stroked the baby's cheek, his eyes glittering with unshed tears. 'She looks just like Jasmina. How could she be anything but beautiful?'

Ethan marvelled at how tiny she was, how fierce and perfect. So did I; I marvelled even more at how much we both loved her.

He whispered stories in Maryam's ear from the first day, stories his mother had told and stories of his own. Some of Ethan's stories were about the daughter of a shepherd and how she learned to be brave defending her flock. The baby always grew quiet at the sound of his voice, eyes open wide and listening. Remembering.

I repeated the same prayer each time I watched Ethan hold our daughter.

Holy Mary, let it always be this way. Let our love be enough to keep her safe and make her brave in times of trouble. Let it make her strong.

Let it always be this way.

I couldn't ask God for more.

Acknowledgements

Who to thank is always important. Who not to forget is even more important, but it's a sure thing that I'll forget someone. Forgive me.

I need to thank my co-workers at Store 2157 for listening to me ramble on about Jeanne d'Arc and actually paying attention, and for cheering me on. Special thanks go to Monique F., who grew up in Lorraine, northeastern France, told me stories about Jeanne she'd heard as a child and brought me photos of houses Jeanne slept in and the annual parade honouring her. Susan Jett, the world's best beta reader, was always there when I needed her advice and friendship and attention to detail. I need to thank the dark cabal on Twitter – Stephen Blackmoore, Teresa Frohock, M.L. Brennan and Lish McBride – for their encouragement and weapons-grade book shilling, Dennis Wright, historian extraordinaire, for answering questions and sending me articles about Jeanne, Mark Lindberg for his opinions and critical eye once I'd finished a draft, Kat Allen and all my friends – just because. This was a tough book to write. Last, but never least, I need to thank my agent, Michael Carr, for talking me off the ledge I kept finding myself on, and never once pushing me over the edge.